THE **writing** CLASS

Also by Jincy Willett

Winner of the National Book Award

Jenny and the Jaws of Life

THE **writing**CLASS

Jincy Willett

Thomas Dunne Books

St. Martin's Press ≋ New York

This is a work of fiction. All of the characters, organizations, and events portrayed in this novel are either products of the author's imagination or are used fictitiously.

The place and time depicted here are real, although the characters and events are not. For example: in this novel, the County of San Diego did not burst spectacularly into flame in October of 2007. This is one of the many ways in which fiction improves on reality.

THOMAS DUNNE BOOKS.
An imprint of St. Martin's Press.

THE WRITING CLASS. Copyright © 2008 by Jincy Willett. All rights reserved. Printed in the United States of America. For information, address St. Martin's Press, 175 Fifth Avenue, New York, N.Y. 10010.

www.thomasdunnebooks.com
www.stmartins.com

Design by Ruth Lee-Mui

Library of Congress Cataloging-in-Publication Data

Willett, Jincy.
    The Writing Class / Jincy Willett—1st Thomas Dunne Books ed.
        p.   cm.
    ISBN-13: 978-0-312-33066-8 (alk. paper)
    ISBN-10: 0-312-33066-9 (alk. paper)
    1. Women college teachers—Fiction.   2. Widows—Fiction.   3. Students—Crimes against—Fiction.   4. Murder—Fiction.   I. Title.
    PS3573.I455 W75   2008
    914'.54—dc22

                                                                    2008009992

First Edition: June 2008

10 9 8 7 6 5 4 3 2 1

FOR **chip willett**

heartyHANDCLASPS

To

M. J. Andersen
Sandy Asirvatham
Norma Cwiek
Carl and Suzie Hammond
Tom Hartley
Dick and Diane Longabaugh
Lil Walker
Ward and Joanne Willett

who slogged through unfinished drafts (of a *mystery* novel, knowing that for years they wouldn't even find out who for pete's sake *did it*) and were cheerful and encouraging and gracious about the whole thing. I wouldn't have been.

To

Sven and Kristin Nielsen

for help with all email and Web site stuff, and who remain entirely blameless for any remaining bloopers.

And to

Tess Link
and
Lisa Fugard

who know why.

THE **writing** CLASS

THE **fat** BROAD

Lumbers into class five minutes late, dragging, along with her yard-wide butt, a beat-up vinyl briefcase stuffed with old notebooks. A contender once, it's obvious, she's got great hair, long and wavy and thick and white gold, but she's pushing sixty, pushing two hundred, and she wears polyester fat pants and a Big & Tall man's white long-sleeved shirt with the sleeves ragged and rolled up. Here is a woman who does not give a rat's ass.

She sits down behind a rickety desk in front of the whiteboard, upends the briefcase, and spreads out the notebooks and papers in a neat line, like a magician's row of cards. She's the teacher. But I knew this. How? Because she's the only person in the room who isn't nervous.

Because she's the dominant male.

She looks up and counts us with her eyes. Seven. She

heaves herself up on her feet and addresses the whiteboard with a green marker:

Fiction Writing Workshop
Amy Gallup

And she follows it up with the numbers of her home phone and cell phone, which if I turned this into a novel or esp a screenplay I'd have to represent as 555-something, which is foolish, which is stupid, but there you are, this is the world we live in, soft and womanish and lowest common D.

I, of course, am not nervous. Yes, I am. Why? I've done this before. I'm a workshop vet, Purple Heart and Silver Cross. I've shown my stories to pretentious morons from sea to shining sea. I've been encouraged by twinkly grandmas, torn apart by gynecologists, talked down to by insurance salesmen.

Write what you know

The interesting thing about women, they get past a certain age and they might as well be men. The Dominant Male. Title? Idea for story?

TORN APART
BY TWINKLY GRANDMAS
PATRONIZED
BY GYNECOLOGISTS

Six more trickle in. The fat broad looks up with studied disinterest. Yes, studied disinterest. It's not a cliché because these workshop instructors don't get paid if they don't fill their quotas. The quota here is ten; any fewer than that and it's no go, we get our $$ back, the fat broad goes hungry, which would do her a world of good, but never mind. So behind her pleasant, scary face the gears are whirring and grinding. I've got to keep ten of these people. Not much breathing space. It's time to go into my dance.

And will she dance with me? Will she walk across that floor, past the losers and wannabes, the loudmouths, the grandmas, the housewives with a million stories in them, the math teachers whose characters for God's sake wake them up in the middle of the night—will she pass them all and pick me? And will it be a fun dance? Will she tell me I'm talented and brilliant and that it's just a matter of time and perseverance, and will she know what the hell she's talking about and will she have any idea how much fucking time and perseverance I've put into it already and will she look right at me and lie and will she for Christ's sake help me out or

2 more, more noise in hallway, here comes another, that makes 16, she must be breathing easier, the bitch

Or will she condescend me to fucking death like that pompous twit at Irvine and that pompous twat at Berkeley or look right through me like Professor Twitmore Fucking Twatface

in Chi with his Recommended Reading list and his fucking
Strunk & White

WRITE WHAT YOU KNOW
WRITE WHAT YOU KNOW
WRITE WHAT YOU KNOW
WRITE WHAT YOU KNOW
WRITE WHAT YOU KNOW
WRITE WHAT YOU

The Fat Broad speaks.

firstCLASS
THE LIST

This is a fiction workshop. We will meet once a week for nine weeks, counting tonight, at the end of which time each of you will have written at least one piece of fiction and submitted it to the group for critique." Amy paused a beat, as she always did. "So anybody who thought this was a balloon winemaking class better throw dignity to the winds and beat feet."

Somebody tittered, but the rest was silence, except for the drone of that cheap standing fan in the back of the room. It was way past time to tweak the speech; balloon winemaking used to get the big laughs. Amy had a thought. "You *do* know what balloon winemaking is."

A generically lovely young woman raised her hand. "Isn't that where they like sail over the vineyards and sort of check out the vines?"

Amy sighed. "Balloon winemaking was a sixties thing. You mixed wine in a bottle, stuck a balloon over the neck, and watched it ferment."

"Yeah," said a guy in the back row, "and after a couple of weeks you got to watch it explode all over your garage."

Big laughs. Blessings on thee, little man. He didn't look quite

5

old enough to remember the sixties, though. Only Amy in all the world was that old. Older even than this stocky, balding little guy with a great wide mouth like a frog. Maybe she could get a routine going with him, a little break-the-ice patter. Maybe he'd help her work the room.

She made a little show of studying her pre-registration list, which she would turn, before the night's end, into her own mnemonic cheat sheet. *Froggie*, she would pencil in next to his name. Amy had a poor memory for faces, let alone names, and needed all the help she could give herself. "And you are . . . ?" She maintained eye contact and let her mouth hang open expectantly.

Froggie wiggled bushy eyebrows and smiled a secret smile.

Oh crap. "You want me to guess?"

"Nah. You'd never do it. I'm not on your list."

That's what you think. Amy shifted in her squeaky chair, raised her voice. "Which brings me to the list. I have here, in my hand"— she waved the pre-registration list—"a list of known . . ." If they didn't remember the sixties, for sure they wouldn't know the fifties. Although, now that she was beginning to look at them individually, clearly there were a few old enough; one woman was more than old enough. "And first among the boring tasks before us tonight is checking your names against this list. Since there are ten names here and sixteen people in the room, my lightning powers of deduction tell me that at least six of you are window shopping." Hands started to go up. "Shoppers who decide to stay with us will register between now and next Monday."

"What if we're undecided?" Froggie again.

"We offer this course every quarter. Winter will come around before you know it." She gave him her frostiest smile, which was unwise. She needed the money; she couldn't afford to alienate potential students (*customers*, the university extension people called them); and Froggie wasn't really out of line. But she hated first nights, hated not knowing if she'd have enough people to run the class (she'd never failed, in fifteen consecutive quarters, but there was always a first time), hated most of all having to work a cold room. In a few weeks' time she'd feel comfortable with these people, and most of them would like her. Right now she wanted them all to buzz off.

Two hands shot up close together. Amy smiled vaguely in that direction and rattled her damn list. "When I read your name, please tell me if I've pronounced it correctly. Between me and the registrar you've got about a fifty-fifty chance." Dead silence.

Amy focused on the first name, which was, of course, surreal. "Tiny Arena?" Amy had long ago learned, from a student named Mary Louise Poop, to keep incredulousness out of her voice and face when reading the class roll.

Sure enough a hand went up, connected to a pale, morbidly obese man in his sixties. Even seated he was clearly way over six feet tall. "Tiny Arena?" Amy asked again, gently, and the man gravely nodded. She relaxed. "You know, I've come across your nickname in fiction lots of times, but in all my years of teaching, you're my first real-life Tiny."

"Actually," the man said, and his voice trailed off into a mumble. He had eyes like Amy's basset hound, red-rimmed, lugubrious. *Tiny = Alphonse*, she wrote.

"I beg your pardon?"

"Tony," the man said. "Actually, my name is Tony."

"But they call you Tiny?"

"No."

"I'm *awfully* sorry." Then why in hell did you nod your head yes, you big dope? Somebody giggled. Not Tony Arena. Amy broke a sweat and kept going, even when she saw the next name. Straight-faced, she looked out over the crowd and said, "Harold Blassbag." *Jesus.*

"Blass Ball," enunciated a visibly annoyed man in the front row.

"Sorry, Blass Ball," said Amy. Blassball? What the hell kind of name was Blassball?

"Blass *Ball*," said the man, even more put out.

"Blass . . ." Oh for god's sake. "I'm sorry. Could you spell it?"

"B-L-A-S-B-A-L-G." He was a slight, fine-boned, annoyed man in a maroon running suit, which would come in handy when he ran back to the registration office, Tony Arena in tow, to demand both their refunds.

"Thank you. Sorry about this. And pronounced Blass Ball?"

"Blass *Ball!*"

"Suggestion!" Froggie waved his hairy arm in exaggerated, locked-elbow fashion, like a small child who has to go to the bathroom. "How about we turn off this fan? It's making a terrific racket back here."

"Please," said Amy, and in a click a terrible quiet descended over a room she had previously thought merely tomblike. "And I'll tell them to put a second *l* in your name, Mr. Blasbalg."

"Harry," said the annoyed man.

Amy cleared her throat. "Ricky Brizza?"

"Buzza."

"Three for three!" cheered Froggie, to scattered applause.

"That was my line," said Amy, who felt already as if she and Froggie had been mortal enemies in another life. "Buzza," she said sadly.

"B-U-Z-Z-A. You got it." The young man smiled at her in a kindly way. "But you can call me Brizza if you want." He looked like a Norman Rockwell paperboy all grown up, eager and full of energy. He was going to stay. And he had short-clipped blond hair, not exactly a buzz cut, but it would do.

"No," said grateful Amy, "I will call you Buzza." She scribbled on her list, fixing Buzza, fixing Tony, decorating Blasbalg with obscenities. "Next," she said, "we have, arguably, Dorothy Hieronymus."

"Here." A plump, pleasant-faced woman about Amy's age raised her hand. "I use dot," she said.

Amy nodded as though this made sense, because by now she basically didn't give a shit. *Uses dot.* "Tiffany McGee." The pretty blonde girl with the winery balloonists. Of course *her* name was just fine. "Sylvester Reyes." Tall, tan, fifties, hiking shorts, sitting in the front row with his legs spread wide. Why did men do that? Simple comfort? No way. "Call me Syl," he said.

Amy shook her head at the next name. "I'm sorry, ladies and gentlemen, but as God is my witness, the next name is Marvy Stokes."

"Right here."

General hilarity. She was working the room at last. Sure, they were laughing at her, but the laughter seemed pretty companionable. This could turn out to be a good group, what with the shared experience of watching its instructor make an ass of herself. What price dignity? Nine hundred and thirty-five dollars a quarter, no benefits. "You're my first Marvy, Mr. Stokes," said Amy.

"And you're my first writing teacher," said Marvy, a Hawaiian-print shirt, chest-hair kind of guy in his forties. "Actually, it's Marvin," he said.

"Hence Marvy," said Amy.

"Right."

"Got it. Frank Wasted?"

"Wah-sted," said another running-suit man in his thirties, this one bright orange. He'd beat out Blasbalg in a sprint: he looked like a lifetime member of Gold's Gym. Maybe a founder.

"Wah-sted," said Amy. Why the hell not? "W-A-S-T-E-D?"

"There's another *A*," Wah-sted offered, reasonably.

"Where?"

"Right before the first one."

"I can't stand it." Amy put her head in her hands. The laughter was delighted, unforced. They were bonding.

"W-*A*-A-S-T-E-D." Muscle Man ticked off each letter on a stubby upraised finger and smiled agreeably. "See?"

"As in *aardvark*."

"Exactamento."

"Edna Wentworth?" Gray hair, thick and permed; polite smile.

"Tiffany Zuniga?"

"Absent."

Amy shot a look toward the speaker, who turned out to be Ricky Buzza. "I beg your pardon?"

"She's coming. She's late. She's a colleague of mine." She's more than that, thought Amy, watching Ricky Buzza turn pink.

"So much for the list," she said, and turned it over so she could write on its back. "Now for the shoppers. Starting here"—she said, pointing stage right—"would those of you whose names haven't been called out and mangled please identify yourselves?"

A handsome, patrician man in a gorgeous cream-colored cashmere sweater raised, not his hand, but a single index finger, as though summoning a waiter. "I am Dr. Richard Surtees," he said.

Well, whoopee. Amy flashed on an old joke, one of the sort where, given a famous line, you were supposed to fabricate a question that changed its meaning. Line: *Dr. Livingstone, I presume?* Question: *And what is your full name, Dr. Presume?*

An equally handsome woman to his left, mid-forties, skinned-back chestnut hair, smiled at Amy. "Ginger Nicklow," she said. Their looks were similarly classical, but the similarity stopped there, and clearly she was unconnected, other than spatially, to Dr. Richard Surtees. She had a thrift-shop elegance about her that beat hell out of wallet-elegance.

"Pete Purvis," said somebody somewhere. Amy looked up but couldn't find him. "I'm here," said Pete Purvis, and sure enough he was, a pale young man in a green sweatshirt, squarely behind poor Tiny. *Tony.* Amy could just see his upraised hand.

Two hands went up in unison, side by side. A couple in matching T-shirts and jeans. "We're the Boudreaus, Sam and Marilyn," said the man. "We're not staying," said the woman."

"Do you want to leave now?"

The Boudreaus shrugged and shook their smiling heads in unison. The first class was free, and clearly the Boudreaus never turned down a freebie.

A tall, slender young woman stood in the doorway, panting.

"Tiffany Zuniga?" asked Amy unnecessarily, as Ricky Buzza was making a clumsy job of clearing his stuff off the chair next to him. When she didn't notice him he patted the seat, thumping it hopefully, like the tail of a happy hound. Taking pity, Amy pointed him out to Tiffany II, who sat down without acknowledging him, whipped a steno pad out of her backpack, and held her pencil poised above it, ready to record Amy's every luminous word.

Amy cleared her throat. "Either one of you is lying doggo," she said, "or I can't add. I've got fifteen names now on my list and there are sixteen of you."

"It's me," said Froggie. "I was on the fence."

"That's perfectly all right, but I'd still like your name."

"I'm not so sure," said Froggie, grinning.

"Rumplestiltskin?" asked Amy.

"Charlton Heston," said Froggie.

Amy just stared.

"Really," said Froggie. "My mother was a religious nut."

"Charlton Heston," said Amy. She massaged her eyeballs as the class bonded joyously all around her. It was early for break, but what the hell. "Take five, everybody. Take twenty. When you come back, we'll get down to business. Be prepared to tell us what books you like to read, and what you hope to accomplish here in the remaining weeks." Amy always got them to name their favorite writers: it was a good icebreaker, and it helped her sort them out in her head. A depressing proportion of writing students didn't actually read much fiction, but few would admit it. Instead, they'd usually profess a deep love of one or all of three writers: Hemingway, Fitzgerald, Updike. Amy had no idea why these were the safe names for nonreaders. Perhaps this would make a good list for her blog.

Charlton Heston walked up to her as the rest filed out. "Can I get you a cup of coffee?"

"Is your name really Charlton Heston?"

"Yep."

Amy sighed and found herself smiling up at him. "You can get me a beer."

"How do you take it?"

"Black," said Amy.

CLASS **list** CHEAT SHEET

~~TINY ARENA = ALPHONSE   TONY TONY TONY~~—took off during break—kill me now

HAROLD ~~BLASSBAG BLASS BALL BLASSBALL~~ BLASBA—L**G**—lawyer!!!, **HARRY**, likes King, Grisham, Turow, zzzzzzz

RICKY ~~BRIZZA~~ BUZZA—young—25?—blond buzz cut—reporter *North County Times*—thing for Tiffany Z—Palahniuk, Bukowski, Pete Dexter

DOROTHY HIERONYMUS—matron—clueless Margaret Dumont book-club type, "I read everything" esp UPDIKE (prob Nora Roberts)—"**DOT**"

TIFFANY MCGEE—blonde airhead, "I don't read a lot but I wanna write"!!!

SYLVESTER REYES—SYL—tall & broad, h.s. football coach, dim bulb?, reads sci fi (or not—didn't name one author, not even H, F, U)—*don't confuse with Frank W*

MARVY STOKES—Hawaiian shirt, balding, brown hair, nice guy, chem tchr, *HEMINGWAY FITZGERALD* prob. Tom Clancy

FRANK WAASTED—~~JOCK~~—NO! works at the U, prof comp lit, tenure?, slumming, Carver, Woolf, Pynchon

EDNA WENTWORTH—old, ret. (?) Schooltchr, sharp, O'Connor, Dickens, Flaubert

~~BOUDREAUS~~

TIFFANY ZUNIGA—pretty, young, job?, snotty, Atwood, A. Carter, Walker, Morrison, blah blah blah

RICHARD SURTEES—"I am Doctor Richard Surtees"—pompous ass, writing NOVEL!! WATCH OUT!! AIEEE!!

GINGER NICKLOW—handsome, 40s, works for some charity org, reads for pleasure (bestsellers & mysteries)

PETE PURVIS—sweet-faced boy, maybe older than he looks, dressed by mother? Tolkien, Rowling, Narnia, wants to write for kids

CHARLTON HESTON—Froggie—smartass—likes Salinger, Roth, Russo

NO CARLA??

Two hours later Amy was speeding up Miramar Road, toward north and home. It was past ten o'clock and traffic was light. Usually she enjoyed the drive, but tonight she was exhausted. Too many new people, too many mixups, and she'd had a hard time committing them to a schedule. In the end Marvy Stokes and Tiffany One, the non-balloonist airhead, had promised to bring in stories for next week, and the arrogant cashmere guy, Dr. Richard Surtees, had bestowed upon Amy a manuscript as thick as her thumb, professionally typed and bound in a plastic cover, no doubt by an overworked medical secretary. "You'll enjoy this," he had actually said, and Amy had actually claimed that she looked forward to reading it.

She never looked forward to reading anything that wasn't bound and marketed by actual publishers, and she hardly ever even looked forward to those. Between her childhood days, when all books were magical, and the unmagical present, something bad had happened, both to the publishing industry and to Amy. The bad thing that happened to Amy was that she had got her first novel published at the age of twenty-two. This was probably not the bad thing that happened to the publishing industry, although it surely hadn't helped. There had just been this steep parallel decline.

Amy also hated, among other things, pulling up to her empty house late at night, squeezing the Crown Vic into the carport, and oozing herself out of the car, the fit being so tight that sometimes she had to back the car out and try again. She hated the sudden quiet, after forty-five minutes of jazz and engine hum, the empty hush of suburban California night. Her neighbors all hit the sack at eight and nine o'clock, so they could be up and going before dawn to beat the grisly morning traffic on the I-15, and all she could hear were her own footsteps and the jingling of her keys, and sometimes, as tonight, the barking of far-off dogs. Her own old basset hound, who barked at will when she was home, never welcomed her with so much as a whine, probably because he was a coward, but possibly, Amy thought, because he begrudged her whatever small comfort he was capable of giving. As usual she had left the living room lights on, but the orange glow behind lowered blinds was only slightly less ominous than pitch black. You could be murdered as easily by incandescent light as in the *pale wash of a gibbous moon,* as her perennial student, Carla Karolak, would put it. What the hell was a gibbous moon? And where the hell was Carla Karolak? She hadn't missed a class for six quarters.

Once inside she went through the usual rituals of locking and double-locking and letting Alphonse in from the backyard, so he could accompany her through the house in search of axe-wielding psychopaths. She needed Alphonse not for protection, which was fortunate, but for company. She didn't want to spend her last, horror-stricken moments on earth alone. Her house was small and cluttered and took only a few minutes to inspect. Amy wondered, as she yanked open the coat closet door, how she could be so full, simultaneously, of dread and boredom. Dread, she guessed, was dreary. Surely they shared a root. She stopped off at her *Webster's Second Edition Unabridged,* to check this out. No, they didn't.

Amy Gallup was a loner who was afraid to be alone. She had never lost her child's fear of basements, and bedroom closets, and the thick darkness under her bed. Over the years she had tried roommates, live-in friends, and husbands, and the lack of privacy in all but her first marriage had driven her crazy, so crazy that these night terrors were preferable. Drinking helped, though getting drunk did not.

She was safe for now, so it was time to give Alphonse his companionship fee. She was heading toward the Milk Bone box in the kitchen when she noticed that her answering machine was blinking "1." It had to be Carla, she thought, apologizing for missing the first class, although apparently not from her home phone, which would have registered on Amy's caller ID. "Private Caller" had left a message of some length. When Carla got chatty, Amy needed a drink. She gave Alphonse his giant biscuit, fixed herself a bourbon on the rocks, and sat down to hear Carla out.

It wasn't Carla, though, unless Carla had managed the call in her sleep. What Amy heard instead was thirty seconds of silence. She moved to press the delete button, since some idiot had obviously misdialed and neglected to hang up. But when she got close to the machine she thought she could hear breathing. Not heavy breathing, directly into the receiver, but erratic, excited breathing, and fragments of whispers, from some distance away. It sounded as though the caller had put the phone down and were talking to himself, or herself, from a few feet away, doing that thing where you whisper your thoughts in shorthand, starting sentences aloud and finishing them inside, censoring your most dangerous thoughts before they make some irrevocable connection. You never do this sort of thing, Amy thought, unless you're very, very upset. Or insane. She imagined, on the fourth playback, that she could hear individual words. *Listen. Pay attention. God damn you.* And, to Amy's great sorrow, because she had practically convinced herself that this was a wrong number, she heard, clearer than all the rest, *Teach me anything.*

Possible contexts, all bad: *You'll never teach me anything. Just you try and teach me anything. You bitch, you actually think you can teach me anything?*

Now it was easy to imagine all sorts of words, obscenities, hateful descriptions, elaborate physical threats. Amy should probably keep the message on her machine as some sort of record, but she knew if she did she would just play it over and over and make herself sick, and things were already bad enough. She hit "delete," instantly regretting it, and replenished her empty glass, and sat down on the living room couch with Alphonse and the manuscript of Dr. Richard Surtees. It was going to be an unpleasant night: the longest in months. Perhaps the doctor had given her something to help her sleep.

According to his secretary's yellow Post-it, Amy was privileged to hold roughly half of something called *Code Black: A Medical Thriller.* Having watched both parents and her first husband waste away in hospitals, Amy was never thrilled by anything medical, but she always tried, when confronted with this genre in class, to put her feelings aside. As she reminded her students, they were each entitled to objective critical response, not a catalog of their critics' tastes.

A quick glance-through told her that Surtees had cast his protagonist in that heroic mold so commonly used by doctors who want to write fiction. Unlike other professionals, physicians rarely viewed themselves with anything approaching ironic detachment—which was probably good for their patients, but not so hot for their readers. Surtees's hero was a world-class neurosurgeon, a black belt in Karate, a distinguished amateur cellist who had studied with Pablo Casals (*"You have a great gift," the old man had admonished him severely, "and you toss it away to save a few insignificant lives!"*), and Merlin the Magnificent in the sack.

The plot of *Code Black* was apparently going to be one of those convoluted deals involving a lot of esoteric medical words and government acronyms (in an ominous footnote, Surtees promised a twenty-page glossary), and would revolve around a worldwide bioterrorist threat amplified by a perfidious liberal cabal hell-bent on imposing socialized medicine on a gullible public.

"'What do we do now,' Senator?" snarled Black, almost spitting in his disgust. "Why, we send each plague-ridden citizen of Manhattan to his primary healthcare provider!"

Amy poured herself another drink, rechecked all the locks, and settled in with Dr. Richard Surtees for dread and drear.

secondCLASS
MAKING STUFF UP

Ordinarily Amy would have been pleased at the small number of drops. The room was almost filled when she arrived, and within a few minutes the rest had straggled in. As far as she could see, she was missing only Tiny Arena, Airhead Tiffany, and the Boudreaus, and she had gained Carla Karolak, no surprise there, sparkling at her from the front row. As promised, Marvy Stokes, helpfully wearing another Hawaiian shirt, had brought in a pile of Xeroxed manuscripts. Amy asked him to pass them out to the class and to her, and asked if anyone had seen Tiffany.

"I'm right here," said Tiffany Zuniga.

"I meant the other Tiffany. McGee. The one who was supposed to bring in a story tonight."

"Maybe she dropped," said Charlton Heston.

"Bite your tongue," said Amy. She regarded the class severely. "There is a special circle of hell," she told them, "reserved specifically for people who promise to bring something in and then renege. I want you all to understand this."

Carla stood up. She had taken to doing this lately, standing up instead of raising her hand or just speaking out. "Take it from me," she told the others, "she's dead serious."

"Why," asked Charlton Heston amiably, "should we take this from you?"

"I've been through this course six times." Carla sat down, then rose once again. "She's that good, people. Take it from me!"

No one, with the possible exception of old lady Wentworth, looked inclined to take anything from Carla Karolak. Carla was clearly in one of her manic phases, and anyone not acquainted with her would likely assume she was some kind of nut. The fact that she was so spectacularly obese that she made Amy look lithe in comparison did not help her credibility either, especially in Southern California, where physical health was synonymous with moral virtue. Carla was a constant annoyance to Amy, mostly because of moments like these, when she was forced to defend her.

"Carla," Amy said, "knows what she's talking about. She also writes dynamite short fiction," she lied. Carla's work was getting better, but that was about it.

"Not anymore!" said Carla, starting to rise again. She was wearing a tight magenta jogging suit of threadbare velour. "I'm back to poetry again!"

Swell. "The point is," Amy interrupted, settling her back down, "that it's inexcusable for any of you to let down the rest of us. I want to make myself clear on this point. If you promise to bring something in and you fail to do so, for whatever reason, then we are doomed to a three-hour class without a common text. We'll spend three full hours twiddling our thumbs, or worse, listening to me drone on and on, or to one of you reading aloud. As I warned you last week, nothing on God's earth is more soporific to the average adult than being read to."

Charlton Heston raised his hand, speaking effortlessly for the whole class. He had that degree of self-assurance. "What if you sign up to bring something in and then die?"

"Then you go to hell," said Amy.

21

He glanced over his shoulder at the nervously chuckling crowd. "She's really strict," he said, in a stage whisper.

"Look," said Amy, "obviously there are valid excuses, but none of them involves failing to notify me so I can make other arrangements. That's why I gave you my phone number last week." She stopped and surveyed their faces, searching out the whispering maniac. Of course there were no obvious candidates. She had a cunning thought. "I can't *teach you anything*," she said slowly, scanning the room for a furtive sign of startled recollection, "in the abstract. I can't *teach you anything* unless you give me something to work with." Zilch.

Dr. Surtees, seated once again in the front row, raised a languid hand. "I took the liberty of bringing twenty copies of *Code Black*," he said, indicating a Nordstrom's shopping bag beside his desk.

"Well, that's enterprising of you. How many pages are we talking about? Not the one hundred twenty you gave me last week—"

"No, the whole thing."

"The entire *novel*?"

"Whoa," said one of the outdoorsy guys, who was either Syl Reyes or Frank Waasted.

"Whoa is right," said Amy. "I appreciate your bringing this in, but you can't expect—"

"I don't," said Dr. Surtees. "I'm merely asking for feedback on the first two chapters. I included the rest just in case anyone wanted to see how it ends."

The middle-aged woman in a fuzzy lime green suit said she couldn't wait to read it. Amy couldn't remember her name, and she'd left her cheat sheet in the car. Typically, Amy didn't nail down the names of all her students until she'd read their fiction. She was trying, though, and getting marginally better at it. Who was this silly woman who rushed to embrace the doctor's novel? Surtees and Marvy Stokes passed out copies to the class and to Amy.

"All right," said Amy, "the deal is, next week we'll have read thoroughly and be ready to discuss chapters one and two of *Code Black* and"—she glanced down at Marvy's manuscript—" 'Nobody Wins All the Time.' Is this a short story?" she asked Marvy, wondering as she did so if it would be possible to go on indefinitely avoiding his ridiculous nickname.

"Yeah. Well, you can tell me if it is. It might be something bigger."

"Fine. Understand that you are each to read each manuscript carefully, and mark it up with your comments, so that you can pass it back to the author at the end of next week's discussion.

"Meanwhile, we are faced with the Problem of the Second Class. We talked about this last week, and I asked all of you to think about bringing in something short for reading aloud and extemporaneous discussion."

Five hands shot up, Carla's first.

"Poem, right?"

"Sorry about that," said Carla. "I know you don't like to deal with them. But it's what I've been doing lately."

"Carla, if you're not doing fiction, then maybe—"

"Don't worry. I've got a story for later. This is just for tonight." Already on her feet, Carla asked if she should read from where she was or come forward. Amy made the mistake of leaving it up to her.

Carla shuffled up front, pausing to send copies of her poem down each row of students, deposited one on Amy's desk, and faced forward. She had, Amy thought, put on a few more pounds since the last quarter. Her magenta sweatshirt was a couple of sizes too small and didn't quite reach what would have been her waist if she had one and displayed a pink roll of midriff. Amy had never figured out whether Carla knew how unwisely she dressed. She was always otherwise well groomed, so it was hard to believe that she chose garish apparel on purpose. Carla was a twinkling mystery to Amy.

"I just finished this one recently," Carla told the class brightly. "I'm interested in brutally honest feedback, so listen up." There were nervous titters; the audience certainly wasn't hers, but probably nobody wanted her to crash and burn either. "It's called 'Engine 101.'"

ENGINE 101

By Karla K

The rope must be new
Or all bets are off

Rope changes when you pull on it
At first it's elastic
At last it's not
Not when you pull too hard

When you pull too hard it breaks.

Upon buying the rope
You should consider its tensile strength
Sometimes expressed in "newtons."
Sometimes in "psi."

Be sure to examine the label.

You must also consider
The maximum safe working load
To prevent tragic accidents
Or whatever.

Suppose you have a working load of
Say
Two hundred seventy-eight pounds.
You could use ⅜-inch diameter twisted nylon
braid

Or ½-inch manila
Or maybe ½-inch sisal
(if you're feeling lucky)

But the first is slippery, like an eel
And the others are scratchy, like bad wool
And none of them feels as good as cotton

You can buy cotton rope on e-Bay
GREAT BUY
½-inch DIAMETER
MAX WORKING LOAD OF 300 LBS

But don't.

They lie.

Carla lowered her paper and regarded the class. Amy, directly behind her, couldn't see the expression on her face, but could hardly miss the expressed reactions of the rest, which ranged from polite dismay through pity to horrified stupefaction. Even Dr. Surtees looked uncomfortable. Carla had really outdone herself this time. Amy didn't know whether to applaud or just put her head in her hands.

"Who wants to go first?" Amy asked disingenuously. "Look, the writer asked for feedback, and even if you're not up to brutal honesty just yet, you are all capable of reacting to what you've just heard." *In fact, you're doing it right now.* "I warn you, I'm going to call on someone in a few seconds."

"Well, first off—" said the outdoorsy guy in the back.

"Excuse me," said Amy. "As it's only the second class, it would be helpful if you would all identify yourselves when speaking up."

"Syl Reyes. Well, first off, I thought it was going to be about a train."

"Why?" asked Amy.

" 'Engine 101,' " explained Charlton Heston. "Charlton Heston," he added.

"See?" said Syl Reyes. "The title is wrong."

Tiffany Zuniga identified herself and explained to Syl that "Engine 101" was a college course, of course, short for Engineering 101. "I think most readers would know that."

"Well, I didn't."

"Actually," said that thrift-shop queen, Ginger Nicklow, "I didn't either."

Amy had to stop this before the little sneaks actually got away with what they were trying to do. "Let's put the title aside for a moment. Let's talk about the poem itself."

"Thanks," said Carla, over her shoulder.

"Well," said Syl Reyes, "my point was, I was so messed up by the title that I couldn't concentrate on the rest of it. I kept waiting for the train."

"Was anyone else similarly distracted?"

A number of them gratefully nodded their heads, including the hypocritical Tiffany Zuniga, which didn't make any sense, unless you knew anything about human nature.

"Then let's hear it again, shall we?" said Amy to Carla, and they all did. Amy found their collective consternation immensely satisfying. *That'll teach you,* she thought.

"All righty," Amy said. "What is the poem about?" Silence. "Tiffany. What is this poem about?"

"Well, that's really not for me to say, is it?"

"Of course it's for you to say."

"Well, how am I supposed to know what she meant when she wrote it?" Amy was definitely getting to Tiffany.

"You're not. You're supposed to know what you heard when she read it."

"The writer," said Carla, "is an authority on his own intentions.

The reader is an authority on his own experience, which includes the experience of reading the writer's work."

Amy hated it when Carla quoted her. First, because she stole her thunder, and second, because hearing her own words from someone else made them sound pompous, which they were.

"This is not to say," Carla went on, "that all readings are equal. There are poor readings and—"

"If you don't understand what you heard," said Amy, "just say so. This is a process, not a test."

"Okay, then, I don't understand what I heard," said Tiffany.

"Good," said Amy. "Now, why is that?" *Gotcha.*

Tiffany looked betrayed.

"Tiffany has given us a good start. Is there anyone here who thinks he understood the poem?"

The buzz-cut reporter, Ricky Buzza, glanced at Tiffany and raised his hand. He reminded Amy of Tom Sawyer, sacrificing himself for Becky Thatcher. "It's about rope," he said.

"Pete Purvis!" said the kid in back of Ricky. "Yeah, it's about rope, tensile strength, and, uh, loads."

"Does everyone agree?"

Everyone looked down or to the side and kept their traps shut, except for Charlton Heston, who regarded Amy with interest.

"Mr. Heston. Charlton? Do you agree? Is this a poem about tensile strength and working loads?"

"Would you mind calling me Chuck? And no, of course it isn't. Who's going to write a poem about rope? It's about—"

"Excuse me!"

Amy searched her class list for a clue as to the identity of that agitated woman in the fuzzy green suit. Studying her baffled, humorless face, Amy flashed on Margaret Dumont in *Duck Soup*, singing "Hail, Hail Freedonia!" *I use dot.* "Ms. Hieronymus, is it?"

"Dot Hieronymus, and I must say something. This is one of the most moving, emotionally wrenching poems I have ever heard. Are we all deaf here? Are we all blind? Are we dumb?"

"Actually," Amy said, "we're all timid. Except, apparently, for you. Dot, will you please tell us what you think the poem is about?"

"I will," said Dot, whose eyes, fixed on Carla, were filling with tears. "But first I want to say, to Carla, that—"

"Wait a minute," said Amy.

"—that we all heard you. That you are among friends."

About half the class seemed to emote along with Dot, and the rest looked ready to bolt. Harold Blass Ball made eye contact with Amy. "Before this goes any further," he said, "I'd like to remind you all that I'm a lawyer, and that this is not a licensed group therapy situation, and that certain liabilities could—"

"Thank you so much," Amy said, "for bringing this up, and I'll get back to it in a sec, but first, will someone please, please, please tell us what they think this poem is about?"

Carla clapped her hands and jiggled. "Wow," she said, "this is so cool."

Dot half-rose from her seat. "Dear Carla," she began.

"Oh, for goodness' sake. The poem is obviously about a failed suicide. The poet herself gives every indication of being happy, and even if she isn't, it's none of our business. We are not friends. We don't even know one another." Edna Wentworth, of all people, briskly retook her seat and gazed severely around her, particularly at Dot Hieronymus. Edna Wentworth, Amy remembered now, was a retired schoolteacher. Amy loved Edna Wentworth. First, for being a bright, no-nonsense woman; and second, for reconfirming for Amy the folly of cliché expectation.

"Exactly," said Amy. "Thank you so much, Edna. Is 'Edna' all right?"

" 'Edna' is perfectly acceptable, but if this is going to turn into an encounter group, I'm leaving."

"Me, too," said Amy. "Everyone, please pay attention. Before we get back to the poem, let's get clear on what we're about. This is a fiction workshop. It is not a journal-writing workshop, or an essay class, or some bogus course on how to get an agent, or a consciousness-raising festival. We're here to write and read and discuss fiction. Fiction is not fact. Though this much should be obvious, to many people, both here and elsewhere, it is not.

"When one of you—Carla, in this instance—brings in something for the class to read, that person has the absolute right to have his manuscript assessed *as fiction*, and each reader has the solemn duty to read it that way. Always. In every single case. No matter what. If, for instance, a two-headed, one-legged leper writes a story with a leprous two-headed, one-legged protagonist, we will not assume that the piece is in any way autobiographical."

"But surely that's unrealistic," said Ginger Nicklow.

"Of course it is. That's the whole point. We are here to write *fiction*. Fiction writers lie their heads off. It's their job. They make stuff up."

"Come on." Ricky Buzza and Syl Reyes spoke at once. Ricky deferred to Syl. "Okay, I mean, we make stuff up, but a lot of it is going to be about our real lives. Right?"

"Of course it is," said Amy.

"Then how can you say that it's all made up?"

"I just told you. Fiction writers lie their heads off."

"She just *lied*!" said Carla Karolak. "Just now! Get it?"

There was a pause, and then most of the class laughed. Even Surtees. Dot Hieronymus didn't look amused, and Pete Purvis, Amy feared, wasn't quite sharp enough to get the joke. "Of course some of what we write is based upon experience. But think about this: If we're going to scour one another's work for autobiographical references, then we'll become paranoid, in short order, about revealing ourselves in our writing. We'll be reduced to bland subject matter, just to avoid embarrassment.

"If we wanted to expose our private lives to public scrutiny, we would write autobiographies or memoirs. Or run for political office. Instead we write fiction. Some is made up out of whole cloth. Some is not. We owe it to one another to assume, in every case, that what we're reading is made up. Does everybody understand this?"

Dot Hieronymus cleared her throat but said nothing.

"I'll tell you something else," said Amy. "When you write, you will find that you sometimes uncover the truth anyway, accidentally, through your artful lies. Sometimes that's the only way to get at it. This may not make much sense to you now, but I promise that it will, if you do your jobs right."

There was a long silence. "So," said Amy, "are we all agreed that Carla's poem seems to be about a failed suicide?"

It turned into an excellent evening. Second class was early to tackle the Making Stuff Up issue, but most of them caught on pretty quickly, and Amy was pleased at how willing most of them were to tackle Carla's poem more or less objectively. Not only did someone—Frank Waasted—zero in on the poem's tone, without too much prodding on Amy's part, but Edna Wentworth helpfully criticized what she called the "forced irony" of the poem. "The poet is cheerful," Edna said, "in a way that forces us to pay attention. I'd rather be seduced." Of course, the others rallied on what they took to be Carla's side, over-praising the poem, going on about how moving and genuine and imaginative it was. Amy followed up on Edna Wentworth's comments by introducing the topics of style and substance, and noting how the style of Carla's poem, breezy and colloquial and offhand, contrasted deliberately with its dark substance.

When discussion died down and it was Carla's turn to speak, she went into her usual self-effacing tap dance, talking more about Amy than about herself, promising the group an ineffable learning experience. Amy could remember actually enjoying Carla's praise, the first couple of times she experienced it. She knew now that this was Carla's way of avoiding the end of the discussion. Carla did not so much revel in the spotlight as come alive there. It was not, as Amy had once thought, that she needed the attention for childish gratification; rather, she needed it in order to recapture her creative energy. Carla never wrote except when she was taking Amy's class. She had probably tossed off this ridiculous poem during the past week.

"Actually, I wrote it a few hours ago," Carla was telling the class. "I had to stop by Kinko's on the way here." She wound up by thanking Edna Wentworth for her critical comments. "You really nailed me," she said gratefully.

After Carla sat down no one else volunteered to read, and Amy got out her exercise book and put them through their paces for the rest of the night. She gave them all a choice among three exercises:

1. Write something from the point of view of the opposite sex. It can be a diary entry, a suicide note, a short-short story, a poem (if you must), a grocery list, or whatever. Anything at all, as long as it's in the first person, and the first person is male if you are female, and female if you are male.
2. Make up ten names, first and last, and write a thumbnail character sketch for each name.
3. Write an opening paragraph for a short story or novel. Make it up on the spot; no fair using something you've already written.

She gave them a half hour and settled back with a library book, a new novel by an old friend from college. Cy cranked his novels out regularly, one every two years, and still got respectable reviews. Unlike Amy, he hadn't gotten published until his mid-thirties, by which time he had a tenured position at UConn and all the time in the world to write. Cy had dedicated his first book, *The Future Lies Ahead*, to Amy ("To Amy, who doesn't believe it for shit"), and she had been touched, even gratified, at the time. It was a sharp and

silly little book in which Lyndon Johnson time-traveled seven minutes into the future at odd intervals, with odder historical results.
Amy and Cy had been lovers when Johnson was president. In fact,
Amy could never think about LBJ without picturing the two of
them one afternoon, naked and stoned, smearing Cy's black-and-
white TV screen with butterscotch pudding until the crafty old
bastard dropped his bombshell about not running for a second
term. They had goggled at each other and then, like chastened
children, had risen and put their clothes on and cleaned up their
mess.

Amy was thinking about Cool n' Creamy Pudding and Cy's narrow freckled shoulders when Pete Purvis raised his hand.

"I think we're all about done," he said. "I've got a character
name."

"Let's hear it," said Amy.

"Well, it's this kid, twelve-year-old kid, his name is Murphy
Gonzalez! His father is Latino, his mother is Irish-American. He
comes from a big family. He's the baby. He's the only kid not interested in sports. He's big on science."

"And you just now thought of him?"

"Well, no, I've been working on this idea for a while. It's a kid's
book. But I never liked the kid's name, which was just Juan Gonzalez. This is brand-new, tonight."

"Excellent." Amy beamed. "Okay, who else came up with something new tonight?"

Syl Reyes came up with "S. J. Quinn," an athletic high-schooler,
muscle bound but "runty." He didn't know what "S. J." stood for.
Amy said he should. "You made him up," she said. "You're responsible for him."

"Like God," said Carla.

"Yes," said Amy. "We are all little gods here. We create people
and set them in motion and determine their fates. There is a certain
aesthetic responsibility to this, bordering on, or at least mirroring,

a moral responsibility. You can never know too much about your characters."

"Sylvester Judd Quinn," said Syl Reyes, reddening. Amy noted, from her class list, that Syl Reyes's middle name began with "J."

There were a few more names. Tiffany came up with a no-doubt-gorgeous, marathon-running Las Vegas district attorney with a troubled past named Heather Francesca. And Edna Wentworth was apparently very pleased to have dreamed up a Miss Hestevold, a censorious, intelligent spinster, curious about her fellow man, who expects the worst and usually finds it. "I like this name very much," said Edna. "I think I'll write about her."

This was going to be a good group. And to top it all off, Chuck Heston did the sex-reversal exercise, which men traditionally avoided (women loved it), and when he read it to the class, Amy actually felt, if for only a moment, as though she weren't wasting everyone's time.

"It's got a title. 'My Pet.' It's really weird. Should I stand up to read it?" Chuck was nervous, which was good. It meant that there was something at stake for him, which, Amy knew, was absolutely essential to a writer's progress. "Do I have to stand up?"

"Not unless you want to."

Chuck kept his seat and read "My Pet."

His name was Mycroft and he had eight knees, at least four too many as far as I was concerned, plus they were bright red, the exact scarlet of the tanager, only Mycroft did not have feathers, and he did not, thank goodness, fly. He was furry. Not the soft fur of a cat, or the springy fur of a dog; not the kind of fur you'd want to stroke. He was furry like a bottle brush. Not a eucalyptus: an actual bottle brush, like you'd use to scrub a bottle. Except that, unlike a bottle brush, he had bristles detachable at will (a terrible thought, that Mycroft had free will), and when he was angry or frightened he would leap straight up in the air a foot or so, from a tense red-kneed crouch, and fling the bristles out sideways, which turned out to be barbed, so that they stuck in your skin and itched like crazy.

Mycroft was Jack's. I was so in love and so excited about Jack moving in with me that when he opened the shoebox and took out Mycroft I didn't scream get the hell out of here with that obscene thing you sadist pervert jerk. I said wow. I said where do you keep him? Jack said Mycroft just roams around. I got spots before my eyes, red spots, but I didn't actually lose consciousness and instead made up a story about a neighborhood cat who was always coming in the window, and how we had to "protect Mycroft." I dug up an old fishbowl and threw in some moss and a couple of rocks, and then that son of a bitch handed Mycroft to me so I could put him in myself and then everything went black and when I came to I had actually gotten Mycroft into the bowl and stuck a piece of screen over it. Jack put the bowl in the bedroom while I slipped outside and threw up in the oleander.

Jack left after eight months and didn't take Mycroft with him. I put the fishbowl in the back hall and got my first good night's sleep since he moved in. Mycroft was harder to lose than Jack. I was going to just neglect him to death, but then I started seeing him in corners and feeling him on my neck, so I started feeding him again, blurring my eyes every time so I couldn't see anything but red spots in motion. I tried to give him away. I had nightmares about flushing him down the toilet, murdering him with a hammer, pouring Drano in the fishbowl. I kept feeding him and he stayed healthy. He lived for five years. When he died I put him and his bowl in the trash.

I miss the way I hated Mycroft. I ran into Jack and his lovely wife last Christmas, and he asked, How's Mycroft? I said he was delicious.

"Wow," said Amy, and there was general applause.

Chuck was actually blushing. "I never did that before," he said.

General discussion went on past the nominal end of class time. Harold Blasbalg wanted to know if Mycroft were a tarantula, and if so, why Chuck didn't come right out and say so, which gave Amy a chance to turn his question around on the group. What was gained by not saying "tarantula"? She reminded them that it wasn't Chuck who avoided the word, it was his unnamed female narrator.

"In real life," Amy told them, "and in fiction, we betray our natures in the way we speak. Chuck's female narrator is a skittish, scattered sort, and also bright and funny. She's making fun of herself here. But I don't think she deliberately avoids specifying the kind of creature Mycroft is. Does she?"

"She's afraid of Mycroft," said Ginger Nicklow. "She's probably phobic."

Ricky Buzza and Pete Purvis asked how she could know that.

"Look," said Ginger, "she blurs her eyes on purpose when she looks at Mycroft. She can't even stand to view him head-on. Not using the word *tarantula* is the same sort of avoidance mechanism. She does it naturally, without thinking."

"I understand," said Dot Hieronymus. "If she doesn't really look, if she doesn't really use the word, then she can pretend he's not there. I understand that completely."

Not everyone else did, and there was a rousing argument, led by Pete Purvis. Finally Amy had to cut them all off because the school janitor was tapping his foot in the doorway. "You're a great group," she told them. "We're going to have some interesting times together."

Dearest Diary:

Since we don't know each other, I'd better introduce myself. I'm a person of the opposite sex, writing from an alien point of view. This may strike you as a dumb waste of time, but hear me out: It is not so much an exercise for the imagination as it is a primer on the vagaries of American speech, particularly as regards men and women, who share an enormous vocabulary and ninety-five. percent of the available syntactical choices, but differ in certain (predictable!) respects. The dialogue of women, for instance, tends to be timid, exact, polite, even judicious, compared to the dialogue of men compare:

Would you mind terribly getting off my foot?
With
Get off my goddamn foot, you fucking bitch!

Revelation of character through language. Word-avoidance, issue-avoidance. At least she didn't say GENDER-SPECIFIC.
She's a slob but she's not bad. I have a little hope.

THE DOMINANT MALE

THE ALPHA MALE

THE OMEGA MALE

THE TERRIBLE BABOON GOD

Carla Karolak waylaid Amy in the parking lot, attempting, for the first time in three years' acquaintance, to cross the line between teacher and student, mentor and mentee. She asked Amy out for a cup of coffee but took it well when Amy begged off. Tonight everything had worked out, and Amy drove home in a buoyant mood, which carried over to her homecoming with Alphonse.

There were no ominous messages on the machine.

So cheerful was her state of mind that she decided to get an early start on Surtees's first chapter.

> Dr. John "Black Jack" Black, F.A.C.P., F.A.C.S., rose from the girl's bed with the alacrity of a young man, though he was forty-two. Glancing back to appreciate her voluptuous curves, the perilous ski-slope of her upturned nubile hip, he strode to the door and opened it . . .

Once upon a time, when Amy was twenty-five and teaching her first workshop, she would have enjoyed a cheap laugh at the ready image of the studly Black Jack Black glancing back at nubile slalom and whanging into a doorframe, but this was now, and it wouldn't be funny even if the rest of her life was sunny and hopeful. She circled "glancing back" and scribbled "watch your participles" in the margin, hoping meanly that the doctor had forgotten what a participle was, and settled in for a grueling read. After ten minutes, at most, she put the thing down and sat down at her computer to check out her blog.

When Amy had still been writing fiction, computers were huge blinking machines housed in concrete buildings, and she did her composing on a typewriter, starting with an old Underwood and progressing to a Selectric, but always using yellow railroad paper for the first draft. She had no idea why they called it that. Railroad paper was her only superstition: she came to believe it a necessary way station for publishable work, and she valued all its attributes— it was porous and limp and you could actually see tiny pieces of wood embedded in the occasional sheet. It was closer to European toilet paper than to Corrasable Bond. Over time it became harder and harder to find, and then, at just the point where Amy's muse, in which she had never wholly believed, took a hike, it disappeared from stores completely. That was the end of her brilliant career. Although she bought her first PC in 1981, she could never bring herself to process her own words on a screen, which was neither yellow nor full of splinters. She eventually became sufficiently computer-savvy to pick up online tutorial and editing work, which was handy when the royalties dried up.

With remnants of creative energy, Amy had taken up blogging a few years ago. She would never have done such a pointless thing on her own steam, since she didn't believe in writing for free, but one of her extension students, Finn Collier, set up a Web site for her which was so easy to use that she didn't see the harm, at first, in just fiddling with available themes and fonts and page setups, just for the hell of it. The student had urged her to peddle her own out-of-print novels, but most of them had disappeared in transit on the move from Maine to Escondido, and the remaining carton full of *The Ambassador of Loss,* which she'd stowed in her carport, had become infested with hornets: she went to retrieve a thank-you copy for that student and got swarmed and badly stung by furious winged ambassadors. So she had nothing to sell and no point to make and, though Amy was chock full of thoughts and opinions, no impulse to broadcast them. But she did have to do something creative, even if it was just some little thing, because she was not writing, and not writing was hard work, almost as hard as writing.

One day she found inspiration in one of her old journals—the very last one she'd kept, during the long final illness of her first husband, Max. She had begun it at his urging, jotting in ideas for stories and fragments of overheard dialogue. It had been so long since she'd looked at these. Of course they were pitiful (*Woman gives birth to the blues. Child foresees ultimate failure*) and cryptic (*knock on plywood: divorced woman learns to use tools—HAMMERHEAD*). In the middle, though, she found a list of "funny-looking words" which she couldn't remember writing down, except that it was the sort of thing she would have distracted herself with during Max's ER visits. The point of the list was that the words *looked* funny, not that they necessarily had comic *meaning.* Looking down the list she saw that some of them *sounded* funny too, but figured that the sound of a word was, in a sense, part of its look. It was a good list—one to which she was ready to add—and she thought, Why not publish it?

No one would read it, but then her stories and novels had never sold big, and that hadn't bothered her. What did bother her about most blogs was their wistfulness. No matter how self-effacing the bloggers were, they clearly believed themselves on some sort of world stage, where they just might be attended to. They needed to communicate. Amy did not. If people stumbled across her site, fine, but it would exist without them, just like her books, whose continued presence in the Library of Congress was her ego's only comfort. To publish in private: she flat-out loved the idea. The title for her site, what Finn called a splash page, and which he set up for her, was:

GO AWAY.

which was centered on a plain white page, in 48-point Times New Roman font. In order to find the second page, you had to click on the period. There she put the subtitle:

A Solipsist's Commonplace Book of Lists

which she thought was probably too cute, but since nobody would read it anyway, it didn't matter.

Clicking on the apostrophe brought her to a page devoted to her actual self, listing her novels and stories, along with the number of copies sold and the date each book went out of print. She pasted into this page an old photograph Max had taken, in which she was hiding behind the trunk of their backyard beech tree, so that only her arms and legs were visible, extended outward like the limbs of Da Vinci's Vitruvian Man. Above the photograph was the title

WHO IS AMY GALLUP?

and beneath it the caption

> An aging, bitter, unpleasant woman living in Escondido, California, who spends her days editing unreadable text and her nights teaching and not writing. Sometimes, late at night, in the dark, she laughs inappropriately.

Her plan was to fill up the next page (which was, according to Finn, virtually unfillable) with lists, and the first one was

FUNNY-LOOKING WORDS
WEDNESDAY, APRIL 14, 2004

Adjectives:
berserk
blotto
gassy
eleemosynary
flocculent

Verbs:
disembosom
buttress
gainsay
lambaste

Nouns:
crabapple
loblolly
kumquat
bomb
blowtorch
flange
lardoon
galoot
poltroon
spittoon
besom
disembosomee
frottage
onus
larb
phlebotomist
philatelist
nozzle
rumpus

FILED IN LISTS | COMMENTS (0)

It was a good list, to which she was prepared to add from time to time, but it was the only blogworthy one in her notebook. For a while she amused herself by searching out her page at the end of a long day (go+away+gallup) and just appreciating the words themselves. She had always loved words as objects in themselves—their shapes, their character. In this list were a disproportionate number of *m*'s and *b*'s and *oo*'s, and lots of double consonants: she had long theorized that words whose syllables were equally accented, like

41

berserk and *poltroon*, were inherently risible, although she had no idea why. The thought prompted the idea for a second list:

FUNNY-LOOKING LETTERS

but after fiddling around for a week and messing with diphthongs and diacritics, she realized that letters, all by themselves, weren't funny at all. Except the Swedish ones, though probably not to the Swedes. But this prompted another, much shorter list

SEXIEST LETTER IN THE ROMAN ALPHABET
SUNDAY, AUGUST 1, 2004

B

FILED IN LISTS | COMMENTS (0)

because staring at all those letters had made this plain. The letter looked like body parts and was actually the first letter of many words which denoted them.

As she played with the lists, she noticed that at the bottom of each, justified at the right margin, was the subheading "Comments." She tried deleting it, but when she'd revisit the site, there it would be, and eventually she figured out that Finn had set it up automatically, assuming she'd want it. She'd have to call the guy, which she really didn't want to do, and ask how to take it off. Or she might go ahead and use it herself, praising and attacking her own lists. Amy had always enjoyed making up names. This was serendipity, or so it seemed, but the next time she checked the site she was shocked to find a "comment" from someone named Compson Fingerle, suggesting that the sexiest letter in the alphabet was *V*.

What shocked her wasn't the suggestion, which was vulgar and obvious, but the published existence of Compson Fingerle. She started to answer him but then stopped, because she had no wish to debate the issue with anyone, especially Compson Fingerle. She amended her list.

SEXIEST LETTER IN THE ROMAN ALPHABET
TUESDAY, AUGUST 3, 2004

B

Runner-up:

V

FILED IN LISTS | COMMENTS (1)

She did this to avoid future communiques, and for a while it worked, but then Myra Kalbfuss nominated *H,* and someone calling himself Sir Underoo submitted *sackbut, dingo,* and *bustard* for the list of funny-looking words.

This was wasn't communication exactly, but it was apparently some sort of *community.* A community of solipsists she could live with, as who could not? But she couldn't figure out how they accessed the site in the first place, and it worried her. She was now forced to telephone Finn Collier, who told her that these people probably found her site by Googling her name. While he was on the phone, she inserted her name in the search box, and sure enough, up popped the usual used-book sites, plus *Go Away.* But why would anyone be Googling her name?

"You underestimate your fame," said Finn.

No, she didn't.

"Or they could have been searching for something else."

"Like what?"

She could hear him tapping at his keyboard. "Galluping bomb does it," he said.

"What??" She typed in this search string and got the question *DO YOU MEAN GALLOPING BOMB?*

"Also blowtorch gas. Try it yourself!"

He was right. "How?"

"Well, your page contains blowtorch, gas, Gallup, and bomb. Somebody typing in some combination of these—"

"But why in the world would someone try to find blowtorch gas?" What a ridiculous idea.

"They probably wouldn't." He tapped some more. "Here, I gotta go, but I'm sending you a link to a Web server stats page. You can keep track of all kinds of cool information about who visits your site, like . . . see, you've had two visits from Indonesia this month."

She clicked on the link and scrolled down a page filled with pie charts and graphs. "Thanks, but this is really a lot more information than—"

"Got it! Okay, scroll down to the Search Term Report pie chart."

"Why?"

"Because it'll show you some of the words and phrases people were looking for when they Googled your site."

Amy found the chart and thanked Collier, who had to get back to work. She stared at the list.

amy gallup 95

gallup 10

amy 9

author amy 9

ambassador of loss 4

monstrous women 2

kumquat flan 1

crabapple flan 1

butt frottage 1

Here she was forced to stop—first, to backtrack through her page and figure out how, for instance, a search for "crabapple flan" had dumped someone on her page. "Flan," it turned out, was nestled in "flange," like a Russian doll. And then to marvel at the fact that in the world, from time to time, people looked for her. She didn't know how to feel about this. Were these doctoral students researching failed novelists? Members of her old high school class, trolling for obits? It was much easier to picture some pallid office drone (or, who knows, dynamic captain of industry) desperately searching for butt frottage, in all the wrong places.

For the time being, she decided, she'd put up with this "community." *Bustard,* she had to admit, was pretty good: she added it, with *Sir Underoo* in parentheses beside it. Credit where credit was due. She changed the subheading "Comments" to "Peanut Gallery" and then to "Kibbitzers," which she left until she could think of something better.

Amy remained incurious about the identities of kibbitzers, whose numbers grew steadily if unspectacularly, so that by now she had forty or so regulars, a few of whom made decent suggestions. Tonight there were no new comments, and, feeling the tiniest bit disappointed, she decided to start a new list, of hybrid novel titles. She'd been thinking about it for a while.

NOVEL HYBRIDS
WEDNESDAY, OCTOBER 3, 2007

Call of the Wild Duck
A plucky dog survives life in the frozen Klondike with the help of a symbolic duck.

Old Man Riverdance
Paul Robeson is kicked to death by stampeding Irish robots.

The Runaway Bunny Jury

Desperate jurors avoid being profiled by ingeniously disguising themselves as birds, flowers, boats, rocks, and fish.

FILED IN LISTS | COMMENTS (0)

There, she thought. Let's see what they do with this.

 **third**CLASS
SHOWING AND TELLING

Gazing around his small, cluttered, dusty private-eye office, Bill Mansfield gave a huge yawn, and then reluctantly unrolled his lanky six-foot-four frame from behind his gunmetal gray desk. "Eleven o'clock a.m.," he thought to himself, "and not a meal ticket in sight."

Nobody Wins All the Time," Amy announced brightly.

"You said it," said Marvy Stokes. "After class last week I got a parking ticket from a campus cop." He waved the ticket around, no doubt trying to find out if he was the only one so abused. "Twenty-five bucks. Can they get away with this?"

Amy collected three campus parking tickets from the group, with the promise to fix them, and the warning that she could only do this once, and yes, the college could in fact get away with that. Marvy wanted to kvetch some more, an obvious delaying tactic which Amy ignored. "Marvy Stokes has bravely volunteered to go first," she told the class.

"No, I didn't. Why don't we start with—"

"So I'm going to lay out ground rules. Here's the deal: While your work is being discussed, you can't interrupt the discussion or even answer questions until the critique is over with." Hands shot up. "Think about it: When you're in the sanctity of your own bedroom, or bathroom, or wherever it is you do most of your reading, the author isn't there leering over your shoulder, thank god. If you start to get bored, he can't object, or claim, perhaps with justification, that you misread a certain line of dialogue or skimmed an important paragraph on page fifty-seven. He can't argue with you or make you feel inadequate. He isn't there at all. Right? All you have to go by is what he's given you.

"So let's base our discussion on the evidence we've got. While we're talking, the author can take notes if he wants to respond to any points. And in any event, when the discussion is over he can respond however he wishes."

"So basically," said Marvy, "I'm the monkey in the middle."

"Actually, no," said Amy. "You're not in the middle. If you're picturing us as some sort of menacing circle, then technically you're outside the circle. You're not here at all."

Amy formally began the critique without further discussion, even though many people obviously wanted to argue about procedure. They always did, at the beginning, and it was more expedient just to go ahead and show them how the system worked rather than defend it. "Nobody," she said, "Wins All the Time."

Dead silence.

"Okay, what happens in this story?"

More dead silence.

"The point being, if we can't agree on what actually happens in a piece of fiction, we can't talk about it at all."

"Well, it's obvious," said Tiffany Zuniga.

"Then you shouldn't have any trouble telling us," said Amy.

Tiffany sighed. "It's a detective story. Okay? There's this private eye, which I don't even know if they still exist on Planet Earth, and this hottie walks into his office and hires him to find her lost poodle."

"Shih tzu," said Marvy.

"Did anyone hear that?" asked Amy.

"I thought I heard 'shih tzu,'" said Chuck Heston, "but it might have been the wind."

"Yeah, could we lose the fan?" Pete Purvis waited for a nod from Amy, and then switched it off.

"Okay, shih tzu. She hires him, at five hundred dollars a day plus expenses, to find her *shih tzu*. He tracks down the dog at some run-down farm in the countryside—"

"Where exactly is the story set?" asked Amy.

"I haven't the faintest idea," said Edna Wentworth. "At the outset we seem to be in a large city, and then we're at a pig farm."

A lot of people chimed in at this point, and Amy let them hash the matter out. The wobbly setting of "Nobody Wins All the Time" was the least of Marvy's problems. Amy studied the class, observed its dynamics, noting with pleasure that Edna was going to be a huge help. This was not going to be one of those namby-pamby groups who, if they had nothing nice to say, didn't say anything at all. They were unusually vocal and energetic.

"What's the difference?" Syl Reyes was arguing. "It's a pig farm on the outskirts of town."

"But it's not a town, it's a big city."

"How do we know this?" asked Amy.

"Because," said Frank Waasted, "Bill Mansfield, this private eye, keeps talking about subways, ghettos, and gridlock." Frank was the other muscle-bound guy, the one Amy at first confused with Syl Reyes. But Frank was sharp and Reyes was kind of dim. Tonight they were both wearing shorts and those clunky brown climbing shoes obviously designed for mountain trails; they were outdoor types, California men, sun-reddened, peeling, way too at ease in their own skin, at least for Amy's liking. But Frank Waasted, who on First Class night had named Raymond Carver as his favorite writer, had done his doctorate on magical realism. Academic types had changed a lot since Amy's day.

Syl continued to wonder what the difference was anyway, since "we all know it's made up," and Amy encouraged a discussion of this issue. "It isn't so much," she finally said, "a matter of being realistic. As Pete and Syl have pointed out, we know we're reading a story, and if we wanted reality we'd go elsewhere." Where, exactly, Amy had no idea. "It's a question of trust. If we're reading something and we can't avoid noticing that our writer has been inattentive, or lazy, with something as basic as setting, we're likely to pull back. He loses his authority, and our trust."

"Can I say something?" Marvy waved oddly, as though trying to spell out his thoughts.

"Later," said Amy.

"It's supposed to take place in—"

"Let's leave this topic and get back to my original question, which was, What happens in this story?"

They had a fine time with that one, because what happened in Marvy Stokes's story was basically up for grabs. A private eye was hired to find a dog, fell in love with a mysterious woman, and uncovered a Byzantine money-laundering scheme involving pigs, methamphetamine, the Grand Cayman Islands, and dog treats. Most of the action took place inside the mind of the bewildered and besotted Bill Mansfield, who, when he wasn't rearranging sections of his lanky frame, was mulling over various sights and sounds to which the reader was not directly privy. Everything of interest happened offstage, including the shattering climax, a three-way pig farm shootout, during which Mansfield was grievously wounded, both physically and psychologically, by the shih-tzu lady. In the final paragraph he was reminiscing in the emergency room of Metro Mercy Hospital. " 'What hurt the worst,' mused Gordo, 'was that she hadn't meant a single word of it.' "

"Then he must have been pretty crazy about her," Chuck was saying, "considering that she shot his kneecap off."

"Yeah, who's Gordo?" asked Pete Purvis.

Marvy started semaphoring again.

"I'm guessing," said Amy, "that Gordo was Bill Mansfield's original—"

"It was 'Gordon,'" Marvy whispered.

"—name, or perhaps it was Gordon, which would explain how Gordo avoided extinction during the terrible time of global change." Amy almost mentioned that Marvy had broken one of James Thurber's six rules for effective storytelling (if you're going to change Ketchum to McTavish, Ketchum should not pop up on the last page). But she didn't, because probably most of them didn't know, or even care, who Thurber was.

It was a decent if rambling discussion. About half the class, including an uncharacteristically subdued Carla Karolak, sat on their hands, and the rest mixed it up. Tiffany objected to the sexual objectification of the shih-tzu lady, whose "buff posterior" was said to be "her most spectacular asset." Edna Wentworth objected to the identical passage, but not for political reasons. "It's clichéd writing," said Edna, "not to mention the unfortunate juxtaposition."

Chuck, Frank Waasted, and Amy laughed at the same moment.

"Juxtaposition of what?" asked Pete Purvis.

"Posterior and asset," said Frank.

"As in," said Chuck Heston, "'Her buff asset was her spectacular posterior.'"

Tiffany pointedly didn't think this was funny. Tiffany was going to be a pain. Amy thought it best at this point to launch into her standard spiel on showing vs. telling. "We can talk about language later," she said, "if we have time. Right now we need to tackle more substantial matters. The problem with this story is that there are hardly any scenes in it. The only ones I can find are the opening scene in Mansfield's office, and that one shot we get of the pig farm. Everything else is described for us within Mansfield's recollection, which is none too specific. We can't see and hear what's happening, because Bill Mansfield is usually in the way."

Amy took a breath, and paused, without thinking, as though waiting for something; at which point she realized she was waiting for Carla, who had heard this speech twenty times and could usually be counted on to pipe up. But Carla was slumped in the back of class, looking down at her untouched notebook, distracted and apparently unhappy. Carla was always moody but Amy had never seen her like this.

Amy wrapped up the critique fifteen minutes later, at which point Marvy told the class that his story was set in Grand Rapids, Michigan, and that when he "cleaned it up" he would definitely mention this. Amy asked him if he had understood the difference between showing and telling, scenes and descriptions, and he said, "I think so," which meant that he hadn't and he didn't care to. When Amy had started out teaching she had taken this sort of thing to heart; now it didn't bother her at all, unless the person showed actual talent, which Marvy so far did not.

At the break, everyone but Carla filed out of the room. "I got a question," she said, without looking up.

Amy sat at the empty desk in front of Carla and scooted it around to face her. "Shoot," said Amy.

Carla doodled on a pad of lined paper. Her doodles looked like blue tattoos: crosses, pagodas, chrysanthemums. "Listen," she said, "I know I talk too much, and I can be a pain in the ass, and I know," she said, looking up at Amy, "what I look like. You know?"

Amy said nothing. Was this going to be another attempt at friendship? Amy never confided in anyone anymore, except Alphonse.

"Here's the thing," said Carla. "It had to be somebody in this class. Had to. Anyway I don't know anyone else, except Mother's bridge people and Mrs. Sanchez and Hilario, the gardener, and my various medicos. Which I realize sounds like a lot of people, but isn't, believe me." Carla was wearing a No Fear sweatshirt. You are too old, Amy wanted to tell her, for legible clothing. "And it wasn't a threat, exactly, so I don't know why I'm so upset. I'm used to people not liking my stuff."

"Did you get a phone call?" *Teach me anything . . .*

"No, God, that would be worse. I got this," Carla said, slipping an envelope out from between the pages of her notepad, "and I'd really like to give it to you. If you don't want to read it I don't blame you, but I've got to stop staring at it."

Amy picked up a ripped-open white envelope, on which was typed Carla's address in La Jolla. There was no return address. A Dr. Seuss Cat-in-the-Hat stamp had made it intact through the canceling machine, despite the fact that its upper right corner protruded beyond the edge of the envelope. The stamp looked as though it had been applied by a small child. "Carla," Amy said, "a lot of people have access to your address. You can find out addresses on the Internet. How do you know—"

"It'll be obvious when you read it. Besides, look." Carla pointed to the first line of the address. "I only spell my first name with a K when I write, and the only people who see my stuff are here. Plus we always exchange addresses in First Class, so chances are it's somebody in this actual class."

"Okay. But you've taken a number of classes from me. What if it's someone from awhile back? It doesn't have to be one of these people here." Amy was beginning to notice how assiduously she was avoiding whatever "it" actually was.

"Just read it," said Carla.

Amy stared down at the envelope. It wasn't very thick. Probably contained only a single sheet, folded three times. She started to open it up when Chuck popped his head in the door.

"Not now," whispered Carla, to Amy.

Amy told Chuck to call in the others and returned to the front of the room, tucking Carla's letter in her pants pocket.

Dot Hieronymus led off discussion of *Code Black* with breathless compliments. Spurred by the doctor's muscular prose ("Black struggled to maintain an impassive countenance, but not even he could quieten the vein that throbbed visibly in his left temple."), she had already torn through half the novel and couldn't wait for the rest of class to catch up. Dot belonged to three book clubs and had read "every medical thriller that ever came down the pike," and *Code Black* ranked with the best of them. For all Amy knew this was true.

"Before we begin," Amy said, "I want us to note that this piece of fiction, as opposed to Marvy's, is part of a larger whole. So it's a fragment, and therefore more difficult to talk about than a short story. We can't complain about loose ends, for instance. We can't demand to understand everything that's going on. At this stage, it would be disastrous if we did get the whole picture, wouldn't it? It's the writer's job, in his opening chapters, to draw his readers in. If, by the end of an opening chapter or two, we don't understand why a character is behaving the way he is, or what somebody meant when he said what he did, that's probably good. We'll keep reading to find out."

"So what *can* we complain about?" asked Frank. His copy of Surtees's manuscript had taken a beating and was covered with pen scribbles. Frank looked eager to complain about lots of things.

"Oh," said Amy, "you can always complain about clichés. And not just language, either. A character can be trite, or a setting."

"Well, here's this black-belt babe-magnet neurosurgeon—"

"Hey," said Ricky Buzza, "that's not a cliché. I mean, I never read about a black-belt neurosurgeon—"

"Come on, he's a *type*, a superhero *type*, and you just know there's going to be a vast conspiracy—"

"Don't spoil it!" said Dot.

"And a big shoot-out, or lobotomy tournament—"

"Don't forget the Illuminati," added Chuck.

Edna Wentworth and Ginger Nicklow smiled and stayed out of it. Tiffany jumped in with Frank and Chuck. Harold Blasbalg, who Amy recalled was supposed to be working on a horror novel, weighed in on Dot's side, as did Syl Reyes, and the rest sat still and watched the show.

Because he was a big shot and because his storytelling, however absurd, was essentially competent and had a certain surface gloss, Amy had expected Surtees to get a free ride. So she was pleasantly surprised by the raucous upbraiding, but after fifteen minutes, during which the doctor took a real pummeling, she figured it was time to even the field. Extension instructors were paid, execrably, to avoid alienating their customers. "As I was saying," she said, "before I was so rudely interrupted—"

"It's not supposed to be Shakespeare," Dot said. Her color was high, and she had managed to smudge printer ink on her ivory jacket. Sometimes people couldn't take debate, rough-and-tumble or no; they either weren't used to being disagreed with or never stuck their necks out in the first place. But Dot seemed invested in Surtees himself. While she lauded and then hotly defended his silly book, she glanced reflexively at the back of his head (Surtees remained composed throughout) as though hoping for a glance back. Sometimes people, usually women, took extension courses to meet singles. "You're not being *fair*," she said.

"As I was saying," said Amy. The class reluctantly attended to her. "You can reasonably complain about cliché characters, settings, even cliché scenes. Tying somebody to the railroad tracks and all. But you can't fairly complain about cliché plots."

"Why not?" asked Ricky Buzza. Ricky was Amy's enabler this quarter.

"Because all plots are cliché. There are no new plots."

Ginger Nicklow spoke up. "I read somewhere, I'm sure it was in college, that there are two basic plots: Cinderella and Jack and the Beanstalk."

"Sex and death," said Chuck Heston.

Syl Reyes wondered what the heck that was supposed to mean.

"Search me," said Amy. "I've heard of this one myself, and I've always wondered. I guess it means you have the quest story and the erotic unveiling story. Most adventure stories, including this one, are quest stories. Although you could obviously have an interior quest, a search for spiritual enlightenment, or a search for the identity of your father's killer, or whatever."

"So *Jaws* is what?" asked Pete Purvis.

"An aquatic unveiling," said Frank, and even Tiffany P.C. Zuniga laughed.

"Getting back to my point," said Amy, "I love it that you guys have gotten so passionate about this piece, but I need to make it clear that it is, as Dot says, not fair to slam *Code Black* for having a trite plot. Whether or not it's unfair to compare it to Shakespeare I leave for another time."

"Okay," said Frank, "but can't we call Black Jack Black a cliché character?"

"Not yet," Amy said. "For all we know he may have quirks and depths we just haven't learned about in the first two chapters." *Sure he does.*

"What about an erotic quest?" asked Chuck.

"There you go," said Frank.

"For this reason," Amy continued, "critiques of fragments—novel chapters, unfinished stories—often center more on language than on structure. Language is the one thing we can safely criticize. A bad sentence can't be redeemed in the last chapter."

Amy led the class through Surtees's manuscript page by page. She landed pretty hard on the dialogue, though without calling it "wooden," and spent a great deal of time trying to convince them that fictional characters should almost always say or ask their lines, rather than hiss, shout, breathe, huff, or spit them. "There's way too much snarling going on here," she said, and when Pete and Dot defended the snarling as vivid she slapped them down smartly. "Even if you were right about this it wouldn't help you," she told them. "The dogs at the gates of publishing houses, called 'readers,' have all been trained to toss unsolicited manuscripts at the earliest opportunity, and they all use the same checklist, fair or not fair. One of the surest ways to turn them off is to have your characters purr 'Good morning,' snarl 'Get lost,' or opine anything whatsoever."

Surtees's cheerleaders reacted sullenly to this speech, but Surtees did not. He was taking notes.

Amy disliked being generous to students like Surtees, who had so little need of her generosity. She had hoped, even expected, that the class would go easy on him, so she could be the one to jump up and down on *Code Black,* but instead she was forced to be the good cop, and actually heard herself praising, however faintly, his attention to physical detail, and the way his characters traveled sure-footed through time and space, and the fact that every scene ended pretty much when it should, and was bound to the scenes before and after it by a neat causal chain. *Code Black* had what creative writing teachers called *narrative pull.* That the tale itself wasn't worth putting down on paper wasn't something Amy was allowed to mention.

In the end all she could do was allow Tiffany Zuniga five full minutes to excoriate the doctor's obligatory sex scene, in chapter two. Tiffany hated that the unnamed woman had "voluptuous curves," yowled like a jaguar "at her moment of ultimate release," and "slipped smilingly out the door" when it was all over. "I mean," said Tiffany, "how convenient is that."

Dr. Surtees, seated in the front row directly ahead of Tiffany, actually smirked.

"Worst of all," said Tiffany, "he uses *bed* as a verb. I hate hate hate hate that."

"Good for you," said Amy, and meant it.

As at the finish of every class Amy made sure that all the marked-up copies had been returned to their authors, and that everyone had received copies of the two stories for the next week, in this case by Edna Wentworth and Ricky Buzza. She waited at her desk until the room was silent, and looked up, expecting Carla still to be there, waiting, but she had left with the others. Amy reached into her pocket for Carla's letter, then thought better of reading its contents here, in this deserted room. Tonight's class had been pretty lively, and she didn't want to end on a downer. Amy gathered up her copies of next week's stories and headed out to her car.

As usual the parking lot, surrounded by eucalyptus trees, smelled like cough drops and was washed in yellow by the low-sodium, Palomar-telescope-friendly streetlamps. The whole group must have scrambled out of there because her car was all alone in its section of the lot. Alone with something on the hood. A plant. A large plant in a wide-mouthed ceramic pot of indeterminate color. A gift, apparently, from one of her students.

Amy knew nothing about plants but guessed that this one was some sort of cactus, like a Christmas cactus, except that it had one great long luminous bud on the edge of one thick branch, or leaf, or whatever you called it, a three-sided job that looked brittle as hell. The single bud was so cumbersome that Amy thought it might break off when she moved the plant into the passenger seat, but it didn't. The plant sat there jutting toward the dashboard, and Amy just didn't like it at all. It looked, she decided, more truculent than succulent, as though already she owed it more than she could pay. Vegetable life was, to Amy, alien life. She found herself hoping that the whole thing would tip over on the ride home, making a mess and giving her the excuse to toss it in the garbage. Sure enough, she hadn't driven halfway across the lot when she hit a speed bump and the pot bowled forward, dumping a cupful of earth on the seat, but the flower still didn't come off. Amy swore and stopped the car and buckled the stupid plant in with the lap belt.

Amy was a bitter, peculiar person, aware at all times of her bitterness and peculiarity, but rarely did this bother her. She was comfortable with her misery. Once in a while, though, something happened to rile her, and it was happening now. Okay, she told herself, so you're a fat middle-aged woman alone in a parking lot, wrestling with a Martian houseplant. Okay, so you're such a misanthrope that you don't even give a damn who gave it to you. Okay, so it's just one more crappy event in an endless, yet terrifyingly finite, stream of crappitude. Suck it up. But there was something about the night, the class, the plant . . . And the sad truth that no one, not even Carla, had stayed behind for her.

Feeling an existential moment coming on, Amy got a Heath bar out of the glove compartment, switched on the interior light, and got out Carla's mystery letter. Amy ate too much and probably drank more than she should, but her only true addiction was reading. The Lawrence Durrell quartet, which she hadn't even enjoyed, had gotten her through the protracted, awful death of Max, and Charles Dickens had seen her through the loss of each parent, and one rainy afternoon, on board a Boeing 727 with faulty landing gear bound for a dubious touchdown in Pensacola, Florida, she had refused to assume the crash position without her open paperback copy of *Revolutionary Road.* Nothing was truly unbearable if you had something to read.

She glanced at the plant, which she could see more clearly in the white interior light. The expensive-looking pot was shiny dark green, and the bud was white with yellow rods, stamens or something, visible through the translucent petals, and it seemed somehow more bulbous, less elongated, than it had just a few minutes earlier, when it had been on top of the car. There was a small white card half-buried in the dirt, upon which was hand-printed the name of the plant,

Hylocereus undatus
(Night-blooming cereus)

but not the identity of the giver. Rather than think too much about that, Amy unfolded Carla's letter.

It was typed neatly on ordinary copy paper, except of course it wasn't typed at all, it was a printout. Nobody typed anymore. Must play hell with forensics, Amy thought, thinking of the Leopold and Loeb ransom note, and how all typewriters were different, but laser printers really weren't, and why was she thinking about forensics, anyway? Well, because here was Carla's letter.

CREATIVE WRITING 101

The wood must be seasoned

Or all bets are off

Unseasoned wood is green and wet
Bark clings to it like a hanger-on
(votary, bootlicker, sycophant, toady)

Bottom line,
Kiddo,
A whole lotta steam
A whole lotta nothing
And in the end
It just won't stay lit

It'll hurt like hell

And the burning will take forever*

Amy sat still for a long time. No wonder Carla had wanted her to take it away. She tried to get her mind around the stark cruelty of the parody and found that she couldn't imagine a set of circumstances that would allow a decent human being to do such a thing. She began to analyze the language, to see if she could figure out who had written it. It had to be somebody her age, or not much

*though you could try kindling . . . manuscript paper might work!

younger. Nobody as young as Tiffany or Pete or Ricky said "kiddo." She pictured Surtees typing this up, and then Edna licking the envelope, and Ginger Nicklow tucking it into a mailbox, and then she shut down the movie. She was in a dark place, trying to get inside a dark mind, and she just wanted to go home. Even an existential moment was preferable to this.

Amy started up the car, stuck a Taj Mahal CD in the slot, cranked up the volume, and drove home the long way, up the coast to Del Mar, where you could just make out the ghost surf pounding in the distance, and then inland through Rancho Santa Fe, past the lake, playing the cut "Ooo Poo Pah Doo" over and over again. Amy liked this drive, especially late at night, the long, sure curves of highway, the solitude. If you lived inside your head, this was the perfect drive, smooth, serene, unconnected. Out of context. Sunlight brought context. Amy was sick of context.

She was almost home when she became aware of the scent of vanilla, a scent she loved, and she rolled down her window and sniffed the air, but the scent retreated, and when she closed the window it returned, more powerful than before. It was vanilla and something else, not gardenia, thank god, but some ridiculously fragrant mystery fruit. She was engulfed in this gorgeous scent, assaulted by it, and the closer she got to her own house the stronger it became. Jesus, she thought, pulling into the carport, I've got to get out of here, there's such a thing as too much of a good thing. Only then did it occur to her that of course it was coming from *inside* the car, it was coming from the plant, and she moved to unbuckle it in the dark and then saw, in a narrow shaft of light from her porch, that its silhouette had changed completely. The plant had, on the drive home, exploded into bloom, into a starburst-collared flower the size of a baby's face, and Amy scrambled from the car and into her house, leaving behind her briefcase, and Carla's letter, and the goddamn night-blooming cereus.

Here's what we're gonna do," said Carla.

It was first thing in the morning, the morning after the blossoming horror, and Amy, having just managed to fall asleep at daybreak, had stumbled over Alphonse to get to the telephone. *"What?"* She was on her hands and knees on the bedroom floor, cradling the cordless receiver with her shoulder, while Alphonse regarded her with doleful mistrust. "Carla? What time is it?"

"It's after nine," said Carla, as though this excused her. "And thanks so much for taking that thing off my hands. I got my first good night's sleep in four days."

"Carla? Did you put a houseplant on my car?"

"Of course not. You hate plants. Why, did somebody give you—"

"How do you know I hate plants?"

"You say so all the time."

Amy couldn't recall saying it once, not in class. Surely she didn't go on and on about her pet peeves to captive strangers. Did she? And why would Carla remember something this boring? Alphonse followed Amy into the kitchen, to remind her of his morning brunch. She always had to toss a slice of whole-wheat bread into the backyard to get him out of the house.

"Plants aren't like us," Carla said.

"Yeah. Yes, that's it exactly." Amy didn't know anyone else thought this.

"I'm just quoting you."

Lord, had the woman been taking down every foolish thing Amy said? Amy closed her burning eyes, propped herself against the refrigerator, and waited for the coffeemaker to cycle through. She hadn't seriously thought Carla had given her the plant, but it really would have been nice if she had. Amy was not at the moment worried about the cactus, or even the poisonous letter. It was morning, and nothing frightened Amy in the morning, because her will to live never kicked in until after lunch. While Carla chattered on about her latest story ("I'll never show it to you even, it's too pathetic, but here's the first paragraph . . ."), Amy conceived, plotted out, and discarded a story idea of her own, in which a homicidal maniac chainsaws into the bedroom of a woman at six in the morning and fails to terrorize her. The story would have been titled "Kill Me Now." "Carla," Amy said.

"Yeah?"

"Why are you calling me?"

"Sorry about that, Chief. You know how I get carried away. Well, I was thinking about our next move."

"I beg your pardon."

"You know. How should we go about it?"

"About what?"

"Finding out who wrote that letter."

Amy was stunned. She had spent a rotten night obsessing about it, the letter and the plant both, back and forth, trying to understand the connection between them, if in fact there was one, rationalizing the outlandishly unnerving effect the blooming flower had had upon her. It was almost five in the morning before it occurred to her that the plant had most likely been a gift, not a threat; that it was probably expensive; and that in any event the giver, however green-thumbed, couldn't have caused the awful thing to go off in her car when it did. And she hadn't been able to deal with the letter at all.

"Carla," she said, "I'm not sure I want to know who wrote that thing."

Carla didn't say anything.

"Think about it," said Amy. "What would you do if you did find out? Challenge the jerk to pistols at dawn? T.P. his car?"

When Carla spoke her voice was small. "I guess I thought *you*'d want to do something."

Amy sighed. "I'll call you back. Let me wake up."

It took Amy the better part of the morning to figure out why she didn't want to deal with the letter. At first she thought her reasons were practical, however weasely. If she knew who it was she'd have to act, and what social horrors would that entail? Asking the culprit to leave class? Amy's position with the university extension people was tenuous enough: her classes barely filled and didn't make them much money, and they would probably welcome an excuse not to use her again. All the ejected student would have to do is complain. Student complaints were customer complaints, and the customer was always right.

But all this was beside the point. What scared Amy was the mere fact of what looked inescapably like recreational malevolence. The poem had been written by an adult, not some teen with an unfinished brain. Whoever wrote the line *bootlicker, sycophant, toady* intended damage, understood how Carla would feel, how anybody would feel, being called such names. The line was playful, offhand, the poem itself a smug, imperious cat stretch. The writer was having fun. Amy had been comfortable in the same room with someone whose idea of fun this was.

Carla can just wait, Amy thought, and spent midday slogging through scut work. Amy derived most of her income from online editing, mostly for a huge reference book company that specialized

in annually collecting and printing curricula vitarum of the famous, quasi-famous, marginally famous, and profoundly obscure.
They called it "sketch-writing," as though what she composed, at a
dollar a sketch, were brief lives, natty little Hirschfeldian cameos,
whereas all she did, hundreds of times a day, was plug information
into data fields, fascinating details like d.o.b., year of m., first
name(s) of c., prin. works, d.o.d.

The nadir of her editing career had come in the previous year,
when she had accidentally been assigned to update her own
sketch. The people she worked for had no idea she was in their
books, which was just fine with Amy.

> GALLUP, Amy. B. Augusta, ME, June 30, 1948. BA in Phi-
> losophy Colby Coll., Waterville, ME, 1969. M. Max Win-
> ston, 1972 (dec. 1988); m. Robert Johanssen, 1989 (div.
> 1992). Author books, including *Monstrous Women*, 1971,
> *Everything Handsome*, 1975, *The Ambassador of Loss*, 1978,
> *A Fiercer Hell*, 1981.

In the year 2006 there had been nothing to update. Why they continued to include her in *American Writers and Composers* was a
mystery, but some day she would open a brand-new edition and
find herself gone, which would be even more depressing than con-
fronting this sorry list of accomplishments.

Amy churned out one hundred sketches in two hours, a personal best, but when she had wrapped up all the batches and
switched off the computer she still had no idea what to tell Carla,
or what do about her class. She felt paralyzed. It was late afternoon
and she hadn't even cleansed her car of that horrible vegetable.

She had to back out of the carport to extract the plant from the
front seat. She had expected that it would be smaller than she had
remembered, but it wasn't, except that the flower had wilted into a
great sullen pout. She placed the plant in the grass beside her front

steps and stared at it in the deep yellow afternoon light. What were the odds that the same person who wrote to Carla gave her this gift? If you looked at it rationally, what did they have in common, besides anonymity? Amy needed a second opinion. Against almost two decades of enforced solitude and every instinct she had, she called Carla back and invited her up north for a drink.

By the time Carla came to the front door, the sun was down and Amy was halfway through the bottle of red she had uncorked for the occasion. And it was quite an occasion: the first time in twelve years that Amy would admit someone into her home besides a furniture mover, plumber, or electrician. Carla pulled up in a silver Infiniti, no doubt her mother's car, and waved at Amy before unbuckling her seat belt and heaving herself out on the pavement. "This is just so cool," she said, grinning, and Amy agreed that yes, it sure was.

Carla exclaimed over the number and breadth of Amy's books, the ingenious homemade wall shelf fixed seven feet off the floor, separated from the ceiling by the length of a trade paperback's spine, which snaked through all five rooms of Amy's house. "I couldn't bear to throw away all my paperbacks," Amy said. "They go back to my youth, childhood even, but I had to get them out of the way. So there they are, out of reach, covered with dust, in alphabetical order."

She had been proud of the shelves when she put them up, back in the early nineties. The shelves were rickety, and made of unfinished wood, the whole effect pleasantly improvisational, something you might find in a grad student's digs. Her second marriage had not yet ended, and she was, she allowed to herself to imagine, working on her fifth novel, as yet untitled. This tiny house, these bookshelves, this not so hot marriage, it was all stopgap, and some day soon she would move back to New England, to a big house in the Berkshires, or maybe the Kennebec Valley, maybe teach in Orono. Anything was possible, and *the future lay ahead.*

"Seriously," Carla was saying, "have you read all of these books?"

"All the paperbacks. About half the hard stuff. For instance, I have yet to read Proust, but I have of course read *The Adventurers.*"

Carla nodded. "Joseph Conrad, right?"

"Harold Robbins. See?" Amy pointed directly above Carla's head, where the Rs were. "I have also read *The Carpetbaggers* and *Where Love Has Gone*, and I cannot bear to part with any of them."

"Wow. They must be really good."

"Why do you want to write?"

Carla put down her wine. "I don't know."

"That's a fine answer. Have you noticed that half my students just 'have' to write, that they're just 'bursting' with stories? It drives me insane."

"Remember that Gretchen person, the girl from Atlanta, who just couldn't sleep at night unless she had committed to paper the events of her working day?"

"Was that creepy or what?"

Carla gasped and laughed. "You told her it was a wonderful habit."

"Well, what was I supposed to say? 'Are you nuts?' 'Get a life'?"

Carla smiled and stared into her wine. Today she was wearing jeans and an oversized white shirt and no makeup, and her bright red hair was pulled back with a denim scrunchie. For the first time Amy could see the pretty young woman in Carla's plump unlined face. "I don't know what to do besides write," Carla finally said. "I tried everything else. Real estate. Art galleries. Venture capitalism. Acting."

"No kidding. Were you in anything?"

"Oh, sure. After my father ran off with that starlet—I told you about that, right?—Mom got a huge pile of money in the settlement, plus she had way too much time on her hands, and she thought, why not put the kid to work?"

"That's what we call a non sequitur," Amy said. "If she had so much money, why not spend it on you?"

"Oh, she did. Acting classes, agents, head shots. I did a ton of commercials in 1983, when I was cute. Mostly local stuff. I was Judy Garland in the Pulgas Carwash commercials, and the annoying kid running through Corky Bean's used car lot, and actually I was pretty effective as a leukemia victim in some hospital spots."

"Jesus."

"And I was an extra in one national ad, which ran for years. I was the white kid in the back row of the Cheezy Chews spot, the musical extravaganza on the space ship."

"Did you like doing this stuff?"

Carla laughed. "You can't imagine how much I hated it. But I couldn't reason with my mother. She kept sending me out, and they kept using me, and in the end I had to make myself unemployable. Do you know how much I had to eat to get this fat?"

This was interesting, even intriguing, but it didn't explain why she wanted to be a writer.

"You really want the truth?" asked Carla. "I never wrote a line before I took that first class with you."

"But you said . . . you were working on a novel, I remember distinctly, you were five hundred pages into your second novel. You brought it with you in a canvas bag, and you took it out and brandished it. It was one of the scariest things I ever saw." The longest of Amy's novels had barely broken two hundred pages.

"I was brandishing my crazy Aunt Mae's failed PhD thesis on 'Jeane Dixon, Sooth or Truth.' "

"But then why—"

"Because you knocked me out. I'd taken a million of these courses, sculpting, computer programming, Sanskrit, and you were the only one that didn't stand up there and bore me to death or lie to me or insult my intelligence."

Amy brushed the compliment aside and focused on Carla herself, who was at this moment a lovely reminder of why Amy had wanted to write in the first place, and why she had kept at it, more or less, as long as she had. Carla was a shining example of what

Amy had called, in her pretentious twenties, the "mystery of per-sonality." Only in art were there clichés; never in nature. There were no ordinary human beings. Everybody was born with a sur-prise inside. Amy's great ambition had once been to make a three-dimensional person out of nothing but her own imagination, like Athena from the forehead of her own father. That no writer had ever managed this was in the beginning no deterrent and in the end no consolation. And in the years after she stopped pretending to write, she had begun, she now realized, to deal with actual peo-ple as though they were puny fictional replicas, with hot and cold buttons, favorite books, overused sayings, and typical outfits.

"Let's think about this," she said, emptying the bottle into Carla's glass. "What sort of person writes a letter like that?"

"A scumbag."

"No. Think like a writer, Carla. Think from the writer's point of view."

"The poison pen letter writer?"

"Yes."

Carla looked thoughtful. "I don't know," she said, "if I want to go there."

"Then why do you want to know who it is?"

Carla looked at her, confused, as thought she couldn't see what one had to do with the other. Amy couldn't either, really.

"Look," said Amy, "they're paying me to take care of you, all of you, to make sure that you get the appropriate experience out of this class, which certainly doesn't include being stalked by post, and you're absolutely right, it's my job to take care of this. If you want me to stand up next Wednesday and demand to know who wrote the thing, I'll do it. As it stands, I have to ask them about the plant, anyway. I figure, if no one admits to leaving it on my car, then it's probably the same person who sent your letter. Although I can't understand the connection. The plant is a *nice* thing. Isn't it? The giver couldn't have known I was going to have a phobic reaction."

"You did?"

Amy had shown the cereus to Carla, without elaborating on it. "What was your idea, anyway?" Amy asked. "When you called me up this morning, I mean. You said you had a plan."

"It was stupid. I was just thinking that if we broke it down, the poem, and paid minute attention to phrases, punctuation, word choice, and all that . . . that by the end of the semester we'd know who it probably was."

"That's not stupid at all."

"I mean, I already ruled out Marvy. He doesn't have the mind for a line like, you know, *bootlicker, toady,* whatever." Carla's gaze fell when she said this, and she looked away from Amy. "And he can't spell, even with spell-check. Plus he's just too much of a doofus."

Amy agreed with her about the wit but argued anyway. Somewhere in the universe, she said, there's a doofus with an intuitive Machiavellian streak, and why the hell not?

"If you say so," said Carla, "but actually I've already picked out my candidate. I really hope it's—"

"Dr. Richard—"

"Surtees!" they both sang at once, laughing. "I think you're wrong, though," said Amy.

"You think it's a woman, don't you?"

"I'd bet on it."

Amy had found the language feminine, and the lancing nastiness, too. It was a relief to hear the same argument from Carla. This was, Amy reflected, the second opinion she had really been searching for. It had not been a mistake to invite Carla here. Amy uncorked a second bottle, of older and tastier wine, and they debated whether it was Edna, Ginger, Dot, or the redoubtable Tiffany, and in no time they were just gossiping about the writing group, sniping, in a not too nasty way, at the various personalities and nonpersonalities ("What's the deal with Pete Purvis, Blob of Mystery?" said Carla) in it, which was terribly unprofessional of Amy, but fun.

Carla talked some more about her childhood and told hilarious stories about an art gallery she had run in La Jolla "for about eight minutes." Amy talked about her books, not the ones she had written but the ones she loved, and she almost talked about herself but pulled back at the last minute. She was amazed that she retained still the impulse to do this. Especially with Carla. Or, why not with Carla, Carla was all right, but no.

In the end she filled Carla up with black coffee and packed her off home with the night-blooming cereus, which Carla had volunteered to take in exchange for the letter. "Hey," Carla shouted out her car window as she backed down the driveway. Amy made a shushing gesture from the front steps; it was almost midnight. "I forgot," Carla stage-whispered. "Wait'll you read Edna's story. It's a knockout."

Well then, Amy thought, let's hope the creep isn't our Edna.

She let in Alphonse and rinsed out the wineglasses, pausing to notice how odd it was to see two of them in the sink, but it was all right. She had actually enjoyed the evening. Of course, she was half in the bag, and she'd have to rethink the whole thing tomorrow, but still. Anyway she'd sleep tonight.

And she would have, if she hadn't remembered, just as she was drifting off, the opposite-sex p.o.v. exercise she'd given them. The only one who tried it was Chuck, and he'd been good at it, feminine language and all. Amy remembered being disappointed that no one else had had a go. Well, be careful what you wish for, she thought, whatever the hell that means, and in a short while she padded out to her computer and fired it up. If she wasn't going to sleep, she could earn. First, she checked Go Away.

Over the years she'd come up with more blog ideas—lists of bad novels and bad poems, unfortunate sentences from her own published novels, particularly idiotic newspaper clichés, ugly flowers, ant species, old lovers. She'd pasted in her own failed stories, annotating them sentence by sentence. She'd made a list of those story ideas in her last notebook, including the ones she still couldn't decipher, like "wommitty—catastrophic misunderstanding—sloms." She enjoyed these entries for a while, but they didn't scare up any response from the kibbitzers, and they filled up quickly anyway. The only open-ended lists were the original three.

Stephen Meyer, Tom Hartley, Kristin Nielsen, Carl Hammond, Marvin Gardens, Casper M. Toast, Absalom E. Sandwich, Bayer Bottomley, and Hymen Payne had offered additions to Novel Hybrids, including *Hey Jude the Obscure, Lord of the Rings of the Nibelung,* and *The Picture of Dorian Gray's Anatomy.* And for the first time, there was a dig, from someone calling himself Herman U. Ticks, advising her to "grow up." She almost deleted the note, but that would be censorship, and also be too close to a riposte, and ripostes were a form of engagement. Instead she invented three hybrids on the spot:

The Bell Jarhead

We are at war with terrorism, racism, and clinically depressed adolescents.

Gone With the Windows for Dummies

Starting the Civil War; Customizing Your Decimated Plantation; That Scary General Sherman.

Stop Or My Mom Will Shoot the Piano Player

A dimwitted cop meets a timid musician with a mysterious past, and together they push Estelle Getty out a window.

She did too have a life, unlike the ultravigorous H. U. Ticks, beavering away at his Nobel Prize–nominated formula for extracting AIDS vaccine and alternative fuel out of his own ass. She had a Life of the Mind.

fourthCLASS
THE WILL DOING THE WORK OF THE IMAGINATION

Of course, none of us chickens had given her the plant. Despite Amy's professed delight with the gift, the class heard about it with expressions ranging from vacancy to mild surprise, not including, in any instance, a flicker of private satisfaction or amusement. For the first time this semester there were absences, Tiffany and Marvy, which was too bad, because it was a small class, and because Edna Wentworth deserved everyone's full attention.

On the other hand, there was Harold Blasbalg. Amy started off the night with "Blood Sky: A Vampire Tale."

> Far off in the night woods Paul Gratiano could hear the ripping howl of carnivorous dogs, feral coyotes, the hooting of predatory owls, the helpless scream of a fat white rabbit. He shivered in his hiding spot, even though the night was hot and moist.
>
> Why had he agreed to meet her here, of all places, and now, of all times?
>
> Why was he here, within this lonely clump of maples, in Central Park at midnight?

Young Pete Purvis loved "Blood Sky," as did Ricky Buzza and Dot Hieronymus who apparently was going to love everything. Pete claimed to have had the bejesus scared out of him by the story's surprise ending, in which the vampire turned out to be Paul Gratiano himself, rather than the sinister mystery gal who finally glided onstage on page nine, only to be eviscerated on page eleven.

"The rest of you are being awfully quiet here," said Amy. "Do I assume that you were each shocked and sickened by the surprise ending?"

Only Carla spoke up. "To be honest, it wasn't that big a surprise to me," she said. "Everything in the story pointed to it. He sits there in the pitch dark, scared out of his wits, waiting for this woman, and that's all that happens until the end. Only the buildup is such a big deal that at some point, around the middle of the story, you begin to suspect that you're being pointed in the wrong direction."

"Exactly in the middle of the story," Amy said. "Can anyone pinpoint the moment?"

Dr. Surtees did that languid waiter-summoning thing with his index finger. Or maybe he was bidding at auction. Christie's, no doubt. Dr. Surtees wasn't a police auction kind of guy. "Page six," he said.

> Paul knew this was dangerous, every instinct in his being decried trusting her. When had such creatures ever been worthy of trust? In all of human history, had they once failed to disappoint? If only, he mourned, she weren't so damnably beautiful . . .

"But wait," said Ricky. "That's explained in the story. He's had a lot of trouble with women, two busted marriages. He's scared to let himself go with her."

Ginger Nicklow said, "That's what you're supposed to think.

But the language here just doesn't sound right. Why 'creatures'? And 'human history'?"

"And 'damnably beautiful,'" said Chuck, "when, on page three, he said she was 'really hot.'"

"Exactly," said Carla. "It's a cover-your-butt sentence. It's there so that, after the mind-blowing surprise ending, the reader can go back to it and say, 'Oh, yeah, why didn't I catch that?'"

"Except that we did," said Chuck.

Dot Hieronymus, looking pretty miffed, wanted to know how you can ever manage a surprise ending if they're so easy to give away.

"You might ask yourself," Amy said, "why you want to surprise your readers in the first place. A surprise ending is sort of like a surprise party. Probably some people, somewhere, enjoy having friends and trusted colleagues lunge at them in sudden blinding light of their own living rooms, but I don't think most of us do.

"We're talking here about the mechanical surprise. The other kind, the organic kind, is another matter." Amy was thinking about little Carla, running through a televised used car lot, screaming "You guys, come on down to Corky's WIGHT THIS MINUTE!" "We get surprised in real life because we can't know everything there is to know. For one thing, we're stuck in our own heads, in a single point of view.

"In Harold's story, we're also limited to one point of view, Paul Gratiano's. But Paul *knows* why he's waiting in the bushes in Central Park. He just doesn't think once about his plans before he acts on them, which is pretty artificial. The writer deliberately withholds information from us in order to achieve his surprise. That's why it's called mechanical, and that's why at least some of us didn't care for it."

"I like surprise endings," said Dot.

"Let's talk about something else," said Amy. "Harold has tried to tell us a scary story. We know that's his intent, because he told us first class that he likes horror fiction, and that's what he wants to write, and his favorite writer is Stephen King. So, ending aside, is this a scary story?"

Now no one spoke up for Harry. Frank Waasted said the story should have been frightening, because it had all the elements, but that somehow it wasn't. Amy encouraged the class to list the elements, and they did: There was darkness, solitude, hooting owls, sudden noises, as when a mugger burst from the underbrush close to Gratiano and attacked a strolling couple. There were dutiful observations of ill winds, and icy fingers, and Paul's retracting scrotum, and viscous pools of blood. The pro-Blasbalg faction defended all these details, except the scrotum, which Dot really hadn't liked. Chuck said that he kind of liked it, although it probably shouldn't have been mentioned twice.

"We spoke last week," Amy finally said, "about telling and showing, and in this story the writer has done a great deal of showing, and yet we aren't scared. This is not necessarily because, as some of you have suggested, many of the shown details are hackneyed. What we're missing here is the sensation of fright, a feeling which we all know to be contagious. If the writer were afraid, then we would be too. What you need to do in this story—a story that aims to provoke a particular response—is imagine, as fully as possible, what it would be like to *be* Paul Gratiano. To be shivering alone in the woods, planning to kill the woman you love. That's the hard work of writing. The imagining."

"Or not," said Chuck. "I mean, what if you don't have to imagine at all? What if you really are a murderer? Then, according to you, you could write on the side, and make the big bucks."

Carla and Amy locked eyes for a moment. What an interesting remark. "Only if you have access to your own feelings and can articulate them. But yes, I suppose you're right."

Amy wrapped up with a short lecture on William Butler Yeats's description of rhetoric as "the will doing the work of the imagination." "All the details in this story, what Frank calls the 'elements,' are rhetorical devices, designed to force the reader into a state of fear, and that's why they don't work so well. As Edna put it the other night, we'd rather be seduced." This got a tiny smile from Edna Wentworth, and on that triumphant note Amy told everybody to pass their critiques in to Harold and take a break.

Harold lingered with Amy to discuss a possible rewrite. "To tell you the truth," he said, "I thought this horror stuff was going to be easy."

"Scary is hard," Amy said. "The only thing harder is funny. You probably thought it was easy because Stephen King is so prolific. But I'll bet you anything he scares hell out of himself every time he sits down to write. That's why he's so good."

"Do you really think this is worth working on?" Harold was serious. Students almost never asked this question. They'd ask, Do you think I could get this published? Safe question, easy answer: I have no idea.

"I think you can do better," Amy said. "If I were you I'd forget the supernatural stuff and concentrate on the psychological. People are creepy enough without tarting them up with batwings and fangs. In my experience."

Harold laughed. "Mine too. I'm a criminal lawyer, you know."

She hadn't. She'd assumed he did civil work.

"I don't usually mention it to strangers. It's my guilty secret." Amy's cell phone went off, and Harold smiled, waved, went out for coffee. Harry was okay.

It was Marvy on the phone, apologizing all over himself, and Amy assured him that it was all right to miss a class or two, as long is it wasn't the class your critique was scheduled for, and Marvy said no, that wasn't it, he was so sorry, because he really liked the class and the way she was running it, but he was going to have to drop.

This had happened to Amy before. She was instantly furious. "Marvy, you got a good go-round with the others. Everybody read your story and spent time thinking about it, and you just said you got a lot out of the experience. And now you're dropping? Before you can do the rest the same favor? Do you know what this looks like? It's horrible for morale."

"Yes," said Marvy, "of course I do, that's why I called you. It isn't that at all." In the pause that followed, Amy could hear the rustle of paper. "It's just that I got this, you know, critique, and it was really out there, you know?"

"You're talking about the written critiques on the returned manuscripts? Marvy, a lot of beginners have no idea what they're doing at first." *Or ever.* "They rewrite your sentences, they dump on your name choices—"

"Actually, I got a lot of helpful comments."

"There you go."

"But this . . . this is just gross. And they didn't even sign it, so I don't know who it was."

Amy leaned back and closed her eyes. "Give me an example."

"I really don't want to."

"Why? Look, this is my job. Please give me at least some idea of what you're talking about."

Marvy sighed and cleared his throat. "Hey, Asswipe," he said.

"I beg your—what?"

"That's how it starts. He also exes out my name at the top of every page and puts in 'Dickwad.' "

To her consternation, Amy had to bury the cell phone in her midriff to blow off the giggles, which had descended upon her with no warning. It soon became obvious that they weren't going to go away. "Lord, Marvy, I'm so sorry," she said, snorting, "it isn't a bit funny, I don't know why—"

"Don't worry about it. My wife's over here laughing her brains out. I would be too."

"If it hadn't happened to you."

"Exactly. And then, remember the part where Bill Mansfield figures out the thing with the dog biscuits? Well, here he puts in, 'You don't know one fucking thing about crystal meth, loser.' "

"This is in handwriting?"

"More like printing, With pencil. And then he gives me—"

"Marvy, is there a comma between 'meth' and 'loser'?"

"No. Then he gives me this printed sheet, the one that starts off 'Hey, Asswipe,' and I'm sorry, Amy, I can't read the whole thing to you, it's just porno."

"You mean it's sexual?"

"Well, not exactly."

"You're talking about profanity."

"Yeah, I guess that's it. He just tells me what I can do with the story, if you know what I mean, plus I *must* have grown up on a pig farm, because yada yada yada, and then finally I should just go jump off the Coronado Bridge." Marvy started to laugh. "You know, it is pretty funny, now that I'm looking at it."

"Marvy, I can't tell you how sorry I am. I've been doing these classes a long time, and nothing like this ever happened before."

Amy's apology continued at length until Marvy was mollified, which hadn't been her intention. She had already given up on getting him back, but by the end of the conversation he promised to return the following week. "I guess," he said, "it takes all kinds."

I'll say, thought Amy. "Marvy, I'm assuming this person didn't sign his work. How many critiques did you get back?"

"Thirteen."

"Including mine?"

More rustling paper. "No, yours makes fourteen."

"But that doesn't add up. We've got thirteen in the class, and you didn't critique yourself."

"No, but somebody must have done it twice. And if I ever figure out who, I'm going to deck the guy."

Amy almost asked him what she had asked Carla, and herself: did he really want to know who it was. But of course he did. Marvy wasn't the greatest writer in the world, but his take on life was refreshingly direct. "I'm not going to knock myself out finding out, but if I do, then I'll deal with it."

Amy asked him to bring in all his critiques next Wednesday and promised to mail him the two new stories, by Dot Hieronymus and Pete Purvis. After he hung up, Amy made a note to herself to mail copies of the new stuff to Marvy and Tiffany, at which point the class began to file in, with Tiffany herself in the lead.

Tiffany leaned over Amy's desk. "I just couldn't deal with the sexism in that stupid story," she whispered. "And I get a real strong feeling from you that you don't want to go there."

"Actually," said Amy.

"And I can respect that. I know you can't pick and choose, you have to let everybody in, and I wouldn't want your job. Anyway, I'm here. I wanted to be here for Edna."

"Thank you," said Amy. Amy wanted to defend Harold, whose work wasn't well enough thought through to be sexist. Tiffany was like Thurber's Miss Groby, the English teacher who combed through every book for unusual figures of speech. "I see by my schedule that you're supposed to bring something in week after next. Are you still going to make it?"

Tiffany nodded and took her seat along with the rest, and the second half began.

Edna Wentworth's story, "The Good Woman," was one of the better stories Amy had received in a workshop. It was told from the point of view of a young married woman who suddenly, without meaning to, has an affair with a cable television installer. The affair is deduced by Miss Hestevold, a retired teacher, a spinster, who lives high on a hill above the young woman's family and notes the too-frequent visits from the cable truck. There was an excellent scene in which the young woman, unaware of being spied upon, drags her little boy up the hill to apologize to Miss Hestevold for having called her a name.

"My son has something to tell you."

Miss Hestevold, unsurprised, only nodded. Up close she was remarkably ugly. The lower half of her face was long and equine, not exactly deformed but still so extreme that it was hard not to stare, and there was white down on her chin and upper lip. She had the large brown eyes of a once pretty woman, which cruelly heightened her ugliness, for she surely had never been pretty. Alice doubted that she had ever even been plain. Miss Hestevold regarded Dougie now with a kind of brutal reserve.

Dougie, wide eyes fixed on the old lady's beard, cried soundlessly, his mouth wide open. Alice squeezed his hand. He was so young and lived so purely in each moment. The immediate and the eternal were one and the same to him, and now he twisted in a universe of shame, without limit or perspective. Alice squeezed and squeezed but said nothing, and neither did Miss Hestevold. Finally he got it out. "I'm sorry, lady," he said. "I didn't mean it." Then he could cry out loud. The tension left his body, and he hung his head, and Alice moved behind him, her hands gentle on his shoulders. She smiled at Miss Hestevold, whose expression did not alter.

"Why are you sorry?" Miss Hestevold asked her son.

Dougie looked up. "Because," he said. Miss Hestevold stared. "Because I called you names." Miss Hestevold waited. "Because I called you poopy pants and—" Humiliated, Dougie started crying again.

"But why," asked Miss Hestevold, "are you sorry for that?"

Why, you vicious old bat. "He's sorry," Alice said, "because he was rude to you and used bad language. He knows better."

Miss Hestevold did not look away from Dougie. "Is that why you're sorry?"

Dougie nodded. "It's wrong to say bad words."

Miss Hestevold nodded too, in his solemn rhythm. "Why is it wrong?"

Alice drew her son back against her body. Dougie twisted his head around and looked up at her in dazed inquiry. "Because it just is," Alice said.

"Because it just is," said Dougie.

Alice opened her mouth to say good-bye, but the old woman sighed and pinned her with disgust, a look that transformed Alice into a powerless child, as unworthy as her son. "It's just wrong! What do you want him to say?" she said, shaming herself with her own whining voice.

Miss Hestevold knelt down then in front of Dougie and smiled at him and took his hands in her own gnarled ones. "Shall I tell you why?" she asked him. Dougie nodded rapidly, in just the way that he would nod to Big Bird on the TV. Though she couldn't see his face, Alice could picture it, mesmerized by the old woman's sudden kind attention. "Because when you call people nasty names, even in fun, you often hurt them. Not always. For instance, you did not hurt me. But this is a risk you run: of making someone else feel foolish, ugly, or sad. Of causing pain without meaning to."

Alice had an absurd impulse to raise her hand and yell, "I knew that!" Obviously Miss Hestevold thought she had Alice's number. Alice was yet another shallow young person who couldn't tell manners from morals. Alice hated to be misunderstood.

"Do you know what 'dignity' means?" asked Miss Hestevold. Dougie shook his head. "Well, you don't have to know. Just remember this. It is always wrong to treat other people as though they were dolls, or toys. It is always terribly wrong to be cruel. Do you understand now?" Dougie nodded slowly. She stroked back his shiny hair with a strong liver-spotted hand. "It was nice meeting you," she said.

Amy liked this scene so much that she wanted to start off by reading it aloud. First of all, old Edna could write up a storm, on top of which the last paragraph could have been composed especially for the moral edification of the creature she was beginning to think of as the Workshop Sniper. But this would have tipped the group off too early about her own feelings, which she liked to reserve until discussion had run its course.

Tiffany led off praising Edna's language, her creative attention to detail, the precision of her phrases. When Amy asked for examples, Tiffany cited the passage where Alice, the brand-new adulteress, confronts her guilt after her absurd new lover has driven off. *[S]he sat up stiffly, like a marionette, and stared down at her good old ordinary pink body, which had just turned on her like a family dog suddenly rabid, and thought that now she must be capable of anything.* "The writer," said Tiffany, "shows us this woman's body as it appears to her, not as it might look to a *Penthouse* photographer." Take that, Blasbalg, Reyes, and Surtees. In back of Tiffany, over her left shoulder, Chuck waggled his eyebrows at Amy, and then actually made rabbit ears on Tiffany's head with his middle and index fingers. What a card. "And a little farther down," continued Tiffany, "her description of the cable man, how his skin is 'poreless, and moist, his body big and sleek, he was simple, tactile, irresistible, like a bath toy, and strong, and hers to do with as she wished.'" Tiffany looked up from the page. "That's sensuous writing!"

"I agree," said Frank Waasted, "although I'm not sure I like being objectified like that."

Tiffany whirled around, almost catching Chuck's rabbit ears. "Oh, come on," she said.

"No, seriously," said Harold, "how would you like to be compared to a rubber ducky?"

Ricky Buzza leapt to Tiffany's defense, immediately pissing her off, and Amy moved to stop it. "Tiffany's right, and you guys are wrong," she said, to a chorus of boos. "Does anyone else want to talk about the language, before we move on to the story itself?"

Just about everyone praised Edna's way with words, including Dr. Surtees, who hadn't deigned to join in earlier discussions. Pete Purvis, bless his heart, timidly complained about a line in Amy's favorite passage, which by this time Amy had read aloud. "I got messed up," Pete said, "by the sentence, 'She had the large brown eyes of a once pretty woman, which cruelly heightened her ugliness, for she surely had never been pretty.' Well, was she ever pretty or not?"

Pete had a point. Technically, Amy said, the sentence could stand: you could coherently say *She had the large brown eyes of a basset hound* without implying that she had ever been a basset hound, or had ever blinded one for that matter. But it was a tad confusing, and Amy thanked him for pointing it out. Now, she said, she wanted to discuss the story as a whole, as a story. What actually happens here, and does the story satisfy?

There were big problems with "The Good Woman," which began so assuredly and then pulled back in the end. The Hestevold woman actually saves Alice's bacon one day, when Alice and the cable guy are going at it and Alice's husband comes home early. The old lady calls out to him and beckons him up the hill, and occupies him long enough for Alice to dress herself and push the cable guy out the back door. Afterward, Alice renounces her lover and rededicates herself to her family, and to gaining the old lady's respect.

But she doesn't achieve it. Instead, Miss Hestevold plays pied piper to Alice's two children, so that they spend more and more time at her place, and even Alice's husband is seduced, chastely, by the charming old bag. The story ends with Alice sitting alone on Christmas afternoon, making peace with her lot. " 'Alice had finally lost the need to confess and simply shared her family with this wise woman who hated her.' "

Ginger Nicklow raised her hand. "There's more to Miss Hestevold than meets the eye," she said, "and I'd like to know what it is. I think the story ends too soon. It's a sad ending, even stark, but it didn't satisfy me. Something's missing."

This was a gratifying moment for Amy. Ginger, who had been holding back, now revealed her analytical intelligence. Amy couldn't have put it better herself.

"I don't think it ends too soon," said Tiffany, "although I do think the last paragraph is maybe too subtle."

"In what way?" asked Amy.

"Well, Alice has finally lost it, right? She's so repressed about sex, and the witch has done such a guilt trip on her, she's lost it completely. And I appreciate the fact that it isn't all spelled out, but I think some readers might miss this. The fact that she's crazy at the end."

"Wait a minute."

Everyone spoke up at once. Thank God, no one but Tiffany had interpreted the story this way. Amy locked eyes with Edna Wentworth, who shrugged her shoulders and smiled, as if to say, *Well, what do you expect from a Tiffany?* Except that Amy had begun to entertain hopes for Tiffany and hated to see them dashed. "I take it that you read this as an impaired perception story?" Amy explained that impaired perception stories, which are fun to write and even more fun to read if you keep your wits about you, are those in which the point-of-view character misinterprets key events, so that there are really two stories, the one the p.o.v. character tells and the one the alert reader watches unfold behind his back. "You take it that Alice is wrong all along to feel so guilty? And that Miss Hestevold is a malevolent creature?"

"Like *The Scarlet Letter*. Yeah."

"Oh," said Amy.

For the last half hour Amy earned her measly wages, guiding them all down the overgrown pathways of authorial intent. Whether Tiffany was on to something or not was not simply, as Ricky argued, a matter of opinion. There was evidence to be sifted and analyzed. In the case of "The Good Woman," nowhere could anyone find proof, or even suggestion, of Alice's irrationality, or of the author's concept of her as in any way delusional. Alice, Amy said, was presented as a more or less ordinary young woman whose feelings of guilt seemed pretty rational. "This is not to say that we want to burn her at the stake," Amy said, and took a breath. *And the burning will take forever.* "Or that we necessarily find her behavior with Calvin Hoving as reprehensible as she does. Well, some of us will and some won't. The point is, this is Alice's story."

"But," said Ricky, "isn't it open to different interpretations?"

"Yes, but you've got to be careful. We each bring to our reading everything we know and believe, about human nature, and psychological and physical laws, about right and wrong, and so forth. About the way the world works. And what we believe shades what we read, and that's as it should be. My *Great Expectations* isn't the same book as Edna's *Great Expectations*, or Ginger's. But you have to be careful. You have to meet the writer on his own terms, and you can't look away from those parts that mess up your interpretation. Here, Tiffany is arguing that Alice is censoring herself into a kind of madness, but I don't see that in, for instance, this passage:

> "And worst of all were the sickening waves of gross carnal-
> ity that didn't go away with Calvin Hoving, that got worse
> and would never go away, no matter how old or ugly Alice

got. She was afraid, not of giving in, but of enduring it forever. Charlie, who had once been too much, was not enough
for her now. No two men or two hundred would be enough.
There was not enough of anything in the world to fill her
up . . .

"Isn't she facing up, here, to her own sexuality? Isn't she really
mourning, not the fact that she cheated on her husband, but that,
no matter how well behaved she is, she is literally insatiable?"

"It's sad, all right," said Chuck, "but it ain't mad."

Edna thanked the class and said that she agreed with Ginger
and Amy. "I don't care for the ending, either," she said, and promised a rewrite before the end of the semester.

Amy passed out the stories for next week, Halloween, and then,
just as they were gathering up their things to go, she asked Edna
and Harold to stay for just a few minutes. She was worried about
the critiques, considering what had happened to Marvy.

"I want to try something new," she said. "If you don't mind, I'd
like to look through your critiques, the ones that just got passed
back to you, before you take them home. Just for a second. I want
to see if everyone's doing his job." In the past, Amy told them, not
altogether untruthfully, students had complained that half their
critiques were just unmarked manuscripts. This is what Amy
wanted to check on, she told them.

There were just eleven manuscripts in Harold's pile, which
made sense, as the class was down one, and sure enough half of
them hadn't been marked up. Chuck, Ginger, Surtees, and Syl
Reyes had all written something and signed their names, Tiffany
had signed hers at the top and written nothing at all, and there
were two other unsigned manuscripts with "Good!" and "Nice!"
written in the margins in various inappropriate places, and that
was it. No "Hey, Asswipe," no snide verse.

Edna Wentworth's pile contained twelve copies. "Have you

looked through these yet?" Amy asked brightly, and Edna said she hadn't gotten the chance. Amy tilted the pile toward her chest and flipped through it, shielding the contents from Edna's eyes. It was like playing poker with a hundred cards. I just can't stand it, Amy thought, if he wrote something nasty to Edna Wentworth. Edna could obviously take care of herself, but enough was enough, and besides, Amy was determined to rescue her class from this creep. She flipped past Tiffany, Chuck, Frank, Pete, Surtees, and there it was, smack in the middle, an unmarked manuscript with a single half-sheet of paper inserted just before the final page, and on it a crude but effective pencil drawing of a naked old woman, masturbating with what looked like a quill pen, and pasted underneath in block letters E. W., and underneath that, *EEEEWWWWW.*

"Guess what!" Amy said to Edna. "There's an extra one here, and it isn't marked up at all. Would you mind if I kept it? I'm giving my own copy back to you, with my writeup, and I'd really like to keep this for my files. If it's all right with you." If it wasn't all right with Edna, Amy was going to feign, or actually experience, a heart attack.

But it was. "Cheerio," said Edna, and she and Harold left together.

Son of a bitch. What was she going to do?

Amy spent the next two days in hibernation. She left her cell in the car, along with the stories for next week, turned off her answering machine, and fixed her phone so it wouldn't ring. On the first day she turned on her television at five in the morning and watched it until midnight. Since the news was almost as alarming as her life, she avoided it, except when broadcast in a tongue she couldn't understand. She watched a lot of local cable access, including two hours of high school academic competition and four of crackpot sermons. She watched Warner Bros. cartoons and reruns of "The Outer Limits" and a Jimmy Stewart movie festival. On the second day she input brief lives from breakfast until dinnertime, and after dinner she turned her phone back on.

She still had no idea what to do, except that she would not call the university people and tell them what was going on. Something bad was happening in her class, and it was probably building up to something worse, but no one in administration had the wit to deal with it. They would play it safe, she was sure: disband the class, refund part of the tuition, cover their ass. And she didn't want the class to break up. It was a good class, one of the best in years. She had two decent writers that she knew of, Chuck and Edna; they were all enthusiastic enough to show up for the first four classes, and so far no one but that other Tiffany, McGee, the drop, had failed to produce work on schedule. That one of their number was a malevolent and possibly unbalanced prankster was terribly upsetting to Amy, and also, she now admitted to herself, terribly interesting.

Unlike Carla, she remained emphatically unenthusiastic about uncovering the prankster's identity, even though she knew that eventually she would probably do so, on purpose or by accident. In truth, she really didn't want to know. When she sifted through the roster, imagining each class member as the One, the Sniper, she began to feel clammy. These were human beings, not fictional constructs. She didn't actively dislike any of them, not even Surtees, and she had begun to feel a little affection for a few, like Marvy, and Edna, and Chuck, and of course there was Carla. Even Tiffany. When she tried to picture Dot Hieronymus, Book-of-the-Month chairwoman of the reception committee, drawing that obscene picture of Edna Wentworth, she felt disloyal, and worse than disloyal, as though she were reducing the woman to, as Tiffany would say, an object. She felt like a pornographer. She wondered if police detectives felt like this. Probably not. They didn't have to deal with people they already knew.

But the malevolence itself, the fact of it, the willingness to act on it—it was pretty damn interesting. Someone in real life was behaving like a character in an old-fashioned mystery, of the *Ten Little Indians* mold, where the back cover of the paperback typically listed the usual suspects:

> Who was garroting the orphans of Glandmoor? Could it be . . .

- Rodney Plank, glowering young barrister, whose family tree has more than one rotting branch? Or . . .

- Hermione Flange, spoilt socialite, with an insatiable
  appetite for heedless thrills? Or . . .

Tiffany Zuniga, lovely, headstrong suffragette, whose ideological convictions perhaps masked . . . a more sinister orthodoxy?

The more Amy thought about it, the more she came to believe that only a writer, or an aspiring writer, would behave in such a literary way. And look at the attention given to style and substance. No two forays alike. You had the oral assault, the whispered phone message. You had the visual, the dreadful cartoon. The crude, high school bully-boy attack on Marvy, and the cutting malice of the poem. If the entire performance were just that, a work in progress, Amy would have to give it high marks.

The first phone call she got was not from Carla.

"Ms. Gallup?"

"Yes."

"This is Dr. Richard Surtees."

As opposed, Amy thought, to Dr. Hymie Surtees, and what had gone wrong now?

"First off I want to thank you for your written and oral comments. You have genuine critical standards, which I very much appreciate."

"You're very welcome." Amy almost added, "So why are you dropping?"

"I'm calling with a proposition. I'd very much like to work with you, privately, one on one, to get this book up to snuff."

"You mean, as a book doctor? That sort of thing?"

"Exactly. I don't have as much time to write as I'd like, and as you've seen I've a lot to learn about editing and refining my work. I'd be willing to pay whatever you think appropriate."

For a moment, Amy was tempted. She could always use money. "I'm flattered, Doctor—"

"Richard."

"—Richard," Amy said, "but I'm not crazy about the whole concept of book doctoring."

"I understand. And you can name your price."

"For starters, I could never guarantee that the doctored book would get published."

"That's not an issue."

"Well, it's an issue for me. It would make me uncomfortable. And also, really, your book should be *your* book, not yours and somebody else's. It's one thing to delegate, say, typing, or billing, but if you want to be a writer, you should own the whole thing."

"And I would very much like to do that, but there are time constraints."

People don't say no to you very often, do they? "Look. It would be different if you were a movie star, or some trust-fund baby with too much time on your hands, and you wanted to *pretend* to be a writer."

"You'd take the job in that case?"

"Well, no, but the point I'm trying to make is that *you* really want to *be* a writer. I can see that. *Code Black* doesn't strike me as a vanity enterprise." Technically, this was true. Surtees was a vain man, but he wasn't self-deluded. And the book he was writing probably wasn't any worse than most published thrillers.

Surtees laughed. "I'm going to take that as a compliment."

"I hope this doesn't mean you're going to drop out."

"Of course not. In fact, I'll probably keep taking your courses, just to go on working with you. It's just that, this way I'll get your help for next to nothing. Are you sure you won't reconsider?"

"I'm sure." Amy hesitated. "Richard, while we're at it, I like to keep tabs on my student critiques, to make sure that everybody's doing his job. What was the level of your written feedback?"

"I have no idea. It was marginally helpful listening to their comments in class, but I just threw away all returned manuscripts, except for yours."

"Ah." *Nuts*. "Okay. Well, thanks for the offer."

The phone rang again before Amy could think about her conversation with Surtees.

"Where the heck have you been?" It was Carla.

Amy's impulse was to tell Carla the truth, about turning off her phone, about the obscene drawing, and Marvy's heckler. "I had to leave town," she said. "What's up?"

"Nothing, I guess." Carla sighed. "I threw away that story."

"What story?"

"The one I read you part of the other day. About the zoo guy, in the yak pen."

"Oh, yeah." Amy had no idea what she was talking about.

"So, there's nothing more on the, you know, thing?"

"Not really."

"Okay, well. I'll see you next Wednesday."

Now Amy felt really guilty. She had spent most of the previous day deciding what to do about the latest Sniper assaults and had concluded, reasonably she was sure, that for the moment they were best kept to herself. She had known that Carla would call and want to know everything, and she had decided it would be better to keep her out of it. Amy trusted Carla and did not seriously imagine that Carla could be the One, but the time they had spent together giggling over the matter and making fun of class members had been, in retrospect, incautious.

Still, she had been tempted to *share*, and she was inclined right now to call Carla back and spill the beans. As if prompted by a higher power, Alphonse muscled past her to the front door and barked viciously at the mailman on the other side. She went through her usual mail-time routine with Alphonse. "Back, Simba, you beast!" she snarled, and Alphonse snarled back, and they kept this up for a while, and then he retired with full military honors for a much-deserved postnap nap. In Amy's mailbox, amid the lottery scams and coupon sheets and free credit applications was an actual first-class letter, and it was from Tiffany the Headstrong Suffragette. Amy, who never expected good news, tore open the letter before she could speculate about it.

Dear Amy,

Something has been bothering me since the first night of your class, and I have been debating whether to talk to you about it, but it's really getting to me. So here goes.

You are a good teacher and I really admire the way you run the class, but you consistently use "his," "he," and "him" when you shouldn't. I'm talking about phrases like "The writer loses his authority," when the writer could be male or female. I expect this kind of thing from Surtees, but not from you.

I respect the fact that you have to deal with all kinds of characters from different backgrounds, but I think you should be more conscientious in your use of pronouns. You set the example for the others. If you don't want to use the female pronoun to stand for everybody, which I'd really prefer, you could at least say "he or she," "him or her," "his or hers," etc. Also, you often use "sex" when you should use "gender."

I know you'll take these comments in the spirit in which they are offered. Other than this really small matter I am very happy with class and look forward to showing you what I'm writing.

Sincerely,
T. Zuniga

Amy, taking Tiffany's comments in the spirit in which they were offered, went to her computer and unleashed a three-page reply, which quickly assumed the form and rhetorical bluster of a third-rate oration. She graciously agreed with Tiffany that sexism lay at the root of the all-purpose use of masculine pronouns, and then pointed out that the sexists responsible for it had been dead for centuries, and that in order to raise their consciousness one would have to raise their bones. She pointed out that "he" was a two-letter monosyllable and "he or she" a dull trisyllabic waste of air and paper space, that the dutiful substitution of "person" for "man" made nouns unwieldy and stupid-looking, that she used "sex" when she was referring to people and "gender" when she was referring to parts of speech, and that in any event she had neither the time nor the heart to give the matter a second's more thought. The phrase "life is too short" was used throughout her reply, at the end of many paragraphs, as a sort of incantation, like *Why say, Sail on, Sail on and On!* She signed off with a vicious obscenity, printed out all three pages, then tore them up and threw them in the wastebasket. Well, at least Tiffany wasn't dropping.

Now Amy did something wildly uncharacteristic. She took out a legal pad and began to jot down an outline. Amy never did outlines, even though she often counseled writing students to do them. Outlines were drudgery, and worse: when you looked at a plot, all plotted out, you were overwhelmed with fatalism and ennui. Now, with fatalism and ennui as her watchwords, she gave her outline a heading:

WHAT ARE YOU AFRAID OF?

She exed this out and wrote

WHAT ARE YOU WORRIED ABOUT?

   I.   The class will find out
       A. And tell Admin
       B. And bolt
  II. Admin will find out
       A. And cancel class
       B. And fire me
 III. The sniper

Amy stared at this pitiful outline long enough to verify that

   A. She really didn't care if they fired her, and anyway
   B. She really didn't think the class would bolt, although
   C. A few of them might rat her out to Admin, but
   D. Not if she headed them off at the pass
   E. Whatever that meant; and
   F. The sniper

was such a huge worry that she couldn't even write anything about him. Or her. There, she'd come up effortlessly with two new lists, neither of them suitable for her blog.

fifthCLASS

"Ewwwwww!" screamed Brittany Micheals, splattering her lunch all over the cafeteria table, "I can't believe you did that, Murphy Gonzalez!"

Murphy Gonzalez stared at Brittany in bewilderment. Well to be more accurate he squinted in Brittany's direction, because his glasses had been knocked off by Brittany's flying orange juice carton. "Huh?" he asked. "What did I do now?"

If Brittany answered him he couldn't hear it, because of the commotion her friends were making. Brittany never traveled alone, always with at least four other girls, Michelle, Ashley, Megan, and Demi, all of whom were now squealing, "Ewwwwwww!"

Murphy felt pretty certain that in a moment or two a cafeteria duty would descend on his table and let him know where he had gone wrong. He shrugged with fatality and went back to practicing his frog dissecting skills.

Amy loved Halloween, and when she had first moved in to her house, she had carved six big pumpkins for Halloween and lined her driveway with them, lit from inside with cheap little flash-lights, just as her neighbors with children were doing. Only two alarmingly tall and uncostumed kids, not from the neighborhood, had showed up. In succeeding autumns Amy ramped up her deco-rations, until the year she actually bought three sets of electrified plastic pumpkins, strewn together like Christmas tree lights, and lit up her shrubs and her palm tree like Broadway; and she had taped silhouettes of witches and werewolves in her living room window, and carved fifteen pumpkins; and this time the little girl who lived across the street actually came to her door, dressed as a Disney creature, some princess or supermodel. But before Amy could greet her, Alphonse did his scourge-of-the-mailman thing, and the child ran down the driveway to her waiting parents. How could anybody, even a little kid, fear Alphonse? It dawned on Amy then that the real bugaboo was Amy Gallup, the Unknown Neigh-bor. In an age when otherwise reasonable people had their kids' treats x-rayed for razor blades, and every stranger was a potential pedophile, it didn't pay to be an Unknown Neighbor. Rather than become Known, Amy basically gave up, although she did continue buying the candy bars, which she always ended up eating herself.

This year, because Fifth Class fell right on Halloween, Amy set out an orange plastic salad bowl full of Mars Bars on her front porch. Maybe if they knew she wasn't here they'd actually come to her house. When she left for class it was already getting dark, and the littlest goblins were afoot, clinging to their mothers' hands. One particularly small ghost was crying.

All the Halloweens in Amy's memory had been thrilling events, where you ran masked and free through magically unfamiliar streets. Amy couldn't remember this part she was watching now, the first and probably most important part, when you had no idea why they were wrapping you up in a sheet with jagged eyeholes and leading you into the dark void. Outside Amy's car window normally overprotective adults giggled at their sobbing, spooked children. The crying ghost had probably glimpsed himself in a mirror, and his mother had said, "It's just you, silly. You're scared of your own self!" and couldn't help laughing when this made him cry even harder. Here was the beginning of a story idea: *Why is the kid crying?* No. *Why is his mother laughing?*

She was late getting to campus and had to park three lots over, because there was evidently some big lecture or theatrical event next door, so that she needed to jog to class, which just about killed her, and she huffed and puffed her way to the front of the room yelling "I know I'm late, sorry, get your notebooks out, is anybody missing?" She emptied her briefcase on her desk and looked up and said, "Oh, my god."

Except for Dr. Richard Surtees, they were all wearing masks. Not cheap masks, either, but the pricey latex kind, the kind that high-tech bank robbers wore in caper movies, except that these weren't Ronald Reagan masks.

"Surprise!" they shouted in unison, their voices a little muffled by the masks.

Amy counted heads. Sure enough, she had thirteen. This was some kind of record: she'd never had a class with such faithful attendance. "I do believe I'll take roll," she said.

"Do you mind if we remove these?" someone said. He was wearing a Bart Simpson mask, and he sounded like Chuck. "It smells really terrible inside here."

"Please wait till I call your name," said Amy. She preserved for the general amusement her New England Stone Face, as she took roll. "Bart Simpson?"

"Here." Chuck ripped off his mask. "Jeez, that was slimy."

"Alice Cooper?"

"Here." It was rather wonderful to watch Ginger Nicklow, thrift-shop sophisticate, whip the ridiculous face of Alice Cooper off her head like a flapper's turban. She shook out her long chestnut hair and fanned her face. "This wasn't my idea," she said, "although it *was* fun."

"Let me guess," said Amy. "This was Carla's doing?"

"You got it." Carla's mask was stunning, a shiny gray replica of the Alien, complete with dual mouths dripping latex acid. She looked like she was balancing a huge phallus on her head.

"That couldn't have been cheap," Amy said.

"Five hundred bucks, actually," said Carla.

Leona Helmsley gasped, "Good lord."

"Edna, is that you?"

Edna Wentworth had trouble removing her mask, which eventually popped off with her glasses inside it. She extricated them and wiped the lenses with a small white handkerchief. "Young woman," she said to Carla, "this little masquerade must have cost you an absurd amount of money."

Carla, who had apparently brought all the masks and passed them out at the beginning of class, declared that she had a walk-in closet full of them. "I'm a collector, sort of."

"So we can't keep them?" This from a giant bloodshot eyeball, a.k.a. Pete Purvis, whom Amy had already recognized by his green hooded sweatshirt, which she had never seen him without. "I love this thing," he said to Carla, and she told him to go ahead and keep it. Pete was probably the same age as Ricky Buzza, but he seemed younger. Pete worked at a guitar store and lived with his dad. Amy knew this because he had appended to his "Murphy Gonzalez and the Frog's Leg" a touching one-paragraph author's bio, in which he mentioned these living arrangements (with an exclamation point!) and claimed that his favorite activity besides writing was playing bass in his garage band, Visibly Shaken.

That left eight (another list!): a gorilla, a fluorescent skull, Jimmy Carter, Mr. Spock, Bozo the Clown, Cher, Leatherface, and Dr. Richard Surtees, upon whose desk lay an empty mask of Saddam Hussein. "Did you choose that one?" Amy asked Surtees.

He bestowed upon her a tolerant smile. "Actually, it was thrust upon me," he said.

"Like greatness itself," said the man with the fluorescent skull.

"Is that you, Frank?"

"I'll never tell."

Amy was having a very good time, for Amy. They liked her. She had been popular with a few writing groups before, but never so soon in the quarter. The nicest thing about all this fooling around was that they were at ease with one another, which was essential to a productive workshop. But fifteen minutes had gone by, and she had to get the class started. In short order she unmasked Frank Waasted, Syl Reyes (Leatherface), Tiffany Zuniga (Mr. Spock), and Ricky "Cher" Buzza. Most improbably, and therefore happily, Dot Hieronymus was the male silverback gorilla. Dot was smiling when she took it off. "I've never felt so empowered," she said.

"All right, you guys," said Amy, regarding Jimmy Carter and Bozo the Clown, who had to be Harry B. and Marvy, sitting side by side in the back row. Amy couldn't recall seeing Harry Blasbalg in jeans before—he always looked as though he drove to class straight from the office—but Jimmy Carter and Bozo were both wearing denim, so obviously Harry must be dressing down tonight. "We've got to get started on 'Murphy Gonzalez and the Frog's Leg' now, and we're not doing it incognito." She extended her arms toward them, like a choir director. "Get 'em off, you two."

Only Amy saw what happened next, the whole tableau, because only she was facing the back wall. The first thing that happened was that Jimmy Carter put his left arm around Bozo and raised his right hand over his head. Almost immediately, the second thing happened, which was that Bozo the Clown collapsed sideways, toward Jimmy Carter, and slipped bonelessly through his embrace and down onto the floor, as Jimmy Carter cried "Oh, no!" with the voice of Marvy Stokes. At this cue the door opened and *Harry Blasbalg walked in* and announced, "Houston, we have a problem."

Amy's reaction time for each event was nightmarishly slow. Each image carried with it such a host of flapping red flags that by the time she had recovered from the first, the next one had already whizzed by, leaving its own afterimage flashing, so that she could not very well step over it to address the impossible sight of Harry Blasbalg in mufti, standing in the doorway with a dead serious expression on his unmasked face. How could Harry be standing there, when he was over here, being embraced by Marvy, and why? Or was Harry embracing Marvy? Why the upraised hand? What was wrong with Harry-Marvy, and who was responsible? Was something *in* the upraised hand? How could Harry be in two places at once? Was it a *knife*? What did he mean by "Houston, we have a problem"? Could this all be an elaborate prank? And *who the hell was Bozo the Clown?*

Amy, though childless, had always imagined herself in a vaguely parental role, however distant, with her classes, and she had more than once entertained the fantasy of rising to the occasion of some outlandish classroom threat, masterfully evoking calm through billows of black smoke, negotiating with terrorists, taking a bullet for her most gifted student writer, or for the most inept, depending on her fantasy mood. She had concocted heroic daydreams since early childhood, and they had persisted all through her promising youth, her marriages, her screwups, and on into the present day. In broken-down middle age she yearned more than ever to be a hero; to be presented, as on Christmas morning, with a grand melodramatic opportunity to redeem her life. It would be, she often thought, like winning a moral lottery. Just last night, as she was trying to sleep, she had imagined herself weaponless, as usual, when some dangerous guy (the Workshop Sniper? Herman U. Ticks?) burst in a door identical to that occupied by Harry Blasbalg. The miscreant was heavily armed and bent on mayhem, but resourceful Amy saved the day by upending a metal wastebasket over his head and whanging on it with a chair.

Now, resourceful Amy stood rooted, mouth agape, as everyone else in the class behaved, if not heroically, at least like rational adults. They made way for Dr. Surtees to see to the stricken clown, over whom even Harry was bending solicitously. Amy found her voice. "Wait!" she shouted. Everyone looked at her. "We don't know who that is!" Everyone looked at her like she was crazy.

Well, of course, they didn't know about the Sniper! The Sniper, Amy was beginning to understand, was somehow involved, and she looked at Carla for support, but Carla was kneeling by the clown, and Surtees was grabbing the mask by its tuft of red hair and yanking it off, and out sprang a thick blond mane as frizzy as Bozo's. "God," said Carla, "look at her face!"

Marvy, Jimmy Carter balanced on top of his head, shook the stricken clown gently. "Sweetie, are you all right?"

"She's coming around," said Surtees. "It looks like an allergic reaction."

Amy finally moved, brushing past Chuck and Tiffany to stand behind the kneeling doctor. The woman lying on her back, wedged between two desk chairs, looked as though she might be attractive, in an athletic, no-makeup sort of way, when her face wasn't upside-down and ballooning with hives. "Excuse me," said Amy. "Would someone please tell me who this poor woman is?"

"Hello, there," said the woman, looking up from the floor. "I'm Cindy Stokes."

At last Amy, the Class Dunce, understood at least the first part of the tableau. "You're Marvy's wife," she said. And everybody had known this but Amy.

"I wanted her to meet everybody," said Marvy.

"I'm so sorry," Cindy said, slowly sitting up. "I've never done that before."

"Was it the latex?" someone asked.

"Probably," said Surtees. "Are you having any airway obstruction? Trouble breathing?"

"Nope. My lips and my cheeks just got incredibly hot and itchy and then I passed out, like a wimp."

"Scared me half to death," said Marvy, helping her to her feet. "I was just going to introduce you to Amy, and then, boom."

Which explained the upraised, knifeless hand.

All that remained was Harry's cryptic warning. Once she'd gotten to the bottom of that, Amy planned to go off somewhere and jump into a well. She had never been so embarrassed.

After Cindy had returned from the bathroom, hives apparently subsiding, to sit beside her husband, and the excitement had fallen off, a thick quiet came over the class, which gazed at Amy, with what expectation she didn't know. Chuck always looked at her speculatively, as though he were trying to figure her out. Now she felt like something on a microscope slide. An apology was in order, but how could she word it? *Folks, I know it looks bad, but, see, one of you, and I don't know even which one it is, is a real nasty piece of work, possibly mentally unhinged, and when the Mystery Clown dropped to the floor, why, naturally I . . .* "Ladies and gentlemen," she began, "there's something I have to tell you." It was all over. She was going to lose them, and her miserable little job too.

"Yes," said Carla. "There's something important you don't know about Amy."

Yes. I'm an ineffectual, irresponsible, paranoid dolt. "When I saw the—when I saw Ms. Stokes pass out, I—"

"It was the Bozo!" said Carla.

"Well, yes." Amy stared at Carla, who stared right back in a very meaningful way.

"Which is totally my bad," said Carla, "because when I was picking out the masks I completely forgot about it."

"About what?" asked Amy.

"Your coulrophobia."

"Her what?"

Carla turned and addressed the class. "Amy has been clinically diagnosed as a clown phobic. To an absolutely crippling degree."

Dot raised her hand. "Oh, I've got that too. I didn't know it had a name."

Amy struggled not to laugh. What a clever girl. To her amazement they seemed to be buying it, or at least willing to entertain the possibility. What was "crippling clown phobia"? Fear of being clotheslined by Emmett Kelly? Even Surtees didn't look skeptical. Now they were all chiming in about how scary clowns were—apparently all the world did not love a clown—and offering their own individual phobic variations. Ginger said she had a morbid fear of mimes. Ricky Buzza looked puzzled for a while, but then perked up. "I get it now," he said. "You were able to control yourself until the clown started acting weird."

"Exactly," said Amy. "That's when I lost it, and I just want to apologize, to all of you, and especially to Cindy." She was starting to feel at ease, and then she remembered Harry, and Houston. Amy sighed. "Harry, what did you mean when you walked in? You said, 'Houston, we have a—' "

"Serious parking problem! And we shouldn't stand for it. These classes cost a lot of money, and tonight I had to park half a mile away . . ."

Amy was suddenly happier than she had been in years. "Harry, you're absolutely right," she said, "and if you want to sue the bastards, count me in. Meanwhile, let's do Murphy Gonzalez."

Dealing with juvenile fiction was always hard. Workshop students were apt to give a pass to everything, on the unexamined theory that kids weren't as discriminating in their reading habits as adults, and any old thing would do, as long as it was sufficiently simpleminded and optimistic. Of course this was false. As far as Amy was concerned, the standards for writing good fiction were the same no matter the age of your target audience. But typically, when dealing in workshop with juvenile fiction, someone would drag in the notions of "age-specific vocabulary," "short, punchy chapters," and "appropriate themes," and tonight was no exception.

Pete had written a likable piece about a sweet quirky kid whose social problems, though predictable, were presented and handled with energy and imagination. Murphy Gonzalez could have just been that staple of modern kids' books, the weird-looking nerd who trips over some convenient plot device and achieves popularity. But Pete's Murphy never gets to the popular part: he's as out of it at the end of the story as he is on the first page. He even loses his semi-girlfriend, another science geek, who forms a middle school chapter of PETA and drops Murphy when he goes to the state regional science fair with his frog-dissection slide show ("To Pith or Double-Pith"). Most remarkably, Murphy never undergoes a change of heart about his frogs, which do not visit him in dreams or crack wise at him from the lab bench; but he does have an African Grey parrot named Margaret whose cryptic advice he values.

Nothing climactic happened in the course of Pete Purvis's twenty-page story, through which Murphy floated from home to school and back again, in and out of scenes, continually distracted by his own thoughts. The writing needed some polish, but Amy loved the piece. To her annoyance, everyone else, with the shining exception of Edna Wentworth, either hated or were indifferent to it.

Dot Hieronymus led the charge against the story's various "age-inappropriate" qualities, and in this she was joined by Marvy and Mrs. Marvy, who also had kids (Dot's two were grown), and Tiffany, who had apparently taken some stupid course in child development. The rest were just lazy. Amy was particularly disappointed in Chuck and Frank, whom she had begun to count on for intelligent in-class feedback. Their few comments were so general in nature that Amy suspected neither had read beyond the first few pages. She was tempted to blast them, and the class in general, for giving Pete less than his due. But she was still so relieved about the identity of "the Bozo" and Harry's anticlimactic announcement that she let the matter slide.

Instead, she allowed Edna the floor. Edna Wentworth must have been a hell of a high school teacher, because she hit a number of complex points right on the head. She praised Pete for avoiding clichés, for his lovely list of girls' names (Brittany, Ashley, Michelle, Megan, Demi), and for the care he had taken to get the details of frog dissection correct. She explained to him the distinction between *fatality* and *fatalism,* and that "Micheals" wasn't as likely a spelling as "Michaels." She did all of Amy's work for her, including solving the mystery of how a "cafeteria duty" could *do* anything at all, much less descend on a table.

"It's an interesting word usage," Edna explained, "which apparently derives from grade school. I never encountered it until about ten years ago. In grade school, kids picked up on the general notion of 'duty,' as in yard, cafeteria, or kitchen duty, but personified it. This must have begun with one child and taken off from there."

"So a 'duty' is a person?" asked Amy, and the other parents nodded that yes, this was true. Cindy Stokes said her son always complained about the yard duty picking on him.

"And I really appreciate seeing this in print," continued Edna, "since it captures what I hope will prove to be an ephemeral, and possibly regional, linguistic anomaly."

Amy went on to heap praises on Pete, who blushed happily, at which point Amy collected all critiques for inspection before handing them to him (this being her new routine) and called a short recess.

After the break, and after Tiffany's and Ricky Buzza's stories had been passed around for the following week's critique, Amy opened discussion on Dot's story, "Gone But Not Forgotten." Amy couldn't help wishing that Dot had been wearing the empowering gorilla mask when she wrote it, an emotionally gruesome Wronged Wife thing which Amy hoped did not correspond in any way with the circumstances of Dot's actual life.

"Here we have an adult story," said Amy, "as opposed to a story for kids. So I expect that those of you who didn't exactly overexert yourselves—"

Tiffany Zuniga actually snorted. "Excuse me," she said, "but in what sense is this an 'adult story'?"

"In the sense," Amy said, "that children probably hear enough about marital discord in their homes without reading bedtime stories about it." She should have realized that Tiffany was going to hate this piece. Tiffany was the anti-Dot.

> Clarissa had arrayed the linen-cloaked dining table with their best china, the Royal Doulton she had selected twenty years ago, when she had been a young bride-to-be. Two wine glasses sparkled in the light of her tall, finely tapered natural beeswax candles, and the air was redolent with the robust, manly scent of bourbon-roasted pork, Jeremy's favorite dish.
>
> It was eight o'clock, past time for Jeremy to return from the office, but then he was frequently late, and Clarissa hadn't really expected him before 8:30, even on this, their twentieth anniversary. Clarissa smiled to herself as she pictured him running for a taxi, cursing the lateness of the hour, anxious to get to her. She wondered what he had gotten her for a present. Whatever it was, or even if it was nothing, it didn't matter to Clarissa. His real present to her, and hers to him, would be unwrapped upstairs, in their satin-slippered bed, after their sumptuously sensuous repast.
>
> Suddenly the front door opened, and quietly closed again. Clarissa smiled once more, this time the smile was for him,

showing her fine white teeth. "I'm waiting, Darling," she called to him.

There was no answer for a long time, and then she could just make out, "I'll be in in a minute." Jeremy sounded tired, distracted, and Clarissa's heart went out to him.

"Whatever you had to do so late this evening," she sang out, "could certainly have been accomplished by your other senior partner, Herb Warminster." When Jeremy didn't respond, she added, "He takes advantage of you, Darling. They all do, just because you're the senior member of the most prestigious law firm in Philadelphia. You really ought to—"

Suddenly Jeremy was standing in the dining room doorway, and he was not alone. Behind him, over his left shoulder, she could see a shiny blonde head.

"Why Jeremy," Clarissa asked, "who's that with you?"

As if in a dream the blonde head materialized in front of Jeremy, attached to the body of Clarissa's younger sister, Rose, who had been a brunette the last time Clarissa had seen her, ten years ago, at an occasion Clarissa could scarcely have forgotten, during which, as a Christmas guest in Clarissa's home, she had thrown herself at her own sister's husband in the master bath.

"Hello, Sis," Rose said, smiling unpleasantly.

Clarissa was dumbstruck. She glanced at Jeremy, whose face was grim, almost metallic, not the face she loved. This wasn't a dream, Clarissa thought to herself. This was a nightmare.

"Clarissa," Jeremy finally spoke, "I want a divorce."

Amy had given some thought to how she would open up discussion. Dot was, on the surface anyway, the most emotionally vulnerable workshop member. She always claimed to love every workshop contribution, even Pete's, which she had actually criticized (a first for her). Somewhere along the line, probably at a young age, she had gotten the idea that you shouldn't say anything at all if you couldn't say something complimentary. Amy had taught workshops full of people like Dot, and these classes were always a waste of everyone's time, especially hers. But here Dot was all alone and exposed. True, Marvy was a very pleasant, look-on-the-bright-side sort, as was Ricky Buzza, but they were guys. Men did not tend to take these sessions personally. Dot would be another story.

So Amy, who could not in good conscience find a single thing to praise in "Gone," had intended to concentrate on stylistic problems and go easy on the more substantial ones. But Tiffany wasn't going to let this happen. "First off," she was saying, "what planet does this woman live on?" Amy hoped she was referring to the hapless Clarissa, not the author. "She's a full-time housewife with a kid in college. She does nothing all day except shop and do lunch and plan candlelight dinners for Jeremy. She has no interests outside her marriage. What does she read? We don't know. What are her politics? We don't know."

"What difference does it make?" Chuck Heston, of all people, rose to Dot's defense. "She's a fictional character, for Pete's sake. You don't have to approve of her."

"It's not a question of approving. I just don't believe in her. She isn't possible."

Now something very interesting began to happen. The class, as one, gathered around Dot Hieronymus, figuratively speaking, and piled on Tiffany Zuniga. Even Ricky Buzza argued with her. Amy would bet the ranch that not one of these people had enjoyed Dot's story, but they didn't want to see the woman hurt. Or maybe they were just annoyed with Tiffany. Or both. "Look," said Frank, "can't we just talk about the story now? So what if it isn't politically correct—"

"Politics," said Tiffany, "has nothing to do with it! It's the woman herself! She's just this pathetic, doormatty, classic passive-aggressive—"

"Excuse me," said Dr. Richard Surtees, raising his finger. "If she's classic anything, then she can't very well be 'impossible.'"

Tiffany looked at the back of his head with loathing. "I never said she was impossible," she said.

"Yes you did," said Pete.

"Hold it," said Amy, glancing at Dot. Dot looked intense, but not alarmed, or hurt; not yet anyway. In fact she seemed to be smiling to herself, just a little. "You're all jumping the gun. Let's first agree upon exactly what we're arguing about. Would someone please tell us what happens in this story?"

"What I said was, or I meant, that I don't want to read about these women any more, the ones who just buy into their own second-class lives."

"Tiffany, please," said Amy.

Carla saved the moment. "A woman, Clarissa, learns that her husband is going to leave her and run off with her younger sister. There's a big flashback, where we see Clarissa and Jeremy on their honeymoon, and we see the birth of their daughter, and all that, but basically the whole thing takes place on the night of the dinner. It ends with Clarissa insisting that they sit down for supper before they leave—"

"How disgusting is that!" said Tiffany.

"—and then she goes into the kitchen and sees that the sink is all backed up, and she takes out this can of Drano. And she just stands there, and her husband says, 'How long is this going to take? We've got a plane to catch,' and she's just standing there crying and wiping her eyes and she says, 'Not long, my darling.'"

"The End," said Syl Reyes. "I thought it was kind of sad."

"Kind of convenient, you mean," said Tiffany. "The pig won't even have to pay alimony! She's going to off herself in the most horrible way possible—"

Dot Hieronymus laughed, instantly silencing the room. It was delighted laughter, unforced, almost but not quite contagious. It was also pretty alarming. Amy tried to make eye contact with her, but Dot kept her head down, and when she stopped laughing she sighed a little and went quiet.

Amy thought fast. "Dot has brilliantly circumvented the 'no talking' rule. While we may not, of course, ask her what she finds so funny, we could take the opportunity to pause here and reflect."

"Well, I don't know," said Marvy, "but did everybody think Clarissa was going to commit suicide? Because I didn't."

At this Dot raised her head and smiled back at Marvy. Her color was high, her cheeks redder than when defending *Code Black*.

To Amy's surprise, the class was about evenly split between Clarissa the Suicide and Clarissa the Cold-Blooded Poisoner. Amy was shocked that even one person, even Tiffany, believed that Clarissa was about to ingest the Drano herself. For Amy, the ending, however melodramatic, was the best thing about the story. Now they all had a fine time wrangling about it. Tiffany scoffed at the idea of a doormat wife suddenly standing up for herself; Syl, Pete, and Harry argued that Clarissa was a killer, but that there should have been some sort of foundation laid earlier in the story. Harry complained that this was a surprise ending, and no fair. And Chuck, to Amy's delight, wondered if Clarissa's character shift, from victim to murderer, hadn't been willed instead of imagined. Moments like this made Amy believe she wasn't wasting her time after all. "It's like the writer wants her to change, so, presto!"

In the end there wasn't time for Amy to discuss stylistic problems. She had all of three minutes left to touch on Dot's stilted dialogue, and specifically why dialogue is generally the worst choice for exposition. "When you're writing lines," she told them, as they started packing up, "you need to focus on the way people actually talk. And when we talk to each other we never explain our terms. We don't say, 'Sweetheart, would you pass me the sugar bowl, which we picked up for a song at that antique stall in Munich'?"

"*I* would never say that," said Chuck, "because I've never been to Germany."

"What would we say instead?" asked Marvy.

"You tell me."

"And we'd never say," said Carla, "Sweetie, your senior partner, Herb Warbucks—"

"Warminster," said Dot pleasantly. She appeared to be extremely pleased with the discussion. Amy had no idea why.

"Gimme the sugar," said Cindy to her husband. "That's what *you*'d say."

"So what do you do," asked Ginger, already on her feet, "if the fact that the sugar bowl comes from Munich is important to your story?"

They were all, spiritually, out the door. Even Carla was busy stuffing masks into a rucksack. Amy sighed. "I'll tell you next week. So long, folks, and Happy Halloween."

As usual she nosed around the empty room, looking for articles left behind. Often students forgot the next week's stories, accidentally-on-purpose, and sometimes jackets, or scarves, and once she found an unsigned three-hundred-page novel, never to be claimed, but tonight there were only a few empty coffee cups for her to throw away. Amy gathered up the two stories for next week, put one in her briefcase and the other on top of it, and started out the door, and there was Tiffany, looking crestfallen.

"I really pissed you off tonight," Tiffany said.

Was this really an apology, or the beginning of an argument? Amy didn't have the energy for either. "Everybody got worked up," Amy said. "A lot of it was just pent-up steam from the Bozo fiasco." To Amy's surprise, Tiffany giggled. "What's so funny?"

"*The Bozo Fiasco*. Sounds like one of those Robert Ludlum things."

"I can't picture you," said Amy, "reading thrillers."

"My mom," said Tiffany. "Robert Ludlum, Frederick Forsyth, all those guys. Sometimes she'd have two going at once." She looked down at her feet. "Look, I know I went over the top tonight. I'm sorry. That Dot lady, that story, it just got to me, but that's my problem, I know."

"Want to walk me to my car?" Amy was sympathetic, even intrigued, but more than that she was exhausted. Together they walked, slowly, down the ramp from the modular classroom building, up the long curving path toward the road that would lead, eventually, to the lot where Amy and most of the others had been forced to park. It was a cool, fragrant night, with a hint of salt breeze, and Amy and Tiffany had it all to themselves.

Tiffany told Amy about her parents, and how her mother had died four years before, and how, armed with a master's degree in Women's Studies, Tiffany hadn't even been able to land a full-time job as a clerical worker. She still lived at home, with her father and her younger sister, and was part-time copyeditor at the *North Country Times*.

"And here I pictured you out there in the corporate jungle, bursting through glass ceilings, right into a corner office with a view."

"That was the plan."

They strolled uphill in silence, past two huge lots still more than half-filled with cars. It always amazed Amy how even this late at night there were so many cars, and so few humans. They hadn't passed a single one on foot. By now Amy was glad of the company. "I hate this walk at night," she said out loud, surprising herself.

"It's creepy, all right." Now they descended into the last lot, where only two cars remained. Tiffany's Saturn was closest. "You should take self-defense classes," she said, digging into her pants pocket. "I've taken tae kwon do and kickboxing, and I don't worry anymore." She stopped and searched her other pockets. "My keys," she said.

"Maybe they're in the ignition," said Amy.

"Never. Never, ever, ever. I've never done that in my life." Tiffany looked stricken, as well she might. By now the classroom—the only place she'd been tonight—was locked up and the custodian gone.

"Have you ever left them sticking in the trunk?"

They were close enough to the car now to see the keys, glinting yellow in the lamplight. Tiffany laughed in delighted relief. "You know what? I even remember doing it! I got my pile of manuscripts from the trunk, and I was really excited about passing them out, and I slammed the top down, and I even thought, Now, don't forget the keys, Stupid!"

Amy stood with her for a moment, as she put her bag in the trunk. "So, you were excited, huh? Does this mean you like what you've written?"

Tiffany smiled. "I like the fact that I wrote anything at all."

Amy smiled back, waved good night, and walked off toward her own car. After a few seconds she turned. "You know," she called to Tiffany, "there are worse things than falling on your face right out of college."

"Like what?"

"Like instant, unearned success. Like getting your first novel accepted by the first publisher you send it to. Like getting your first rejection slip at the age of thirty-five."

Tiffany laughed. "You're breaking my heart!"

"Later," said Amy, turning back.

Well, this was nice. Tiffany was a decent girl after all. Tonight even Surtees had been almost likable. Amy loved it when someone turned out not to be a jerk. She often wondered if this trait prevented her from being a better writer. Once she'd gotten a story rejected by the *New Yorker* with the comment, "People simply aren't this noble." But they *were*, she thought now, on this lovely night, after an absurd and invigorating evening among people who just wanted to get their stories down on paper, leave some little mark, make themselves distinct. They were all, potentially, noble. In the distance, Tiffany's car started up and drove off. And essentially kind, Amy thought. Maybe not always, especially if you gave them a chance to think about it first, but look at what happened tonight, with Cindy Stokes, and then with Dot's foolish story, which could have been a disaster, with indignation, hurt feelings, God knows what all, but instead look what happened. Everybody went home happy.

She heard, off in the distance, the hysterical squeal of brakes, and then the gunning of an engine, and she looked back to see if it could be Tiffany's car. At first all she could make out was a small car entering the far end of the lot at an unsafe speed, at least for speed bumps, and sure enough it hit three of them, bottoming out each time in a pitchless bang, the third time with an attendant rattle that sounded like a dislodged oil pan, and still it careened forward, coming straight for Amy.

Resourceful Amy did not, of course, move an inch. She was paralyzed, but her mind was humming right along, and what she was thinking was that even if she could move she'd never be able to get out of the way in time. Perhaps, when she was younger. Not now. Oh, well.

The car was close enough so that she could see it *was* that Saturn, it *was* Tiffany, and then it swerved to Amy's left, and braked so hard that she could smell the rubber burning twenty feet away. In the abrupt quiet Amy heard a funny, muffled, high-pitched *eeeeee*, like a cartoon falsetto, and then Tiffany opened her door and tumbled out on the asphalt, and it was a scream, *EEEEEEEE*, but still so thin a sound and so odd that Amy felt like she had all the time in the world, how bad could it be? And then Tiffany got on her feet and slammed the car door and, without looking in Amy's direction, pointed at her own backseat window and began to scream full-throated, with all the overtones, a scream to wake the dead. She stood stiff, jackknifed forward at the waist, and pointed and screamed and screamed as if she were trying to kill the whole car with her voice alone.

Amy, taking all this in, suddenly realized that she wasn't afraid yet. She would be soon, but right now she was feeling good, strong, charged with the electric joy of not having been run over. She wasn't afraid, and she could move again, and she was, being a human being, potentially noble. Amy ran to Tiffany's side and embraced the poor shrieking girl. "I'm here," she said. "It's all right. I'm here, and it's going to be all right." She repeated this many, many times, until Tiffany stopped screaming, and just cried, shuddering and coughing; until at last she managed to say, still pointing, "Look."

Amy looked at the car window, but she could see only the reflection of an overhead streetlamp. She opened the driver-side door and peered inside, but all she could see was a pile of books on the passenger seat and deep shadow in the back. She would have to open the rear door to look back there, and so resourceful Amy, still unafraid, sat in the driver's seat, and it smelled like cough drops in there, overwhelming, like the nightbloomer only different, and she turned and reached around back to pull up the lock, and there, on the backseat directly behind her, she could finally see, eye level, impaled, and propped straight up on a eucalyptus branch, the head of Ted Bundy.

After all the speed-bump-scraping, brake-squealing, and prolonged high-decibel screaming, including a final two-tone duet, not a single campus cop showed his or her face. Nor, for that matter, did anybody else. Amy and Tiffany remained the only players in an asphalt arena. Eventually there would be the problem of what to do next, but first Amy had to extricate herself thoroughly from Tiffany's car, which had one of those shoulder belts that automatically tightens around the driver the second he sits down, so that when Amy, after wasting countless precious seconds processing visual information, at last recognized a human head, a smirking face, Bundy's smirking face, and attempted her escape, she actually plunged headfirst onto the pavement, her lower body anchored inside the car by a snarl of safety webbing. How ironic was that?

Amy had always feared that she would die in an embarrassing manner, knowing, as her sad life passed before her, that not even the kindest soul could possibly hear the circumstances without laughing, like people who died horribly in chocolate vats and on public toilets at the DMV, and that poor man who was bludgeoned to death at a Friendly's. Now sure enough, here she was, immobilized by a lifesaving device, awaiting a grisly death at the hands of a monster who, now that she thought of it, had been electrocuted at least twenty years ago, at which point she noticed that Tiffany wasn't screaming any more, she was yelling. "Mask on a stick! It's a mask! Mask!" Of course it was.

By the time Tiffany had helped Amy free herself and they were both upright on the asphalt, they began to laugh and did not stop for at least five minutes. Every so often Tiffany would manage to gasp, "It isn't funny!," which would set her off again, and Amy too. Amy could not recall ever having laughed this hard. She did not feel, as the cliché would have it, as though her sides would split, but rather as if something high in front, her breastbone maybe, would buckle, or maybe her heart would just seize up. This was "hysterical" laughter, and finally experiencing it confirmed her most deeply held belief: that all laughter, except possibly the nervous tittering sort—which was counterfeit, really—stemmed from the same source: an accidental glimpse behind the curtain of denial at the Real Deal, an uncontained porridge of nothingness and stars through which meteors, comets, entire galaxies whiz like shaving-cream pies.

In the end Tiffany was the one who got the Bundy mask out of the backseat and placed it on the hood of her car. It had been modeled on the most notorious snapshot of him, where he's smiling mischievously beneath a gaze certainly calculated to terrify. Even flattened out like this it was pretty unnerving. "All right," said Amy. "How is this possible? Carla brought the masks. Am I supposed to believe that she saved this one? That Carla did it? It just can't be." Amy was almost positive of this.

"Carla brought two whole duffel bags full of these things. Everybody got to pick what they wanted, but there were a whole bunch left over."

Amy didn't remember two duffel bags.

"She kicked them into the back of the room," Tiffany said, "behind the last row of chairs. They were too bulky to keep with her."

"So anybody could have gotten to it."

"No, they couldn't," said Tiffany. "We kept the door closed during class, and anyway, if anybody from outside had come around, even during break, we would have seen him."

"Right."

Amy was suddenly aware that she was cold. The fall night air was damp, oppressive, and everything, the wrinkled skin of her own hands, Tiffany's shiny auburn hair, the peeling eucalyptus trunks, the pink bougainvillea, the asphalt, the mask, everything was ugly in the yellow light. Tomorrow she would have to tell administration about the Sniper. But right now, Tiffany had no idea. Tiffany believed that a stranger had played this awful joke. Amy didn't have the heart to tell her the truth. "Let me drive you home," she said. "I'll come get you tomorrow and bring you back here for your car."

But Tiffany insisted she was steady enough to drive herself. After arguing with her, Amy helped her clear the car of eucalyptus bark and leaves. They opened the windows and doors to air it out and waited awhile in silence.

"Are you sure about this?" Amy asked.

Tiffany nodded and got in the car. She cranked the windows back up and made sure the doors were locked. She started up her engine, put the car in gear, and fiddled with the knobs on her radio for about two minutes. Then she turned her radio off and cranked down her window. "You live in North County, right?" Amy nodded. "Well, would you mind just following me home? Oh, forget it, it's nuts, I'll just—"

"Of course I will," said Amy. Good for you, she thought. If it were me, I'd tough it out until I got on the road and then have a panic attack.

Amy got in her car and followed the Saturn out of the lot, out of the campus, west to the sea, and north on Torrey Pines. She was glad to see they weren't going to take the interstate. It was past

midnight now, on a weeknight, so for long stretches they had this dark road to themselves, and she had no trouble keeping the girl's lights in her sight. She kept her radio off and her window up, and they stayed close, separated by a few car lengths, as the road curved in and out with the contour of the shore. Only in California would this pass for intimacy, a nearness literal enough to stave off the jitters. On nights like this, Californians liked to tailgate, and when Amy first came west, she assumed they were being obnoxious. It took her awhile to understand that they were just lonely.

Sudden white fog closed in when they reached Encinitas, and they had to slow way down, crawl their way east, away from the water, past invisible flower farms, fields of cloud, and occasional street signs, wonderful names, Vesta, Dionysus, Olympus. No Buena Vista Cul-de-Sac, no Via Del Luxurio. Amy just drove. What a pleasure not to think at all. Zephyr, Calypso, Demetria. Eventually they came to Andromeda Way, where Tiffany lived, in a little wooden house with a fig tree in the front yard. Amy watched while Tiffany walked to her house and opened the door, and waved, and went inside.

She planned on taking hours to get home, floating on these enchanted roads until she somehow found herself further inland, but when she had gone a few miles east the fog lifted, and she had no choice but to pick up speed, so she was in her own driveway by two o'clock. She got out of the ticking car and stood at the base of her porch steps. The orange Halloween bowl had been licked clean of chocolate bars. Amy listened to Alphonse not bark, and looked through her window blinds at her illuminated house, and she realized that she couldn't go in. Or shouldn't. Not now, not in the dark. She wasn't exactly afraid at the moment, but she knew that, once inside, she would have a terrible night. The Bundy mask was in the trunk of her car, but there was something much worse in her house.

So Amy spent Halloween night at a pancake joint, which she

shared with hospital workers off shift and a sad-eyed old man in a pea jacket. She ordered a huge meal of waffles and sausages, which she drowned in terrible syrup and pushed around on her plate, and she drank cup after cup of bad coffee, and read her student stories for next week, which of course would never happen, because the class was kaput.

As dawn approached she drove back home and sat on her front steps, waiting for first light. The only constellation Amy had ever been able to recognize was the Dipper, and there it was, down near the horizon, dipping away. And close by, right under the handle, something once alive with light—a burning rock, a shooting star— traced a little thumbnail arc and winked out. The moon was long gone, but the stars were still up there, not twinkling, but winking, in the great purple slapstick sky. You have to learn to laugh at it, she thought. The first time you see it—when you're tiny and dressed up in a sheet with jagged eyeholes—it isn't funny at all.

November 1, 2007

<merge address>

Dear <merge name>,

By the time you receive this you'll undoubtedly have been notified by the Extension people that our Fall Fiction Workshop class has been officially cancelled, and that your fee will be completely refunded. I have no idea what reason they gave you for the cancellation, although I'm sure it was maddeningly vague and insulting to your intelligence.

I have been asked—no, instructed—by the Extension people not to do what I'm about to do, which is to explain, to the best of my ability, why the class had to be cancelled. There are a number of reasons why I'm going to do this, but they all boil down to one: I owe it to you. You're the best class I've had in years: the most fun, the most industrious, the most surprising (in more ways than one). You deserve better than to be left hanging.

What happened was that someone—someone in your class—frightened another class member half to death last night. This unknown person has been playing games with me, and with some of you, all semester. The pranks started off relatively small, with an odd phone call, the occasional mean-spirited note, and so on, but until Halloween I didn't detect any real escalation. This is my excuse for not alerting all of you: that I had no sense that this person (my term: The Sniper) was building up to anything even remotely dangerous. Halloween night changed all that. A serial killer mask was propped up in the backseat of a class member's car, and could well have caused a serious accident. As it happened, the prank was not fatal, merely terrifying, but enough is clearly enough.

I have two stories to read and mark up—Tiffany's and Ricky's—and I plan to go ahead and mail the markups back to them. I encourage the rest of you, if you can spare the postage, to do the same. (I trust you still have your address lists.)

Five of you haven't had your class go-round yet. I'm thinking of Syl

Reyes, Chuck Heston, Frank Waasted, Carla Karolak, and Ginger Nicklow. Please feel free, over the remainder of the semester, to mail me your fiction, and I'll send you back a critique. And the rest of you—if you want me to look at revisions, or if you get inspired to write something else, I'd be happy to oblige. It's the least I can do.

I wish you all the best for the upcoming holidays.

Regards and regrets,
Amy Gallup

P.S. It occurs to me that this very letter reads like some sort of prank. I wish it were. I'm also all too aware that one of you, reading this letter right now, is responsible for all this. What I don't know is if you, the Sniper, have won, or lost. The really odd thing is that, whoever you are, I find that I can bear you no real malice, since you're a member of a group of which I have grown quite fond.

Say, there's a story idea! Do me a favor, one of you, and run with it.

A.G.

From: "Carla Karolak" <karlak@bmbx96.com>
To: "Amy Gallup" <gallopingamy@jupiter.net
Subject: Are you crazy they're gonna fire you
Sent: Saturday, November 3, 2007 9:30 AM

:-O Who was the class member? Edna? Which mask was it? The Bundy mask, right? I just thought somebody snagged it. Why didn't you call me, for gods sake? Why do we have to quit? This is horrible! Pick up your phone!!!! <worrylines>

From: "Amy Gallup" <gallopingamy@jupiter.net>
To: "Carla Karolak" <karlak@bmbx96.com>
Subject: RE: Are you crazy they're gonna fire you
Sent: Saturday, November 3, 2007 5:00 PM

Sorry, Carla. I'll put my phone back on the hook tomorrow, maybe. Depends on my mood, which remains black. It was Tiffany, and it was the Bundy mask, which I've got in my trunk if you want the)(*#$& thing back. We have to quit because the Sniper obviously isn't going to. Some stuff happened that I didn't tell you about—a rude, unsigned "critique" of Marv's thing, and a dirty cartoon of Edna, which thank god I intercepted. The mask in Tiffany's car was really frightening; it was propped up in the backseat, and she didn't even see it until she was almost to the main road.

Somebody's crazy, and it isn't me, and I really don't care if they fire me anyway.

Amy G.

November 5, 2007

Amy Gallup
964 Jacaranda Drive
Escondido, CA 92025

Dear Ms. Gallup,

Three of your students from Course #LA097798382 called our office this morning and demanded that the class be resumed. It emerged in these conversations that you have apparently notified every class member about the cause of cancellation, which we had expressly asked you not to do.

Be advised that you will not be asked to teach for us in the future.

Yours truly,

Lauren McDoo
Executive Assistant to the Associate Dean
College of Extended Studies in the Creative Arts

From: "Carla Karolak" <karlak@bmbx96.com>
To: "Amy Gallup" <gallopingamy@jupiter.net>
Subject: RE: RE: Are you crazy they're gonna fire you
Sent: Monday, November 5, 2007 12:15 PM

I just got off the phone with Harry Blasbalg who actually called that little snot at the ext office and THREATENED TO SUE if they didn't let us continue the class. (Whodathunk it?) He was calling everybody on the list, and so far everybody agrees with him! He was going alphabetically, so that's only Ricky and Chuck and me, and Harry, but really, I don't see how they can turn us down.

BTW nobody's mad at you about the sniper.

PLEASE hook up your phone. We need to talk. I do anyway.

From: "Amy Gallup" <gallopingamy@jupiter.net>
To: "Carla Karolak" <karlak@bmbx96.com>
Subject: RE: RE: RE: Are you crazy they're gonna fire you
Sent: Tuesday, November 6, 2007 6:24 PM

They fired me.

Not to worry, though. In the Fall Catalog I count six other extension writing classes this semester alone:

Go Publish Yourself!

Finding Your Inner Story

Finding Your Voice

Finding the Perfect Agent

Finding a Subject for Your Memoir

Finding Your Own Ass with Two Hands, a Map, and a Compass

Okay, I made up two of them, but there really are a slew of courses, and I'm sure the gang would be welcomed into any or all of them with open legs, since it must be killing those SOBs to give back all those $$$.

Take it easy, Carla. Don't worry so much.

From: "Killjoy" <kkkiiillllrrrooooyyy@hotmail.com>
To: "Amy Gallup" <gallopingamy@jupiter.net>
Subject: RE: RE: Are you crazy they're gonna fire you
Sent: Tuesday, November 6, 2007 9:06 PM

>What I don't know is if you, the Sniper, have won, or lost. The
>really odd thing is that, whoever you are, I find that I can bear
>you no real malice, since you're a member of a group for which I
>have grown quite fond.

What would it take, I wonder, for you to bear me "real malice"?

Well, obviously I've lost, haven't I.

Amy had been traumatized in late childhood by an old movie she saw on her family's RCA console TV, in which a mad pianist's hands were severed after death and proceeded to crawl around a drafty old house at night, strangling people. Frankenstein was tragic, and Bela Lugosi cracked her up, but for some reason the spectacle of white hands moving crabwise across a bedspread stopped her breath. She took to keeping the door of her closet firmly closed and sleeping with the bedroom door open, to catch the light from downstairs, and insisted, over her mother's practical objections, upon dust ruffles beneath her mattress, around which dust collected in dingy clouds. She pretended to find the dust ruffles feminine and cozy, but really they were just flimsy barriers beyond which lurked the malign viscosity under her bed. Behind those pink curtains the pale hands waited, squatting, flexing, mulling their midnight itinerary.

It was the fingers that frightened her the most, not the gory, indecent stump, which in those days had yet to be rendered realistically on screen and so could not really be imagined. Fingers were intelligent. "You have smart hands," her grandmother used to tell her, when Amy would deal the cards for Authors and Crazy 8s and

Hi-Lo Jack. Hands could be smart or stupid, and the hands capering hypothetically beneath her bed were brilliant. They knew all about Amy.

Most nights young Amy slept well, but at least one night a week, sometimes two, she was terrorized by the creeping hands. She never saw them, of course, not even out of the corner of her eye, but often she heard them scampering across the floor, the bureau, and on one memorable occasion the window by her bed, a velvet tapping so subtle that it seemed composed for her ears alone, in some obscene code. At twelve she didn't worry at their symbolism. She had enough on her plate, those long nights, without torturing herself with deeper meanings. All she knew about the hands was that they were out to get her and could be kept away only through constant, wretched vigilance.

In time, though, she came to know something worse: that they weren't really under her bed, or behind the closet door, and that they weren't even *hands*. They were something else entirely, and they lived inside her mind. This came to her one long night when she came awake from a deep sleep to a crisp, hyperreal afterimage, one severed hand perched on her night table, index and third fingers extended toward her, playing a slow trill on the night air, and when, before she had emerged so fully from sleep as to be paralyzed with fright, she sat up and switched on the table lamp, the hand remained, three-dimensional, solid, and absurd. It was just as she had always imagined it, but smaller, or more compact, and frankly stupid-looking. A ridiculous object, and she blinked it away, and there was her blond night table, lightly and evenly blanketed in dust.

Of course there were no severed hands crawling around her bedroom at midnight. She was protected by laws biological and physical. She had been terrified of nothing in this world. Amy was a self-conscious child, never more so than when she was alone, and she was given to formal observations, the most cogent of which she wrote down in her journal, which at that stage was only a three-volume set. Now she got out her pen with the multicolored refills, opened her journal, selected lavender ink, and wrote

> What a goon I've been! I've been living inside a B movie all this time. Think of all those nights, all that lost sleep . . . But perhaps it was all worth it. I've just realized something truly profound. I really am "the Captain of My Fate"! Good night, sweet dreams, Onward to the Morning!!!

She slipped the journal back into its bedside drawer, switched off the light, settled in for the first carefree night in recent memory, and an hour later bolted awake screaming from the worst nightmare she had ever had in her whole life: the first of the tarantula dreams. They chased her down hallways, up spiral staircases, through all the upper rooms of unfamiliar houses, multiplying as they scampered, and always, in the end, surrounding her, nibbling at her bare feet, and they must have been albinos, because they were as pale as they were huge, and coated in luxuriant platinum fur. Her mother and father were both at her bedside, calling her name, shaking her into consciousness. They told her that she'd been screaming for ten minutes.

Amy had two more realizations that night, neither of which she wrote down. First, she literally was, as her parents often told her, her own worst enemy; and second, she missed the hands already. The hands were fictional. But there really were tarantulas in the world; and beneath their disguise lurked something else, and something worse beneath that. Onward to the Morning, indeed.

Sometime during the six nights between Halloween and the following Tuesday, when she got Killjoy's e-mail, Amy must have dozed off, but her only evidence of this was that she hadn't gone completely insane, which was supposed to happen to you if you were critically sleep deprived. After spending Wednesday night at the IHOP she had harbored faint hopes for an exhausted sleep on Thursday, but it didn't come, and she survived that night in bed watching television. By Friday evening she had consumed a bottle and a half of sour merlot, which knocked her out for two hours. For the rest of that night she was too sick for night terrors, but by late Saturday afternoon she had needed to turn on every light in her little house.

Flipping Carla off like that, breezily assuring her that she wasn't worried about being let go, had somehow made things worse instead of better. She was sick about being let go. She had been disrespected by an executive assistant to an associate dean, on top of which she had lost her last direct contact with humankind.

She roamed her house and attached garage day and night, dragging Alphonse with her, attempting to believe that they were alone and safe. She tried to go out once to shop for groceries, and realized that even at high noon she didn't have the nerve to leave the place unattended, for fear of what would slip in. By Monday she had emptied the freezer and was down to ancient cans of soup, cream of potato, tomato, corn chowder, with no crackers, and no milk either, which made the oatmeal (the only cereal left on top of her refrigerator) pretty tough to choke down. Alphonse ate well, as she always bought his kibble in bulk, but he missed his snacks, the Vienna Fingers and Cheez-Its, the giant soft pretzels, the cold cuts and havarti, not to mention dinner-plate leftovers, and he took to sitting motionless at her feet, staring at her with simple hostility. He had never pretended to love her, and now he drilled her with the basset gaze of hate. She didn't blame him. For all he knew, she had the good stuff hidden somewhere and withheld it now out of unfathomable human spite.

Amy was a loner who hated to be alone, but before the Sniper entered her life, she had kept her nebulous fears at bay, taking them out once every month or so, walking them in the night air, letting them trash the occasional night's rest, and then they had always tucked themselves away (like spiders) until the next time. The Sniper had let them loose, apparently for good. And Amy still didn't know what it was she feared. It wasn't spiders, it wasn't hands, and if she were ever to identify it, in some blinding midnight epiphany, it would turn out not to be that either.

Finally hearing from Killjoy the Sniper allowed Amy to sleep through the night. The downside was that now she could dream again. The blond tarantulas were back, from a ten-year hiatus. Or maybe they'd never left. When she was married to "Bob," at least during the time when they shared a bed, he would often complain about the noises she made in her sleep. Little yelps, he called them. She sounded, he claimed, like an old-time cartoon character, singing. He called her Steamboat Willie.

She'd never been able to figure out what they stood for—the tarantulas, the hands. Oddly for a writer, Amy was bored by symbols. They ruled the night, and they sprouted in her fiction, when she wrote, but she figured they were no business, really, of hers. They were the product and property of her subconscious, which she pictured as a little man in a projection booth whose matinees she preferred not to attend. The little man threw severed hands at her, and then tarantulas, because he figured she wasn't ready to look at what they really, really meant, and that was just fine with Amy. He knew what he was doing, she was sure.

Still, except for the one nightmare, which stirred her only briefly, she slept deep and awakened early Wednesday afternoon to the officious clicks of Alphonse's overgrown nails on the hardwood floor of her bedroom. She staggered to the back door, let him out, waited until he was finished, let him back in, filled up his dish with dry food, and lurched back to bed, passing along the way her answering machine blinking "35." This was fifteen more than it had been at midnight, which was bad. She had planned on wiping the messages without reading them, once the number stopped growing, and the class gave up. It had to be class members calling, mostly Carla, because nobody else ever called Amy. She slept dreamlessly, deeper even than before, the kind of sleep into which time disappears, and then the doorbell rang.

It was probably a Mormon, or some poor soul hawking tamales out of the trunk of his car, or her neighbor Mrs. Franz, who was losing her mind and sometimes forgot where she lived. But the bell rang again, and then three or four minutes later, a third time, and now Alphonse clicked out into the living room and began to woof at the front door, and there was nothing for it but to open her eyes, locate her slippers and put on a bathrobe, and find out who the hell it was.

Never mind who. It was dark in Amy's room, even with the reading lamp on, and the rest of the house was darker still. How long had she been sleeping? And why was she opening her front door to an unknown caller in what was apparently the middle of the night? Because, Amy guessed, as she tried to focus on the figure standing with its back to her on her front porch, her circadian clock was off and she had early-morning courage. *Kill me now.* She spoke. "Do you know what time it is?"

The figure simultaneously jumped a foot and whirled around off balance, colliding with her decrepit Christmas cactus and knocking it to the cement. "Jesus," said Chuck Heston. "Give a guy some warning."

Amy stared for a moment, and then said, "Seriously, do you know what time it is? Because actually I don't."

Chuck squatted and began to scoop dirt back into the pot. "It's time to get a new plant."

"Because I've been asleep, more or less, since Tuesday night."

"I'll make you a deal. I'll tell you what time it is if you tell me what day it is."

Rumplestiltskin. Amy remembered now making a wisecrack about the fairy-tale dwarf the night she first met Chuck, and here he was on her front porch making enigmatic bargains. Amy was suddenly aware of how she must look, which was much worse than usual; and how, even if she had wanted to, she couldn't very well invite him into her filthy house, which hadn't been cleaned or picked up or even aired out in a week and must reek of burned pizza, old basset, and flop sweat. "I can't invite you in," she said. "I'm sorry."

"It's Wednesday," said Chuck, rising to his feet and brushing potting soil off his jeans. "Wednesday is class day. They sent me, by the way, because I'm the only one who lives near Escondido."

Chuck wasn't making any sense at all. "But didn't you get my letter? Oh, no." Amy had a distressing thought. "Chuck, I sent a letter to each of you. Don't tell me you didn't—"

"We decided to blow off your letter."

Amy just stared. The last human being who had stood on her porch, besides the mailman and Mrs. Franz, was Carla; and before her, she couldn't remember anyone.

"Actually, Carla decided to blow off your letter, and she browbeat the rest of us into joining her. The class must go on."

"Chuck, that's sweet, but we don't have a classroom, and anyway—"

"I just came from a pretty good classroom. We all got together tonight at Carla's place, in La Jolla. She's got a great house with a view straight down into the water, and a living room the size of Petco Park. We can meet there next week, too."

"When you say 'we all,' who are you talking about? Surely not the whole class."

"Just about. Surtees didn't make it, but he sent regards, and said he was in. The only one we didn't hear back from was Dot Hieronymus. Carla's going to call her again tomorrow."

"Chuck." Amy didn't know where to start. She was gladdened,

absurdly so, by the gesture. She felt valued. She could not remember feeling that way for a long time, perhaps ever. "Aren't you all forgetting something?"

"We'll pay you exactly what we paid the extension, which they returned already, only now you'll get the whole amount."

"I don't mean that. I mean . . ."

"Oh! You mean . . ." He waggled his eyebrows three times.

"It's not funny. You didn't see Tiffany in that car, screaming her head off. We can't all pretend it didn't happen."

"Want to know something interesting? Tiffany was your other cheerleader. She and Carla talked the rest of us into it. And if the screamer isn't worried, what's the problem?"

"It's *escalating*. That's the problem, Chuck. Okay, right now everybody's excited about carrying on and meeting in a new place, and so on, and that's cute, but sooner or later they're going to start looking at each other, and wondering: 'What if it's her? How do I know it isn't him?' And you won't, either, unless the Sniper stands up and confesses, and fat chance of that. It's going to end with everybody freaking out everybody else."

"How do you know," asked Chuck, "that it isn't me?"

"I beg your pardon?"

"You don't know, do you?"

"Chuck, that's seriously not funny."

"I'm not trying to be funny. I'm just pointing something out. Do you or do you not know if it's me?"

"I *don't* know. Obviously. Look, this is really annoying."

"Exactly! I'm annoying you, and sorry about that, but look what I'm not doing. I'm not freaking you out. Am I?"

Amy was startled to realize this was true.

"It's weird, isn't it?" Chuck grinned. "We all noticed it tonight. The absence of freak. There we were, relaxing together in this, by the way, amazing retro conversation pit, the kind where you sink into these huge couches and chairs and can't get back out without flailing around, and we were about an hour into it when Frank mentioned that, actuarially speaking, the Sniper was one of us. There was this real brief pause, and then somebody asked him to pass the nachos. Then Pete Purvis asked if we should maybe talk about it. And there was another pause, and then Harry B. said, 'What's the point? Whoever it is, they're not going to admit it.' And then he asked if anybody was worried. And nobody said anything, and then they went back to planning the schedule. We're going to meet in different people's houses. Carla nominated your house for the last class."

Amy sagged against the doorframe. "I don't get it," she said.

"You don't have to," said Chuck. "Look, you got everybody worked up. Face it, you're a good teacher. They don't want to quit, and they want to go on working with you. And if you want to know the truth," he said, backing down the steps, "I think they're kind of enjoying the whole Sniper thing. It's exciting, in a dirty sort of way."

"That's what I'm afraid of," said Amy. She had no idea if this was true.

Chuck opened his car door. "So. Next week at Carla's. We're doing Tiffany's thing, and Ricky Buzza's, and Syl's bringing in something to pass around for the week after. And somebody else is too. I don't remember who."

"You never asked me," Amy called after him, "whether I'd do it."

"Seven o'clock sharp," Chuck called through his window as he backed down the drive. "See ya, Teach!"

Amy slowly closed the door and shuffled back to her bedroom. She lay on her back, trying to figure out if she was worried or angry or even happy, and eventually decided that it was a three-way tie. Only then did she remember that she hadn't locked the front door. Then a tiny miracle happened: the absence of freak. She just walked calmly to the door and locked it.

There was, tonight, nothing to be afraid of. And she was still of value. Amy closed her eyes and slept, without spiders.

GO AWAY

FUNNY-LOOKING WORDS
SATURDAY, NOVEMBER 10, 2007

buckaroo

hartebeest

flummox

FILED IN LISTS | COMMENTS (53)

KIBBITZERS
Selma B. wrote:

How about "chard"?

WEDNESDAY, OCTOBER 31 AT 6:22 PM | PERMALINK

Marian Haste wrote:

"Gallup" is pretty funny.

FRIDAY, NOVEMBER 2 AT 2:22 PM | PERMALINK

NOVEL HYBRIDS
SATURDAY, NOVEMBER 10, 2007

Little Women Who Run With the Wolves
. . . try valiantly but can't keep up, which is probably just as well.

The Scarsdale Diet of Worms
Drastic weight loss through unrecanted heresy.

Suddenly Last Summa Theologica
The prolonged agony and hideous death of an effete young man at the hands of ravenous street urchins brilliantly sums up all that can be understood of Christian theology.

Beast in the Jungle Book
On his deathbed, Mowgli is horrified to realize that he has wasted his entire life in the damn jungle.

National Blue Velvet
Dennis Hopper does something unspeakable with Elizabeth Taylor's ear.

Jurassic Mansfield Park
Fanny and Edmund avert their eyes while Mary and Henry Crawford are slaughtered by velociraptors.

20,000 Bottles of Beer Under the Sea
Al Gore attempts to befriend a giant squid. A struggle ensues.

FILED IN LISTS | COMMENTS (21)

KIBBITZERS:

John Q. Public wrote:

A Christmas Carol Channing, featuring "Hello, Jesus."

Song of the South Beach Diet: "Mr. Bluebird's On My Shoulder, which must be why the scale says 239 pounds."

Hardy Harharr wrote:

Northwest Passage to India. Mrs. Moore narrowly misses getting butchered by Abenaki Indians and gets really creeped out.

Your Number One Fan wrote:

r u supposed to be funny?

sixthCLASS
THE INEXORABLE LOGIC OF METAPHOR

Carla Karolak lived in a huge gray house on a bluff overlooking the Pacific. Amy knew the sea was close by because she could hear the surf thundering not too far away, and the salt smell almost knocked her over. The house itself was clearly visible, spotlit from stem to stern by an elaborate network of security lights. Carla's nickname for it—The Birdhouse—had led Amy to expect some sort of multilevel structure with multiple doors and little windows, like one of those elaborate purple martin motels people build back East. Nothing could have been farther from the truth. The center of the house was a round structure, a tower, going up a full four stories, topped by a conical hat. As a child, Amy had longed to live in a house with round rooms. The tower was of a modest diameter, but from each side swept long curving wings, symmetrical, double-to-single-story, each tapering to a point. The entire house, end to end, was as long as a passenger train. It suddenly occurred to Amy that from above, in the daytime, the house must look like a huge stone bird in flight. The Birdhouse.

There were at least ten cars in the roundabout driveway and easily room for ten more. The northern wing was lit from inside, and through a long oval window she could make out Chuck, Ginger,

Harry B., and Carla standing in front of a fireplace, sipping what looked like wine. They looked happy. Far to the right, through a smaller window, Marvy and Syl Reyes crouched before an open refrigerator, apparently very much at home.

Amy rang the bell. Nothing happened, and she was about to ring again when it was opened by a gaunt older woman Amy had never seen before, standing in a pale silk dressing gown, gazing at Amy with disdain. "You're the teacher," she said. Amy, still fumbling for a response, was reminded of Mrs. Danvers, the gargoyle of Manderley.

Suddenly she got it. "You're Carla's mother," Amy said. "How do you do—"

"Go back to bed, Ma," said Carla, and then, to Amy, "I'm sorry, I thought I left the door open."

"You probably did." Amy didn't barge into people's houses, whether the doors were open or not. Barging was a California thing.

"She rang the *bell*," said Mrs. Danvers to her daughter, making it sound as though Amy had left a flaming bag of dog poop on the step.

Carla ignored her and pushed Amy on ahead, down a curving hallway into what had to be her section of the house. The dark wing was Mother's.

"I'm terribly sorry," Amy called back, but there was no response.

"She'll be fine," said Carla. "Here's Amy!"

They had come around the curve into a huge red room full of sofas, pillows, and people, all of whom seemed inordinately pleased to see her. The fire in the fireplace was even more welcoming here than it had been through the window, there were open wine bottles and platters of fruit and cheese, and they had saved the nicest seat in the room, a huge high-backed comfy chair and a huge comfy ottoman on which to rest her feet, all upholstered in maroon paisley, like a giant necktie. The entire room looked as though Carla had decorated it when she was twelve and under the spell of the Arabian Nights. There were keyhole shapes everywhere, alcoves stocked with candles, stuffed animals, statuary, and the walls were flocked in deep red velvet.

"Hideous, isn't it?" Carla handed Amy a huge goblet of red wine. "Drives Ma batshit. You should see her side of the house."

"Minimalist? All-white?"

"And not just any old white. 'Bleached bone.'"

Amy was counting heads. She had twelve. "Who's missing?"

"Dot."

"So she's dropped?"

Carla shrugged and stared down into her wine. "I guess so. I keep leaving messages."

Edna approached. She was dressed oddly, for Edna: bundled up in an oversized sweater, evidently hand-knit, and gray sweatpants. She carried a box of tissues. "Would you mind if we got started soon?" she asked, her voice quite nasal. "As I'm sure you can tell, I've got a cold, and I'd like to get to bed at a reasonable hour."

"Of course," Amy said. "Why didn't you stay home? I could have mailed you the stories for next week."

"Wouldn't miss it for the world," said Edna, actually patting Amy's knee. Then she straightened up and clapped her hands. "We're starting now," she announced, in what had to be her public high school voice, and immediately people took their seats.

They were arrayed around her, their faces ruddy and expectant. Ruddy with wine, some of them, but also with cheer. Dr. Surtees, who had been chatting with Frank Waasted, was the last to take a seat, and he didn't hold himself apart from the others as usual. He had, for now, dropped his class pretenses, and seemed to be genuinely enjoying himself.

"We've got a lot to talk about tonight," said Amy. "But before we start, I wonder if we ought to talk about why we're here. You must have questions, and it's probably best that we get everything out in the open."

"Oh, let's not," said Harry Blasbalg.

"Yay, Harry," said Tiffany, raising her glass.

"Seriously," said Harry. "We've already talked about it. That's what we did last week."

"Well, you didn't talk about it with me."

"What's to talk about?" asked Frank. "We all know the deal."

"One of us," said Chuck, "has a screw loose."

"You make it sound so benign," said Amy. "You weren't in that parking lot the other night."

"No, but I was," said Tiffany, "and I'm with Harry. There's nothing to talk about."

"Come on!" Amy was stunned. Nothing to talk about? "Look at all of us sitting here, convivial as all get-out. Hail-fellow-well-met—"

"—and all the other hyphens," said Chuck.

"And all the other hyphens. Except that chances are one of us has, as Chuck says, a screw loose."

"And the rest of us do not." Edna blew her nose and regarded Amy censoriously. "Which story are we discussing first?"

"Ricky Buzza's," said Amy. "And we'll get to it in one minute, I promise you." They were all giggly and chummy and full of what looked to her like bravado, and it made her very uneasy. They were acting like it was some kind of game, or worse, as though they were in one of those stupid haunted-house movies, where a criminal mastermind with nothing better to do orchestrates thrills on cue. "Look, there's something wrong here."

"We're all adults, Amy," said Dr. Surtees, smiling fatuously. He had never called her by name before. "We can take care of ourselves."

How do you know? "Do you have any idea," she said, beginning to feel desperate, "what's going to happen next?"

He shrugged, an elaborate, pretentious, European-style shrug.

"Just do me one favor," said Amy, looking around the room. "Humor me. Turn to the person to your right and ask yourself the obvious question."

Chuck turned to Ginger. "Would you please pass the cheese?"

Amy waited until the laughter died down. "How do you know the Sniper isn't Ginger?" she asked him.

"I don't. And she doesn't know it isn't me. Look, we really have gone through this already. We've got the picture. One of us is a homicidal maniac. Mwa-ah-ah-ah."

Frank said something under his breath, and Carla shushed him. Apparently others around him had heard what he said, because the room was suddenly quiet.

"What did you say, Frank?" asked Amy.

"I said, 'And one of us isn't here.'" Frank looked straight at her.

"Ah," said Amy.

Now it made sense. They were all so jolly and relaxed because they'd apparently decided who it probably was: the only class member who hadn't shown her face since Halloween. Case closed, then. Nothing to worry about. Amy tried to figure out how she felt about this, and as she did she gazed out over their heads, and at the oval window opposite. *Sometimes*, thought Amy, *there's God so quickly*. And she raised her right hand and waved at Dot Hieronymus, standing there framed in the white light, peering in at everyone. "You'd better head her off," she said to Carla, "before she rings the bell."

"Who?" asked Carla, and then turned to see. "Oh, jeez."

As it turned out, Dot did ring the bell before Carla got to her, and in a minute they could all hear Carla's mother complaining bitterly. "I can't *have* this," she was saying, over Dot's and Carla's greetings, and she followed the two of them into the living room. "Are you all here now?" she asked the group. "Is anyone else coming?"

"We're very sorry," said Amy.

"Good night, Ma," said Carla, and her mother stalked off. "Don't pay any attention to her," she said, and then fell silent, regarding Dot.

Dot, formerly a tasteful taupe and ivory gal, was swathed this evening in shades of turquoise and aquamarine, some kind of flowing lounge outfit, and wearing lots of orange makeup. "Did I miss anything?" she asked. She had sprayed herself with industrial-strength Youth Dew. Dot seemed to have turned some kind of corner, socially.

The rest were wonderfully subdued. They made more room for Dot on the center sofa than was actually necessary and looked to Amy for guidance. Serves you right, she thought. "Where were we?" she asked, to deep silence. "Frank? Chuck? You were saying—"

"Could we start now?" asked Ricky Buzza.

"Yeah," said Chuck. " 'Crystal Night.' "

" 'Crystal Night' it is," said Amy.

Herk Romano had a face as wide open as the grilled tuna sandwich at Chumpy's and a deceptively slender physique, and he had always looked younger than his twenty-seven years. People liked him, but they also thought he was a light-weight. He looked like the proverbial college kid, everybody's favorite nephew. So they were usually caught off guard when, in the middle of a random conversation, he suddenly flashed them the contents of his wallet.

Herk Romano had the best arrest record on the Trona City Vice Squad.

Whistling tunelessly he swung his japaleño green Mini Cooper into a visitor parking space in front of KUSP Studios, and catapulted out of the driver's seat in one fluid motion. In no time he exited the fourth-floor elevator, a dozen yellow roses in one hand, and two Ani DiFranco concert tickets in the other. From the end of the hallway, where the studios were, he could just hear Crystal signing off for the day with her memorable catch phrase "Tomorrow is another day!"

Yeah, and today isn't so bad either, Herk thought to himself as he watched her walk toward him. She wafted his way like a sunbeam on an endless afternoon, slim hips swaying like waves on an angry sea, causing Herk to think, for the thousandth time, that the sun literally rose and sat on that amazing derriere. Today was the day he was finally going to finally ask Crystal Molloy for a date.

Dot raised her hand. "May I begin? I just want to say that I enjoyed this story from start to finish. I read it in one sitting. And I also want to compliment this writer on his use of metaphor. This is definitely one of the best stories we've seen so far."

"Thank you, Dot," said Amy. "Who else?" Dot always complimented everybody on their "use of metaphor."

It was really pretty amusing how they all sat there, mute, the ones who liked the story (there must be one or two) and the ones who didn't, all of them afraid to speak. "Come on, people. Okay, you asked for it. You know how much I hate calling on you." Pete Purvis had taken his billfold out of his pants pocket and was studying its contents intently. "Pete!" said Amy.

"What?"

"Do you agree with Dot?"

She expected some lame delaying action, but Pete surprised her. He was a surprising guy. "Actually I was looking at the contents of my wallet." He leaned around Syl and addressed Ricky directly. "When you said, 'flashed the contents of his wallet,' were you—"

"Gong!" yelled Carla.

"Yeah," said Syl. "You're breaking the rules. He doesn't get to speak until we're all through."

"Okay, what I'm getting at is, the natural thing to say is 'flashed his badge,' not 'flashed the contents of his wallet.' I mean, I'm looking at my wallet, and if I flashed it at anybody they'd just see my Visa card and this picture of my girlfriend." Marv and Chuck inspected the picture of Pete's girlfriend.

"But if you had a police badge," said Dot, "they'd see it, instead of your Visa card."

"Maybe, but it still sounds wrong."

"*Flashing the badge* is a cliché," said Dr. Richard Surtees. "Obviously, Rick was trying to get around it."

"So," said Amy. "The moral is what?"

"Better the devil you know," said Ginger Nicklow.

"Would someone tell me," said Amy, "what happens in this story?" She always had to ask this, because no one ever willingly committed to a simple summary. It was so much easier to blather on about the use of metaphor, and whether the names of two characters were sufficiently distinguishable, and other trivial matters, than to think about the thing as a whole. "Someone besides Edna," she added. Edna was her mainstay.

"There's this guy. Herk," said Chuck. Frank Waasted snorted, and quickly looked down at his shoes. "He's a vice squad cop, and he's in love with this TV newswoman. She gets kidnapped by the, I don't know, pimp mafia, and he rescues her. That's it."

"Yeah," said Syl. "It's like a cop show."

"Is that good?" asked Amy.

Syl stood up for Ricky. It's probably not supposed to be, he said, but what's wrong with a good story? "Crystal Night" was "a real page-turner."

"Does everybody agree with Syl?" asked Amy.

There followed the uncomfortable silence that usually preceded a negative feeler. Harry B. cleared his throat and mentioned that the story was "kind of long." This gave them something to talk about for a while, as Ricky's story was almost forty pages in length, twice as long as Amy's suggested page limit for group critiques. Dot, Surtees, and Syl defended its length. For one thing, it was forty pages of slam-bang action, involving a car chase, a gun battle, a plummeting elevator, and a lot of heavy breathing. "Also," said Surtees accurately, "it's really the only finished piece that anybody's handed in so far. It's got a beginning, a middle, and an end. When it's over, you know it's over. We're not left with a lot of unanswered questions."

"And that's good?" Amy was prodding more than usual, partly because it was fun to watch them squirm, and also if they didn't stop pussyfooting around one another the class would founder. She gave them a full minute, and sighed. "All righty," she said. "Now, Dot has complimented the author on his use of metaphor. Would anyone care to discuss the author's style?"

Ginger raised her hand. "Could we talk about the title?"

"Why?"

"Yes," said Carla. "Was anybody but me a little bothered by it?"

Oh, for Pete's sake. "We'll get to the title in a minute. Right now I want to talk about—"

"Actually," said Harry B., "it's borderline offensive." He had the grace to look embarrassed, but he persevered anyway. "It's an obvious play on words. Crystal Night? *Kristallnacht?*"

"Yeah, right," said Syl.

"What's wrong with a play on words? Obvious or otherwise?" Carla started to answer. "Let Syl explain," said Amy, who was willing to bet a thousand dollars she didn't have that Syl had no idea what *Kristallnacht* actually meant.

Syl thought hard. "It's German?"

"Some words really shouldn't be fooled with," said Carla. "You said so yourself. Remember? Three years ago, when that surfer dude passed around that disgusting Nazi story—"

"Carla," said Amy. "Do you agree with Dot? About the author's use of metaphor?"

Carla locked eyes with Amy and nodded, almost imperceptibly, in Dot's direction.

"Dot," said Amy, ignoring the nod. "I'm afraid it's up to you. Could you give us an example or two of the metaphorical turns you most admire?"

Now Dot looked almost as luckless as Syl. She began to shuffle through the story, pausing occasionally, only to shuffle on.

"As I've advised you all, fifty thousand times," said Amy, "you're supposed to be marking up these manuscripts like crazy. I happen to know that most of them return to their authors in pristine condition. Dot, if you really liked something on the page, you should have written something in the margin—"

"Here's one!" Dot held out a single page, triumphantly. The rest of "Crystal Night" had cascaded around her dyed turquoise shoes. " 'Herk's devotion to Crystal went far beyond the physical. Even more than her delectable physique and her impish grin, he adored her mind, which leaped and gleamed like the rainbows in Silver Creek.' " She looked up and out over the class. "Isn't that just lovely?"

"No," said Tiffany. Everybody froze except Ricky Buzza, who blushed and hung his head. "She's got a mind like a fish. What's *lovely* about that?" Tiffany, the obvious inspiration for Crystal Malloy, was apparently more annoyed about this than she was worried about setting Dot off. "Not to mention the sun *sitting*, as opposed to *setting*, on her legendary buttocks." Tiffany was basically a nice person, but like most pretty girls she wasn't sentimental about unwanted attendees.

With this, the group shifted free of its paralysis, some rainbowing all over poor Ricky's metaphors, some (all guys) springing to his defense, while Dot complained to anyone who would listen that the metaphor had nothing to do with fish, it was about rainbows, and nobody bothered to explain that they were rainbow *trout,* until Edna finally spoke up. "If we're going to talk about metaphor," she said, "could we please address the logic of 'wafting like a sunbeam' while at the same time 'swaying like waves on an angry sea'?"

Amy, happy to comply, launched into her Extended Metaphor lecture, pausing midway through to fish the battered copy of Fowler's out of her briefcase, and then regaled them for fifteen minutes with some of her favorite passages. This shut down everybody but Dot, who valiantly rose to Ricky's defense. It wasn't right, she said. Metaphorical language makes us free. If you're going to impose all these rules, then what's the point?

"No one's imposing rules," said Amy. "It's not like deciding where to put the salad fork. Metaphors dictate their own logic. People notice when this logic is violated. They laugh at lines like 'rising out of the ashes like a burst bubble,' not to show off, but because of the silly picture it creates."

Dot opened her mouth to argue, but left it open, apparently distracted by thought, and Amy used the opportunity to steer the discussion back toward the substance of the story which, though clichéd, wasn't as vulnerable to attack as its style. Ricky had endured enough abuse. After another half hour, during which Marv and Syl and Dot stood fast in defense of "Crystal Night," Amy closed discussion and announced a break. Ricky Buzza, given a chance to speak, said nothing. He just got up and went outside and stood with his back to the window and his hands in his pockets. He was soon joined by a few others, but he didn't seem to be talking to any of them, and they were kind enough to leave him alone.

During break, people formed small groups outside in front and all around the huge room, leaving Dot conspicuously alone on the couch. Amy sat down across from her. "Carla had trouble reaching you by phone," she said. "We were all worried that you'd left us."

Dot was belting into a plate of tortilla chips and guacamole, with a side of chipotle dip. Ricky's story still covered her feet. She seemed disinclined to move, or gather up the story, or do anything more complicated than scoop and crunch. "I've been away," she said, not quite meeting Amy's eyes. If she was aware of the group's attitude toward her, she didn't seem bothered. She was a bit more vacant than usual, but happy enough. Contented, like a cow, and ruminating. This close, the Estée Lauder was overwhelming, and heat rose from her expansive bosom, which had been dusted with, Amy guessed, Youth Dew Bath Powder. "Are you working on anything new?" Amy asked.

Dot smiled a secret smile and nodded. "Oh, yes. I'm trying something completely different." She smeared the chipotle on a long chip, snapping it in two, then made a sandwich out of the halves, fastidiously, her little fingers arched out as though she were sipping tea. She was absolutely absorbed in the food and paying as little attention to Amy as she could without being outright rude.

Amy was beginning to think the group was onto something here. She cleared her throat. "Dot," she said, and this time waited for the woman to stop her damn crunching and look at her. "Is there anything you want to ask me about this Sniper business? I realize it must be of some concern, and—"

Dot smiled so widely and so suddenly and so inappropriately that Amy almost shrank from her. "Isn't it exciting!" she said, one plump hand on her chest.

"Well, that's not the word I'd have chosen—"

"My husband and I did two murder cruises, and this is much better than either of them. This is real."

Amy wanted to ask Dot about her husband. She realized that she had been assuming, based on Dot's story, that her husband actually ran off with a younger woman. She knew better than to do this, but something about Dot Hieronymus just brought out cliché expectations in everybody. Now she was going to have to ask some lame question about the guy, ostensibly out of friendly curiosity, but really to find out if he was still in the picture. She was still working on it when Dot stopped crunching and licked her lips.

"Harrison loves murder cruises," said Dot. "As do I."

"Really."

"So much so that I'm working on a mystery-cruise script right now. There's this contest. I entered it last year and got some really good comments on my script. This time I'm going to win. Especially if you help me out. And the others, too, of course." Dot seldom made eye contact when she talked, and when she did, immediately afterward she glanced away and fluttered her lashes. It looked involuntary, an old girlish habit. Beneath the makeup and the affectation Amy could see the young woman Dot had been, lustrous-eyed, sensuous, confident of male attention. Spoiled by it, probably, so that now, in middle age, she had no resources. Except Harrison.

"We don't usually do scripts," Amy said.

"Here's my idea," said Dot, leaning into Amy. "I could pass out the scripts, and there'd probably be parts for almost everybody. We could read through it and—" The rest was drowned out by a burst of laughter from Marvy, Syl, and Dr. Surtees, huddled near the entrance to the hallway, and then another more raucous burst as they continued to crack one another up. One more time and they'd wake the old Kraken next door.

Amy stood up. "Sounds fine," she said. Then, because she'd stood so abruptly, she added, "Is there a part for me?"

Dot smiled and fluttered and deftly flicked tortilla crumbs out of her cleavage. "Of course," she said. "There's a great part for you."

Tonight, for a number of reasons, Amy had a hard time starting up again after break. One problem was that all the wine and Dos Equis, combined with general nerves over the presence of Dot "Madman" Hieronymus, unfocused the group, and even though Amy gathered them all together and sat them down, she had trouble commanding their full attention.

Another problem was Tiffany herself, who disavowed the piece before Amy could start discussion, apologizing to everyone for "dumping it" on them. Just two weeks before, she had been happy for having written "anything at all." Amy debated whether to call her on it. Tiffany's piece was unfinished, untitled, self-indulgent, plotless, and rambling, but intelligent too, and likable in spite of its flaws, like Tiffany herself.

Before she could say a word, though, Ricky Buzza cleared his throat. "So we all, what? Wasted our time reading it?" His copy of "Untitled" was rolled up in his fist like a bat. Ricky Buzza was the third problem.

Tiffany glanced around at him, perched on the arm of Edna's

comfy chair, looming over her. She looked shocked, as well she might.

"I don't know about the rest of you folks," he went on, "but I spent an hour on this story. I read it twice." "Folks" was an odd word for someone so young to use, but then Ricky was in an odd mood. He was paler than usual, with spots of color on his high cheekbones. "So I'd like to spend at least five minutes talking about it."

"I didn't mean—" said Tiffany.

"Terrific. If nobody minds, I'd like to read the first paragraph." Amy opened her mouth to stop him, but Ricky was too quick.

> "6:15 a.m. The sun slants in on Maggie's eyelids, prying her awake, and there's nothing to do, no snooze alarm, no suit hanging ready on her open closet door, no open closet door, no water running in the shower, no NPR echoing from the bathroom, no Jake. Maggie rolls onto her stomach, burrows back into the dream, the small white boat on the water, and someone was helping her on board, someone with arms out-stretched, but no, no more, and who it was in the boat she doesn't know, and now the boat is gone, and she's awake, and alone, and she's lost her job, and Jake is gone. Today is the worst day of the rest of her life."

Ricky looked up from the curled page. "Two things," he said. "One, it's very rhythmic, like poetry. That's why I wanted to read it out loud. Two, it's very economical. She's just lying there in bed, wak-ing up, but look at how much we learn about her." Behind him, Edna Wentworth smiled broadly, as though Ricky were her own pupil.

"Like what?" This from Harry B. "That she likes to feel sorry for herself? Because that's pretty much what she does for fifteen pages."

"We learn," said Ricky, "that she had a boyfriend, or a husband, named Jake, and that he left her, probably the day or night before. We also get that she's lost her job, probably recently."

"And," said Carla, energized, "we learn that whatever Jake does for a living, he wears a suit, and he listens to NPR in the bathroom, so he's probably educated, and so is she. We learn her social class."

"We get all this," said Ricky, "in five hundred words. I just wanted to mention that." He handed his marked-up copy to Tiffany, then sat back, obviously finished.

"So," said Marvy, "educated people listen to NPR in the bathroom?"

"What's NPR?" asked Syl.

Dr. Surtees laughed. "You a Limbaugh man, Syl?"

At the mention of Rush Limbaugh, Ginger and Carla made identical faces, and Amy knew that she ought to say something to keep them from becoming fractious, to settle them back on track, but she was still puzzling over Ricky Buzza, his sudden, bitter blossoming this evening, his articulate defense of Tiffany's piece. She'd long ago written him off as an earnest kid, the juvenile lead. He'd been lying doggo. Still, how could he have written something as bad as "Crystal Night" and be so perceptive a critic? And when did Surtees start clapping guys on the back and calling them by their first name? Dot wasn't the only one who had turned a corner tonight.

Now Ginger was speaking up, holding forth at some length. Ginger was usually pretty terse. She was agreeing with Ricky about Tiffany's stylistic skills. "On the other hand," she said, "you can't get around the fact that fifteen pages later, the point-of-view character, Maggie, is still in bed. She hasn't done or said anything, or interacted with anybody. She hasn't even taken a shower. Nothing happens here. Nothing outside her head, anyway."

They wrangled for fifteen minutes over whether Maggie had an epiphany (she hadn't), and for another ten over whether "Untitled" was really a story at all or a vignette, and Amy didn't need to explain the difference between the two because Carla did so neatly, from memory. With one notable exception, everybody got into the act. Edna offered measured praise for the piece's linguistic cleverness,

Chuck and Frank backed her up, and the slackers—Harry, Marv, Syl—whom Amy could usually count on to say nothing unless they liked a story, complained that if nothing happens, it isn't finished. Only Dot was silent. Apparently she was unimpressed by this writer's use of metaphor, or by anything else Tiffany had accomplished.

Amy didn't have to do a thing. She marveled at the group's new focus and energy. They were functioning on a college level now, not merely an extension level. They were thinking and talking like scholars-in-waiting. She stopped paying close attention to the discussion—clearly they didn't need her—and just watched them. Ginger and Chuck were particularly animated, backing up their praises with examples from the piece, but Syl stood up to them. "All I know," he was saying, "is, say, I'm riding on a bus, and the guy next to me strikes up a conversation, and it's going to be a long ride, you know? So this could be a good thing. But then he says, I woke up this morning, and my alarm clock was on the fritz, and my girlfriend left me, and then I had two slices of French toast, and the phone rang, and—"

"—and it was a wrong number," said Marvy.

"—it was a wrong number, and I went out and bought a newspaper, and the Iraqi death toll—"

"—yeah, what's with the Iraqi death toll?"

"It's an NPR thing," said Dr. Surtees, making a lot of people laugh, including Amy.

Tiffany was laughing too. When Syl finally ran out of gas, she raised her hand and spoke up. She thanked everybody, and apologized, too, for "pretending that this piece didn't matter. It matters a lot," she said. "Thanks for taking it so seriously."

"So finish it already," said Syl, and Tiffany promised she would.

The evening was suddenly over, and all Amy had to do was get everyone to pass critiques back to Tiffany and Ricky, and then ask Syl and Ginger to pass out stories for the following week. Syl and

Ginger demurred, claiming that they were putting on the finishing touches, and promising to mail them out to everybody in a day or two. The class would meet at Syl's condo in La Mesa, the directions to which he'd Xeroxed and passed out.

Amy stood with Carla in the circular driveway, watching as the last two cars drove away. Carla was jazzed. "I thought they'd never leave," she said. Amy, too, had noticed a general reluctance to leave such a welcoming, comfortable spot. Carla's half, anyway. "Did you catch the deal between Ricky and Tiffany? What was that all about? Where did that come from? And how about old Dot?"

Carla wanted Amy to come back inside for coffee and a post mortem on the evening, but Amy begged off. She was too tired, and she wanted to concentrate on the strides this group had made, not on its social intricacies and certainly not on the Sniper, whose importance had receded considerably, at least for now. Apologize to your mother for me, she said, and pulled away, leaving Carla standing square in a spotlight, waving at her with both hands. She looked a shade thinner, around the middle and in the face, and Amy tried to recall what she'd seen her eat. Was Carla on a diet? Was everybody turning some sort of corner, socially?

Well, not *moi*, thought Amy. She put in her CD of Gould playing the Bach French Suites, and coasted home to the Fifth, the one with the amazing gigue that sounded like hunters tantivying in counterpoint, turning their tunes inside out and upside down, cracking beautiful jokes. She tried to focus on the evening's events, but the music was too wonderful. What a happy man Bach must have been. All the way home she pretended to play.

And when she saw her answering machine blinking "1," she pressed the button without taking a deep breath, or even closing the front door behind her. Carla must have started talking before the beep. "—Andromeda strain! Exactly! Call me when you get there!"

If an Andromeda strain was some sort of muscle pull, it couldn't be all that bad, judging from Carla's excitement, and anyway Amy wasn't inclined to call people after ten o'clock. Alphonse woofed at her from the back steps, his censorious face glaring at her through the bottom panes of her French door. He had cataracts, and his eyesight had never been all that great anyway, but he always knew where she was, and disapproved. She let him in and gave him a hunk of aged New York cheddar, and was just locking the front door and congratulating herself on the casual way she did it when Carla called again.

At what precise point had she become the sort of person to whom answering machines chanted "Pick up! Pick up!"? Was she grateful now, after years of solitude, to be demanded by anybody, even Carla? "You gotta be home by now," said Carla. Amy sighed and picked up the phone.

"Did you see all the delivery trucks? You must have passed them on the road."

"What delivery trucks?"

"Two from Dominos, three from Round Table, and one from Little Caesars. And one from Mikey's Wood-Fired, here in town, which must have cost a pantload."

"Pizza?"

"Exactamento! Seventy-six personal pizzas!"

"You must have been terribly hungry."

Carla snorted. "Do you see what this means?"

Despite the lateness of the hour, Amy was beginning to. "Who were they addressed to? You personally?"

"Ma had a total meltdown. The bell rang about twenty times."

"Who paid for them? Were you stuck with the bill?"

"Nah. They were all paid for with a credit card. I couldn't get any of the guys to tell me who, but I bet we could find out tomorrow. They were just sent to this address, only to different names. One was for me, and one for you, and one for Tiff, and I forget the others. I wrote it down. The point is, it's over! Or it will be pretty soon."

"Carla, I don't know what you're so happy about. In the first place, you're stuck with a million personal pizzas—"

"—which I'll drop off at Balboa Park tomorrow. This'll feed the homeless for a week."

"And in the second place, it's not like the Sniper at all. It's more of a high school prank. Plus it happened so late that nobody even found out about it but you."

"That's what I'm trying to say! It's like that movie where this mutating virus came from deep space, and it was really terrifying, it was going to wipe out humanity, but then it kept on mutating until it was totally harmless. That's what's happening to the Sniper!"

Amy sat down at the telephone table on a little chair she hardly ever used because it was absurdly small, even for a thin person, and also because she almost never talked on the phone. Alphonse sat at her feet, regarding her with raised eyebrows. This was something she'd seen other dogs do when their owners were on the phone. The dogs figured, reasonably, that they themselves were being addressed, at greater length than usual and with a puzzling variety of sounds and facial signals. This was the one occasion where they were treated, apparently, as peers, not ignored or patronized or ordered around. Now even Alphonse regarded her with mild interest, as if she were something more complicated than a food god. "I have no idea what you're talking about," Amy said. Alphonse cocked his great long head. "The Sniper is no longer intent on wiping out humanity?"

"Exactamento!"

"Lovely. I'm going to go to bed now."

"But this is so interesting!"

Not to Alphonse, who slumped to the floor, his glossy brown ears arrayed flat on either side, like airplane wings. "It's my bedtime, Carla. I'll call you tomorrow."

After her hot bath, she called him to bed for the night. For the first time she could remember, she hadn't made him follow her through the house while she poked in closets, but he seemed neither disappointed nor grateful. The only routines that meant anything to Alphonse involved eating and sleeping and going outside, and he did that only to relieve himself. Some dogs loved to run and explore, patrol and hunt and kill. Before Alphonse she'd had a big Bernese who could play Frisbee by herself; and when she and Max were first married, they inherited an addled dachshund who used to drag rocks up from the beach and secrete them underneath the living room couch. But to Alphonse, the outside world was just one giant toilet.

He slept on a mat in the corner of her small bedroom. It was a comfort in the dark to hear him snoring, and in hot summer to hear the jingle of his collar as he swatted his fleas. He was too short to jump up to her bed and too heavy to lift. She'd tried once to lure him up there, arranging a stairway of hassocks and chairs, and he made it all the way up and nosed around her bedspread. But there were no smells there but her own, no variety, nothing to pique his interest. He wouldn't lie down, and after a while he descended to an altitude more to his liking. She yearned for him to sleep with her, toasting her feet with his great deep-chested body, like the leggy, finer-boned dogs of her childhood. She would have killed for animal warmth. She settled instead for his little sighs and groans in the night, and the occasional cloud of basset gas that would pass over her on its way to the ozone.

Seventy-six personal pizzas? It didn't fit, really. Where was the malevolence in seventy-six pizzas? The nasty, intelligent prodding at individual flaws, the searching out of vulnerabilities? It had to be some kind of ploy. A distraction, a misdirection, masquerading as a parting shot.

The telephone rang now, softly, from the living room. It was the middle of the night. Even Carla wouldn't be calling this late. Amy lay still and let the machine get it. She listened to her own message, and then to the click of the phone at the other end. A minute later the ringing started again. She lay still, on her back in the dark, and waited through ten calls in as many minutes. She was not threatened in the least. She was seriously pissed off, though, and the eleventh call brought her to the phone, which she picked up and held to her ear, waiting. This, she thought, had better be good.

There was a long pause and then a woman's voice, familiar but hard to place. She sounded like she was in a box, maybe an old-style phone booth, and the connection was terrible. She wasn't alarming at all: she sounded, instead, alarmed. Possibly frightened. She said, "Do you have any idea what's going to happen next?" Amy pressed the receiver to her ear and held her breath. There was some sort of commotion in the background, rasping, clicking. Giggling, maybe. The woman spoke again. "Do you have any idea what's going to happen next?" And then she said, "Do you have any idea what's going to happen next?"

The familiar voice was Amy's own, higher-pitched, cheaply taped just a few hours before, when she'd asked Dr. Surtees this question. She placed her finger on the receiver button, ready to silence the looping voice and unplug the phone, and then suddenly she didn't. "No," she said, "and my refrigerator isn't running. Also, I don't have Prince Albert in the can. Nor do I have Elsie by the jugs, or Aunt Jemima by the box, but thank you so much for asking. Are you taking a survey? Is there anything else you'd like to know? At one o'clock in the morning? You miserable, useless, pitiful, waste-of-space-lonely-ass piece of shit?"

She slammed down the phone, shaking so badly that it missed its cradle. She was still breathing hard when she got back to bed. Amy hadn't lost her temper for thirty years, except only once, when Max was in horrific pain and his morphine was past due and she came upon the two nurses chatting at the nurses' station, shooting the breeze, one of them leaning back against the console where the light from Max's room blinked white. Amy closed her eyes now and tried to summon the dull moon face of the younger nurse, who had actually rolled her eyes while Amy tore into her, but the face was gone, along with the name, a Portuguese name, once clearly visible on the plastic ID tag pinned to her uniform. She was gone, gone, along with the faces of her college professors, her old lovers, her mother, her father, and Max himself, and "Bob," and the Bernese, long gone. She couldn't remember any of them, really. Just facts about them, fully digested. The sound of the phone when it rang again was almost welcome. She heard herself announce her own name and phone number and invite the caller to leave a message, and she heard herself ask, from very far away, if she had any idea what was going to happen next. In a minute she would rise and unplug the phone, because she had a pretty good idea what was going to happen next, but she was wrong, it didn't ring again, and she slept.

Dearest of Diaries

I will say here, however it might disappoint those romantic souls who revere the intellect of anyone who takes pen to paper, that I have never seriously aspired to create, or unearth, an entirely novel way of expressing my own modest perspective—to find, as some would have it, my own voice. My ambitions are far more humble. Though of course I would rejoice at loftier accomplishments, though I would doubtless enjoy the blandishments of literary scholars, though, if truth be told, I have more than once allowed myself to dream of critical fame, I would settle, tomorrow, for far less. I would be content simply to see, on a single occasion, a work of my own in print. This would be enough.

There was a time, I must admit, when my goals were somewhat loftier—when I intended to publish book after book, a small library of my own making, beginning with collections of stories, and then longer pieces, novels, trilogies, more collected stories, an early, hopeful memoir, and later another, rueful and replete with the inevitable disappointments, crowned ultimately with the complete collected stories—and to fill these volumes with the fruits of my own hard-won wisdom. I never expected to make vast sums from these publications, for to do this one must be fashionable, and to be fashionable one must have one's finger on the pulse, no, the very groin of societal preoccupations;

but I would earn enough, I was sure, to live in simple comfort.

Alas, dearest of D's, I might as well have wished for the moon; for despite an early flurry of promises from The Atlantic, from Harper's, from Sewanee, from The Paris Review . . . despite tantalizing, eyelash-batting, come-hither, personally composed, and actually hand-signed rejection letters, recounting agonized editorial sessions in which my stories engaged hand-to-hand with others for territorial supremacy, in one such battle losing only by winning, whereupon it was discovered that a recently scheduled updike story featured—O, what are the odds?—a whale-watching scene, as did my own, and although the scenes were really nothing alike, his being the opportunity for yet another snapshot of marital discord, and mine being the occasion of a child's awful death and his mother's simultaneous false epiphany—although Updike's scene could have been relocated and rewritten in ten minutes, no five, and my own was central to its story—although the stupid I-looked-at-my-wife-and-suddenly-realized-she-was-thirty-five tale had been told fifty thousand times already and mine had never once appeared in print

> . . . it was ultimately decided, with deepest regret, that we had to pass on "Watching the Whales." Still we have every confidence that you'll see it published elsewhere, and we look forward to receiving more short fiction from you.
>
> P.S. Have you tried *The Atlantic*?

Thus did the high point of my literary career come and go while a roomful of strangers dripped mayonnaise on my manuscript and used it as a coaster and would have wiped themselves with it if they hadn't had to send it back to me in my hand-stamped handwritten 9×5 manila envelope, folded as always neatly in two. And I did try The Atlantic and they were impressed, but not very, and I tried Harper's, and Esquire, and got a nice note, and I tried every lit journal in the book, all forty-seven. And nada.

And still I kept writing, and I kept sending the stories out, never stapled, always fastened with a jumbo paper clip, with the two-sentence, professional cover letters and the folded brown SASEs, and the stories got better, and the responses got worse, because by now the competition, though (or because) unreadable, pointless, unfathomable, and trendy, was fierce, and the personal responses got shorter and shorter and then stopped, and then came the form letters and cards with the pencil scrawls on the bottom

Sorry, Thanks, Try Us Again
Sorry, Thanks, Try Us Again
Sorry, Thanks, Try Us Again
Sorry, Try Again
Sorry, Try Again
Try Again
Try Again
Try Again

Try Again
Try Again
Sorry
Sorry
Sorry

Until in the end they weren't sorry any more, not in the least.

And one day "Watching the Whales" came back to me in a ripped SASE, the crumpled upper-right corner lolling out, smudged and bruised, like the bare shoulder of some not-quite-ravaged virgin in an old gothic. It had been gone so long I had lost track—two years, perhaps, or three, and for all I knew it had been around the world, like a kidnapped garden gnome, posed at the foot of the Eiffel Tower, slapped down on the oaken bar of an Irish pub, gaily flourished from the window of a tour bus in Ankara. And here it was, returned to me, and I actually smiled just to see it again, safe at home.

And then still smiling unclasped the envelope, coaxed it open, upended it and shook it gently, waiting for the little rejection slip to waft out. Hoping for one last "sorry" for old time's sake. But nothing. And then I looked, and there was no rejection slip, and no writing on the manuscript, no coaster ring, no coffee splotch, no indication anywhere that a human being had actually read it. Nothing.

And worst of all: the jumbo paper clip was gone.

So.

No Turkish bus for "Whales," no global jaunt, no public or private airing of any kind. It had languished for years in the bottom drawer of some metal desk, or high on a wall shelf, buried underneath dusty piles of old "literary" journals, the ones they hadn't been able to sell to the mommies and great-aunties of the "writers" they "publish," and when the "editors" were evicted from their old digs and relegated to a basement closet in ye olde alumni relations building, some indentured servant—a freshman on scholarship, a first-year grad student—had noticed the envelope, the uncanceled stamps—had put it on the top of the "what do we do with this shit" pile. And a month or a year later what they did was pillage it, rob it of the only thing it contained which was of value to them—a good, untarnished, once-used jumbo paper clip—and stick the envelope in the out box.

Bastards.

The only reason they didn't take the stamps was they didn't have the patience to steam them off. These people knew nothing about patience.

Well I wrote them a letter. And then I tore it up and wrote them another, and then another, and the letters got longer and longer, and I tore them all up. I tried high dudgeon, I tried low dudgeon, I tried blasphemy, profanity, and scatology, separately and at once, I threatened their superiors (who must, I said, be legion), I appealed to their better selves, I lectured, I even sank to humor—"imagine my surprise, gentlemen, when, one cloudy afternoon, from my rustic, battered mailbox issued . . ." This last one was particularly sad, as comedy has never been an arrow in my quiver, but not much worse, really, than all the rest, and it took me the longest time to realize the problem.

They were all signed.

What was I thinking? I was **nobody** to them. A mere wannabe, one of tens of thousands. My name was meaningless, my signature worthless, and any thoughts issuing from me to them were of no interest, except, of course, to the police, if I were ever to, as we all say nowadays

"Act out."

In the end I settled for a simple, elegant prank, a single jumbo paper clip mailed to them anonymously in a plain white envelope.

An okay idea, but hardly satisfying. I sent them another, and then set up a schedule, sending one on the first and third Wednesdays of every month, for six months running. And not just to these particular miscreants. There were so many, and I had all their addresses.

I started to mix it up, sending three clips one month, and a small boxful on the fifteenth of the following month, and then back to one, and then lying low for three months. And then I took a Polaroid of a paper clip, with a background of black construction paper, and sent it out in one of my "9x12's," which gave me an idea, so that the next time, when I sent some of them three boxfuls, all jumbo, I enclosed also a SASE, only the address wasn't, of course, mine, but in each case the home address of the director or the "acquisitions editor."

I was beginning to enjoy myself. It was a simple enough matter to learn the home addresses of employees—university secretaries being so grotesquely underpaid that they'll happily divulge any information just to prolong conversation with a kindly stranger who doesn't talk to them as though they're zoo animals, what with their quaint high school diplomas and associate degrees—and in no time I had branched out from paper clips (which, truth be told, were beginning to bore me) into other areas. The problem with paper clips was that by now they had surely become an office joke. "Guess what I got in the mail Saturday?" (much forehead-slapping, groans, etc.). I was the "paper clip wacko," or just "the wacko," as in, "anybody hear from the wacko lately?" Paper clips may pique the interest, but they don't exactly draw blood. Know what I mean, D.D.?

So I experimented. Nothing explosive, no poisonous substances or dead animals. I'm a deeply creative person. I wrote a series of pornographic vignettes and submitted them as the work of the head of the department of women's studies at another, considerably more prestigious, university. This was particularly enjoyable for me, as the professor in question, in her position as advisory editor of a well-known journal of contemporary fiction, had on more than one occasion seen fit to pass, without comment, on my own efforts.

It was an interesting experience to write, for once, without even the slightest hope of publication—to write for a practical purpose: to cause confusion and distress. For once my work had utility! Eventually, though, it proved exhausting, and I adopted a no-frills approach, not pretty, and certainly devoid of wit, but then so were the recipients.

Dearest D., one day, after a prolonged battle with an abscessed tooth, I decided to go ahead and have the poor thing pulled. And when I heard it clink in the little kidney-shaped pan, I had a thought. What do you do with them? I asked the dentist. Funny you should ask, said he, reaching into a nearby drawer and coming up with an old brown paper lunch sack translucent with grease within which jingled what sounded like glass beads. I'm a pack rat, he said, blushing. The blush was particularly startling because of the deathly pallor which had transfigured him since my last appointment. He was suddenly dying—adult leukemia—and had been droning on, during my procedure, about a hastily-arranged-for replacement who would soon be attending to his patients. His recitation had been quite dry, even droll ("I was really dreading retirement anyway"). But now, as he held aloft his own personal skull of Yorick he looked misty. "I had an idea, once," he said, "but now, for the life of me, I can't imagine what it was."

I had an idea, too. After ascertaining that he intended to discard them, I began to work out in my head an elaborate, as they say, "scenario," involving a fictitious eccentric artist in the family who was always on the lookout for new materials. Absurdly, though, he interrupted my machinations with a blunt offer. "You want 'em?" Indeed, I did. I started to explain about cousin Itt and his oddball biosculptures, but the dying man waved me off. Curiosity was no longer, if it ever had been, among the bags he carried.

The teeth were wonderful. Some had been cleaned, some looked like they'd been through a rock polisher, but quite a few, to my delight, were untouched, flecked with blood and adorned with unmentionable blobs and strings. There were baby teeth and old yellow teeth, flat teeth, and long teeth, and many of these shiny with silver. One, an enormous molar, retained a gorgeous cap of purest gold. I considered returning it to Dr. Death, who had obviously overlooked it—I am not a greedy person—but then could not resist keeping it for some glorious future project, involving, perhaps, the making of jewelry in my spare time, and in my own home! I could already visualize it: Berenice's locket, or perhaps a black velvet choker . . . And maybe, if I could figure out how to pierce them, a string of wisdom pebbles, like pearls.

In the true creative life, one inspiration can detonate another. The wastebaskets in barber shops and beauty salons are, it turns out, a veritable treasure trove. Nail and hair clippings do not qualify technically as biohazards, though their presence in a FedEx box, artfully arranged, might well prove hazardous to a person's psychic equilibrium. Picture an ancient robin's nest lined with coarse gunmetal gray strands of old-lady hair, casually braided, coddling a small family of stained incisors.

And one jumbo paper clip.

I felt like God. Not the personal-relationship god, the one who watches the sparrow fall, but the god of the deists, who set the planets and their elements in motion and then took a nice long nap. Well, I wasn't exactly napping, but I didn't see any birds hit the windshield either, nor did I hover, even long-distance, over the scenes of my revenge. It was pleasant to imagine them—shocked little cries, sleepless nights, abrupt resignations—but really I had no idea what, if any, damage I was doing. It was enough, for quite a while, just to nudge those spheres out of their orbits.

And then it wasn't. I was Googling late one evening, keeping my fiction market files current—for every new outlet that opened up, it seemed, five went under—no, I had not abandoned hope, D.D., nor have I to this very day—when I stumbled across the news of an apparent suicide in academe. An untenured lady in one of the midwestern groves, whose jobs had included, it seems, interim editorial directorship of that institution's literary rag, the Brickbat Quarterly. (I am not making up that name.) Usually colleges hush up that sort of thing, suicide being thought contagious to the kiddos and therefore alarming to the alums, but in this case they couldn't really manage it, as the woman had defenestrated herself, landing on a passing shoal of undergraduates, who managed to sustain fairly serious injuries without effectively breaking her fall. She had jumped from the fourth-floor window of her office, no doubt a rat hole crammed with unsold Brickbats, not to mention unsolicited manuscripts, one of which had come, awhile back, from me. She had been for some time, according to the terse online obit, noticeably despondent.

Of course it wouldn't have been any one thing. For instance, she had worked at the place untenured for six years, and was forty-two and single. There were no quotes from bereft colleagues or students. And we can surmise, from the damage she visited on the kiddos, that she was a porker. Put it all together and you've got sufficient cause. Still, a person like that could slog on for years. Forever. Unless one little thing happened, a single unexceptional provocation, just one more dead letter in the out box . . . I tried to remember what I'd most recently sent her, and honestly could not. I narrowed it down to three possibilities: a tasteful paperclip necklace arranged on a lustrous hennaed bed; a Brickbat Quarterly rejection slip saturated in ancient fish blood; or a heart-shaped Whitman Sampler containing, among nougats, jellies, and carameled cashews, a dark chocolate cherry cordial into the base of which I had inserted a child's bicuspid.

Whichever it was, it couldn't have cheered the poor woman. I made no attempt to delude myself on this score. I had caused injury, possibly dental (imagine, Dearest D., crunching down into a tooth not one's own!!), possibly mortal, to a despondent soul, and one whose offenses toward me, while considerable, were not capital in nature.

I willingly, and with eyes wide open, took upon myself whatever moral responsibility I had in contributing to this human being's death. I felt, and feel, no guilt, but assumed it nonetheless, as a plain fact, and resolved never again to meddle with the private lives of strangers.

It's so much better, really, when you know them, and you can watch them up close.

And why limit yourself to the publishing end of this sordid business, when the woods are thick with competitors, deluded and otherwise, not to mention their facilitators, who encourage, advise, and teach them? I'm not a deist after all. I like to watch. And I, too, have no idea what's going to happen next.

Just between you and me and the brickbat, Dearest of D's, I'd have given anything to see her fall..

seventhCLASS
THE ELLIPTICAL QUALITY OF SPEECH

Syl lived in a condo. Having never visited one, and on the basis of Syl's high-energy, dumb-jock persona, Amy had expected some kind of bachelor colony, a warren of wet bars, whatever they were, and gyms and pool rooms, and a parking lot full of Hummers and sleek little sperm cars. But the building was genteel running to seedy, a white stucco two-story scribbled with bougainvillea, no doubt magenta (the common San Diego variety)—it was hard to tell in the dark—and what cars she saw were for the most part well-kept sedans, some junkers, and a few vans with handicap plates. She didn't recognize a single car and checked her watch. She was five minutes late for class. Where were the others?

"Where are the others?" asked Syl, peering beyond her as he let her into his place.

He sat her down in a worn brown velvet La-Z-Boy and poured her a Diet Coke, pausing at a window on his way back to scan the parking lot. "I don't get it," he said. "We can't both have the wrong night. Can we?"

Amy didn't see how. "I called Ginger last Sunday, right when I called you. She said she was coming." Amy had called them both because neither one had mailed her a story to discuss. Both apologized and promised that they'd have copies to pass out on Wednesday, and that they'd read from them out loud, and take whatever instant feedback they got. Amy hated this and would ordinarily have insisted on rescheduling; but this was not an ordinary group, and discipline had obviously broken down because of the Sniper's shenanigans. She'd left it up to both of them to make the necessary calls to the other group members, and Syl was now insisting that he'd called his half of the list, and Ginger had assured him that she'd called hers.

"I just talked to Marvy on Monday," Syl said. Syl was distraught. He had obviously cleaned up his living room—Amy could see vacuum tracks on the carpet—and there were three huge bowls of fluorescent popcorn and nachos side-by-side on his coffee table. The condo was roomy, underfurnished, and impersonal. There was nothing hanging on the walls, no photos propped up on the cherry veneer Target workstation (identical to Amy's own). On the floor, arranged in a semicircle at Amy's feet, were large plaid pillows, obviously brand-new. If it weren't for the crumbs the vacuum had missed and the smell of old burned pizza and beer, Amy would have wondered if he'd moved in today, just for the occasion of the class.

Syl's place was familiar to Amy, in a way that reminded her of the taunting tape recording of her own voice. It wasn't her place, but a rough facsimile, and recognizable once you adjusted for the absence of books and basset. He must be divorced, she thought, divorce being the only reason she could come up with for a physically fit though balding man in his late thirties, with what sounded like a decent job, to be living like an undergraduate. The only thing sadder than Syl at this moment was the prospect of making conversation with him. "Something's up," Amy said. "We should call Carla. She knows everything."

"I just did," said Syl. "Her phone is busy."

Amy got out her class list and phone, and dialed Frank's cell. It rang unanswered. "Try Chuck," she told Syl, and she herself dialed

Edna's home phone. Edna was the only member of the class, and possibly the only citizen of San Diego County who didn't own a cell phone. Edna's phone rang and rang.

"She's not answering," said Syl.

"I know," said Amy. "I mean—*Chuck's* not answering?" They stared at each other for ten seconds. "Something's up," said Amy.

"You think it's—"

Amy's cell phone rang, a tune she'd actually selected and downloaded, in less unsettling times, for her own amusement: the *Twilight Zone* theme. *Nee-nee-nee-nee, Nee-nee-nee-nee.* Syl stared at her with that constipated look that people get when they're forced to process too much information in too short a period of time, and even though he wasn't the sharpest tack in the box, Amy could hardly blame him. It didn't help that by the time she'd fished the damn phone out of her pocketbook she was giggling uncontrollably. She couldn't even say hello.

"What's so funny?" It was Carla. "Did you do this on purpose?"

"Do what?" Amy asked, trying to settle down.

"He's not home! Plus nobody else was there either, so I went to your house, because it's only a few miles away, and—"

"*Who's* not home?"

"Chuck! Who do you think?"

"You went to Chuck's?"

Carla swore. "Of *course* I went to Chuck's! What do you—" There was a sharp intake of breath. "Oh no."

"Look, Syl and I are sitting here, and nobody's—"

"*Syl? Oh!* I get it! I get it! Christ, I am so freaking clever I can't believe it."

"What?"

"*You* didn't send the e-mail, did you? Telling us to meet at Chuck's?"

"Wait a minute. You got an e-mail from me? How is that possible?"

"So let me get this straight. You're at Syl's, and who else?"

"Nobody."

"You're alone with Syl."

"What's that supposed to mean?"

Carla remained silent. Syl regarded Amy like a drowning man, then looked at his cell phone with the same expression, as it suddenly played the theme from *Peter Gunn*.

"Don't be ridiculous," Amy said.

"Give me a minute," said Carla. "I'll round up everybody and get them to Syl's pronto." Amy could hear screeching tires as Carla took off, probably backing out of Amy's own driveway. Amy sincerely hoped that poor old Mrs. Franz wasn't wandering the street. Probably not—it was winter, and she usually figured out where she lived by the time the sun went down. "Carla, watch out for—"

"Sit tight!" Carla rang off.

Meanwhile, Syl was nodding into his phone. "Uh-huh. Uh-huh. Just a minute." He looked up at Amy. "Chuck says that everybody except Carla's at Carla's, and the old bat just threatened to call the police."

Amy sighed. It was really kind of scary that she basically understood what Syl was saying. Chuck and "everybody" (except, apparently, Carla) were milling around Carla's house, having been directed there by the Sniper. No doubt the doorbell had been rung many, many times. "Tell Chuck," Amy said, "to tell them to come here."

"But that'll take—"

"About an hour. I know. But we've got to regroup."

"Guacamole?"

It felt as though they had been sitting in excruciating silence for fifteen minutes, which meant that it had probably been only a few. Five, maybe.

"I got guacamole, green salsa, red salsa, and bean dip." Syl seemed a little happier, or less anxious, now that, in theory, people were actually coming to his condo. "Also Pete's Wicked and Miller Lite."

Amy said, "The Sniper e-mailed everybody, making believe it was me. I've been sitting here trying to figure out how."

Syl crunched on a giant corn chip. "Who's your provider?"

"I have no idea what that even means."

"What's your e-mail address?"

"It's—oh, I see. It's a Hotmail address. So that means that anybody can just get online and—?"

"They'd need your password."

"I give up. Is this guy psychic or what?"

Syl got up and left the room, returning in a minute with his three-ring binder, which he always brought to class but hardly ever, Amy noticed, wrote in. He opened it and glanced at something. "MonstrousW," he said. "MWomen. FiercerH."

"Those are the titles of my—well. No, I don't use the titles of my novels for my stupid password."

"How about a title and a publication year?"

"Nope." It had never even occurred to Amy to do that. "You'll never get it," she said confidently. "There are just too many possibilities. Nobody, not even the Sniper, is going to waste hours going through every permutation—"

"Alphonse," said Syl.

"What?"

"That's it, isn't it?"

"How the hell did you do that?"

Syl smiled, with pity. "Pet names. Oldest trick in the book. I should have gone there first."

"But I never talk about Alphonse."

"You talked about him during the first class. Carla was asking about him, and you told us all about basset hounds, how they have these huge feet."

Amy was shaken. "And you wrote that down?" My god, she thought, how she blathered on about her private life.

"No! Why would I do that? I just remembered it. It's a cute name." Syl crunched. "We had a cocker once, named Joe."

"When you were a kid?"

"No, me and Eileen." Syl clapped the salt and grease off his hands and stood up. "I'm having another beer. Want one?"

Amy accepted beer in the bottle and was quiet for a while. That the Sniper had been able to impersonate her online was somehow more upsetting than that he, or she, had screwed up the entire evening. "Are you good with computers?" she finally asked.

Syl shrugged. "It's getting to you, isn't it?" He stood up and walked over to the parking-lot window. "Hey, if it really bothers you, you could get online and check out your mailbox." Syl switched on his computer monitor and beckoned to Amy.

She didn't see what good it was going to do, but she signed on anyway. "I never save my sent mail," she said, "so I don't know what's going to look different." Sure enough, when she took a look at her Hotmail inbox, it was full of the usual spam, Viagra and hot stocks and computer dating services. Somebody, the Sniper, had seen this. How pathetic. She was about to sign off when Syl, hanging over her shoulder, pointed out that there were three "sent messages" listed. The Sniper, apparently, wanted Amy to view his handiwork, and had saved the messages accordingly.

There were indeed three Sniper letters. One had been mailed to Pete, Ricky, Ginger, Tiffany, Chuck, Surtees, Edna, Harry B., and Marvy, from, of course, <gallopingamy@hotmail.com>:

> Sorry—there's been a change of plans. Syl's going to be out of town, so we're all meeting at Carla's, at the usual time.
>
> See youse all there!

"Youse?" What the hell was that? A second letter was sent to Carla, worded exactly the same, except that it told her the meeting was at Chuck's. And a third letter was sent to Frank, telling him that the class was meeting at Dot's. Amy printed out all three and stared at them. "My head hurts," she finally said. "What could possibly be the point of all this? Why not send everybody to Carla's?"

"There's one missing," said Syl. "There's thirteen of us, right? Now, according to this, eleven people got phony e-mails, plus me, that's twelve."

"Dot," said Amy.

"No, Dot's here."

"Her *house* is here. Frank's supposed to go to her *house*. But the Sniper didn't send her an e-mail. Or if he did, he didn't save it. I hate this."

Amy excused herself and went to the bathroom. Syl had thick brown towels and a matching brown rug and toilet seat cover, and he used some personal aerosol product called "Axe." Jesus. Who would put something named "Axe" on his bare skin? There was a pile of *Maxims* on a wall shelf painted brown. *Story idea: bathroom tours of lonely single guys.* Amy herself was hit with a wave of loneliness so sudden that she closed her eyes against it. Through the door she could hear Syl talking to someone on the phone.

"That was Marvy," Syl said, popping two more beers and handing one to Amy. "They haven't left yet. They're waiting for Carla."

"We ought to just call it off."

Syl shook his head.

"Seriously. By the time they get here it'll be way after nine. We'll never get anything done."

"Sure we will! Besides, everybody's psyched."

No, *you're* psyched, Syl. You poor lonely brown-toweled bastard. "While we're waiting," she said, "why don't you give me a copy of your story?"

> John Blovio had a huge problemmo. His slabonast was
> jammed, there were six Raggmots on his tail, he had a hang-
> over the size of Phimiander IV, and Cinnamon Sominoid
> was on the rag.

Amy flipped through the pages, of which there were barely four,
triple-spaced. Blovio apparently had, or at least used, a silver
thrummox, which clanged against the spaceship's floor like the
Belles (Bells?) of Cumberling whenever he cursed and threw it
down, which he did twice in the first two pages.

"Does this have a title, Syl?"

"Well," he said, blushing, "it's got a working title, but it's kind
of silly."

Sillier than what? "Hit me," she said.

"Close Encounters of the Worst Kind."

"Funny," Amy said.

"No, it's not," said Syl. He slumped back into his brown sofa
module thing. "Can I be honest with you?"

"Please do."

"I'm really not interested in writing."

Thank God. "Trying to get back in the swing, huh?" Syl looked
startled. "Look, this is an extension course. At least a quarter of the
people in any given class are just looking to hook up with somebody." Amy took a swig of ale. "They're usually pretty easy to spot
because they don't turn anything in. You're a good sport, Syl. You
actually bothered."

"Sort of. Are they ever, you know, successful? Hooking up?"

"No clue."

"How about you?"

"I beg your pardon?"

"You married?"

What was the man asking? Amy had been attractive once, but
she hadn't been propositioned in so long that she felt, suddenly,

like a huge rusted mechanism. You have made, she wanted to say, a category mistake. "Twice, actually," she said.

"Divorce," said Syl. "It's a killer. Eileen and me were married for ten years. Two kids."

"Actually, I was widowed the first time."

"One day she wakes up and tells me, 'I want to go on with my life.'"

"As opposed to . . . ?"

"Well, yeah! Two kids, five and eight, plus this great house in Del Mar."

"Which she's living in now?" Syl wasn't interested in her. Syl was just emptied out. Amy had a pretty good idea why Eileen had wanted to get on with her life.

Amy tried to recall the last time she'd listened to the life story of a relative stranger. She'd been a hermit for so long that it was hard to recall the details of the conversational life. It was coming back to her now, though, and quickly: she had *never* had the patience for listening to the life stories of relative strangers. This was small talk, and small talk used to make her break out in cold sweats. She remembered now leaning up against a stuffed Moose in some restaurant in Bangor, one of Max's hangouts, enduring the chatter of some businessman, the father, she now remembered, of one of Max's friends. A carpet salesman, and he went on forever about the crummy mileage he got on his Monte Carlo, on account of he had to lug around a ton of carpet samples. "I got carpet samples up the wazoo," he said. His name was Carmine something, and when she complained later, bitterly, to Max, he said what he always said. "So use it, Amy. Use it all. Write a cool story about Carmine and his great wazoo." Max knew she never did that. She never *used* people in her fiction. She never wrote, for instance, about Max, his happy life, his terrible death, and the kindness that passed for love between them. "My first marriage," she told Syl, "was a Vietnam marriage. I married Max to save him from the draft."

"He was Vietnamese?"

"He was from Augusta, Maine. We were best friends. He was gay."

Syl got that intense, constipated look again. "Was he a U.S. citizen?"

"Yes, a gay American citizen, from Augusta, Maine. See, in the sixties, there was this brief window of opportunity, where married guys were actually exempt from the dreaded *Greeting*." Syl's gaze turned ever blanker. "He and I were close friends in high school, and he was looking down the barrel of—"

"How did he get citizenship? Wasn't it hard for those guys?"

"What do you mean? He was born in Maine."

"But his *parents* were Vietnamese?" Syl, apparently hearing something, sprang to his feet and went over to the window. "Nope," he said.

"He died of AIDS in 1989."

"Huh," said Syl.

Amy fought back the sudden urge to tell somebody, even Syl, about Max. How comfortable she had been with him. Not happy—Amy had never been happy—but peaceful. What had begun strictly as a marriage of convenience had soon turned into a utopian living arrangement. To the surprise of both, they were perfectly compatible in all respects but one, and the house they rented in Waterville had many bedrooms. She learned to cook and he to keep house, and their house was always open to friends and lovers. They lived together for seventeen years and didn't have a single serious argument. Amy did secretarial work while Max got his doctorate, and then he supported her, more or less, as a professor of Romance languages without portfolio, working untenured at Colby and Bowdoin and U. Maine, while Amy wrote a raft of stories and then a novel, and then two more, and sold them all, for modest sums, with very little effort. Everything was so easy.

Too easy. Max said they were cheating life, the way some people cheat death. She managed to bypass all the drama and heartbreak of faltering affairs and marriages begun in delirious lust, those couples whose wedding receptions were already haunted by the ghosts of their older disappointed selves. She and Max valued each other, delighted each other, leaned on each other when the ordinary world let them down. She slept around, not as much as Max, but enough to keep herself satisfied. She was cheating life, yes, but she was also young and talented and lucky, and there would be time, later, if she wished, to fall in love. Time ran out, of course. Max got sick in 1985, and she cared for him until he died, four years later.

"You know what's funny," said Syl. "I can't raise Frank. I keep getting voice mail."

Amy consulted her e-mail printouts. "He's supposed to be at Dot's. Did you try Dot?"

"It's ringing." From across the room, Amy could hear Dot saying hello. Syl, apparently prepared only for busy signals and voice mail, stared at the phone.

Amy grabbed Syl's cell phone and said hello. "Is Frank there?" she asked.

"Frank who? Frank Waasted? Why would Frank be here?"

"Because—" Amy looked at her printouts again and closed her eyes for a moment to concentrate. "Dot, did I send you an e-mail?"

Dot apparently didn't think this was an odd question. She also didn't sound very happy. "Yes, and at the last minute, too, and I finished my mystery play in a rush and spent all night last night at Kinko's getting ready to pass it out in class. I guess I can mail it out for next week, but it's going to cost me a pretty penny, I can tell you."

"Dot, bear with me for a minute. What did I tell you about tonight's class?"

"Only that it was canceled. You didn't say why. And I wouldn't mind knowing, actually—"

"Go ahead and mail them out."

"What? I don't understand why—"

Amy didn't either, but she needed to get off the phone. "Mail them out tomorrow, okay? And I'll call you and let you know where we're meeting next."

"But—"

"Dot, I'm sorry. I'll chip in on the mailing costs. I have to go." Where the hell *was* Frank?

It was almost ten o'clock by the time they showed up, making a huge racket in the parking lot, arriving in a caravan, slamming car doors and calling out to one another. Carla, jumping up and down like a little kid, waved at Amy standing in the window. "Ma went completely berserk!" she yelled.

"Oh, *man*," said Syl, "most of my neighbors hit the sack at eight thirty." He ran down the stairs, shushing people as they climbed.

"Here's the deal," announced Carla, plopping herself on one of the big floor pillows, while Syl passed out beer and diet soda, and got everybody seated. "Dot never came. And neither did Frank."

"Where's Ginger?" Amy asked. Ginger was bringing the other story for tonight.

"Ginger came, but then she bailed," said Carla.

"Well, did she leave copies of her story with somebody?"

Edna, the last to make it up the stairs, sat next to Amy. "In my opinion," she told her, "Ginger hadn't brought anything to leave."

Amy slumped back in her chair. "Then what the heck are we here for?"

"We've still got Syl, right?" said Marvy.

While Syl passed out his half-assed four-pager, Carla leaned forward and whispered to Amy. "I think Ginger's gone for good. She made a big thing tonight, shaking her head and all, tons of body language, about how this was turning into a waste of time because of the Sniper and all. But I'm with Edna. I think she froze up and didn't write anything and left without admitting it. Good riddance, right?"

"Cool!" said Marvy, looking at Syl's pages. "It's science fiction!"

"Ladies and gentlemen," said Amy. She had to repeat it three times before everybody shut up. "Loath though I am to encourage the mass exploration of *feelings*—"

"Hear, hear," said Edna.

"I am compelled to find out how tonight's alarms and excursions have affected you all as a group. It seems to me that, what with Ginger giving up, and Frank who-knows-where, not to mention Dot Hieronymus—"

"Mention away!" said Chuck, to rowdy applause.

"On top of the fact that we've wasted most of the night, and God knows how much gasoline—"

"What did I tell you?" Carla had turned to face the others. "Didn't I say she was going to do this?"

"Hell, no!" This from Dr. Richard Surtees, hail-fellow-well-met, newborn regular guy and then some. Richard "Hell, No!" Surtees. Amy had liked him better when he was a pompous ass. "We're not quitting! In fact—and we were just talking about this before the drive over—we'd like to extend this class past the semester limit, and on into the New Year!"

Amy closed her eyes and listened to the huzzahs. Edna leaned in and said, "I think you may be outflanked."

Yes, Amy thought, but by whom? "All right," she said. "We've got exactly four pages here to talk about, unless anybody's got something ready. And while we're at it, who brought something for next week?"

"I've got a revision," said Edna, "but it won't be ready that soon."

Harry B. said he too had revised and expanded his vampire thing. Tiffany and Ricky both said they were working on something. Surtees, of course, "always had a chapter ready," although, curiously, he had stopped bringing shopping bags full of copies with him.

"Never fear," said Amy, "because Dot will be mailing out her mystery play, and you should all have a copy by midweek."

"Oh, that's priceless," snorted Harry B.

"What's that supposed to mean?" asked Amy, who knew perfectly well what he meant. It was time they brought it out into the open.

Harry B. exchanged looks with Carla and Marvy and Surtees. The rest glanced down. Nobody spoke for a full half minute. Amy was reminded of First Class, those awkward moments when nobody wanted to stick his neck out and everybody waited for someone to step up. Nobody, everybody, and someone. *Idea for a story*: three pronouns in desperate search of an antecedent.

In the end, it was Tiffany who spoke out. "We think it's her," she said.

"She," said Edna.

"The Sniper," said Carla.

"On the basis of . . . ?"

"Rampant weirdness." Tiffany had enough class to look ashamed. "Okay, that doesn't mean anything, but look at what happened tonight. Where is she? Everybody else gets called out and sent on a wild goose chase, and there's Dot, holed up in her house. Probably giggling away in the dark."

"Ewwww," said Carla.

The playground phenomenon. Amy had seen it countless times, though never under such peculiar circumstances. If you got a group of adults together in class, and the class coalesced, worked together successfully as a group, sooner or later there would emerge an agreed-upon patsy, rampantly weird, or maybe just rampantly untalented, or rampantly something else that didn't fit in. Usually all that happened was that the outsider's stories weren't taken seriously, or were routinely patronized. This was worse. They were ganging up on Dot.

"The Sniper," Amy said, "is a complex, tricky individual whose next moves have so far proven, at least to me, unpredictable. Does that sound like Dorothy Hieronymus to you? Any of you?"

"No," said Carla. "But then you're always talking about how surprising people are. About how, ultimately, nobody is predictable, least of all to himself. You say there wouldn't be any point in writing fiction otherwise."

Did Carla come to her classes with a tape recorder? There was an unsettling thought, for more reasons than one. "My point is, if she's so brilliant and cunning, why is she home tonight, when everybody else is being sent all over San Diego County?"

Chuck said he'd been thinking the same thing. "Maybe," he said, "she's been set up."

"Hey! I like that!" This from Syl, who indeed looked delighted.

"And where the hell is Frank?" said Chuck.

"Yeah!" said Syl. "Maybe it's Frank!"

Tiffany raised her hand. "Carla says, and I agree, that the Sniper seems to be morphing into a less angry, much more playful state of mind." Everybody seemed to agree, except possibly Chuck, who looked thoughtful. "I mean, look at tonight. Okay, we all wasted a lot of time and gas, but it was sort of fun. And the gag was clever, too, as though the person were showing off—for all of us. It just doesn't seem so personal any more, and it doesn't seem nasty at all. Not like before."

Amy thought about her phone call the other night, her own taped voice razzing her in the dark. The tireless way in which the Sniper had dialed and dialed and dialed. That had seemed both personal *and* nasty. These people were enjoying themselves way too much. "Would somebody please try calling Frank again?"

"I've been trying every ten minutes," Chuck said unhappily. "I talked to him just yesterday. He was definitely coming tonight, because he'd finished something, and he was going to bring it with him."

"You guys hang out, right?" asked Tiffany. "I mean you knew each other before?"

"Actually, no. I only know Frank through class." Chuck looked at Amy. "Actually, he said he was bringing something *interesting*. I couldn't get him to talk about it. I was kind of surprised, because I figured Frank for a looky-loo."

So had Amy. Frank Waasted was bright and an asset to class discussions, but he struck her as way too guarded to stick his neck out. He had signed up to bring in something for Last Class. Looky-loos often did that, and then deferred, at the last minute, to class members who wanted a second go-round.

"This is what we know," said Carla. "The Sniper told Frank to go to Dot's. But Frank *didn't* go to Dot's."

"According to Dot," said Tiffany.

"Oh, what's that supposed to mean?" Chuck looked really put out. He seemed to agree with Amy that some of these people were treating Frank's disappearance, along with the other nonsense, as some kind of mystery romp. "The woman has a husband, for Christ's sake. Do you think the two of them have Frank stowed in their fruit cellar, like Mrs. Bates?"

"Ewwww—"

"Carla! Everybody!" Amy had had enough. "This is what we're going to do. We're going to read Syl's piece, silently. Unless Syl wants to read it out loud?" Syl did not. Syl didn't even want his piece discussed, which was too damn bad. "Then we're going to discuss it. Then we're going to discuss, briefly, whether we're meeting next week, and if so, where. Then we're going home. It's late, and I've had it."

For ten minutes the only sound was paper scraping on paper. Chuck, she noticed, used his cell phone periodically, apparently re-dialing Frank, but he was discreet about it. Edna, Chuck, and Dr. Surtees marked up their copies. The rest read with almost identical expressions of sullen boredom, the teacher, what a poop, having ruined their good time. When Amy called for discussion to begin, the silence persevered. It wasn't just sullenness, she realized— without Dot there to start off with her usual encomium to the writer's use of metaphor, no one knew quite how to begin.

Pete Purvis cleared his throat, startling Amy. She hadn't noticed him. In fact, she seldom noticed Pete. He had a way of blending into the wallpaper. "I'm going to go out on a limb here, Syl, and guess that you aren't really a big sci-fi fan."

Marvy, standing in for Dot, announced that he thought "Close Encounters of the Worst Kind," though just a fragment, was a "really great, high-energy start," and that he hoped that Syl was going to finish it soon.

"Why?" asked Pete. "All he's done is made up a bunch of words. Blimmix. Thrombocopter. He doesn't even show you what a thrombocopter *is*."

"You're right," said Syl.

"Raggmopp!"

"Actually," said Dr. Surtees, "it's "raggmot.""

"Who cares?"

"I'm with you," said Syl.

"What do you mean, 'I'm with you'?" Carla waved her copy in his face. "It's *your* story, for God's sake."

"Yeah," said Syl, "but I'm not really serious about it. I just wrote it, you know, because it was my turn. It doesn't matter to me."

"Well, it matters to *me*," said Edna, regarding Syl censoriously. "I just spent ten minutes reading it."

"And it's vulgar," said Pete. What an odd word for Pete to use. "The way it talks about this girl, Cinnamon, like she's just some bimbo. It's disrespectful."

Pete Purvis seemed genuinely angry. He was talking like a feminist, which apparently he was, which shouldn't have surprised Amy. She thought back to Pete's story, its essential sweetness. Pete wrote very well from a child's point of view. In Amy's experience, writers who could do that were often innocent themselves, and sometimes in a creepy way. But Pete was likable. He lived, she now recalled, with his dad.

Amy let Pete and Edna bat Syl around awhile longer, and then closed discussion without adding to it herself. This was the first time she had ever done so, but she felt no guilt. The evening, like Syl's idiotic story, had been a complete waste of time. "Where are we meeting next?" she asked.

"My place," said Carla. "Everybody knows where it is."

"But your mother!" said Amy. "The poor woman. We can't impose—"

"You're not imposing," said Carla.

"But it's her house," said Edna. "She has a perfect right not to have strangers tramping around—"

"The hell it is!"

"Well, half hers, then."

"No, it's not. It's all mine. I paid for the whole thing. I let her live in half the house, but it belongs to me. I can have class there every week if I want." Carla looked and sounded like a truculent thirteen-year-old.

Amy wasn't crazy about the idea of returning to the Birdhouse, but since no one else was offering she didn't argue. "Is everybody clear on what we'll be reading for next time? Dot will be mailing out her mystery play."

"But we've already done one of Dot's things," said Tiffany.

"Yes, but none of you has brought anything for next week. We'll be lucky to have the play. Besides," Amy said, packing up her stuff, handing Syl back his execrable piece without so much as a scribbled word, "maybe we can act it out. Put on a show in the old barn." Collective groans, led by Carla. "Or," Amy said, "we could disband right now."

"Wait a minute," said Marvy. "Nobody wants to give up. Right?" The rest nodded.

"Why on earth not?" asked Amy. "Don't you see what's happening? Discipline has broken down completely. Everybody's on edge. Even if you all hadn't been sent to the wrong place tonight, we only had four pages to talk about, and even they were, according to their own author, not worth the effort. No one brought work to take home and read. I'm not used to working like this," Amy said.

"And good for you," said Edna, with a smile that was almost warm. "That's why we value your leadership."

Traitor, thought Amy. Edna, of all people, should have let her go. Edna was a real teacher. Edna would never have put up with the Sniper, or with Carla, either.

Amy sighed. "Ground rules," she finally said. "No more e-mails. If there's a change in plans, I'll call you each personally. Now, who's bringing copies of something next time, to pass out for Last Class?"

"But wait," said Carla, "it's not going to be Last Class, remember? Because we're extending—" Amy glared at her, and she had the good sense to shut up. "Okay. I'll bring something."

"Me too," said Chuck. "And I think Frank has something also." He fired up his cell phone again.

"Hey, everybody," said Syl. "Just because the class is over doesn't mean you all have to leave."

He might as well have fired a starter pistol. Instantly they were all on their feet, gathering up bags and notebooks. They hadn't touched the nachos, or any of the dips. The expression on Syl's face was openly sad, and nobody but Amy was looking. And then Amy looked away. She was fresh out of sympathy.

"Bad night," said a voice in her right ear, and a hand lighted on her left shoulder. It was Dr. Surtees, standing behind her, his arm actually around her, as if they were old friends, or worse. It took effort not to brush him off like a spiderweb. Amy hated to be touched. "Listen," he said, oblivious, "I can send out a chapter this week, if you think it would help with morale."

Whose? "If you like," Amy said, speeding up, joining the line clogging Syl's stairwell. She tried to move past Marvy and Pete and widen the buffer between herself and Surtees, but there seemed to be a serious clog in the line. "What's the holdup?" she asked.

"Hello? Frank? Hello?"

Chuck had apparently gotten Frank on the phone. What had people done before cell phones? When exactly had it become so damn important to keep in touch?

"I'm Chuck Hes— Who are you? Where's Frank?"

Amy muscled her way down the echoing stairwell to Chuck and began to pass him, but he put a hand on her arm. What the hell was going on? Why was everybody touching her?

"Frank Waasted," Chuck was saying. He looked alarmed. "Who is this? Hey, buddy! Would you please hand the phone to Frank?"

Chuck tightened his grip on Amy's arm. Apparently he wasn't going to let her go, and they were all going to stand in this wretched stairwell all night. Amy grabbed the phone and held it to her ear.

"—wasted, all right! He's hammered, man."

The speaker sounded pretty hammered himself, or else baked, and also very young. "Hello?" Amy said, momentarily unsure of herself, about to make demands of a complete stranger. Then she pretended to be Edna Wentworth. "Young man! Where are you, and where is Mr. Waasted?" All she got back was laughter and scraping noises. She could hear a girl's voice in the background, in front of another constant sound, like hissing. Then she heard the girl say, "Why don't *you* . . . ?" in a querulous whine, and then more hissing, and then the girl began to scream.

The scream wasn't loud, because she was too far away from the phone, but it was prolonged and high pitched. Not a squeal, but a scream; and then the boy's voice, shouting, "Are you sure?" and "How do you know?" And then, after a minute or so, nothing but that hissing.

"What is it?" asked Chuck.

Amy shook her head and didn't look at him. She focused inward, on the hissing sound, which was beginning to remind her of something. A conch. The cell phone was like a conch shell. *I've got the conch!* said poor Piggy, and he was right, too, for all the good it did him. She was listening to the ocean surf.

"Lady!" The boy's voice was at once stronger and less sure. "Your friend's got something wrong with him." "*He's dead!*" the girl was screaming. "He won't move, Lady. His neck—" "*He's dead!*"

"Where are you?"

"Moonlight Beach. Lady, your friend is definitely probably dead. We gotta take off." The conch went silent.

She had to say something. She should ask where Moonlight Beach was. She should ask if Frank had family. She should dial 911. Amy held up the conch. "Would someone please take this goddamn thing away from me," she said.

It turned out that Moonlight Beach was in Encinitas, just a couple of miles west of Tiffany's house. Everybody knew this but Amy. The first thing they all did, after Syl herded them out of the stairwell and out into the far corner of the parking lot, was hash out whether or not to call the police. Amy and Edna were all for doing this immediately, but Harry B., the criminal lawyer, cautioned that since all they had to tell the police was that some unidentified joker had claimed that another unidentified man was dead, the police wouldn't be inclined to race to the beach, blue lights and sirens akimbo. "But we have to do *something*," said Carla, at least five times. And she was right.

Thirty minutes later the entire class, minus Syl, who stayed behind but extracted a promise that they'd keep him informed, and Marvy Stokes, whose wife had insisted he come home immediately, pulled into the deserted Moonlight Beach parking lot. There were the usual tall yellow-gleaming streetlights, but beyond their pale sickly circles was booming darkness, toward which they all walked, at first in silence and in a straight line. There was no moonlight on this beach now. Amy's ears told her that they were approaching the water's edge; still it was a shock when a cold wave lapped at her toes. She couldn't see the water at all, not even starshine on the waves. Only the parking lot was visible from here. They had to take on faith that if they turned left, they'd follow the coastline to the south, and if they turned right they'd be heading north. She had no idea what lay in either direction except water, and a little sand, and many rocks. She could barely hear herself think over the noise of the surf. She was inside the conch.

"What do we do now?" asked a voice in her ear. Chuck, she thought. Someone, Carla, splashed past her and into the water. "Frank!" she called. "Where are you? Frank?"

"He's not in the water," said Amy. "That wouldn't make any sense. The guy on the phone said he was *wasted*. You wouldn't say that about somebody who was drowning. Would you? He must be on land somewhere."

"We should fan out." This from Dr. Surtees.

"What does that mean?"

"Half of us go south, half of us north. Walk in a line perpendicular to the water's edge, about ten or fifteen yards apart."

"But we can't see a damn thing!"

"Sure we can. It just takes awhile for your eyes to adjust."

As soon as he said this, Amy saw that it was true. She could see the doctor's outline right in front of her, black against a blacker sky. She could see Carla's squat cutout against the dark water. "I'm going north," she said, and headed right.

Carla, Chuck, Pete, and Dr. Surtees went with her. The others— Edna, Tiffany, Ricky Buzza, and Harry B., went south. Edna called out, before they could get too far. "If you don't mind a suggestion," she said. "Perhaps it would be best if each group stayed together. Perhaps no one should go off by himself. At this point." You're right, Amy shouted back, and of course she was. Amy should have been the one to think of this, to say it. The obvious, common-sense warning.

It was slow going in the dark. The beaches here weren't sandy, at least not here, north of San Diego. Every summer they imported tons of sand and poured it on the rocks, and every winter the sand washed away. Amy took off her shoes and stepped gingerly. She positioned herself farthest inland, next to Chuck, though far enough away from him that they couldn't converse. They all walked slowly and maintained a straight line down to the water, which she could see more clearly now, along with the silhouettes of lighted ships far out from shore. Off to her right, for a while, was the parking lot, with buildings and volleyball courts. In time, though, the lot winked out, blocked by something big.

"Bluffs," called Chuck. "Sandstone bluffs."

Amy looked up. "How high?"

"Thirty, forty feet," said Chuck.

"What's up there? Condos? Houses?"

"Some. There's a public park up there too, somewhere."

"Well, maybe Frank's there. Is there a way up?"

Dr. Surtees heard them and came closer. "No way up," he said. "The bluffs are very unstable. You shouldn't walk too close beneath them, and you shouldn't walk on top of them either, too close to the edge. They crumble."

Looking toward the bluffs, Amy could see nothing at all. "How far away?" she asked.

"Close enough," said Chuck.

"Not really," said Amy. "We're not close enough to see anything,"

"Close enough for safety."

They walked forward for another minute, and then Amy broke away from the line. "This is stupid," she said, not bothering to raise her voice. Either they were looking for Frank or they weren't. She walked toward the bluffs until she could begin to make out their contours. From a hundred feet away they looked pretty solid; not crumbly at all. There was nothing on the ground beneath them but more rocks and sand. She continued heading north, noticing that the others had followed and adjusted the line accordingly. No one had thought to bring a flashlight. In fact there had been no discussion at all of what to do when they got here, or indeed what their true purpose was. They were here, by default, to "help Frank," a man about whom none of them knew much, except that he was smart and pleasant and a faithful class member. And that, according to Chuck, he had planned to bring something *interesting* to class tonight.

The rest were silent and far enough away that it was easy to imagine herself alone, stumbling improbably on an alien beach in the salty darkness, far from home, light-years from her own life, that had ended so long ago and so quietly that she hadn't noticed. In her first published story Amy had observed, with no earned understanding of why she was right, that remembered lives were like strings of Christmas lights, each twinkling in its own fixed important Moment, separated from its neighbors by dark necessary strands. When she was a child these moments came thick and fast; and still they glowed, from far away, clustered in an enduring tangle, brighter than any in the long, hopelessly straight line that led to where she was. While everyone else tried to live "in the moment," Amy learned to hide from hers. It was the only thing she worked at, really. Her last moment had come two years ago, and of course by accident, when a student named Rudolf Minge, to whom she had scrupulously given the sparest and most generic of encouragements, had invited her to spend Christmas Eve with his large family, at the end of which interminable evening she had found herself caroling in the parking lot of a Mormon nursing home, linking hands with Minges, the sound of her own voice high and young, a child's voice in an aging woman's body, and when she closed her eyes she was fourteen years old and president of her Pioneer Fellowship and deeply in love with her minister, and all her futures were curving, rolling roads. I'm having a Moment, she thought, and tried to stomp on it, but it stayed lit, evil and tiny and bright, so that thereafter she had only to run out of Fritos or lose her cable connection or wake up at three in the morning, and there it was, *the world in solemn wonder.*

Now came another Moment, one where she led a troupe of virtual strangers on a pointless midnight search for a man intimately unknown to any of them, and the worst thing was that there was no foreseeable end to it. How could she call it off, and when? The muscles in her calves, so unused to exercise, were cramping up, and she was cold and slowing down. It seemed as though the rest adjusted their speed to match hers, probably out of pity, and her breath was getting short, too, and what would happen if she had a heart attack with all of them watching. Goddamn Surtees, he'd probably bring her back, the bastard. She was crying in the windy dark, no sound, head down, letting the tears drop and dry. She felt like a great balloon tied down by this string of people, and if only they weren't there. Up she could lift, up and up, off, away, and gone. She hated them suddenly, every single one of them. She had to be alone.

Amy stopped. "I'm beat," she said to Chuck. "I'm going to rest for a while."

"We'll wait with—"

"Please," said Amy. "Go on. I'll catch up."

Chuck hesitated, and then began to back off, toward the rest. "It's only another quarter mile or so. We'll be back in ten minutes."

She watched their backs as they went on, moving faster now, away from her. Even Carla trotted with ease. Well, she was young. The other southward-moving line might have already turned around and be on their way back. Amy wanted to sit down, but not on these sandy rocks. If she got all the way down, she'd have to get herself all the way back up, which these days involved getting on her hands and knees first, like some broken-down swayback farm animal. She wandered toward the shoreline and then thought better of it. There were things out there, in the water. Things like hands.

She turned around and scanned the rocks for one big enough to sit on, and there it was, in the light of the slivered moon, at the base of the bluff. She must have walked right past it, a pair of boulders, or maybe a trio, close together and high enough off the ground so that she could sit without collapsing. She craned her neck and scanned the top of the bluff as she approached it. There must be artificial light up there, far back, because she could make out snarls of iceplant draped along the edge, blooming pink, the only color in view. The wall of earth below came straight down to the beach. Now that she was closer she could see that its surface was indeed porous and loose, and she could easily imagine it crumbling, catastrophically, in a mild earthquake. Now, for instance. No, she had to get a little closer. Now it could happen: the very last Moment. A long sexy rolling canter deep beneath her feet, no rumble or rattle (out here there was nothing to rumble or rattle), and then a few tons of earth would shear off and drop silently, painlessly, like God cutting a birthday cake. Happy birthday to me.

Amy looked down at the boulders. She couldn't see them so clearly now; they were in her shadow, or maybe the stars were hiding. But she was almost there, and she was feeling better. It was not like her to be so morbid. She was spending too much time in company. In her whole life, even in childhood, she had hardly ever cried, and it seemed to her now that every time she had, she had been in company. Alone was so much more civilized.

The boulders converged in a convenient shape, like a chair, with a square back flat against the bluff, and a crooked seat and slanted legs. When Amy got close enough to take a seat, the boulders reconverged, into a different shape. This happened not gradually but instantly. Amy blinked twice, three times, but couldn't manage a third convergence. The shape remained what it was, and all the light in the world wouldn't change it. The seat was a lap, the back was a torso, the legs were legs, and it had to be Frank, but she couldn't be sure, not without looking at the face, and you needed a head for that.

Carla was not helping. Everyone else was quiet as they waited in the parking lot for the police and the ambulance, which they could see approaching in a formal line a mile up the highway. Carla was shaking and crying and it took Ricky and Pete to hold her still while Surtees checked her pulse, "Just in case." Of what? She kept saying "Oh my god," rhythmically, and it seemed as though she'd been doing this for a half hour. Amy wanted to slap her. Carla, she recalled, was the one who had thought the Sniper mystery was cool. On top of which, *she* hadn't even seen Frank's body.

Carla hadn't been alone with it in the dark for five minutes, turned to stone and staring, unable to move or make a sound or process a thought or do anything but go on staring, seeing more and more of Frank, who looked nothing like a pile of boulders. Frank had died wearing running shorts and Nikes and a sweatshirt and a watch. Frank wasn't headless, literally. Frank's head was just bent so far back that not even his jawline was visible above his neck. Amy couldn't recall ever noticing that Frank had such a freakishly long neck. Probably he hadn't. Not before.

Amy had been unable to move in any direction. Her ancient options—fight or flight—apparently shorted each other out. She was paralyzed, and noticed it, and went on breathing, shallowly and slowly. She had no urge to scream, although it would have been nice to tell someone about Frank. And then, magically, a cell phone appeared at her feet—well, at Frank's feet—and she was able to reach down and pick it up and turn it on. For his cell phone screen Frank had selected a beach at sunset. The last caller was Chuck. (She had misheard that shrieking girl. She hadn't screamed, "He's dead," but rather "*His head! His head!*") Amy selected Chuck's name and hit "enter." On the second ring Chuck answered, sounding very, very relieved. "Where the hell are you, man?" he asked. "He's right here," said Amy. And when Chuck asked her where that was, she could only repeat, here. He's here. Her voice had been calm, though. She hadn't lost it, like Carla.

Now, as she watched the lead police car roll to a stop, Amy began seriously marshaling her thoughts. She had quite a story to tell them, and she guessed it was best to start in the foreground—this night, with all of the class here, looking for Frank and finding him—and then work back, naturally, filling in the story of the Sniper as the police asked the logical, inevitable questions. *Who are you? Who are all these people? Why were you all here? What were you worried about, again?*

"We have a thought," said Edna, into Amy's right ear.

Tiffany, at Amy's left, said, "We assume you're going to tell them everything?"

Amy looked at them. They were calm and alert. They looked like Amy felt. "Of course," said Amy. "Why wouldn't I?"

"I agree," said Edna. "But our thought is we probably shouldn't call him 'the Sniper.'"

"Oh, Lord," said Amy. They were right. "Sniper" meant something specific to a cop. Things were bad enough without calling in S.W.A.T. teams and the FBI. Ahead of the crowd, Carla broke free, chugging toward the police. "Somebody grab Carla," Amy said, in a voice she'd never used before, and Chuck and Pete each took an arm and turned Carla back toward the group. The class formed a loose circle, and they all looked at her. "We need to talk," Amy said.

"I'm way ahead of you," said Harry B. "There's been a lot of speculation lately about the Sniper—"

"We're not calling him that!" said Amy and Tiffany and Edna.

"Whatever. The point is, we have to look at this rationally. On the one hand, somebody in the group is playing head games. Tonight another group member is dead. Is there any reason to assume that these two things have anything to do with each other?"

Carla looked at Harry as though he had lost his mind. "What do you mean, 'any reason'? My God! Who else could it be?"

"We don't even know yet what happened to him," said Dr. Surtees. "Obviously his neck is broken, but we don't know if it's by accident or—"

"Accident!"

"The point is," said Harry, "we've got to tell them why we're all here, and we can't be hysterical when we do it."

Everybody looked at Carla. "What?" she said. "I'm not hysterical! What's the matter with everybody?"

"Here they come," said Harry, coming to stand beside Amy. "If they ask, I'm your lawyer."

"You mean, lie?" What an extraordinary suggestion.

"Of course not. I'll actually *be* your lawyer. If you want me to."

"Why would I—"

"Which one of you called the police?" The cop was a little taller than Amy and carried a gun. So did the other three with him. She couldn't see their faces, since the light was behind them.

"I did," said Amy. "Would you like to see the body?"

Behind her, Tiffany started giggling. The cop craned his neck to get a look at whoever found this situation so damn funny. "I'm sorry," said Tiffany, "it's just that—" and she was off again.

"Steady on," said Edna.

"It's been a long night," Amy said, by way of explanation. She could feel her own hysterics lurking just offstage, waiting to grab hold at any moment. "Why don't we all—"

"*Would you like to see the body?*" gasped Tiffany.

"I know," said Amy, "it sounds like, 'Would you like to see what we've done to the nursery?'"

"It really has been a long night," said Harry, stepping manfully into the breach.

"And we're tired," said Amy, looking closely into the cop's deep-set eyes, "and I don't know what I'm saying. I'll show you where it is."

All the time Amy was leading them back to Frank's body she thought about the deadpan expression on the cop's face. He was young and clean-shaven, and of course in uniform, but he had old eyes, and he reminded her of Dr. Scherm, her Bangor psychiatrist, whose company she had kept for two months after Max died. That same studied blank expression, except that in the case of the $100-an-hour man it was a professional affectation. She had loathed Dr. Scherm for it, but she sympathized with the cop. Police spend half their time getting evaded and shined on and lied to. Amy, for instance, had always considered herself a law-abiding citizen, but just now she and her law-abiding cohorts had been discussing how much information to withhold from these people.

"He's over there," she finally said, pointing.

The police huddled over poor Frank and waited for the ambulance guys, who followed with a stretcher. Amy couldn't hear what anybody was saying, but they were all shaking their heads, and then one of them must have said something funny, because two of the cops threw their heads back and laughed. Occasionally the lead cop looked over in Amy's direction, but he never waved her over.

"This is going to take forever," Ricky said. "The crime scene techs haven't gotten here yet, and you know what a big deal that's going to be."

"I'm not so sure," said Harry.

Amy had no idea what a crime scene tech was, but listening to Ricky and Harry argue, she learned that when there was a suspicious death, nobody could touch the body before it was specially photographed and measured and generally assessed, in a high-tech way, for the subtlest clues. This was according to Ricky. Harry kept saying, "Yeah, but this is Encinitas." Apparently, whatever Harry meant by that, he was right, because before long one of the ambulance guys unfolded a long black thing and disappeared with it into the knot of uniformed people.

"Oh, my God," said Carla. "It's a body bag!"

Amy prepared herself mentally for the sight of Frank Waasted's body, shrouded in black plastic, as they carried it past her on the stretcher. It took a long time to materialize, and when it did it was both less and more than what she'd prepared for. From a distance the long plastic bag looked like a python with eyes considerably bigger than its stomach. And up close it still didn't look like a shrouded body. It was as if someone had shoved an armchair into a big and tall garment bag. The carriers had a tough time balancing it on the stretcher. "Rigor," said Dr. Surtees.

Amy watched as they tipped Frank into the ambulance, which almost immediately started up and drove out of the lot, followed by two of the cop cars, leaving one. The lead cop, practically as an afterthought, checked back with Amy and the group.

"Here it comes," said Amy. "We're not calling him the Sniper, but we have to fill him in on what's been happening. Calmly."

"I really don't appreciate this," said Carla.

"We've got your number," said the deadpan cop, "and you've got everyone else's. That right?"

"Yes, of course," said Amy, "but don't you want to—"

"Tomorrow," said the cop. "Or Friday. Depends on what the coroner says."

"Officer," said Chuck. "This is wrong. This man shouldn't be dead."

"Tell me about it," said the cop, who obviously didn't want anybody to tell him about it.

"Do you at least get that he was supposed to be with us in class tonight, and he was supposed to actually bring something for everybody to read, and that this was a man who was absolutely totally punctual, by which I mean that if he said he was going to bring something he was going to bring it, and now he's horribly dead?" Carla's voice was unpleasantly pitched, but she wasn't hysterical anymore.

The cop sighed. "I can tell you this much." He looked at Amy and away from Carla. "His car's back there." He pointed up, toward the top of the bluff. "Parked at a picnic area a half mile down, more or less directly above where the body ended up. There's no sign of a struggle up there. But that's where he was."

"So, he fell?"

"One way or the other. Happens more often than you'd think." He turned away and headed for the car, which had already started up. "I'll get back to you," he said over his shoulder.

"Don't strain yourself," muttered Carla, "you smug bastard."

After the car drove off, Carla turned to Amy. "We have to go up there and look around," she said. "Maybe he left something."

Harold warned that they shouldn't disturb a crime scene, but Ricky and Chuck agreed with Carla. "It's the least we can do," said Chuck.

It was after three in the morning. "Suit yourselves," said Amy. "I'm worn out and probably in shock, and I'm going home to see my dog."

She left them standing there, without even a promise to get in touch. Of course she would, but she had to get away. She was numb on the drive home, and when she let herself in, her little house was warm, and her little big dog was grudgingly happy to see her. She made herself a giant mug of real cocoa, got into bed, and settled in for a long insomniac wait for dawn. The shock would wear off any minute and she would take what had happened to Frank into herself, and it would change her forever. There were emotions to be experienced. Perhaps fear; perhaps even terror. Certainly sorrow. With any luck, she wouldn't suffer long in the dark. The sun would rise in a few hours and help put it all in some kind of perspective. It was odd, she thought, how stoical she felt. She closed her eyes, just for a minute, and slept deeply.

In fact, Amy would have slept until noon, had Carla not called her, raving about a FedEx box she'd just gotten from Dot Hieronymus. "Of course I didn't bring it into the house," she said. "I'm not even sure it's safe to leave on the front step."

Amy, half asleep, didn't understand how the phone could still be ringing while Carla yammered in her ear. Then she heard Alphonse click down the hall to the front door and realized that the ringing was her doorbell. "Hang on," she said, and returned in a minute with her own FedEx box. "We'll open them together," she told Carla.

Carla said something absurd about a bomb, and also "Happy Thanksgiving, by the way."

Amy was staring at a 9×12 letter-sized cardboard envelope stuffed to a width of perhaps half an inch. "Can you honestly picture Dot horsing around with plastique?"

Carla admitted that she couldn't. "But then I wouldn't have pictured her shoving Frank off a cliff, either."

"I'm opening mine," said Amy, as she pulled on the cardboard zip-tab. Either kill me now, she thought, or bring me a cup of black coffee.

"What if it's not a bomb? What if it's something poisonous, like an asp, or a—"

Amy slid the manuscript out onto her chenille bedspread as Carla said "tarantula." Actually it slipped out in four discrete layers, one per syllable. Still the cardboard envelope remained distended, certainly from having harbored a manuscript that had to be at least sixty pages long, but Amy went ahead and smashed it with her fist anyway, twice. Of course, in the rational world a tarantula would have been squashed in transit; they weren't shapeshifters. Except in dreams.

"Oh, my God," said Carla. "It's—"

"The Workshop Murders." Carla and Amy spoke in unison.

"Oh, my God," said Carla. "Do you realize what this means?"

Amy was staring at the second page.

DRAMATIS PERSONAE

CLEMENTINE SCRIBNER	writer-in-residence and professor of fiction, Ivy University
JOHNNIE MAGRUDER	young hotshot reporter (secretly working on a gangster roman à clef) at the *Daily Eagle*
ZIRCONIA CUMMINGS	beautiful young graduate student, working on a doctorate in art history, and toying with a historical novella on Lady Jane Grey
PERSEPHONE DARKSPOON	well-to-do widow, blocked on the third novel in a mystery series
DR. P. T. MERRIWETHER	renowned neurosurgeon, working on a medical thriller
CASSIE BUNCHE	eccentric performance artist, working in multimedia
HESTER SPITZ	owner of a small bookstore, likes to enter short story contests

MELVYN RUMBELOW	retired computer software magnate, working on a screenplay
GEORGIE RUMBELOW	his nephew, working on a science fiction trilogy
FANNY MAKEPEACE	retired Methodist missionary, working on memoirs
JAKE WISEMAN	mob lawyer, playing his cards close to the table
VITO LASAGNA	Wiseman's most important client
CAPTAIN MANLEY	of the cruise ship *Aurora Queen*
STEWARD	

"Thirteen!" said Carla. "Oh my God! There's exactly thirteen! And look—"

Amy scanned the names. "Dot's cleverer than she looks," she said. "*Zirconia*. A flashy, worthless pseudogem. So much for Tiffany. And poor Edna's a missionary. *Makepeace*!"

"Thackeray!"

"I don't think so. She's made Edna the peacemaker, the sexless guardian of the moral order. That's another way of shooting down the opposition."

"Okay, Jake Wiseman, the mob lawyer, is obviously Harry B. And Magruder is Ricky Buzza. And Dr. Merriwether, guess who . . ." There was a sharp intake of breath. "Cassie *Bunche*!! Oh, man! What a bitch!"

Amy had been waiting for that discovery, and while she was waiting, doped out that Syl was probably Vito. There were no thugs in the writing group, and Syl had the most muscle. And the nephew, Georgie, had to be Pete. He and Ricky were the youngest guys in class. Which left Melvyn Rumbelow, the Captain, and the Steward, to be matched up with Chuck, Marvy, and poor dead Frank. "Marvy" and "Melvyn" sounded an awful lot alike.

Carla agreed, and it was apparent to both, even without saying it, who would play Persephone Darkspoon: Dot Hieronymus, the dark lady herself.

"We can only hope," said Amy, "that Hester Spitz is a throwaway part, because Ginger's long gone."

"Yeah. What?" Carla quit rattling her pages. "We're not going to put this thing on, are we?"

"Where? In the old barn? No, but I did tell Dot to mail these out, and the only way I can see to deal with it in class is to read through it as a group."

"*What!?*"

"I know, it breaks the rule. But plays are meant to be spoken. It won't be like reading a short story out loud. Besides, it's likely to be the least painful way to get through it."

"Amy, how are we supposed to get together like nothing's happened, with Dot right there, and put on this stupid play, when—"

Amy lay back and closed her eyes. All this from the Carla, the cheerleader who had bullied Amy into continuing the group privately, against all her instincts. "Carla, I don't expect we'll ever meet again, at least not outside a police station or a court of law. I was just thinking like a teacher. Excuse me all to hell." Carla started to apologize, or maybe argue, but Amy cut her off and hung up. She wanted very much to pull the phone jack out of the wall, but didn't, because the police would surely call, and she had to be responsible.

Two days went by, and the police never called once. At least they never called Amy. Another thing that didn't happen was the wearing off of shock. In time Amy understood that she hadn't actually been in shock at all. She could no more feel Frank's death than she could experience, in depth, her own unanchored solitude. All she could *feel* were hurt and anger, both of which were absurd under the circumstances. She felt abandoned. This was an unpleasant surprise, as was a breakfast phone call, on the third day, Saturday, from Dot Hieronymus, who wanted to know where and when the next meeting would take place. "I've e-mailed everybody," she said, "but no one has replied as yet. Am I to assume," she continued querulously, "that we're not meeting on our regular night? Any information would be very much appreciated."

"*I* just assumed . . . ," began Amy, and then realized that she hadn't assumed anything. She had just cut them all loose before they could formally do the same to her. "Dot, after what happened to Frank, I assumed no one would be interested in meeting again."

Dot was silent for a beat. "Of course I read about the accident," she said, "and of course I feel badly about it. But I don't understand what this has to do with the group. I went to a great deal of trouble and expense, not to mention writing out all those addresses on the envelopes, and the FedEx expense. This is . . . not acceptable."

Amy began to remonstrate with Dot, pointing out that it wasn't grief that shut the class down, but rather fear and anxiety over personal safety. Dot interrupted, saying, with some asperity, that "this Sniper character" was obviously just a prankster, and people were being silly, and it just wasn't acceptable. Every time she used the word "acceptable" it seemed to gather resonance, as though she'd never used it before, at least not in this way, and was learning to enjoy it.

As Dot picked up steam, Amy tried very hard to imagine that she was listening to the rantings of a murderer. In person, Dot had always spoken softly, but now she achieved the old-fashioned, high-pitched singing voice of a movie matron. Amy pictured Spring Byington, *December Bride*, swathed in flowery chiffon, hard-charging Frank Waasted and shoving him off the edge of a cliff; Spring Byington inviting Frank to peer over the side, and then kneeing him in the rear. No, Spring would never knee or shove. Perhaps she had pretended to take his picture and simply asked him to take a couple of steps back. Frank, way too young to have seen *Auntie Mame* at an impressionable age . . . Amy interrupted Dot. "I'll get back to you," she said.

From: "Amy Gallup" <gallopingamy@cox.net
To: Writers
Subject: What do we do now
Date Sent: November 24, 2007

Hello. This is Really Me. I've got a new e-mail address, as you
can see. It shouldn't be as easy to break into as the Hotmail
one. If you have any doubts, call me up to verify.

I need to hear from all of you, either by e-mail, or phone, or in
person. I need two questions answered:

1. Have the police contacted anyone about Frank? I feel like
   I've fallen down a rabbit hole.
2. Do you have any interest in going on with the group? This
   may sound like, and probably is, an insane question, but I
   have to figure out what to tell Dot, who has sent you all her
   play. I fully expect that you don't want to continue, but I'd
   appreciate your verifying this.

It was no doubt stupid to ask about Frank in an e-mail. E-mails
were apparently immortal and could be retrieved and used as evidence. But of what? Amy had tried and tried and failed to come up
with a serious legal misstep on her part. She'd given the damn cops
her name and phone number. She'd been standing right there in
front of them. She had found the body, for God's sake. And she'd
been as inconsequential that night as she was to her own self, and
now to her class.

Amy took Alphonse for a walk. She hadn't walked him since
spring. Summers were impossibly hot and fall often more so, since
fall was Fire Season, when the Southern California scrubland, usu-

ally with the aid of arsonists or lost hunters with flare guns, would ignite, and Santa Anas would blow the flames westward through canyons and Indian reservations and hillside developments, and the sky would swirl with the colors of an old bruise. Sometimes ash floated down like snow. But Fire Season was probably over now, and evenings were cool. Amy fixed Alphonse to his long red leash and dragged him outside and up the hill, past the well-kept oleander bushes and green gravel lawns of her neighbors. Amy hated to walk even more than Alphonse did, but she couldn't take another day alone in the house.

Alphonse enjoyed the smells and disregarded everything else— the cats, the Rottweilers, even the Gomezes' insane grass-mowing goat, which they had inherited when they bought their house, a former meth lab. (In San Diego County, Amy had learned, even the nicest neighborhoods included meth labs.) Amy yanked Alphonse across the street just as the satanic goat lunged at them, stopped short by his chain. By the time she had reached the top of the first hill she was wheezing, her calves cramped solid, and she had to stop to get her breath. It was nice, actually, to be distracted with pain, and so she determined to keep climbing, and after a half hour she and Alphonse sat panting on a flat rock at the top of the last hill. From there they could see for a mile all around—strip malls to the north and west, clusters of dirt-colored roofs, sixteen steepled churches, and all of it dotted with eucalyptus and pepper and fruit trees.

The last time she had been up here, Amy realized, she had been with "Bob," her second husband, on the day they had decided to buy the house. They had been half in the bag, both of them, at the time, and "Bob," surveying the view, had told Amy that joke about Christ on the cross shouting down to Simon Peter, "I can see your house from here," and even though she had heard it twice already, and both times from "Bob," she had actually laughed out loud. It had been June and jacarandas tall as elms were in splendid bloom, the landscape studded with little bursts of periwinkle blue, her favorite Crayola color. Amy, never before or since a tree lover, had been seduced by those very jacarandas and the pin-cushion pink blossoms on the silk trees, which grew everywhere like weeds and smelled like cotton candy, and by the cough-drop eucalyptuses, into believing that Southern California was indeed an enchanted place. Too bad it hadn't been Fire Season.

Robert Johanssen had been Max's attorney, as well as the lawyer for two of Max's friends and, in the last year of Max's life, a frequent visitor to their house, helping with "will and estate stuff," according to Max. Max had more than once tried to ex-plain, and Amy refused to hear about it. Denial at that time was like a gently swaying hammock, comfy and hypnotic. Of course Max was dying, she knew that, but the house was so lively with laughter and music and people going in and out, and she kept herself busy feeding everybody and pouring wine. She even be-came a decent cook by figuring out how to coax Max into finish-ing a meal. Robert Johanssen took to hanging around more and more during the last year, silently helping Amy with the dishes and the cleanup, sharing late-night vigils when Max's health went into sharp decline. Amy hardly noticed him. She assumed he was there for Max.

Which was odd, as Max paid little direct attention to him, and always referred to him, behind his back, as "Bob," acting out the quotes with voice and eyebrows, as in, "What have you been up to with 'Bob'?" "Why," Amy finally asked, "do you say his name like that?" "Because he asked me to call him 'Bob,'" said Max, "and, as you know, I'm an amiable human." As it turned out, "Bob" wasn't there for Max—he was there for Amy. "He's in awe of you," Max said, grinning evilly, "and your creative genius." But why, Amy had wanted to ask, did Max find him so ridiculous, but at that point

Max began to cough, and they never picked up the thread of that particular conversation. Max only mentioned him to Amy one more time, in the latter days. "He's got piles of money," said Max, "does our 'Bob.'" He made Amy look at him. "You could do worse," he said.

She had married him six months after Max died, for no good reason except she had to get away. "Bob" wasn't sexy, and he wasn't funny, and he wasn't smart, and he wasn't even particularly attractive, in addition to which Amy had never aspired to wealth. But she went with him anyway, because he offered her a quick way out of her empty house and her paralyzed life. "Bob" was hell-bent on real-estate investment in Southern California, which was pretty far away from Maine. They'd buy a little house and a lot of land in North County San Diego and watch it double in value in six months, a year tops.

"Bob" may have had a pile of money to begin with, but as soon as he invested it, the real-estate market went into free fall, and then they were stuck together in that crappy little house, and within two years of their marriage, "Bob" was gone. Nothing of him remained, in the house or anywhere else. She couldn't remember what he looked like naked, or the sound of his voice, or a single thing he had ever said to her. Except, apparently, that silly Calvary joke. Four years later she got Alphonse from a local basset rescue. She had a more fulfilling and complex relationship with him than she ever had with "Bob."

Sometimes, as now, as Alphonse lay sleeping on the rock, smacking his gums in reverie, she would cup and stroke his great forehead in her palm and sing, way under her breath, a nonsense song about a basset hound who was always around and belonged in the pound. A child's song in a child's voice, and while she sang it, and while she listened to herself sing it, she would feel herself thaw, just a little bit, enough for tears to begin way in the back of her throat, in plenty of time to stop them. Which she did. They stayed there until nightfall and then traipsed back downhill toward home.

As they came around the bend above her driveway, she heard a baritone voice sonorously intoning what sounded like a sermon. "Shipmates, this book, containing only four chapters—four yarns—is one of the smallest strands in the mighty cable of the Scriptures. Yet what depths of the soul does Jonah's deep sealine sound! What a pregnant lesson to us is this prophet!"

It was, in fact, the sermon given at the Seaman's Bethel in *Moby Dick*, and the voice was that of Orson Welles, issuing from a white SUV parked in front of her house, and in the driver's seat was Edna Wentworth. "Edna!" Amy was absurdly glad to see her. Edna clicked off her CD player and leaned out the window. "Sorry to show up unannounced," she said, "but you took your phone off the hook and we couldn't get through to you."

"I sent an e-mail—"

"Hate the things," said Edna. "How are you?" Edna looked closely at Amy, with that expression of kindly curiosity, though nothing so intrusive as sympathy. Maine, Amy remembered, had been chock full of women like Edna—weathered, no-nonsense, competent as hell. Of course Edna drove an SUV. She probably changed her own oil.

"I'm just fine. Why don't you come in?" The house was dusty and cluttered with soda cans and books, but she couldn't be rude to Edna.

"You've had quite a fright," said Edna, shaking off the invitation.

"Well, we all have."

"You're the one who found him."

"Yes." To her horror, Amy found herself, once again, on the verge of tears. "This is my dog, Alphonse," she said.

"We're planning to meet Friday night, at Carla's house, at the usual time. Can you make it?"

"Look." Amy knelt and stroked Alphonse, hiding her face until she could compose herself. "It makes no sense to go on meeting," she said, rising. "Carla was right about that. I'm sorry if I've given you the impression that I needed—"

"Carla's version was somewhat different," said Edna. "We've been assuming that the reluctance was yours, not hers. In any event, it makes every sense to go on. We're writing, every single one of us, and we're learning from you. You're a fine teacher."

"But—"

"And we've got a cracking good mystery on our hands!" Edna started up the ignition.

"Edna! People could get hurt. One of us is already dead, for God's sake. This isn't a game."

"Tell that to the Sniper," said Edna, backing out into the street. At the bottom of the driveway, she called, "See you Friday, then?" and she was off.

Amy might have stood there, staring after Edna, for hours, but Alphonse was hungry and pulled her into the house. She filled his water bowl and fixed him a real meal of leftover ham and roast chicken. She put Peggy Lee on the stereo and began to pick up the living room. She dusted all the books on her shelves. By midnight, she was singing "Big Bad Bill" loud enough to wake the dead.

She was so game, she was ready to face her blog, which she'd avoided since being asked by some illiterate moron if she was "supposed to be funny." This was what they called "flaming," and rather than endure it she had been prepared to call it quits. But good old Edna had thickened her skin.

GO AWAY

FUNNY-LOOKING WORDS
SATURDAY, NOVEMBER 24, 2007

> prepuce
>
> piebald
>
> knothole
>
> obnubilate

FILED IN LISTS | COMMENTS (53)

NOVEL HYBRIDS
SATURDAY, NOVEMBER 24, 2007

The Martian Chronicles of Narnia

The Lion, the Witch, and Ylla K.

Gentle Ben Hur

Thrill to the heartwarming saga of a 600 lb. brown bear who befriends a lonely young boy, wins a chariot race, and witnesses the crucifixion of Christ.

FILED IN LISTS | COMMENTS (22)

Well, one out of two wasn't bad, but she was definitely running dry. It was time for a new list. She glanced down at *Kibbitzers*, because sometimes they made some pretty decent suggestions, and there it was.

YOUR NUMBER ONE FAN WROTE:

U R THE ASSIEST ASSHAT IN ASSVILLE

FRIDAY, NOVEMBER 23, 2007 AT 5:36 PM | PERMALINK

Amy had a number of competing reactions, all simultaneous, so that she had to tease them apart like a knot of lamp cords. The first was, Well, yes, I probably am. The second, When did we start using *assy* as an adjective, and where did *asshat* come from? And finally, Is Your Number One Fan the Sniper?

The third question came seemingly out of left field, and she couldn't figure out why, since it should have occurred to her earlier, when he asked that impertinent question. It was certainly possible. The Sniper was a good mimic, so textspeak wouldn't be a problem. Fan was a flamer, and so (in spades) was the Sniper. But the longer she stared at this phrase, the more she found herself liking it. It made her smile, and in a way that only the verbal constructs of the very young could do (and the Sniper never did). She used to keep a notebook, long since misplaced, devoted solely to overheard dialogue from children and teens. For instance, she loved the music in the various inflections of "dude," from its use as a noun of direct address, to the expression of complex thoughts, from *Hey, You!* to *What the hell did you do that for?* to *That was seriously cool* to *So sorry you just screwed up your entire life*. She loved the fact that now they routinely told each other to "shut up" when the person being addressed hadn't even said anything. And "asshat" was hilarious. On the one hand, it was appropriate to mourn the degradation of language, the shelving of all her lovely words, even the funny-looking ones; still, literate or no, the young took on the world fresh. The Sniper was anything but dewy. The Sniper wasn't her Number One Fan.

Amy stared at the phrase some more and then doubt began to creep in. Maybe "the assiest asshat in assville" wasn't as minty fresh as all that. Amy didn't hang around with kids; for all she knew, *everybody* was saying it, and if that were the case, then it could have wafted up to the Sniper's generation, whatever that was, like the noxious "bling." After worrying at the question, she typed into the Google search box, and was immediately and wonderfully rewarded by a no-hit page containing the answering question

DO YOU MEAN THE *EASIEST ASSHAT* IN *ASHVILLE?*

Why yes, Amy said out loud. That's exactly what I meant! and she shut down the computer and hit the sack. Frank Waasted was horribly dead, evil stalked her little group, and her life was a dark tunnel to nowhere, but there was joy in Ashville, where apparently resided the easiest of asshats. She drifted off composing a brand-new country and western song: "She's the easiest asshat in Ashville, but I love her just the same."

eighthCLASS
THE BRUTAL TYRANNY OF FACT

When Amy arrived, the whole class, minus Dot, was already in Carla's living room. Dr. Surtees was standing in front of the fireplace, leaning on the mantel. "We told Dot we were starting at eight o'clock," said Carla, handing Amy a glass of wine and a sheet of paper.

"This is what we know," said Surtees, reading off the top line of the paper. Clearly he had written the thing—his letterhead was at the top, followed by "This is What We Know."

1. The Sniper is sufficiently tech-savvy to play e-mail pranks
2. The Sniper is sufficiently agile to grab a mask out of Carla's bag on Halloween, and then put it in Tiffany's car during break
3. The Sniper is sufficiently strong to push Frank off a cliff
4. The Sniper is clever, quick, and not necessarily insane

The class nodded, as one, after every point, except the very last one. "Is that your professional opinion, Doc?" asked Chuck. "And anyway, so what?"

"I was thinking the same thing," said Harry B. "Nobody in class is a drooling maniac, so whether or not the guy is insane is beside the point, except later, in court."

Tiffany spoke up. "We know a lot more than that. The Sniper isn't just clever. He—or she—is a brilliant writer."

Syl snorted. "Have you seen what he wrote on Marvy's story?"

"Yeah," said Marvy mournfully. " 'Way to go, Dickwad.' Oh, gee. I'm sorry, Edna!"

"I have taught high school children for forty years," said Edna.

" 'Dickwad' is just what I mean," said Tiffany. "The same person wrote 'Way to go, Dickwad,' and those clever e-mails."

Carla looked sharply at Tiffany.

"Nice point," said Chuck. "I'm not sure that he's brilliant, but he's a real writer." Chuck looked right at Amy. "Do you agree?"

Amy sank back in her chair. "He's creative," she said. "He has more than one voice. He's a chameleon. He's funny."

Actually, the Sniper's sense of humor frightened Amy more than anything else. The parody of Carla's poem had been witty, the rudeness of Marvy's critique outlandish, and she was still, for some reason, fixated on that "youse" in the Sniper's counterfeit email. "Youse" was like a spectral elbow to Amy's ribs. Dangerous, malevolent people should not be amusing. In order to be humorous, you had to have perspective, to be able to stand outside yourself and your own needs and grudges and fears and see yourself for the puny ludicrous creature you really are. How could somebody do that and still imagine himself entitled to harry, to wound, to kill?

And there was something else—something missing from "This Is What We Know." Some aspect of the Sniper that they were forgetting, and it nibbled at the far edges of Amy's mind.

"And why," asked Tiffany, "are we using the masculine pronoun?"

Syl and Dr. Surtees, spiritual brothers, rolled their eyes, but Ricky Buzza supported Tiffany, pointing out that it didn't take great strength to push somebody, at least from behind; and Marvy said, "And anyway, if we think it's a guy, why did we tell Dot, who's not a guy, to come an hour late? What are we doing here, people?"

As Marvy asked this reasonable question, Amy was looking at Pete Purvis, who hadn't said a word, and who looked disturbed. The baby in the group, Pete came across as a gentle soul, averse to even mild conflict. Whenever the class would argue the merits of a piece, Pete would stare tensely down at his notebook, and sometimes directly at Amy, clearly wishing she'd do something to calm the waters. Amy couldn't imagine Pete as the Sniper. "What do you think, Pete?" asked Amy. "Why did you guys give Dot the wrong starting time?"

"I didn't have anything to do with it." Pete took a resentful breath. "In fact, I think it's kind of mean. Nobody likes her, because she's—she doesn't fit in. She's out of the loop." One of the men muttered something, and another one snickered. "Yeah, okay, loopy," Pete said, over his shoulder. "But mainly she's just not in the clique. That doesn't make her the Sniper."

"Look at that story she wrote," Carla said. "Doesn't that creep you out? The devoted wife poisoning her husband?"

"As I recall," said Amy, "nobody called the story creepy at the time. Half of you thought the wife character was going to commit suicide."

"Right!" said Pete. "But now you know her a little better, and you're all ganging up on her because she's different."

Amy, remembering the Murphy Gonzalez story, guessed that Pete knew quite a bit about being different.

"We're ganging up on her," said Harry B., "because, as far as anybody knows, Frank went to her house that night. Alone. At the Sniper's invitation."

"Which we know about, how?" asked Chuck. "The same way we know about the other misdirections that night. The Sniper left an easy trail to follow, in Amy's inbox."

What a horrible term. "Chuck makes an important point," said

Amy. "You've all just agreed that the Sniper is clever. How clever is it to leave a line of breadcrumbs right to your door?"

"But you could turn that around," said Dr. Surtees. "The breadcrumb trail could be the most brilliant misdirection of all."

Everybody started speaking at once, except for Amy, who poured herself another glass of red. They were still, most of them, treating this as an exercise, or worse, as though they had fallen into a TV script. Surtees especially seemed to relish a kind of detective role, as in a rousing game of Murder. She had arrived at Carla's this evening expecting a somber, fear-chastened group, and here they were, squabbling over procedure. "Let's talk about writing," said Amy.

Everybody shut up.

"When I was a child," she said, "I loved to read mysteries. Agatha Christie, Ngaio Marsh, Ellery Queen. I even went through a John Bradford March period, where every mystery involved somebody getting throttled behind a deadbolted door."

"Ah," said Dr. Surtees, nodding wisely. "Yes. The Locked Room—"

"In other words," continued Amy, "every murder was physically impossible. That was the fun of the whole thing."

"Precisely," said Surtees.

"When you're fourteen years old. If you try to read one of these books now, you'll be amazed at how preposterous they are. I'm not only talking about the mechanics of the murder. I'm talking about the characters themselves. They're all robots, willing to take human life for the silliest reasons. And worse, they don't just shoot them when nobody's looking. They set up the most elaborate Rube Goldberg strategies, where even the tiniest mistake would bring the whole edifice down on their heads. They plan murders the way real people plan weddings."

"Yeah," said Chuck. "We're talking as though the Sniper were some Machiavellian genius, with nothing but time on his hands."

"Her," said Tiffany. "*Her* hands."

Somebody, one of the guys, muttered, "Oh, can it."

"What other reasons do you people have for suspecting Dot?" Amy asked. "Besides the breadcrumb trail thing."

There was a protracted silence while they all tried to recover the moment when Dot had distinguished herself, suspect-wise. "I think it was the last time we were here," said Marvy, "and she came late and she acted kind of strange. Like she had this secret."

"And I heard her say something to you about how *fun* it was, about the Sniper," said Tiffany.

"'Exciting,'" said Amy. "Not fun. Exciting. Which did not at the time distinguish her attitude from everyone else's."

"No!" said Carla. "It was before that night. Remember, when we were trying to regroup after the Halloween thing, with Tiffany and the Bundy mask, and nobody could get her on the phone, and later she said she'd been busy, or something."

"Well, case closed!" said Pete. "Call the cops! Jeez, you people are cold."

"I'm inclined to agree with Pete," said Amy. "Dot Hieronymus doesn't fit in. But why does this make her a suspect? Why, while we're at it, isn't anybody talking about Ginger Nicklow? Ginger disappeared from the group the night Frank died. Why isn't that a big honking coincidence?"

"I'm way ahead of you! Because I talked to her two days ago," said Carla, "in person, at her house in North Park, and she had definitely moved on. She told me she'd taken the course for fun, and she stopped having fun even before the Sniper screwed everything up. She said she hadn't written anything, and she couldn't think of anything to write, and now was as good a time as any to bail. She says Hi." Carla waved to everybody.

"Why did you go to her house?" asked Chuck. "How did you manage that?"

"Mapquest," said Carla, "plus I needed to look her in the eye, to make sure. She's got three kids and a husband."

"So what? Dot's married, too," said Pete.

"Yeah, but Ginger's husband is a Presbyterian minister." Somebody snorted. "And anyway, you should see the books in her house. Wall to wall *non*-fiction. Theology, history, saltwater fish. There's a whole bookcase full of gardening guides. The only fiction I could see was *The Da Vinci Code*, and they were using that to prop up a piano bench. She's not the Sniper, guys."

Amy sighed. "So, let me get this straight. We've decided, as a group, that the Sniper is a somewhat gifted shape-shifting male or female who's not nuts." She took a long sip of wine. "And who isn't married to a clergyman."

"Shape-shifter?" asked Syl.

Nobody bothered to answer Syl. They sat still for a long while, listening to the fire, looking down at the floor.

Finally, Harry B. cleared his throat. "Motive, means, opportunity," he said. "We can't begin to discuss means and opportunity, at least as far as Frank is concerned, until we know more about the t.o.d."

"Well, we know something about the t.o.d. already," said Dr. Surtees.

What the hell was the t.o.d.?

"We saw them carry away the body at midnight, in full rigor," continued Surtees. "And we know that under normal conditions a body doesn't reach that state before at least six hours."

"Full rigor?" asked Amy.

"They couldn't get him to lie down in the stretcher," whispered Carla.

"Perhaps if they'd asked him nicely . . ." Amy was gratified to hear Edna Wentworth chuckle.

"Which means," said Ricky, "that Frank couldn't have died after six o'clock."

"So he was killed around suppertime," said Carla.

"Not necessarily," said Dr. Surtees. "The *latest* he could have died is six p.m. But he could have died much earlier that afternoon. Rigor doesn't descend on the body all at once. It takes as much as twelve—"

"Yes," said Carla, "but earlier in the afternoon it was daylight, and somebody would have seen the body, probably. So it had to be suppertime."

"Which means," said Chuck, "that we're all on the hook. Because we didn't begin to congregate at Carla's until seven."

"And *I* wasn't even there," said Carla. "I was all by myself, tooling around Escondido. Which I can't prove."

"So nobody has an alibi," said Harry B.

Almost everybody spoke at once, because almost everybody had an alibi for at least part of the time between noon and six on the day Frank died. Except Edna and Amy didn't, because Edna and Amy were loners. And then it turned out that nobody had the entire six-hour period covered, rock solid. Most had managed to be alone for ninety minutes, here and there, and only Marvy claimed to have actually had supper, with his family. The rest had apparently counted on Syl's chips and dip. Carla's alibi before she left for Escondido was her own mother, with whom she hadn't exchanged a word or glance for weeks. "I mean," said Carla, "if I'd actually driven off, she should have heard the motor, but chances are she was watching the soaps or Montel anyway. And even if she'd heard me," she continued cheerfully, "she'd probably claim she hadn't. Ma wouldn't alibi Mother Teresa."

All this time business was giving Amy a headache. She had always hated dealing with timelines in her fiction, often ignoring them altogether and counting on copyeditors to fix any mistakes, which usually they did, although in *Monstrous Women* she had managed to graduate a character from high school at the age of eleven and kill off another in the Korean War in 1946. No one had noticed until the birth of the Internet and the emergence of blogs, more than one of which were manned by obsessives intent on illuminating every inconsequential error ever committed to celluloid or print. "Why should I care about this novel," one of them asked, "when the author cares so little about it herself?" Amy had responded with a three-page letter advising the blogger to spend her time scouring the classics for timeline errors, which, "though plenteous, have magically failed to prevent readers from *caring* about them." Actually, Amy had no idea if Tolstoy and Dickens and Proust were slobs like herself—the Count probably had serfs to check his facts—but it was fun, for a while, to imagine that they had been, and the letter, when finished, was the best writing she had done in a long time. She decided against sending it, in case the blogger actually took her up on the challenge; and in the end she threw it away when she realized that as a matter of fact she had not cared all that much about *Monstrous Women*.

Amy thought about alibis, good and bad. "Alibi" itself was such an odd-looking word, a tall, slim marble slab of a word. What was the value, really, of an alibi between lovers, friends, or family members? Except for Carla's awful mother. *Idea for a greeting card*: "Will You Be My Alibi?"

"Amy, what do you think?" asked Chuck.

"I think Dot will get here in five minutes, and then we can get on with the class."

"You're no fun," said Chuck. Chuck often looked right at her, as he was doing now, with what seemed to be interest, and something else—appreciation? Fondness? Chuck liked her. Amy couldn't imagine why, but she was beginning to respond in kind. She knew nothing about Chuck except that his mother had given him that absurd name for religious reasons, and even that was probably not true, a joke, well worn. Maybe she just had a thing for Charlton Heston, who had been a kind of male pinup in his day, undressed in his most illustrious roles, his chest burnished to a high gloss. Or maybe she was a prescient gun nut.

"So, most of you come to class without eating supper?" Amy asked. "Why? No wonder people are fainting in class."

"I think better on an empty stomach," said Syl, of all people, "and anyway, now that we're not meeting at UC, there's always something to eat during break."

"Tonight, for instance," said Carla, "we're having three kinds of pizza, courtesy of—"

"Pizza!" shouted Amy. "That's it! I knew there was something missing!"

Understandably taken aback, Carla said she could heat it up now, if Amy was hungry.

"No! I mean, when we were listing all of the Sniper's attributes, we forgot something. Something important. The five hundred personal pizzas! It bothered the hell out of me at the time, and then, with all that happened afterward, I just forgot about it. But the pizza prank—it's significant. It was a radical departure from everything the Sniper had done before, and it in no way foreshadowed what he—or she—was about to do."

Carla's hand shot up. "It wasn't five hundred. It was seventy-six."

"What difference does that make?" The class was responding oddly. Most, like Chuck and Harry B. and Tiffany, looked puzzled, but Syl and Marvy and Dr. Surtees were staring down at the floor, while Carla continued to wave her hand. She didn't so much wave it as punch the sky with it, the way little kids do. Amy wondered if Carla had ever had a boyfriend, or even a sexual thought. "The point is, this Sniper, who had been up to this moment—and afterwards—malevolent, hurtful, ingenious, unpredictable—suddenly plays a frat-house prank, no more frightening than a midnight call for Prince Albert in the can.

"I believe," said Amy, warming to the subject of the Sniper's identity for the first time that evening, "that the night of the personal pizzas could have been a turning point for the Sniper. He was ready to quit. The personal pizzas were a kind of white flag. (There, by the way, is a perfect example of a mixed metaphor!) And then something must have happened after that night, something that enraged the Sniper all over again. What was it? Any thoughts?" Amy sat back, feeling rather like Ellery Queen, her favorite detective, back in the day.

"That's such a really, really great idea," said Carla.

"Hardly," said Amy. "I should have thought of it sooner. Now, what we have to do is—"

Marvy stood up. "I have something to say," he said, and it was clear from the look on his face that it wasn't going to be easy.

"Is anybody else confused?" asked Tiffany. "What was the Night of the Personal Pizzas?"

"It was a seventies drive-in flick," said Chuck, "with Sam Jaffe and Diane McBain."

"I did it," said Marvy.

"Not by himself, he didn't," said Dr. Surtees.

Syl stood up next to Marvy. "We all did it," he said.

Amy couldn't process this. She felt as she had the evening that Bozo the Clown fainted and *Houston, we have a problem*. Apparently these three men had done it, but she couldn't get her mind around what exactly they had done. To what were they confessing? Surely they hadn't killed Frank?

"*They* sent me the pizzas," said Carla. "That was what I was trying to tell you! I figured it out a couple weeks ago, because I know this kid Austen who works at Mikey's Wood-Fired? And Dr. Surtees used his credit card there to buy some of the pizzas. And then I forgot to tell you. In all the excitement."

"We just thought it would be funny," said Syl.

Amy stared at the three of them long enough to fluster even Dr. Surtees. She felt like an idiot. Everyone was instantly subdued, their eyes studiously not focused on her own, with the exception of Chuck, who looked as though he actually did think it was funny. He was probably the only one not embarrassed for her. Well, good for him. Amy rose and took her goblet over to the sideboard for a refill. She stooped and peered through her own reflection in the window. "I suggest," she said over her shoulder, "that you all get out your scripts." The doorbell rang then, a new seasonal tune: *We Gather Together*, as, almost simultaneously, Carla's mother thumped on a distant wall and shrieked like Medea.

"Here's Dot," said Amy.

Dot came outfitted in an ancient silk middy blouse, a pleated navy wool skirt, and Topsiders. She blew into the room, flustered and happy, laden with a stack of brand-new scripts. "You can throw your old ones away," she announced. "I've had to revise, given our recent change in personnel." She carried a small stack of Grizzly Mystery Cruise pamphlets, which she passed out to everyone, along with the new scripts, her wafting Youth Dew blanketing the room like ground fog. The pamphlets looked homemade compared to the usual glossy foldouts. Grizzly Mystery Cruises apparently were conducted in British Columbia. Their logo was a jocular bear in a deerstalker hat. Dot explained that she and Harrison had taken their first cruise on their honeymoon, and a second one on their last anniversary. "And that's when I got the idea," said Dot, "to write one of my own plays for their next cruise. They're always on the lookout for new scripts!"

"How much?" asked Carla, and when Dot didn't answer, repeated, "How much? Per script?"

"Oh, not for *money*," said Dot, waving at the pesky notion of pay as if it were a fruit fly. "Just for a lark. And the experience, of course."

"I've heard of these affairs," said Edna, "but I've never been able to figure out how they work."

"Yeah," said Marvy. "On the one hand, there's supposed to be audience participation, and on the other hand there's a script? I don't get it."

"It's a series of setpieces," said Dot, "and they're played out all over the ship at different times. At dinnertime, of course, there's a lot of drama, but it's continued later on deck, and in designated staterooms." She went on to explain that although it was scripted, there was a lot of improvisation, too. "Usually, the murder happens on the first night, and on the last night, the murderer is revealed. It's great fun!"

"But in your own play," said Amy, "there are references to three earlier murders."

"Four, actually," said Dot. "I wanted to try something different: a serial killer mystery cruise!"

After a dead pause, Tiffany asked, "Is it a coincidence, then, that there are just enough parts for everybody in the class? Or at least, there would have been, before Frank and Ginger—"

Dot laughed. Her laughter, in that hushed room—for no one had so much as shifted in his chair after her entrance—reminded Amy of some particularly unpleasant and notorious event which she couldn't quite place, except that it had something to do with New England. "Of course it's not a *coincidence*, Tiffany," Dot said, leaning just a little on the name. Dot didn't like Tiffany, who, Amy recalled, had been really snippy during the critique of Dot's piece. "I adapted this especially for us. The original has only a cast of eight. And this second revision has twelve, not fourteen. And I've made some fairly extensive changes. It's practically a brand-new play!"

"Well," said Edna, "but you personalized these characters to fit each one of us. And surely the original play isn't about a writing class."

"Oh, but it is!" said Dot. "You see, I've taken many, many writing workshops. You'd be surprised how many."

No I wouldn't, thought Amy, although she *would* be surprised if any of the other classes had actually encouraged critical reading. Dot was ideal prey for the sort of writing guru who praised everybody's use of metaphor whenever a metaphor, however exhausted, was actually used. No doubt Dot had been told more than once that her work was publishable, and Dot, hearing identical assurances given to others, had believed in her heart of hearts that she was the only one not being patronized. There was a local industry devoted to Dots: weekend writing conferences, during which the Dots could pay extra to have a real-live literary agent actually read one of their paragraphs; expensive weeklong retreats in Anza-Borrego or Julian or Ensenada, where the Dots could locate their inner voices; and at least three annual fiction-writing contests which the Dots could enter at will, for a hefty fee. Amy was willing to bet that in Dot's living room an entire wall was devoted to framed literary awards, including Third Runner-Up Best Unpublished Romance Manuscript.

Five years ago Amy herself had by invitation entered one of these contests, under the impression that the event was genuine, and at the "awards banquet" her own short story—the last she had written; probably the last she would ever write—came in second, behind some excrescence entitled "If It's Tuesday, Why Am I Wearing My Saturday Panties?" The banquet itself she recalled in bitterer detail than the ceremony: not a banquet at all but a buffet of stale cheese cubes, Brazil nuts, carrot sticks, and large breaded mushroom-shaped objects, and she had endured one of her Moments there when, as she hoisted one of these toward her mouth, a large piece of raw chicken liver dropped from the bottom like a bomb and slithered across her paper plate, its surface so shiny that she could see herself in it. She had instantly committed it all to memory, the pattern on the plate, the color and sheen of the liver, the color and texture of her own disgust, the whole tableau, so that she could tell Max about it later. This was, absurdly, the first and last time that Amy forgot he was dead—as though the insult to her dignity had been so brutal as to rip out a wide swath of memory— and all that had kept her from bolting to her car, thus missing the award ceremony, was the thought of Max laughing his ass off.

"Dot," she said now, "you do realize that we can't perform this whole thing tonight."

"We'll see," said Dot.

What was that supposed to mean? "This is fifty-plus pages. We'll be lucky if we can do twenty."

"I think you'll be pleasantly surprised," said Dot, "at how fast the time goes by."

"Let's just get started," said Marvy, nervously clearing his throat and rising once again to his feet, to mumble, "Georgie, put that confounded comic book away."

"No, no, no!" Dot flew toward Marvy, almost toppling him. "You must be seated at table!"

"But aren't we just *reading*—" said Marvy, continuing to regard Dot, as they all did, slightly askance, as though he'd get a more accurate assessment out of the corner of his eye.

"The entire room must be rearranged," announced Dot, and Carla, to Amy's surprise, decided to go along with this. In three minutes, with the help of all the men, two dining tables had been improvised and around them arrayed her mother's bridge chairs. At the longer table Dot seated Marvy, Dr. Surtees, Tiffany, Pete Purvis, Amy, and Dot herself, right next to her. Edna, Carla, Syl, and Harry B. squeezed around the smaller table. "I don't have a chair," said Ricky Buzza, and Dot assured him that he and Chuck wouldn't need them.

"Now," said Dot, keenly surveying her stage, "now we begin!"

Marvy sighed deeply. "Georgie," he said, "put that confounded comic book away."

"Say it like you mean it!" said Dot.

"Dot, we're not actors," Amy reminded her. "All we're doing here is a read-through."

"Who's Georgie?" asked Harry B.

"GEORGIE! PUT THAT CONFOUNDED COMIC BOOK AWAY! Sorry, everybody, that was way too loud," said Marvy.

"Stay on script!"

"Gosh, Uncle Melvyn," said Pete Purvis, "this isn't a comic book. It's the illustrated classic *King Solomon's*—"

"Begin again," said Dot. "This time without the extra comments, and remain in character."

"Give me a break," said Syl.

"Georgie, put that confounded comic book away!" Now Marvy actually made eye contact with Pete, a.k.a. Georgie Rumbelow.

"Gosh, Uncle Melvyn, this isn't a comic book! It's the illustrated classic *King Solomon's Mines*, by H. Rider Haggard, and it's way cool."

Dot—Persephone Darkspoon—laid a cold, plump hand on Amy's forearm and chuckled. "At least it's a book, and not a video game. Eh, Professor Scribner?"

Amy declined, in spite of the stage directions, to chuckle back. "My sentiments exactly," she read.

"Dr. Merriwether," said Dot. "What is your considered medical opinion on the subject of video games and the development of young minds?"

Dr. Surtees stared balefully at his script. "It all depends, Mrs. Darkspoon, on the game itself and the frequency of play. And of course the quality of the young mind to begin with. Young Georgie here has already demonstrated a great verbal acuity in the first two volumes of his science fiction trilogy, *The Archives of Corinthia*."

"Ha ha ha," said Tiffany, deadpan. "Doctor, I beg to differ. Verbal acuity in outer space. As if. Georgie's got a fine imagination, I'll grant you, but surely it would be better applied to real people in real settings, tackling real problems." She was rolling her eyes like a fifteen-year-old.

"Speaking of real people," said Edna, "how is your historical novel on Lady Jane Grey coming along, Zirconia?"

There was an extended silence, during which Tiffany was supposed to say "Actually, Miss Makepeace, it's a novella," but sullenly did not, until Amy, partly as a matter of principle and partly to head off Dot, shot her a dirty look.

Johnnie "Ricky Buzza" Magruder strolled in from the hallway and announced that Zirconia's book was brilliant. "Next to *Grey Lady Jane*, my own puny efforts are seriously paltry," he said.

"Don't sell yourself short, kid," said Syl. "I'm a big fan of your woik."

Now, at Dot's italicized stage direction, everybody leaned stage right, and after a two-second pause, straightened in their chairs again. The rolling-ship effect was marred by the fact that half of them didn't know where "stage right" was. "Whoa!" said Pete Purvis. "That was some wave!"

Again, everyone leaned one way or the other. "I say," said Dr. Surtees, "we might be heading into a real—"

"Stage right," said Dot, pointing toward the hallway, "is over there." Her color was high. "If you don't all lean the same way, you'll spoil the illusion!"

This time they all leaned in the same direction. "I say, we might be heading into a real nor'easter!"

Captain Manley—Chuck Heston—strolled onstage from the hallway, past the diners, toward the far corner of the room. "Not to worry, ladies and gentlemen," he said. "The *Aurora Queen* could shrug off a force ten gale!"

Ricky, standing center stage (between the two tables), for some reason pretended to fiddle with a pipe. "So—you're a regular reader of my column in the *Daily Eagle*, eh, Mr. Lasagna?"

"Yeah," said Syl. "And I hear youse are writin' somethin' special, on the hush-hush. Yeah. A crime novel, or so my spies tell me. Starrin' a real gangster type."

"Yes," said Harry B./Jake Wiseman, "and you should be advised that my client here, Mr. Vito Lasagna—"

"I have a question," said Tiffany. "This is supposed to be a writing class. It meets regularly. They all know each other. So why does Jake have to use Vito's last name, or remind everybody that he's Jake's client? It's blatant exposition in dialogue."

"You're wrong, dear," said Persephone Darkspoon. "This is a performance piece. The rules are different for performance pieces."

"I'm not so sure," said Edna.

"Well, I am. Characters in Shakespeare always find a way to let you know who they are, and what their backstory is. If you look at *Hamlet*, for instance, you'll see that."

"I'll also see," said Edna, who usually stayed above the fray but was obviously irritated now, "that Shakespeare's exposition is accomplished with a certain degree of *skill*."

Pete Purvis joined in, objecting that nobody, including Dot, should be held to such a high standard, at which point Amy wadded up a napkin and lobbed it at the other table, bouncing it off a surprised Harry B. She locked eyes with him and pointed at her script. Harry looked down at his own and found his line. ". . . my client here, Mr. Vito Lasagna, made his wishes known at the beginning of this class. To wit: What happens in writing class stays in writing class."

"Kopisky," said Syl menacingly.

"*Capisce*," whispered Dot.

"Yes," said Amy, "and you'll recall, Mr. Wiseman, that I cautioned you at that time against making any such assumptions. This is a writing class, not a confessional." Amy was startled to realize that Dot, like Carla, actually paid attention to her in class, at least often enough to swipe her own words and use them in this silly play.

"But you understand, Professor," said Harry B., "that my client—for reasons of his own, which shall remain nameless— likes to play his cards, as they say, close to the table."

Chuck Heston's piggish snort emanated from behind a divan in the corner of the room, where he was apparently waiting out his reentry. "Sorry, Dot," he called out, "but what they *say* is 'close to the *vest*.' If you played your cards close to the table, you'd be hunched over like Quasimodo."

"*Bing-bing-bing-bing-bing!*" sang Carla, in a high register. "I'm tapping my glass with a spoon!"

"No improvising," said Dot, waving off Chuck's advice. Dot was starting to look disappointed by the read-through.

Carla stood up. The group's only professional actor, she was at ease with herself, and actually seemed enthusiastic about what she was about to do. She didn't put ironic quotes around her lines, like Amy and Tiffany and Dr. Surtees, and she didn't plod through them like the rest. Amy wondered if Carla secretly missed the spotlit life. "Before we all dig in," she said, "to our fantastic nine-course meal on our first evening of this fantastic three-day cruise on the *Aurora Queen*, courtesy of the generous Dr. P. T. Merriwether, we need to take a moment to commemorate this occasion. We're all here, on this wonderful evening, for one reason—to honor Professor Clementine Scribner, who, in her brilliance, generosity, and wisdom, has guided us all through the perils and pitfalls of bad writing—past the whirlpools of purple prose, far from the rocky shoals of cliché, braving the typhoons of mediocrity, ever ready to do hand-to-hand combat with the pirates of overextended metaphor."

"*Excuse me!*" said Dot.

Carla grinned. "Ever ready," she amended, "to do hand-to-hand combat with the pirates of poor taste."

All said, "Hear, hear."

"Hold on," said Edna. "Someone's missing. I count ten, and there should be eleven. Ten class members and Professor Scribner." Edna, apparently neutral in the Dot Wars, simply read her lines without fuss.

"Yes, where's Hester? Hester Spitz?" asked Marvy.

"I left her lying down in her stateroom with a slight case of mal de mer," said Carla, "but she promised to be here at seven on the dot, with a brand-new story for us all to read. It's nonfiction this time, and she said it was going to knock our socks off!"

"Well, she's not there now," said Edna, "because I looked in on her before coming down for dinner."

"Captain Manley!" called Amy, toward the divan. "Would you mind doing us a favor?"

Chuck crawled out of hiding and laboriously got to his feet. His face was flushed, and obviously not from exercise. Chuck was enjoying himself way too much. "Yes, Professor Scribner?"

"Could you possibly initiate a search for our missing friend? I'm so sorry to trouble you. Meanwhile, who's got Hester's cell phone number?"

"I'm on it, Chief," said Carla, ad-libbing the "Chief," whipping out her own phone and punching in seven numbers actually specified in the new script.

"I'll return shortly," said Chuck, swaggering toward the hallway with his thumbs hooked in his belt loops, looking more like a pint-sized John Wayne than a cruise ship captain. He had just disappeared from view when a cell phone went off from some distance, probably on the outside of the front door. They could barely make out the theme from *The Pink Panther*. Dot must have planted the phone there before she came in: Carla, as scripted, had dialed the number of that phone. Amy would have been impressed at Dot's farsightedness, except that she was distracted by the idea of the phone abandoned and ringing, like Frank's in the sand at Moonlight Beach. Hester Spitz had clearly bought the farm—and again this was a smart move for Dot, given that Ginger herself had dropped out. Dot could have as easily murdered Frank's character, the unnamed steward; she'd been tasteful enough, just, to avoid doing that. Still the obvious parallels she'd deliberately incorporated into the play—the missing class member, the worried calls to Frank, and the phone itself, ringing all alone, a few feet away from the corpse—were nasty. Amy was always telling her classes that fiction is written in cold blood, and here was Dot, of all people, doing just that. Or worse.

Chuck reentered, holding up Hester's cell phone. "I've just had a disturbing conversation," he said, "with Mrs. Spitz's spouse." He managed to say this line straight-faced, only to lose his composure immediately afterward. To his credit, he bent down, pretending to fuss with the laces on his running shoes. His shoulders shook rhythmically.

"Where did you find her phone?" asked Dr. Surtees.

"In the companionway, near her stateroom. Her husband's been trying to contact her for an hour. He says she never goes anywhere without her cellular phone, and he's quite anxious." Chuck managed this muffled, gasping speech from a crouching position.

At this point Dot's mystery narrative began to unfold predictably, over the course of fifteen dialogue-choked pages. Everybody in the room voiced a lengthy opinion on Hester's whereabouts, and, given the wild pitching of the boat, a growing concern about her safety. Much was made of the mysterious socks-jettisoning manuscript she had planned to spring on the group. Finally Edna wondered aloud if, as Hester had been so unwell, she might have gone on deck to clear her head and fallen overboard. The class then managed, on cue, to lean first stage right and then all the way stage left; then half of them rose as one and followed Captain Manley offstage to "investigate this possibility." They were supposed to lurch as they did so, but only Carla was able to do this convincingly. Marvy and Pete staggered with their arms straight out to the side, as though walking a tightrope; Tiffany defiantly slouched out ahead of the pack; and Ricky, following close behind, attempted to stumble and right himself but was only partly successful, knocking over a large silver plate of crudités. Those remaining onstage attempted to reassure themselves that Hester was perfectly okay.

Only Persephone Darkspoon was pessimistic. She delivered a somber speech about fate and bad things happening to good people. "We want to believe that life is fair," she said. "That the righteous are rewarded and the guilty punished. Hester Spitz is a fine woman, a nice person, a good mother, a faithful wife. She's a decent soul, and surely she deserves the best that life has to give her. And that, my friends, is why I fear the worst."

Carla screamed, from the hallway wings, "She's dead! Oh, Dear God! She's dead," making no attempt to modulate her cries, so that her mother's distant imprecations followed the group as they rushed back into the room. "Poor Hester!" sobbed Carla, collapsing in Chuck's arms, as Marvy and Pete assumed masks of grief and Tiffany announced in a bored monotone that Hester had indeed gone overboard, but "not all the way. She's hanging from a rope off the stern."

"Well, haul her up, for pity's sake," said Dr. Surtees. "She may still be resuscitated."

"Not with a broken neck," said Chuck, prompting more bleating from Carla.

"You mean—" exclaimed Harry B.

"Yes!" cried Carla. "She's hanged herself!"

"I'm afraid not," said Chuck.

"Her hands and feet were tied," said Tiffany. "By which I guess I'm supposed to mean that her hands were tied together and her feet were tied together, rather than all four—"

"You mean—" exclaimed Ricky Buzza.

"Murder," said Persephone Darkspoon, in a deep register, rising to her feet. Everyone turned to face her. Even Tiffany. "Murder most foul!"

Carla and Edna dashed to the kitchen for intermission refreshments while the rest remained more or less as they had been at the end of Act One. With the exception of Tiffany, they had apparently begun to enjoy themselves. Dr. Surtees and Syl were laughing together and the rest were poking through Act Two, as though anxious to start up again, and practicing their sea-rolls and lurches.

Next to Amy, Dot sat as silent as Buddha, frowning, eyes closed, hands folded on the table. Amy couldn't imagine what was wrong. True, she had taken a certain amount of razzing, but it had been mostly good-natured, and by now Dot should have been pretty happy about the whole thing. Of course, the play was awful, but surely Dot didn't know that. Amy leaned toward her and spoke. "It's going well, don't you think?" Dot opened her eyes and regarded Amy, for a second or two, as if she were a total stranger accosting her on a bus. "You were right," said Amy, feeling the beginnings of panic. "I'm sure we can run through the whole thing tonight."

After a long teetering pause, Dot blinked, returning to present company, and gave Amy a polite smile. "That would be nice," she said.

Nice? Only a short while ago, Dot had swept into this room breathless with anticipation, and now she seemed disconnected from her surroundings and disengaged from Amy's response, or anyone else's, to her play. Dot was, Amy realized, an interesting woman.

And she should have known that. It was an article of faith with Amy, with most writers, that there were no uninteresting people. That the dullest aunt at a family reunion, the gabbiest passenger on a plane, had, whether or not they knew it, a thousand stories to tell, each more stimulating, more enlightening, than the one before, and all of them better than true. Amy saw that Dot's story, the one she was living this very moment, was horribly sad. She was lonely in a way that Amy was not. Amy had Alphonse. Amy even had Carla, and, Edna, and Chuck, and the rest. And the memory of Max. She didn't know what this meant, but she did know that compared to Dot she was the toast of the town.

But what about Harrison, her husband, who was apparently willing to go on more than one of these grisly grizzly deals? Why, Amy wondered, if this guy was the uxorious type, was the woman so deeply unhappy? Maybe she was bipolar or hormonal or both, and for sure she wasn't getting enough sleep. There were hollows around her eyes, beneath flakes of pink powder and turquoise eyeshadow. Had she always looked so empty, so fragile? Amy had never looked directly at her before, not from up close. Like everyone else, she had regarded the woman askance, or from a safe remove. Clumsily, she reached out to Dot. Not literally, of course, but she poured two glasses of red and handed one to her. "You should have brought Harrison with you tonight," she said. "I'll bet he'd enjoy this! Next class, why don't you . . ." She had to stop, because

Dot was staring back at her, hard, as though sizing her up; as though Amy had just called her outside to settle things once and for all. There was such a thing, Amy decided right then, as being too interesting. "It was just a thought," Amy started to say.

"My husband left me four years ago," said Dot. "On our twentieth wedding anniversary." She took a sip of wine and made an ugly face. "He ran off with my younger sister, actually, whose name is actually Rose. They're living happily in Phoenix now. Actually. I want a sandwich and a piece of cheese." She said this last to Carla, who was walking by with a food tray, and when Carla bent down to present her with choices, Dot gathered up food with both hands and resumed talking once Carla had left. "They'd been at it for years. I had no idea until they told me. I was a total innocent." For a long moment she focused on the food, taking great bites, as though ravenous, as though she'd starved for a week. "You thought my story was all made up," she said. "You said it was unbelievable. You were wrong." She stood up suddenly and bent over Amy, her fists on the table. "You don't know shit," she said.

Amy watched Dot Hieronymus stalk off to the bathroom, wineglass in hand, and refused to acknowledge her own emotional response to the moment. She was good at that. It would be a simple enough trick to turn what had just happened into an intellectual dispute. Not *entirely* wrong, she argued silently. You didn't *actually* poison them. You didn't *actually* kill yourself. She wanted to say this, not in her own defense, since Dot had really really nailed her, no doubt about that, but in defense of aesthetic fundamentals. Okay, on the one hand Amy stood justly accused of reducing a fellow human being to a cartoon creature. But still. That Dot's story had been based on fact didn't make it credible. Fact exerted a tyranny over beginning writers, sapping them of the will to make things up, seducing them into complacency. They didn't understand: it was the writer's job to fashion truth out of fact. Dot probably should have killed the bastard, but she hadn't. Assuming Harrison really was happily living in Phoenix. Dot scared the hell out of Amy. Actually.

Right before ten o'clock everyone assumed his place for Act Two. The tables had been moved away, and Carla's chairs, pillows, and sofas arranged in a wide arc. Although the actors were still game, their general mood was subdued, partly because it was getting late and their bellies were full, but mostly because now the drama played out like an interminable game of Murder, with the detective—in this case, Captain Manley—stolidly interrogating each person in turn about where he had been at various times, and who could vouch for whom, and it was impossible to keep track of it all, let alone care who was telling the truth and who was lying. Carla and Ricky tried to inject some life into their lines, with uneven results, and the author herself sat in the very middle of the pack exuding such odd, negative vibes that even Syl glanced at her with concern.

Amy wanted to call a halt, send everyone home, get as far away as she could, to be alone with her thoughts about Dot and Harrison and her own colossal cluelessness, but there were only ten pages to go, and the show must go on.

"I hardly knew the dame," Syl was saying, "and anyways, she seemed decent enough. Why would I want to off her?"

"Maybe," Carla said, "because she was on to you, and she was about to spill the beans."

"Exactly," said Dr. Surtees. "What happened in writing class wasn't going to *stay* in writing class. Eh, Lasagna?"

"Why, I oughtta—"

"Sit down, Vito," ordered Amy. "And the rest of you. You're all turning on one another like jackals. Don't you see? This must be part of the murderer's cunning stratagem: to divide and conquer. Don't make it so easy for him."

"Or her," read Tiffany, and the class was startled into laughter by the wit of this line, which was so very Tiffany.

"Good one!" whispered Marvy, to Dot.

Tiffany glared up at her. "You don't miss much, do you?" she said, off-script. She had drunk more wine during intermission and was becoming belligerent. Amy tried to catch her eye.

"Kindly don't improvise, Tiffany," said Dot, not looking up from her page.

This new mildness, in sharp contrast to her earlier vehemence, was alarming to Amy, who would have gone off-script herself to defuse the looming confrontation, but Chuck saved the day. Instead of speaking his next lines from a standing position, he squeezed in between the two women on the couch. "I'm intrigued, Miss Cummings, that you say 'her,' because I have every reason to believe that you are correct. And how, I'm beginning to wonder, did you know?"

"I'm afraid you're barking up the wrong tree, Captain," said Edna. "Our Zirconia can't abide sexist language, even when it works to her advantage."

"I must second Miss Makepeace on that point," said Harry B., "it's really just a matter of principle with Zirconia," and the rest chimed in, piling on Tiffany, and apparently enjoying it, too. Even Edna smiled, just a little, at Dot's clever little revenge.

"What did you mean just now, Captain?" Tiffany asked. Steam was not literally shooting out of her ears, but it might as well have been. "Whom do you suspect?"

"It's really quite simple," said Chuck. He rose and began to pace in back of the seated crowd. "You see, when Young Georgie here returned to the stateroom he shares with his father, in quest of his dog-eared copy of *King Solomon's Mines*, it was four bells—six o'clock in the evening, to you landlubbers—and he passed three people on the way back: Mr. Lasagna, Dr. Merriwether, and Mrs. Darkspoon."

"Yes, we know that," said Amy, "and I fail to see what that has to do with—"

"Be patient, Professor Scribner. The gentlemen were answering calls of nature, and Mrs. Darkspoon was on her way to the ship's library, where she had left her asthma medication. Within fifteen minutes, all three had returned to the table, and after that point no one left until we sent out the search party for Mrs. Spitz."

"We've been over this before, Captain," objected Dr. Surtees.

"*But,*" said Chuck, neatly stepping on the doctor's line, "we've failed to notice the one piece of the puzzle that doesn't quite fit! You'll recall that, according to Mr. Rumbelow, the billiard room on deck two had been locked between noon and, to the best he can recall, three forty-five. And Miss Makepeace has assured us that within fifteen minutes two cigarettes were smoldering unattended in an ashtray on the third-deck promenade . . ."

Kill me now, thought Amy, who had begun to count numbers as they rolled by: three, fifteen, one, two . . . If she made it through the evening intact, she planned to add a footnote to her short list of fiction-writing homilies: *Arithmetic is the death of story.* Six more pages and it was all over. Six was a cheerful number.

"So it's inescapably obvious," said Chuck, "that the only one among you who could possibly have left Musky Rose lipstick on that smoldering cigarette—the only one with a genuine motive for shutting up Hester Spitz once and for all—the only one clever enough to frame Lasagna—was also the single person with dark eyes that beckoned to me every evening as the meddling hussy flaunted that obscene snapshot, threatening to sell it to the tabloids and leave me and my darling baby daughter twisting in the wind!"

Chuck's momentum had been such that he made it all the way to the end of this extraordinary speech without stumbling. Now he stopped and stared at the page, and flipped to the previous page, and back again. The room was silent, almost reverent, as they all held their breath in wonder. Which, in a way, was appropriate, since without miraculous intervention Dot could never have written such a sentence. She was a surprising woman, but not, unfortunately, a surprising writer, and Amy opened her mouth to point out the obvious—that there must be a page out of place or missing in Chuck's script—and instead, unpardonably, Amy laughed. It wasn't so much the obscene flaunted snapshot or the baby in the wind, or even the echo of Chuck's stentorian, impassioned nonsense; she got stuck instead on the mental image of framed lasagna, and she lost it, and so encouraged the rest to lose it along with her. Even Pete.

Too bad for Dot, who had almost gained entry to the clubhouse, who had come so close to being one of the gang, and who now jerked to her feet, her script sliding from her lap onto the carpet, and walked out into the middle of the room, her back to them all. Amy made herself ready for what was bound to be a wicked confrontation. "Come on, Dot," said Marvy. "We're not laughing at you! Chuck just lost his place, is all."

"Yes," said Amy. "Come back. Let's finish this."

Dot turned around and faced them. Her face was a terrible dark color, almost maroon, and her eyes bulged white.

"Dot?"

Dot hugged herself tight and fell to her knees, shaking the room, the tip of her tongue protruding between her lips, in sharp pink contrast to the eggplant hue of her skin.

Dr. Surtees, shouting "Call 911," embraced her from behind, the Heimlich maneuver, but Dot wasn't choking, at least not mechanically. She stared straight at them unseeing and toppled sideways, slowly, as he eased her on her back. She didn't flail, she didn't gasp, she just went down, and as he worked on her all that moved were her hands, clenching, opening, and clenching again into fists, until, just before the ambulance came, they opened for the last time and stayed that way, in permanent bloom. It all happened very fast, and it took forever.

Howdy, Amy!

Depending upon when you notice this, I slipped it under the door either before class or later last night, whilst you slept, or perchance in the a.m. on my way to work at _____, but you didn't hear me because you were in the shower. Actually, no, I figure you for a sandalwood bath beads kind of lady.

Say, maybe you could ask your neighbors to describe my automobile, or my actual person? That's assuming I parked on the street and didn't stroll up to your door in heavy disguise. Maybe, on the other hand, you don't know your neighbors well enough to ask. You're not the sociable type, are you? And what's with the "Buzz Off" doormat? Are you really plagued with unwanted visitors?

Anyhoo, about Frank. Basically it was an accident, but then so was Velcro, so there you go. Frank was a decent enough chap, but too curious for his own good. Instead of spending his time profitably, Making Stuff Up, Finding his Inner Voice, and Avoiding Exposition in Dialogue, he decided to Spillane his way to the truth about what you people are calling The Sniper. Turns out he had an old friend who's an assistant pooh-bah for one of the more infamous literary snotrags (you'll forgive me if I don't name it here), and he was shooting the shit with this guy (or gal) one evening and happened to mention the antics of Moi, and before you could say Jack Robinson the gal (or guy) said, "Hey! That kind of sounds familiar!" (Lit snotrag assistants are nothing if not blindingly articulate.)

And wouldn't you know that a week or so later Our Frank got an actual letter from this creature, the gist of which I will reproduce here:

Frank—

It was so fabulous to hear from you!

Thanks for sending that writing class list (sorry, it went it to the wrong department, so it took awhile), and sure enough, I recognized the name of this whacko[1] I was telling you about. _____ _____ [2] used to send us a story a month, back in the day, when I was a lowly unpaid reader. Every first Monday, you could set your watch.[3] Not a bad writer, actually, though rather conservative for our taste—psychological realism, linear plots, and so on—but _____ sort of knew _____ way around a sentence, and I always figured that sooner or later we'd take one.[4] Then we got this incredibly vomitous thing in the mail.

It looked like a perfectly good dictionary,[5] brand-new—I thought we'd ordered it—but when I opened it up it had been hollowed out with a razor, and then packed with long, coarse, dirty white hair all rolled up in a ball. This was bad enough, but when I took out the hair (yes, I actually took out the hair—what can I tell you, I was twenty-one!) it unraveled, and inside it was a pile of *teeth*. Gross! The secretary thought they were human (I'm sure they were canine)[6] and got so upset that we had to give her the day off.

Of course the package was unsigned, and there's no way we could legally prove it came from ____. Still, _____ lives in a small town in _____—the only one of our contributors to send us manuscripts from there—and although the package was postmarked in _____, the Whacko (you say The Sniper, and we said The Whacko—let's call the whole thing off!![7]) had forgotten to take the store sticker off the dictionary, and the store was in _____. So we were pretty damn sure.

And then we never heard from _____ again! No more Monday manuscripts.

Now that I think about it, that was the creepiest part of the whole thing.[8] The smart move would have been for _____ to keep sending those

1. Read "wacko." Note that our lit queen (or king) can't spell.
2. Sorry, can't include this, but anyway it was misspelled. Naturally.
3. Sure, if you set your watch by a calendar.
4. Bullshit!!!! Bullshit!!!!
5. It was Fowler's *Modern English Usage*, but what the hey.
6. Wrong again!
7. What a card!
8. No, the "creepiest part" was when the bleeding teeth fell out of the hairball. *Quelle poseur (or poseuse)*.

manuscripts, right? To throw off suspicion? Anyway, we couldn't prove anything, so that was that.

So you guys have your hands full! You better tell your teacher, and let her deal with it. That's what she's paid for.

And let me know what happens! Maybe over dinner, the next time you're in town? My treat!!

P.S. Are you still with B_____? Give her my regards!

Well, turns out Our Frank was a real straight shooter, by which I mean that he couldn't bring himself to, as he put it, "go over my head" to you without first giving me a chance to explain myself. He called me that morning and said he wanted to meet with me and talk things out. What things, I asked, and he declined to say, except that it concerned the class, of course. It was he, swear to Gawd, who suggested meeting at Moonlight Beach, because it was close enough to his department so he could dart out at lunchtime, have this weird confab, and make it back in time to do whatever it was he did.

I tried to imagine a benign explanation for this rendezvous. Imagination has never been my strong suit.

So there I am, sitting at a picnic table, gazing idly down at the surfers, their wet boards glinting in the winter sun, or maybe it was their wetsuits— no, I tell a lie, it was cold and off-and-on drizzly, and I had the whole place to myself, more's the pity, and here comes Frank, loaded for bear, and he plunks this stupid letter down in front of me and invites me, with a palm-up flourish, to read it.

Naturally, I try stonewalling. "And you actually believe this?" I ask. "Doesn't your friend's conclusion strike you as a bit tenuous? Yes, I did, in fact, submit a number of stories to this journal. I take my writing seriously, Frank. When I finish a story I'm satisfied with, I send it out to a carefully honed list of journals, one of which this one used to be, before this twit came on board. So it's hardly surprising that _____ recognized my name. And honestly, can you picture me cramming a dictionary with hair and teeth?"

"I can now," says Frank.

I still can't figure out what he meant by that. The only thing that makes sense is that just seeing me there made some tumblers fall into place. I all at once looked like the sort of individual who would bombard simpletons with grotesque packages, and make obscene phone calls, and write poison pen letters, and of course he was right, but still it was unnerving. Apparently my mask had slipped.

And I was going to keep denying everything—it works for the politicians, so why not for me—and I got to my feet and fixed him with what I hoped was a baffled, pitying look, and opened my mouth to make my excuses—I'm busy, I would say, and I have a dentist appointment, and if you're determined to press the issue to the group, I won't stand in your way, although you're likely to make an ass of yourself. Sorry, Frank, I would say, then I would make a point of shaking his hand, good sport that I am, but I've got to get going, and then I said it, "Sorry, Frank," and I moved to shake his hand, and he did the most extraordinary thing. He flinched.

Then he stood up and grabbed the damn letter off the table and backed away from me. I had done nothing to provoke this response. In fact, I'll go so far as to say in all honesty—and I almost never do that!—that I've done nothing to provoke any response of any strength from any person on any occasion in my entire life. I am a civilized human. Acquaintances and strangers regard me mildly, and why not? I'm hardly a terrorist. I took another step toward him, my hand still extended, and damned if he didn't take another step back.

At this point I'll admit that I began to enjoy myself. In light of what happened, this sounds bad, but imagine yourself suddenly absurdly endowed with a peculiar superpower: you go to lick a stamp and fire shoots from your tongue, or you think about a boysenberry milkshake and one appears in front of you. Could you resist materializing, or incinerating, one damn thing after another, for the sheer hell of it? Of course not, and neither could I stop advancing on Our Frank, in modest increments, my nascent hearty handclasp proffered robotically, because—the look on his face!! He was trying, literally straining, to stand his ground, but he couldn't do it, he had to move away. From me! What a silly man.

Again I moved toward him, widening my smile, out of simple mischief, I swear. There's something that happens, though, when you bare your teeth on purpose, your teeth like unsheathed swords, and some ancient memory wakes, and sure enough his eyes widened in reply, and still he moved back. It would have been easy enough to get around me and hotfoot it to the parking lot. Hell, he could have pushed me out of the way. What was I going to do—grin him to death?

Finally Frank backed up against a tallish shrub, a row of which lined the rim of that little park. Beach hibiscus. Past his head and shoulders I could just make out the gray sea, or maybe just the gray mist. Except for the ridiculous expression on his face he made a pretty picture in that delicate gray light, embraced as he was by green leaves and crepey yellow flowers, and I was inspired then to extend my other arm, one last little nudge for the noodge, and then I would clasp his shoulders and give him a little shake and finally speak, breaking the spell. "Frank," I would say. "What in the world is wrong with you?" Or "How about we get a nice cup of coffee and talk this out?" Or "Get a grip on yourself, man!"

This is what I'm trying to explain to you. The shrub was an optical illusion. It was there, of course, but there wasn't much to it: more space than substance, really. The shrub was for show.

So when Frank began to disappear into it, in slow motion, the effect was more magical than alarming. I can see it still in my mind's eye. I'm looking at it right now! Time-lapse, shutter-shutter-shutter, as Frank blends in, becomes one with the hibiscus, his face, those misted leaves, his eyes, replaced, first one, then the other, those pale yellow blossoms crimson at the center, and then just his hand reaches out toward mine, and time stops.

And then he's gone.

Nobody hears. There is nothing to hear. No cry, no shout. Nobody walking on the gray beach below. No consequences.

Well, until tonight. Because, blameless as I am for Frank's death, I did cause it, and found in the experience something I could take away. A happy unintended goal, better than Velcro, more like the discovery of penicillin. Okay, I liked it. I stood there in the Frankless vacuum and tried to locate horror, grief, guilt, and up popped joy.

I'm seeing it again now as I write to you, shutter-shutter-shutter, and again right now, as you read this.

Or maybe I'm seeing something else: what happened tonight. Which was not an accident.

You can do it too! Close your eyes and there's her face, and there, and there again, and gone.

Enough about me. See you soon!

P.S. Love your dog.

Amy wasn't sure who called the ambulance, Carla or Dr. Surtees or maybe Chuck, or Pete. Harry B. had called the police from his cell phone, but they hadn't arrived by the time Amy insisted on riding along with Dot in the ambulance, and for some reason she had been allowed to do this. Perhaps she had looked so distraught that they assumed she was a close relative. Amy had no idea how she looked. The medics attached tubes and plastic bags to Dot and, once they'd assured themselves that Amy wasn't going to get hysterical, they talked about the Chargers and their Super Bowl chances, and generally behaved like the technicians who'd taken Max on his final ride. Amy remembered now how she had loved those guys for their offhand grace, their calm attention on the only thing that mattered, coaxing out one more breath, one more beat. "She's dead?" asked Amy, and the older one said, "Doesn't look good, ma'am." With Max, there had been a chance—not of saving him, but of keeping him alive for a few more hours, and they'd let her hold his hand. She couldn't bring herself to reach for Dot's, who deserved better than Amy.

When they got to the hospital, Amy trudged behind the gurney and heard herself explained to the resident as "the sister." She watched them working over Dot's body in a muddle of wrinkled pastels and beat-up machines, and though they spent a long time poking and pounding and beeping, Amy could tell they were just satisfying a set of protocols. Dot had been gone from the moment she fell to the floor in Carla's living room.

"I don't know," Amy said, when asked about Dot's closest kin. "I'm just her teacher," she said. They asked her for Dot's Social Security number and home address, which was when Amy realized she hadn't brought Dot's purse with her. The resident, a magenta-haired young man who had obviously been practicing his "seen it all" expression for future use, sighed and began to turn away. "She was married," said Amy. "I'm not sure she's divorced yet. Maybe not. Her husband's name is Harrison." There, let them wake up the heartless bastard. "Yeah, Harrison what?" asked the resident. Amy now blanked on Dot's last name. It was the name of an artist. A Dutch artist. Brueghel? She desperately free-associated and came up with Corrie Ten Boom. "What was the patient's last name?" asked the resident.

"Hieronymus." Dr. Surtees appeared at Amy's shoulder like a cartoon angel, or devil. "The lady's name was Dorothy Hieronymus." He turned to Amy. "I'm so sorry. I should have ridden with you, but she had passed, and I thought I could be of greater assistance with the police. They turned out to be as dense and rude as this young man here." Dr. Surtees flashed some badge-thing at the resident, who lowered his eyes, nodded, and took off.

Amy didn't like hearing a euphemism like "she had passed" from a physician. It sounded smarmy, and besides, yes, he really should have come along in the ambulance. Maybe he could have saved her.

Dr. Surtees touched Amy familiarly, for the second time in as many weeks. He was rubbing her shoulder. As though they were old friends, or worse. "She was gone," he said in her ear, "ten minutes before the ambulance got there. Whatever she took stopped her heart."

Whatever she took. Was he right? Had Dot done this to herself? "But they could have gotten it going again! They can always—"

"No, they can't. That's only on television. Her heart just seized, like a car engine after it's run dry of oil. You don't come back from that."

"How do you know this? She's only been dead for a few minutes!"

"Amy," he said, smiling in a pitying way, "it's after one in the morning. You've been here for over two hours. Let me take you home."

She almost did. But when he touched her again, taking her arm to lead her outside, she remembered that right now she should not be alone with any one of them. Especially this one. She shook herself free and told him she had a ride. She waited another forty-five minutes, until she was sure he had left the parking lot, before calling a cab.

After the terrible death, after the shrieking ambulance, the hospital, and the cab ride, Amy was grateful to be home. She locked the screen door and deadbolted the front door, sloughed off her coat and called Alphonse. For a moment she just leaned back against the door and closed her eyes. If she could just stay this tired, she could fall asleep before the night's events and their implications began to churn. She went to hang her keys on the wall but they slipped off onto the floor, and when she bent to pick them up, she saw the envelope. AMY was printed across it, in great bold black letters, each lower case and carefully formed around an imagined square, like a child's attempt at calligraphy. She called Alphonse again. She listened for him in the silence. Nothing, not even the sound of her own breathing. Just before screaming his name, she heard him bark from the backyard. Yes! she remembered now, she had left him outside tonight, and for the time it took her to let him in, she didn't think of anything else. His nose was cold and he was more annoyed with her than usual, shrugging off her welcoming hands and trotting to his favorite spot in the middle of the living room rug, where he began to wriggle on his back and make snarfling sounds.

Amy sat down beside him and began to read.

When she put the letter in her pocket, she was flushed, hyper-alert, and holding herself very still. That was all: she didn't process it, didn't allowed herself to, just held the text in the front of her mind, the way you do things you have to remember for a limited period of time, like license plate numbers. The Kit Kat Clock on the fireplace wall clicked and whirred, Alphonse scratched his back and snarled *Ong ong ong ong ong*, and in a minute the phone would ring, or maybe the doorbell, and the next thing would happen. *Howdy, Amy!*

For the first time she started to think hard about who the Sniper was. Before now she had not been able to bring herself to do this in any methodical way, she'd left that to the class, because it had seemed somehow disloyal to each of them. Now she imagined Carla, Chuck, Pete Purvis, grinning horribly, stalking Frank in the mist, making him one with the hibiscus, and what a striking image that was, and how frightening, if she allowed it out of the front of her mind. No, not Pete. Pete was just too young, and so was Ricky, and Tiffany, too. The Sniper was no kid. He knew too much—about pop culture, dated slang, human nature. But then, as Carla would argue, the Sniper was also a good writer, and good writers can cultivate different voices. And that was another thing—how many of these people were good writers? Could Syl Reyes be so diabolically talented that he could write this letter as well as that excrescence about John Blovio and his huge problemmo?

Sleep was obviously out of the question, and she couldn't call anybody for hours. Except the police. Amy needed to show them this letter, and if that meant they had to schlep up to Escondido at four in the morning, it was too damn bad, because she had allowed this to go on long enough. She would call the La Jolla police. She wouldn't be put off again. This, along with a cup of oolong, made her feel energized, even perky, and she got out her phone book and looked up the number.

A half hour later, having abandoned the phone book, trolled the Internet, and spoken to five robots and three actual human beings at various stations in La Jolla and downtown San Diego, she was no closer to connecting with someone on whom she could unload the terrible contents of this letter, not to mention her own conscience. Three times she started to dial 911 but couldn't bring herself to finish the call, because this wasn't an emergency, at least not yet (or not anymore), and she didn't want to come off like a crackpot.

Eventually she got it through her head that there wasn't a "La Jolla Police Department," because La Jolla was part of the city of San Diego, *ma'am*, and when she'd finally gotten hold of a "Sergeant Colostomy"—this couldn't have been his actual name, but it was as close as she could make out, because the man seemed to be chewing on something doughy—and begun at last to cultivate official interest in the Sniper, she'd made the mistake of mentioning Frank Waasted and Moonlight Beach, and their conversation had immediately deflated. Frank's "incident," according to Sergeant Colostomy, was "County," which meant the Sheriff's department, and apparently the sheriff and the police, like the cowman and the farmer, had certain communication issues. She knew he was going to tell her that someone would be getting in touch. She couldn't stand it.

"Communication issues! You want to hear communication issues! Listen to this: He says, and I quote, '. . . blameless as I am for Frank's death, I did cause it, and found in the experience something I could take away. A happy *unintended goal*, better than Velcro . . . *Okay, I liked it.*'" Amy paused, giving them both time to take in this grotesque sentence. "'I stood there in the Frankless vacuum—'"

"Who wrote this, ma'am?"

"Who do you think? Who have we been talking about, Sergeant? This person in my class who has murdered two people!"

"And you may well be right, ma'am, and someone will be in touch—"

"No! No, they won't! They didn't get in touch when Frank died, even though I talked to them right there on the beach, and you have my name and number and my—"

"Ma'am," said the sergeant, obviously using his professionally soothing skittish-mare voice. "What you just read to me sounds, and don't take this the wrong way, like something you'd read in a book. You say you people are writers?"

Amy pressed a hand over her mouth and waited until she'd be able to sound like a rational person. "This is not a creative writing exercise, Sergeant Colostomy."

"That's *Colostomy*, ma'am." Amy was going deaf or crazy or both at once. "And I'm sure it isn't. What I need for you to do right now is this. First, it's almost five in the morning, and you need to go to bed. I need for you to give me your phone number, and I promise you that someone from the department will—"

"Never mind, thank you so very much," said Amy. "I don't *need* to take up any more of your time." She hung up the phone and screamed, "You patronizing moron!" Alphonse, who had been snoring splayed on his back, rolled over and trudged off to the bedroom, and as he clicked away, the phone, still in her lap, rang merrily. Just when did authority figures begin to frame every command in terms of inappropriate private yearning? *I need you to calm down. I need you to step away from the bomb. I need you to lie down on your stomach with your arms outstretched and name the sitting president.* Amy picked up the receiver and shouted, "And you know what? If your name isn't 'Colostomy,' it ought to be!"

At the other end of the line there was a sharp intake of breath, but no other sound. The silence went on long enough for Amy to look down at the caller ID readout. It wasn't the police. It was a "Private Caller." Amy held the receiver still and didn't breathe, and neither did the caller. Eventually there was a tiny mechanical click, followed by static, and then Dot's voice, only higher and younger because of the cheap recording made just hours ago. In life, Dot had been unable to write a sentence that wasn't false. Now she sounded like Cassandra on the palace steps. "We want to believe that life is fair, that the righteous are rewarded and the guilty punished." The recorder clicked twice and she said it again. Amy leaned back and heard her out. After a few more repetitions, the caller fast-forwarded to "Murder. Murder most foul!" and from there to Chuck ranting about the meddling hussy flaunting the snapshot, and then that endless three-second pause and then the first laugh, her own, *ha ha ha*.

Amy hung up delicately, so that the Private Caller wouldn't know she was gone, and waited for him to figure it out. This was her only weapon—to deny him the satisfaction of a response.

This was, she reckoned, the Sniper's third call. The first time had been when she got home from First Class, and there had been that odd message on her machine, the angry whisperer: *Teach me anything.* At the time she had wondered (wondered!) if the caller had been one of those strangers who'd shown up in the classroom that night. Later, she had, of course, connected the call with the Sniper, especially when she got the second call, taunting her with her own recorded voice: *Do you have any idea what's going to happen next?* And now this. Something bothered her, like a tickle way in the back of her mind—something about the calls. She sat still and waited for the thought to form, and waited, too, to become frightened. First the letter, and now the call, and what was next— well, obviously a home visit. But outside her living room window she could hear her neighbors starting up their cars for the dawn commute, and she could see them, too, not just their lights, but the colors of the cars. The sun would be up soon, and Amy just couldn't be afraid in the daytime.

That was silly. Monsters killed in the sunlight as easily as under the stars, and the last throes of their victims couldn't possibly be assuaged by glimpses of vibrant color and the cheerful gossip of nesting birds. If anything, surely the contrast would make it worse. Still, there would be that time lag, that slow appreciation of danger, the tuning out of all that sunny busyness. You wouldn't be so ready to believe the worst. With any luck, the whole thing would be over with just as you began to wonder why that nice young man had an axe in his hand.

It would be hours before Amy could call Harry B. or Carla, and there was no way she could sleep. She made herself some coffee and sat down at her computer, and began to go through the stories and novel chapters the class had turned in this semester. This would either put her to sleep or refresh her memory about each of them. Now that she had this letter, she would read each piece— except Dot's—with an eye for Sniper clues, looking for similarities of speech, of rhythm, maybe even idiosyncratic use of imagery or overuse of specific words. She would become the world's first creative writing forensic specialist.

By midmorning, she had compiled three lists, one of bad writers, one of good writers, and one of in-betweens. On the bad list were Harry B., Marvy, and Syl. On the good list was Edna, Tiffany, Chuck, and Pete; and in between lay Carla, Ricky, Dot, and Dr. Surtees. She began to compose separate Word documents, addressing each group in detail.

THE GOOD

Edna:
- favorite writer in class
- Example: *The immediate and the eternal were one and the same to him, and now he twisted in a universe of shame, without limit or perspective.*

- Could be the Sniper because

  - Doesn't suffer fools.
  - Has been writing a long time (Sniper: *I take my writing seriously, Frank. When I finish a story I'm satisfied with, I send it out, to a carefully honed list of journals*)
  - Sniper: *"I am a civilized human."* So is Edna.

- Can't be the Sniper because

  - Disgusting drawing of Edna.
  - snotrag, boysenberry shake, bullshit!!
  - It's Edna, for god's sake.

Tiffany:
- Example: *. . . and there's nothing to do, no snooze alarm, no suit hanging ready on her open closet door, no open closet door, no water running in the shower, no NPR echoing from the bathroom, no Jake.*
- Nice rhythms, loves language.
- Could be the Sniper because

  - Could have put that Bundy thing in own car.
  - Temper, attitude.
  - *Today is the worst day of the rest of her life.* Clever. Notices everybody. Lives with father. (What does that mean?) Drinks too much.

- Can't be the Sniper because

  - Young. How long can she have been sending out stuff? Five-six years?
  - All wrapped up in being Tiffany. Can't see her impersonating people.

Chuck:

- Leprechaun—mischievous, charming, at ease with self.
- Hasn't brought in anything since that exercise in Second Class.
- *Mycroft was Jack's. I was so in love and so excited about Jack moving in with me that when he opened the shoebox and took out Mycroft I didn't scream get the hell out of here with that obscene thing you sadist pervert jerk. I said wow. I said where do you keep him? Jack said Mycroft just roams around. I got spots before my eyes, red spots, but I didn't actually lose consciousness and instead made up a story about a neighborhood cat who was always coming in the window, and how we had to "protect Mycroft."*
- Could be the Sniper because:

  - Charming! Psychopaths are charming.
  - Can do point-of-view female!!
  - Frank's buddy; Frank would trust him; Frank would feel most betrayed by him, and maybe most afraid. Chuck Heston in the mist??

- Can't be the Sniper because:

  - He's funny. Sniper is not funny. Sniper is amusing.
  - He's a really nice guy, a kind person.
  - I like him.

Pete:

- *Murphy Gonzalez stared at Brittany in bewilderment. Or to be more accurate he squinted in Brittany's direction, because his glasses had been knocked off by Brittany's flying orange juice carton. "Huh?" he asked? "What did I do?"*
- Sweet kid, only not a kid, but he's still pretty young. Dot's only defender. Obviously a reader, not a doer.

- Could be the Sniper because:

  - There's a hurt, watchful quality there.
  - Stood up for Dot just before killing her? Diabolical enough.

- Can't be the Sniper because

  - No evidence of smarts—not stupid, but not obviously sharp like the others.

THE BAD

Harry B.

- *Paul knew this was dangerous, every instinct in his being cried out against trusting her. When had such creatures ever been worthy of trust? In all of human history, had they once failed to disappoint? If only, he mourned, she weren't so damnably beautiful . . .*
- Writes crap.
- Could be the Sniper because:

  - Knows the law; knows all about police jurisdictions! Could have purposely killed Dot and Frank in different cities.
  - Sniper letter: *your teeth like unsheathed swords, and some ancient memory wakes . . .* Kind of lurid.

- Can't be the Sniper because:

  - *Reads* crap. Harry doesn't care about books.

Marvy Stokes:

- *Gazing around his small, cluttered, dusty private-eye office, Jack Mansfield gave a huge yawn, and then reluctantly unrolled his lanky six-foot-four frame from behind his gunmetal gray desk. "Eleven o'clock a.m.," he thought to himself, "and not a meal ticket in sight."*
- Sweet guy, nice wife.

- Could be the Sniper because:

  - Technically any of them could.

- Can't be the Sniper because:

  - It's Marvy.

Amy stopped. What was happening to the list was what happened to every list Amy had ever tried to keep. Grocery lists, lists of expenses, class lists, address books, irregular French verbs—they all petered out or got aggressively misplaced before they could fulfill any sort of function. There was something about them that offended her on the deepest level. If she couldn't hold a group of things or people or ideas in her head, then the hell with it. Even her blog lists were drying up. She'd never been able to take notes in class either, or bring herself to jot anything in the margin of a book, even a book she loved, or one she despised. Why had she become a writer, if she hated writing so much?

All she was doing with this list, even with all the hunting and cutting and pasting and the cute bullet points, was saying, It can't be Edna, because it just can't, and it can't be Marvy either, and it can't be Tiffany because she's Tiffany. She'd succeeded in organizing the class into three neat subdivisions, but so what? She already knew that the Sniper was a good writer and a talented impersonator. Even if she could tease out rhythms and phrases from the Sniper letter and identify their counterparts in classwork, it wouldn't prove anything. All writers, good and bad, stole from one another with both hands. On top of this, she was making up nonsense rules: *The Sniper can't be funny.* Who says? *The Sniper can't be a good person.* Well, duh, but he can certainly come across that way. *The Sniper can't have a nice, ordinary family.* Sure. Just ask those people in Wichita.

It was time to make some phone calls, this time to real people. Carla first.

She got Carla's machine, and was just about to hang up and work out what message she should leave, when someone picked up and said, "Who's calling?"

"Carla?"

"Who's this?" The woman sounded furious. It had to be Carla's mother.

"Mrs. Karolak? I'm—"

"I didn't take that bastard's name."

"I beg your pardon?"

"My name is Massengill."

Of course it was. What a deep thrill it would be, Amy thought, to introduce Carla's mother to Sergeant Colostomy, and she swallowed a laugh, hiccuping into the phone.

"I said who is this?"

"I'm Amy Gallup, Ms. Massengill, and I teach Carla's—"

"I know who you are." She must have let the receiver drop to the floor, because there were three dull bouncing clunks, through which Amy could hear her calling Carla from some distance away. "Carla! That woman's on the phone!"

She kept bellowing, but Amy held her receiver far enough away from her ear so that she wouldn't catch the particulars. Amy had a horror of overhearing herself being spoken about. Max had always found this hilarious. "What are you so afraid of?" he would tease her. "That you'll hear some haunting unfaceable truth?" No, it wasn't that. It was metaphysical, really. If others referred to her, then she must be a member of human society. Of course, she knew she was in fact a member of human society, but she had always preferred to live as though she were not. Amy wasn't shy. "I'm socially disconnected," she told Max, who agreed. "You're off the hook," he would say, and she'd respond, sometimes out loud, "Except to you."

What an unpleasant woman Mother Massengill was. Perhaps, Amy thought, she should be added to the List.

"Amy?" Carla was breathless. "Are you all right?"

"I've had a letter," Amy said.

Carla knew right away who the letter was from, and when Amy explained about trying to call the police, Carla knew what to do. "Fax me that letter," she said. "I'm calling Harry B."

"I don't know how to do that," Amy said, "and anyway, what can Harry do that I can't?"

Carla said that Harry had connections. He knew people.

"Yes," Amy said, "he knows other lawyers. He defends criminals. Why would that place him on a first-name basis with policemen? Besides," she added, hating to go down this road, "why are we assuming he isn't the Sniper?"

"Because look," said Carla. There was a long pause. "Now that we know it isn't, you know, Dot . . ." She waited for Amy to interrupt, but what was the point of that? They certainly did know that it wasn't Dot, and Amy was tired of defending her anyway. "I have a short list," said Carla, "and I'll bet you do too."

"I have a *list*. The only reason it's short is that I ran out of energy."

"And Harry B. isn't on it. Am I right or am I right?"

"I don't own a fax machine, and I don't feel like going out and finding one."

"So call Harry, and read it to him."

Amy almost agreed, but then she thought of how poorly her last reading had gone, with Sergeant Colostomy. "I'll type it into an e-mail right now. I've got his address."

"Copy me in," said Carla. "And why don't you just scan it and attach the JPEG?"

"Are you serious?"

Amy hung up and got to work. It was unpleasant, typing "Howdy, Amy," and all that followed. She felt like the Sniper's stenographer (idea for a novel title), and wasted a lot of time figuring out how to include those damn footnotes in the body of an e-mail.

At the end of the letter, she wrote, "This is what arrived today. Advice appreciated," and pressed the send button.

All of a sudden she felt almost giddy, as though having successfully accomplished some form of communication was all she had needed to relieve her of the weight of the Sniper's letter, and she grabbed Alphonse's leash off the hook and called to him in the next room. The early day was sunny, the shadows were gone, and a little exertion might help her to nap. "Walkies!" she trilled, in British dog-lady falsetto. Alphonse loathed walkies. "Doughnut!" she called, in a much softer, seductive voice, and there he came, barreling around the corner. Alphonse wasn't really that gullible. Like Pascal, he had decided that faith in a good outcome was, on the whole, the way to go. "Walkies first, you big sap," she said, snapping the leash on his collar, and they were halfway out the door when the phone rang.

"Pick up pick up pick up pick up." Carla keened like a kindergartner. *Pick me pick me pick me!*

Amy picked up. "I'm on my way out. I'll call you back."

"No! Harry's on the line with me and we have to talk!"

It couldn't have been more than ten minutes since she'd sent the e-mail. Carla must have been hovering like a yellow jacket over her virtual mailbox, must have phoned Harry B., who must instantly have read his copy, and together they had managed a miraculous tandem phone call, and for what? The day was new, there was tons of time, and *then* would do just as well as *now*. "Do you ever worry," asked Amy, "that within the next twenty years, the noun *anticipation*, and all its synonyms, will join the ranks of archaic words, like *nonce* and *eftsoons*?"

"She is so cool," said Carla, apparently to Harry B. Why didn't they just talk to each other and leave her out of it? "Tell her," said Carla.

"Hi, Amy," Harry said. "How carefully have you read this letter?"

"Well, I haven't memorized it, if that's what you mean. Carefully enough, I'm sure."

"Assuming that the letter within the letter is accurately rendered—"

"Why would we assume that?" Amy asked. "He didn't enclose the actual letter, Harry. I'm sorry if I didn't make that clear. He 'quotes' from the letter, and quite selectively, too. If you're getting all excited about the fact that the editor asks him if he's 'still with B_____,' I wouldn't get my hopes up. Chuck says Frank wasn't 'with' anybody—his father's still living, in Washington state, and the body is being shipped back up there."

"Yes," said Harry, "but assuming that Frank had girlfriends in the past, it shouldn't be hard to locate them and ask them if they can figure out who "B" is. Once they identify B, they've got a shot at finding the editor who wrote the letter!"

Amy stopped and thought. "Hard for whom? Harry, if we were television detectives, with access to enormous flashing databanks, and we could just plug in a couple of nifty variables—"

"No, sorry, we didn't mean that," said Carla. "Obviously *we* can't do it. But the cops can!"

At this Amy laughed airily. Of course the cops could do this, if one could actually attract their attention. She explained to Carla and Harry about Sergeant C., and *The Runaround, Part Deux.* "I'm sure you're right," she said, "and I can even imagine that some day, perhaps in my lifetime, some cop somewhere will get around to the letter and zero in on its writer, and all that. But right now, I'm going to walk my dog."

"No, no, no!" cried Carla.

Harry B. cleared his throat. "Amy, you're missing the point."
"Which is?"

"That the Sniper is getting sloppy. Or beginning to lose it."

"Think about it," said Carla. "All this time, with the nasty notes and the Bundy mask and all of the rest of it, not one slipup. He's been a regular criminal mastermind, zigging and zagging this way and that."

"And now this letter," said Harry, "which he's tried to modify to protect himself, whereas what he should have done was not tell you anything about it at all."

"Exactly!" said Carla. "Why share this information with you? How is this in his best interest? Well, it's not, except that he really, really wants you to know about him."

Amy dropped the leash and sank down at the telephone table. They were right. She had focused so tightly on the narrative of Frank's death, and the threats to her own well-being and that of Alphonse, that she'd missed this obvious fact. The Sniper had wanted her to know how Frank came to die.

She had no faith that the lit snotrag backstory was factual even in outline, but she did believe that the scene described on that overlook at Moonlight Beach was perfectly honest, at least from the Sniper's point of view. Frank had had something on the Sniper, and had brought it there with him, and had died as a result of the Sniper's miscalculations. The Sniper had not known his own strength—the strength of his own presence, unmasked. He had not realized he was a monster until he saw the truth in Frank's "ridiculous" expression. He probably did not formulate the decision to hurt Frank, let alone to kill him. He was too busy reveling in his own power. All he meant to do—all he thought he meant to do—was . . . "The letter!" Amy cried.

"Right," said Carla. "The letter is a dead giveaway—"

"No, I'm talking about the other letter. The letter Frank brought to the meeting. God, I'm so thick. What happened to it?" She ran to the computer and retrieved the Sniper's note. " 'Then he stood up,' " she read to them, " 'and grabbed the damn letter off the table and backed away from me.' Well, what happened to it?"

Harry said, "Maybe the cops found it on the beach. They might have bagged it and it's sitting on a shelf somewhere."

"There was no letter on the beach," said Amy. "There was nothing on the beach but Frank and me and that awful cell phone. I don't know much, but I know that."

"Well then," said Harry, "it got left at the overlook. Which means that it probably got picked up with the trash."

"Wait!" Carla said. "The hibiscus bush! It's in the hibiscus bush! There could still be scraps left! I'm on it!"

While Harry talked Carla down—there had been solid rain off and on since Frank's death, so the idea of legible scraps was ludicrous—Amy closed her eyes and waited, and as she did a crisp image came to her of the hibiscus bush with Frank's hand sticking out of it like a Christmas ornament. She didn't need to consult the letter to recall the Sniper's last glimpse of Frank: . . . *and then just his hand reaches out toward mine, and time stops.* Only now she could see quite clearly that the hand wasn't empty. There was a letter in it. And just as she knew that the Sniper's description, as far as it went, was accurate, she also knew what had happened to that letter. "You had time to grab his hand," she said. "And instead you grabbed the letter."

"What?"

"I'll call you later," she said. "Leave me alone for now, Carla. I mean it."

Amy and Alphonse walked and walked until he lay down in a parking lot and refused to budge. They were over a mile from home, in a strip mall with a Ralphs and a Staples and a pizza place where, according to the neon slogan, the dough was so fresh that you cooked it yourself. She had succeeded in blistering the balls of both feet but not in putting the genie (that hand, that letter) back in its bottle, and she knew that no matter how long it took her to get back, her house would be no kind of refuge. So she took her time. She gave him ten minutes, and then crooned, "Doughnut," and he lumbered to his feet and trotted out ahead of her, pulling her home. She stopped at a doughnut stand halfway there and bought him a raised glazed. A passing jogger censoriously regarded the tableau this made. Amy glared back and almost tripped the woman.

She had planned to take her time getting home, but as she watched Alphonse lick sugar off the grass she realized that it was already afternoon, and soon the shadows would begin to lengthen. She needed to get inside before that happened.

When they got home, she locked and double-locked, and checked the answering machine, and dragged Alphonse through all the rooms and the garage. No window was left cracked open. She cleaned the house and laundered the bedding and towels and straightened out the kitchen cabinets. She kept moving. Night came quickly anyway, as it always did out here in the West. No twilight, you turned your back once and then you were mugged by this sudden darkness, and then there were endless hours ahead of dark and dark and more dark, and this was going to be a bad one, Amy could tell, because when she switched on all the lights it didn't help one bit. Even with the blinds down and curtains drawn she felt on display, in some diorama: *Frightened Suburban Woman*. She fed Alphonse but could not feed herself, and the wine parched her throat. She tried watching a movie and had to stop, because she couldn't hear past the noise of the television. She tried reading but could not hold so much as a sentence in her mind, so abrupt was every creak and clock tick in the house, so unnatural the sound of her own breathing. When the phone finally rang, as she knew it would, it was a relief.

Private Caller said nothing.

Amy's heart pounded in her ears. Her whole body pulsed as she stood rooted, gripping the phone, waiting for the next thing to happen. Without planning to, she opened her mouth. "You had time to grab his hand," she said, "and instead you grabbed the letter."

Private Caller said nothing.

The pounding stopped like magic. She had amazed herself with the sound of her own voice. She was talking to the Sniper and she wasn't huddled in a ball or shrieking in terror. What she was doing, actually, was writing dialogue, for the first time in years. "You think you're clever, and you're absolutely right, you are," she said. "It's too bad, kid, because you'd be a better writer if you weren't." What next? "You say you take your writing seriously. Tell me, have you figured out yet why you don't get published?" What would happen now? Would he slam down the phone, race over, and chop her up with a meat axe? What the hell, thought Amy. "Because I know you're not published. Not once. I know that much."

There was a tiny gasp from Private Caller.

"And would you like to know why?"

It was actually heartening to hear these fumblings, the dropped receiver, the far-off rummaging—the sound of the Sniper, not in control. Then of course those tape-recorder clicks, and Dot's voice, intoning *Murder most foul*, etc. "Shut that stupid thing off," Amy said. "Right now, or I'm hanging up."

Private Caller shut off the recorder.

Okay, genius, Amy thought. What do I do now? "What I'm going to do now," she said, "if you'll get off the damn phone, is contact everybody in class and decide on a date and time for our next meeting. So you can expect a call from me shortly. Won't that be interesting?" Amy looked at her calendar. "It's short notice, but I don't see offhand why we can't meet this coming Wednesday, at the usual time. We'll meet here at my place. I know you know the way. Don't be late," Amy said. "We'll be discussing your work."

She began dialing just as soon as she hung up. It was already eight thirty, and she had a lot of calls to make.

ninthCLASS
EPIPHANY

Of the ten remaining class members, Carla turned out to be the hardest sell. Though she clearly planned to perpetuate a relationship with Amy, whether Amy wanted it or not, she seemed genuinely shocked at the suggestion of a Last Class. Eventually she allowed that a smaller hand-picked group might be okay—Chuck and Edna and Harry B. and Marvy, but that was all, not even Pete and Ricky, who were really nice guys. "You realize, don't you, that I actually hosted a *murder*? I hate to even walk through my own living room now. I can't sleep without a buttload of Xanax." Amy stood fast. It had to be everybody, and it had to be Wednesday, at her house. In the end, Carla got on board, so enthusiastically that she threatened to capsize the boat. She wanted to arrange for catering and cleanup afterwards, money was "no object," and she'd send up some extra chairs, because Amy's house was, you know, pretty cozy, and besides she didn't want Amy to lift a finger. "Absolutely not," said Amy. "No food, and especially no drinks, unless people want to bring their own. Think about it, Carla. What happened the last time we passed the bottle?" Carla thought about it. "Jesus," she said, "this is serious, isn't it?" Yes, it was.

Carla was right about the "cozyness" of Amy's tiny house: in its present cluttered state, there was no way she could fit eleven people in the living room. Amy basically dwelled in her bedroom and dining area, which she had made into an office. The living room had been for years a way station between the two—a convenient place to drop laundered clothes, shopping bags, junk mail, and all the books that wouldn't fit in her bookcases. Amy spent a full day emptying it of everything but furniture. She piled loose books on the already jammed shelves lining the walls, and when they threatened to break, she moved the rest into what was supposed to be her spare bedroom, a de facto attic (Californians didn't believe in those) that contained table lamps, mirrors, two yet-to-be assembled twin beds and half a truckload of unpacked cartons from her move west with "Bob."

Once she settled into the work, it was almost fun to come across titles she'd forgotten she had—the two-volume history of the world by H. G. Wells, Max's gardening books, the works of Saki, Stephen Leacock, Coppard, and Chesterton. Then there were armfuls of books she had never even opened, written by authors who had once blurbed Amy's books in anticipation of return blurbs from her. Those she glimpsed now as she stacked the piles—promising readers illumination, delight, "unpretentious wit" (whatever the hell that was supposed to mean)—had been, like all her blurbs, carefully written so as to avoid bald-faced lying. The "If . . . then . . ." construction had served her well. *If you long for a languid, sensuous trip down the Ancient Nile, this book is for you!* On the other hand, if you'd rather have your gums scraped than time-travel down a croc-infested river, you should read Flaubert. *For all those readers still mourning the death of the locked room mystery. . . .* She stopped to stare at a somber book jacket for something called *Christmas Tremens.* "A must-read for the adult grandchildren of alcoholics." She had to have qualified this goofy claim in some way, but the publisher had cut her short and she hadn't even noticed. What a lazy, angry writer she had been. They'd stopped asking her for blurbs at some point—probably right after *Christmas Tremens*—but she'd kept all these stupid books, because the blurbs themselves were her only published work since *Fiercer Hell*.

She set aside the mound of blurbage, and when the room had been sufficiently compacted to allow for more overflow from the living room, she carted these books back in there and piled them by the fireplace. Wednesday night was supposed to be cold. She wouldn't have to buy kindling.

On Wednesday morning she signed on to her e-mail account to broadcast directions to her house, and there was something in her inbox from Sniper4758, with an attachment.

> Since we're doing "my work," I thought you should have more. I attach excerpts from my most recent journal entries. Feel free to distribute them to the kiddies, or keep them to yourself. You may treat them either as fact or fiction. I thrive on criticism. Especially from asskissing wannabes. Especially from you you big fat vicious washed-up no-talent bitch

Attached was a rambling document, but with subheadings: one was "The Fat Broad" and the other three were undated diary entries. "The Fat Broad" had apparently been spewed during First Class. Amy caught her breath: only a few class members had brought laptops with them. But as she continued reading, she noticed an increasing number of typos and missing words; by the last page, there was an entire line of alphabet soup, where the Sniper's fingers had been on the wrong keys and he hadn't even noticed, or bothered to correct. This was a transcription, probably typed in one sitting, probably very recently, and the Sniper had become angrier and less controlled with each page, *you big fat vicious washed-up no-talent bitch*. The originals, Amy figured, were handwritten.

Amy now forwarded the Sniper's attachments to the rest of the class (subject line: Last Minute Reading). Then she made enough hard copies to pass around tonight, along with copies of the Sniper's letter.

One hour before class was to begin, Amy started up a fire in the fireplace and sat down in her newly habitable living room with a cup of hot tea. She tried to focus on how she was going to conduct tonight's critique, a problem she'd been putting off ever since throwing down the gauntlet to the Sniper. Her hope was that magically, with the whole class focused on these pages, a coherent portrait of their author might shimmer into common view. Amy had been teaching long enough to have seen something like this actually happen.

A student would submit a piece for class discussion that was shockingly incoherent. The student would have sat quietly through classes, hanging back noticeably reserved but otherwise apparently normal, only to pass out some full-blown psychotic world view for class critique. Madness would rise from the page like swamp gas: nameless characters would begin to connect and then drift askew into rhyme and repetition. There would be eyes and mouths and many jagged edges, and literally nothing to talk about except pathology, and of course Amy couldn't allow that. The first time this happened, she considered calling class members ahead of time, to warn them against being too honest in their responses, but she couldn't think of a way to do this that wouldn't insult their intelligence, and so she approached next class with great dread. But a small miracle happened: One class member talked about the parts she "liked," the characters or metaphors or events that worked for her. When she stopped, another took up the thread of criticism, elaborating about what the first had said, and adding to it, and then another, and another, and gradually the class fabricated a sort of ghost text, woven on the spot from the threads of social desperation, the weave eventually so tight and even that latecomers could jump in gamely and embroider the edges. And when they were done, the crazy guy was actually smiling. He told the class, "You all really got what I was trying to do," went home happy and, to everyone's relief, never returned.

This happened three separate times over the years, and in pretty much the same way. The most striking part of the whole phenomenon was the untouched purity of the ghost text, each contributor laboring alone, with no idea what the literal text meant. United in a common purpose—to propitiate the mad—they were wonderfully, intuitively creative. Unlike the six blind men of Indostan, they could not only describe the elephant from trunk to tail, but will the beast into life right on the spot. Carla had been in one of these classes. "Jeez," she had said privately to Amy, after class was over, "I must be an idiot. Everybody understood that piece but me! Between you and I," she had whispered, "I was just winging it."

Winging it: the key to creative inspiration. Maybe what writers really needed wasn't encouragement, mentoring, or even stern deadlines, but immediate, ratcheting anxiety. Make something up and make it work, or you'll be sorry. Perhaps tonight they could do the same thing with the real Sniper text—the narrative behind these hateful scraps and wadded-up spitballs. And then what? Amy had no idea.

Syl and Pete were the first to arrive, standing green and somber beneath her porch light, Syl with his collar turned up like Sam Spade. "Mind if I look around the back?" he asked.

"Sure, but what for? The only thing you're going to find is—" Syl had disappeared around the corner. "Dog poop," she said to Pete Purvis. "Did you two come together?" They both lived in La Mesa and sometimes shared rides.

"I wanted to, but he wasn't up for it. I think he's kind of paranoid." Amy led him into the living room. "Wow," said Pete. "Look at all those books." He walked over to the bookcases and began to check out her library, running his fingertips lightly over the spines. "You've got *Once and Future King*," he exclaimed. "I love that book!"

"You love books, period. I can tell by the way you touch them." He was a sweet boy, even younger up close than sitting in class, and there was no way he could deliberately hurt anybody. Pete had been tough to convince about Last Class, because of Dot. I just don't have the heart for any more of this, he had told her, and she thought, Good for you. But she'd leaned on him anyway, and here he was, thumbing through her ancient inherited copy of *Girl of the Limberlost*.

Syl banged on the back door. "It's clear," he said.

"Clear of what, Syl? What were you looking for?"

Syl shucked his coat onto Amy's computer chair. "You never know," he said. "He could have gotten here early. Ahead of the pack."

"Like you?" asked Amy, and was heartened to hear Pete laugh. Outside her front windows she could see the other cars arriving, as if in deliberate caravan or funeral cortege. She stepped out onto her porch and counted them. Ten people, ten cars: nobody trusted anybody. Across and down the street her neighbors came to their windows. Amy never had visitors, and now she had a parade of them, parking halfway up the hill, scurrying silently toward her in the dark. She found herself wishing she could have cooked for them, picked out wine and beer—planned for a bright evening, as she had once done with Max, in the days their house was full of funny, odd people, all with appetites and stories to tell. In those days, she had never stopped to feel affection for any of them (except for Max); she was too busy trying to top her previous menu or steer conversation or arrange meetings between potential couples— what Max called introducing Tab A to Slot B.

She was gripped now, if not by affection, at least by a rush of sentiment. She didn't want the Sniper to be any of these people, not even Dr. Creepy Surtees, who had gone up a tick in Amy's estimation when he played that stupid pizza joke on Carla. Sure, he was an arrogant jackass, but not too arrogant for a Prince-Albert-in-the-Can moment with his new public-golf-course buddies. And not Harry B., walking thoughtfully behind Tiffany, taking care not to come abreast and spook her. Tiffany's shoulders were rounded, her arms folded tightly in a shield, and she walked with her head down, an anxious child on her way to catechism. Ricky walked beside her without speaking, and in back of this pack was Chuck, and behind him was Marvy, and someone else. He'd brought his wife, whom Amy hadn't seen since the night of the Halloween masks. Carla, bringing up the rear, caught up with them and started chatting with Mrs. Marvy, who was apparently beyond suspicion. Amy couldn't think why.

When she'd gotten them seated there was a long, incredibly awkward pause, broken, of course, by Carla. "Here's the plan," she said.

What had Amy ever done without Carla and her plans? Tonight, Amy was winging it, and up stepped Carla with a plan.

"You know how on First Class we always go around the room and introduce ourselves? Well, we'll go around the room now and explain why we're not the Sniper. I'll go first." She waited for somebody—Amy—to object, but no one did. "Okay," she said. And after awhile, "I'm blanking here."

"Just start the sentence," suggested Amy, "and see what happens. This is how we write."

"But we're not writing now," said Marvy. "This is real."

"Doesn't mean we're not writing," said Amy. "You know how I'm always trying to get you people to think about the difference between fiction and reality? Now is as good a time as any to take that question seriously." Amy snapped her fingers twice. "Come on, people."

"I'm not the Sniper," said Carla, "because . . . I'm not an angry person. The Sniper is the angriest person in the universe. I haven't lost my temper since eighth grade. Plus if I were going to kill any-body, it'd be Ma."

"Why is it good," asked Ricky, "that you haven't lost your tem-per since eighth grade? That sounds dangerous."

"And *you're* not the Sniper because . . . ," said Amy.

"Because I'm not a creative writer. No, it's true," said Ricky, as though someone had rushed to contradict him. "I took this class because I write for a living, and I thought it would be supereasy for me, being a pro and all. But my fiction sucks. The Sniper is a real writer," he said.

"You haven't written enough," said Edna, "to know whether or not you suck. Also, should you be the Sniper, you might be affect-ing amateur status in class." Edna, regarding Ricky kindly, clearly didn't think this was likely. She turned to address everyone else. "I'm not the Sniper, because I'm old." This time, people did protest, but she waved them away. "I'm in reasonably good shape for my age, but still, I can't be running around in the dark with house-plants and masks, pushing people off cliffs."

"My husband is not the Sniper," announced Mrs. Marvy. "He was home with me when Frank died, and then after that woman died, he came home and stayed in bed all the next day." Marvy was tugging on her sleeve like a little boy, trying to speak up for himself, but she ignored him. Mrs. Marvy (Cindy, Amy remem-bered now) was indignant: the game, pleasant gal who had come to sixth class in Bozo the Clown getup was here to protect her man, not so much from the Sniper as from Amy and the others. ". . . the very idea," she was saying, "means that you don't know my husband at all. It's bad enough that he had to go through this stuff, these deaths, but this is the last straw! To be put un-der suspicion, as though he were anything but an innocent victim—"

Harry B. cut her off. "He's not being treated any differently from the rest of us," he said.

"I tried to explain that," said Marvy. He leaned toward Amy and whispered, "She's just very upset."

"Who else isn't the Sniper?" asked Chuck.

"Me," said Syl.

"Me neither," said Pete. "And here's why."

"Wait a minute," said Carla. "Syl can't get away with that. You have to give a reason."

Syl rummaged through the papers he'd rolled in his jacket pocket. It took him awhile to scan through them and find what he was looking for. "This is from that thing you sent out today. 'Well.'" he read slowly, stumbling over many words, "'I wrote them a letter, and then I tore it up and wrote them another, and then another, and the letters got longer and longer, and I tore them all up. I tried high dudgeon, I tried low dudgeon, I tried blasphemy, profanity, and scatology, separately and at once.'" Syl looked up. "I'm not dumb, and this is just, what, three sentences, and you can't even understand them. There's four words here that nobody knows what they mean, or maybe they do, but not me. What's a dudgeon? I hate this kind of shit." Syl was getting as worked up as Mrs. Marvy. "This is the way people write when they want to make you feel stupid."

"Syl," said Pete, "nobody wants you to feel stupid."

"I think you may be wrong," said Amy, delighted. "Actually, Syl's on to something."

"And you're what—surprised?" asked Syl, quite steamed.

Amy regarded Syl directly, giving him her full attention, realizing that she hadn't done this before. None of them had. "I'm pleased," she said. "What you just did is what I've been trying to get you to do all semester—read with your own eyes, listen with your own ears. That was a genuine critical response to the reading, Syl."

"Hear, hear," said Dr. Surtees, clapping a hand on Syl's shoulder. "And while we're at it, I'm not the Sniper, either. I'm much too busy. I have a full practice, a busy social life—my wife sees to that—and in my off-moments, during the last nine weeks, I've re-vised two thirds of *Code Black*." He reached into his briefcase and drew out a manuscript which looked to have doubled in size.

"That doesn't prove anything," said Tiffany.

Harry B. spoke up. "None of what's been said—nothing anyone could say tonight—*proves* anything one way or the other. That's not the point."

"Well then, what *is* the point?" asked Cindy Stokes. "I mean this is ridiculous."

"The point is," said Amy, "that everyone in this room, with the exception of you, wants to be a writer." Cindy wasn't helping. "Some want it more than others, but everyone who comes to a writing workshop believes that he has a story worth telling: that he knows something that no one else knows or will ever know, unless he tells that story and does it right. The Sniper is one of us. The Sniper, like the rest of us, wants to be taken seriously."

"And that's what we're doing tonight," said Chuck.

"Why aren't you the Sniper, Chuck?" asked Amy.

Chuck looked away, toward the dark fireplace. "Why don't we have a fire."

"Not until you've—"

"A fine idea," said Amy. She watched Chuck arrange five small logs just so, allowing just the right vertical and horizontal space between them to nurture the flames. When he asked for kindling, Amy pointed to the blurbage.

"No!" shouted Carla and Tiffany at once. "Are those your books? You're burning your own books?" Carla looked for a moment as though she were about to throw herself in the flames ahead of the books; then her expression shifted radically, as though she were about to say "Cool!" Either she winked at Amy or she experienced some facial tic. Carla must be on something tonight. Tiffany was just horrified, jolted out of whatever lugubrious state she had ar-rived in.

Amy assured them that the books were not her own and explained about the blurbs. "This isn't tragic," she told Tiffany. "I'm cleaning house. As you may have noticed, I don't do that very often."

"But it's a sin," said Pete, "to burn a book."

"Pete, this is not the Reichstag fire. Look at these titles. Read them and weep."

Cindy Stokes thought she'd read something by the author of the Nefertiti whodunit, but when pressed admitted that it couldn't have been very good or she'd remember it for sure.

"But they're *books*," said Pete. "How can you do this to *books*? Don't you love them?" Pete looked like he was going to cry, if not soon, then later on tonight, when he was alone. Pete Purvis was a melancholy boy. Amy was willing to bet that his best friends were girls, smart girls, but that he'd never had a girlfriend in his life. If he didn't move out on his own, away from home, he'd become a middle-aged boy and then an old boy. Or was she just making him up? "How would you like it," he asked her now, "if someone burned *your* books?"

"Here's the thing," said Chuck. "You can't just set them on fire. First, you'd have to take the covers off, because they're full of toxins, and you don't want to gag everybody. Plus they'll really gunk up your flue. And if you try to light the book as is, it won't catch, because there's no air between the pages. What you could do," he continued, taking *The Marchpane Cicatrix* off the top of the pile and laying it out flat on the hearth, "is rip them out a few at a—"

"Stop!" Marvy's voice now joined in the chorus, and she thought she heard Harry B. as well. Did the majority rule here? How sentimental they all were about the printed word. If Amy ever taught again, she would devote an entire class to the journey of a novel from Platonic ideal to its shimmering manifestation, first in the subconscious and then the right frontal lobe, then in notebooks or computer screens, then in manuscript copy, in proofs, in hard cover and soft, on retail and library shelves, on remainder tables and in bins, and ultimately, with the exception of a handful of copies whose accidental survival would give them spurious value, in the great maw of the pulping machine.

"Surely," said Dr. Surtees, "we are all united here in our love of the printed word."

Oh, you ass, thought Amy, and was about to squash him flat when Ricky Buzza saved her the trouble.

"Hey, you all recycle your newspapers, right? Well, those are full of printed words, and some of them are mine. I don't see any of you getting all worked up about that."

"Newspapers," said Edna, "are designed to be ephemeral. Books are not."

Amy remembered that on the night of First Class she had inadvertently banded them together in shared enjoyment at her awkwardness with names, her mispronunciations and misapprehensions, the slapstick of the wobbly fan in the back of the classroom and the deafening silence when she'd had the thing turned off. She had known then that this would be a good group; and here, after all they'd been through, they were reunited now, armed against her and her Philistine book-burning ways. She would miss them. It was nice to forget, just for the moment, why they were all gathered here.

She sighed and told Chuck to put the book back in the pile, and sent Syl to the store room for some newspapers. Everybody leaned back in relief. But Amy was on a roll. She would have none of that. "When they pulp them," she said, "they wash them with caustic soda. It's called 'de-inking.'"

"That's terrible."

"For God's sake," said Amy, "they're not boiling puppies."

On cue, Syl returned with a stack of the *North County Times* and Alphonse, who had been so quiet in the back of the house that Amy had forgotten about him. Everyone exclaimed over him, as he nosed happily among their feet, purses, and backpacks. People meant food. Alphonse loved people. Amy grabbed him by the collar and began to drag him away, to a chorus of protests. They all liked dogs, probably more than they liked Amy at this moment, except that one of them did not, and she couldn't be watching him all the time. The Sniper could slip him poison in a hunk of cheese, hamburger, brownie (she'd imagined them all), and she couldn't trust the rest of them to watch him every minute.

"They wash what used to be the books with caustic soda and ash," Amy continued, taking her seat, "and after a while the ink lifts off and floats to the top like black silk. And is sluiced down the drain. They recycle the paper, but not the ink. This is what happens," she said, looking straight at Dr. Surtees, "to all our wonderful words."

"And you know this how?" asked Harry B.

She knew, because when her last book got remaindered, her publisher offered her five hundred copies at a buck apiece. It was either that or the pulp machine. "I told them to pulp them, as long as I could watch." Edna said that must have been distressing. "They pulp them at a factory in Newark. It was instructive," said Amy. "It smelled awful."

For a long minute they all listened to the crackle of the fire Chuck and Syl had made, and the impatient clicking of Alphonse's nails behind the closed door. Into this silence, Carla rose and advanced on the fireplace, holding out a copy of the Sniper's manuscript. What on earth was she doing?

"So what you're saying," said Chuck, "is that even if hell freezes over and we get published, in the end it's pointless, because—"

Carla smiled at Amy, as if sharing some private joke, and chucked the manuscript onto the log pile, where it flared up instantly and began to curl into ash. Then, very much on stage, she turned and faced the class. "It will hurt like hell," she said, "and the burning will take forever." She peered at her audience, panning deliberately from face to face. Everyone regarded her with identical expressions of alarm, and no wonder. Carla seemed to hold her breath for a minute and then slumped a little. "Oh, well," she said, "it was worth a try."

As she resumed her seat, Chuck wondered, on behalf of the group, exactly *what* was worth a try. "I guess it won't hurt to tell you," Carla said, glancing at Amy for verification. Amy kept her own expression blank, while she tried to imagine what Carla was up to. "You all know that the Sniper wrote a mean parody of my poem, the one I read in Second Class, but only Amy, me, and one other person here knows what it says." She extracted a wrinkled sheet of paper from her backpack and cleared her throat. "The wood must be seasoned," she read,

> *Or all bets are off*
> *Unseasoned wood is green and wet*
> *Bark clings to it like a hanger-on*
> *(votary, bootlicker, sycophant, toady)*
>
> *Bottom line,*
> *Kiddo,*
> *A whole lotta steam*
> *A whole lotta nothing*
> *And in the end*
> *It just won't stay lit*
>
> *It'll hurt like hell*
>
> *And the burning will take forever*

"And then he added, at the bottom, 'you could try kindling . . . manuscript paper might work!' When you started on the book-burning thing, I almost didn't get what you were doing," she said to Amy, rolling her eyes at her own lack of acuity. "But then, of course, I got it. It was a great idea!"

Chuck didn't think so. "Did you honestly think that the Sniper would lunge into the fire after a bunch of Xerox copies?"

"Well, as Carla said, I thought it was worth a try. I was looking for what they call a tell." This was pretty ironic, as anyone who actually played poker would know Amy wasn't doing anything of the kind. She'd completely forgotten the poem until now. She'd read it through only a couple of times and filed away in memory its nasty tone without holding on to its content. The kindling idea had been her own, a coincidence. At least she thought so.

"And?" Chuck seemed genuinely cross.

"And, to get back to what we were saying, one of the instructive differences between fiction and real life is that in real life the curtain only comes down once, and almost never when it should. Of course it's lovely to get published, especially the first time: to get that acceptance letter, that formal, you should pardon the expression, validation; to watch the book take form and color; to hold it in your hands.

"But there's no space break in the real world. Life goes on. The thing sells or doesn't, gets reviewed or not, lasts one year or twenty. You become a better writer or you don't, you keep writing or you stop. Chances are excellent you'll live long enough to be out of print but not long enough to know if what you wrote was any good. All you can be sure of is that it's an artifact, like an hourglass or an arrowhead, and just about as likely as any other artifact to be stumbled across and appreciated. Or totally misunderstood. Robert Nathan wrote this terrific book—"

"We understand," said Carla, getting her second wind. "You're pretending to talk to all of us, but you're really talking to the Sniper."

Actually, no, but judging from the sullen faces before her, this was as good a time as any to switch gears. "Who wants to start?" she asked. She reached underneath the pile of blurbage and pulled out the Sniper's work, paper-clipped as neatly as any other student manuscript. She scanned their faces as she did this: she *had* placed it there, in the mound of kindling, as a deliberate insult. But the insult paled in comparison to Carla's dramatic gesture, and of course they were all busy dutifully retrieving their own printouts. There were no *tells*.

"We need to talk about the dominant male thing," said Chuck. "It's interesting."

"I don't get it," said Syl.

"The Sniper is threatened by Amy," said Edna, "and sees her as a dominant male, which implies, to me, that the Sniper wants to challenge for dominance."

"It's so typical," said Tiffany, roused, at least momentarily, from her funk. "If she's a threat, then she must be essentially male."

"That's assuming that the Sniper is a guy," said Harry B., "which, as I recall, is exactly what you don't want us to do."

"Thank you so much for reminding me." Tiffany leaned forward as if about to stand up and then slumped back in her seat. "I need to say something. I haven't slept since the night Dot died. I keep hearing my own ugly voice in my head, taunting her. I was so angry at Dot, and that's no excuse, but she just pushed all my buttons, and she was a sweet woman, I know that, and I'm just a hopeless bitch."

Amy promised herself that if she and Tiffany remained in touch, she would tell her some day about her own final conversation with Dot, who was anything but a sweet woman, at least not by the time she died. Right this minute, though, she felt no need to reassure Tiffany, who thought she knew just how tiresome she was being right now, and who was wrong about that. Tiffany felt bad, all right, but there was a smidgen of pleasure in this exploration of her own guilt. She was on stage now, and where there's drama, there's crap. As Dot would say, Tiffany didn't know shit.

"Anyway," said Chuck, "the Sniper's first encounter with the group, with Amy, and she's this dominant lowland gorilla. What's up with that?"

"Baboon," said Harry B.

" 'Terrible baboon god,' " quoted Ricky.

"Actually," said Pete Purvis, "that's pretty good."

"I must agree," said Amy, "since the phrase apparently res-onated with most of you. Now, I'm going to throw out a question that under normal circumstances I would never ask. Is this person a good writer?"

"Just wondering," said Marvy, "but why would you never ask this question?" Marvy's face was guarded. His wife nodded, as if to encourage him.

"Because in all the years I've taught, I've never once had a stu-dent ask me, publicly or privately, if he was a good writer. They'll ask about their chances of getting published, but never if they're worth publishing. No one wants to hear the answer to that ques-tion. *I* certainly don't."

Carla said, "It's like, 'Do these pants make me look fat?' "

Nobody said anything, probably because Carla was wearing wide-ribbed Christmas-red stretch pants, and besides, people asked *that* sort of question all the time.

Dr. Surtees cleared his throat and thumbed ostentatiously through the Sniper's pages. "He obviously knows his way around a sentence," he said.

"What the hell does that mean?" Ricky might have still been chafing about the doctor's professed adoration of everything in print, or maybe he was worried about Tiffany, or even fed up with her. "He uses ten-dollar words. He's in love with his own verbal smarts. Listen to this: 'I might as well have wished for the moon; for despite an early flurry of promises from *The Atlantic*, from *Harper's*, blah, blah, blah . . . despite tantalizing, eyelash-batting, come-hither, personally composed, and actually hand-signed re-jection letters, recounting agonized blah blah blah,' I mean, come on, it's precious as hell. Number one, I don't believe this guy just barely lost out to Updike, whales or no whales. I don't believe he was ever considered seriously in the first place. He's just jerking off here. Pardon my language."

This was great—a direct hit, and the Sniper must be outraged. Amy scanned their faces intently, but except for Ricky himself, who was really exercised, they all wore the same closed-off expressions as Marvy. When one spoke, they looked at the speaker, but not at her. They were, she slowly realized, closed off to *her*. What had she done? She had to get them back.

"Or how about here," said Marvy, "where he tells about Frank's death. The description is spooky and you can really see it in your head, Frank blending in with the leaves and flowers."

"It's horrible," said his wife.

"Yeah, but what I mean is, it's too horrible. I mean it's perfect. Is that what you mean by 'precious'?" he asked Ricky. "I mean, if I killed somebody and then tried to write about it, I'd be all over the place." Nobody said, Yes, but you're not a writer.

Chuck poked the fire, causing the thinnest avocado log to roll off and rest against the spark screen. While he located the right fireplace tool to pick it up with, the class watched silently. There was something about a fire. During that last Augusta winter, when Max got too weak to stand easily, Amy took over this chore, and noted that gatherings always hushed while she attended to it. There was something primal about this shared attention, this impersonal automatic focus that transcended intellect and age and station in life. Writers and grad students and their toddlers and "Bob" would watch intently, their heads idly swiveling as one. We are hard-wired for it, Amy decided; and when Max stopped watching, she knew he was pulling away for good. There was a story in it somewhere. Fire-watchers.

"Let's talk," Amy said, "about authorial intent."

"Where's the bathroom?" asked Syl.

The bathroom was in the closed-off part of the house, with Alphonse, which posed a problem Amy hadn't considered. She couldn't very well walk Syl to the bathroom. It would be socially odd. Amy had always been fascinated with the equivalence between risking one's life and risking social suicide. She had once kept a file on real life people who had literally died to avoid embarrassment, like the man who wouldn't take his pants off in public even though they were on fire. Surely his was not a heroic death, and yet she couldn't help respecting his choice. Syl opened the hallway door and Alphonse once again plunged into the room, resuming his earlier quest. What to do? "Doughnut," she whispered, luring him first into the kitchen, where she gathered up half a loaf of stale bread and then broadcast the slices out into the backyard, slamming the door behind him. He wouldn't like it out there, but he'd be safe, and it was easier to explain than walking Syl or anyone else to the bathroom.

"Here's what strikes me," said Harry B., "about the Sniper's writing. Some of this is private stuff, a journal or diary, and some of it is communication, with you, with the group. But there's no difference in what you call the "voice," is there? It's all the same. My point is, he always writes as if somebody's going to read it."

"Is this part of a critique," asked Amy, "or are you playing detective? What we're doing here is assessing the work, not trying to identify the writer."

Harry looked confused. This was not the way to get them back. She was way off her stride, she was losing them; this would have been a bad teaching night even if lives hadn't hung in the balance. Book-burning had been a horrible idea, along with the forced march to the pulping machine. "Sorry," Harry said, "I didn't make myself clear. I think I'm on the same page as Ricky. This is showoffy stuff, from beginning to end. Even when he's all alone, writing for himself, he's showing off."

For a while the class argued with Harry, Ricky, and Syl, who were united in their disdain for the Sniper's talent. Alphonse interrupted at regular intervals, woofing deeply at the back door, and

Amy, worried about upsetting the neighbors, was about to let him in when he finally settled down. Carla defended the parody of her own poem, saying that there was "truth" in it, because the original poem was pretty lame. Marvy was impressed by the Sniper's ability to sound "educated and flowery" in the journals and letters and like a high school thug when ripping on Marvy's own story. Chuck surprised Amy by praising his description of Frank's last moments in the hibiscus bush. "I know, this is going to sound cold. But that's a great scene."

Chuck was right: it did sound pretty cold, and Amy was reminded right then that Chuck had never explained why he wasn't the Sniper. He'd just changed the subject. The only piece Chuck had ever submitted to the group was that in-class exercise he did during second class. Point-of-view female. "The Sniper," said Amy, "is a gifted mimic. A chameleon, and while that's a helpful talent to have, it's a minor one. Helpful in the sense that you might create minor characters, what Forster called flat characters, with ease, but of no help at all in creating one with depth."

The mere mention of Forster, whom Amy revered, put the kibosh on what little energy the group had managed to recover. They were mugged by torpor, and in the ensuing silence the firewood popped, lobbing a spark over the top of the screen. Amy, only a few feet away, sat still and watched it burn a hole the diameter of a pencil eraser in the carpet she and Max had picked out at Jordan Marsh and which she had made some effort, over the years, to keep in decent condition. It was a good wool rug in the Aubusson style, and Amy had loved it right away and prevailed upon Max to buy it with her, even though he hated blue. "It's a *warm* blue," she had claimed, to the nodding enthusiasm of the salesman, and Max had continued to twit her with this phrase for years. She'd be chatting or refilling drinks and she'd hear, "Yes, but it's a *warm* blue," to a new conquest, or somebody's wife or husband. She'd lugged it all the way to California, she'd tended to it while everything else in the house slipped beneath archeological layers of dust, and now she just watched it burn.

And so did they. Thanks to her ineptitude, not one of them gave a damn. First she'd bullied them into coming, then did this foolish tough-love thing in class, and now they were too defeated, confused, and bored to stir. It was over. When she suggested they call it a night, not one of them argued with her. Not even Carla.

I'm sorry, she almost said, as they roused themselves and began to gather their stuff together, for dragging you all the way out here for nothing, but she didn't trust her own voice, and Edna saved her from it, leaning close and saying, "This was a good idea," as though she could read Amy's mind. Could they all? Was she really that pathetic?

"Yes, it was," said Pete. "I didn't think so in the beginning, but I'm glad we all got together again. I'm really gonna miss you guys."

"No, you won't," said Carla, "because there's no way this is the last class." She was wrong, but Amy was not about to argue with her. She wanted them all out as quickly as possible. All the while she had planned for this evening, she had dreaded its close, the fear which was sure to follow. The only thing she was afraid of now was bursting into tears in front of them. Amy, who never cried, was undone—by a tiny burn hole; by the echo of her own foolish, droning voice; by the feeble fellowship of kind souls (all but one) in her cheerless little house. "Can we see that basset again?" asked Carla. "Just once?"

Anything to get her out of there, and Amy grabbed the leash from its hook. She'd keep him right by her, where he'd be safe. She opened the back door and scanned the yard. "Come on in," she yelled. Amy never called him by name; they were too close for that. She listened for the jingle of his collar in the dark, but nothing. "Doughnut!" she announced, and when he didn't come, she said it again. She'd never had to repeat this magic word. Something was wrong.

The back floodlight had burned out long ago, and it took her forever to find a working flashlight. Carla asked her what was going on, but she ignored her as she hunted through every kitchen drawer for batteries, and by then they had all caught on, and they spilled out into the backyard with her, calling his name. He didn't know his name. He was the Great I Am. *Doughnut*, yelled Carla, and Ricky, and Tiffany, they were chorusing the secret word, *Doughnut, here boy, Doughnut*. She played the light over the overgrown shrubs and eucalyptus that lined the fence, where Alphonse went to do his business and check out passersby.

Everybody in the neighborhood knew Alphonse, and half of them fed him treats—why else would he bother hanging around the fence?—so why hadn't she seen the danger? The Sniper must have set it up before class, before they even came to her house, while they were walking down the hill, yes, the bastard had tossed a poisoned tidbit over the chain-link, and just waited. A perfect setup: simplicity itself. What difference would it make whether he ate it tonight or tomorrow? Sooner or later, he'd find it. The Sniper was like God the Clock winder, he didn't have to see the looks on people's faces when they opened up obscene boxfuls of teeth, or witness that poor nameless woman jumping out a window. He didn't need to see her good dog convulsing in agony. It was enough to set the gears in motion, and she'd been crazy to hold this class, and she'd gotten Alphonse murdered.

Chuck grabbed the flashlight from her hand and climbed into the oleander, along with Carla and Pete. She watched the light dart back and forth over the leaves and dirt like a hound on the scent, her own stalwart hound, and listened to them calling to each other and stumbling over roots and sprinkler heads, and waited for the silence that would come when they found him. "I don't think he's here," said Chuck.

Of course he was there, but she needed to find him herself. It was the least she could do. She was competent enough to find a dead dog in her own backyard. In the dark, someone took her arm. "Amy, I'm so sorry," said Syl.

"Don't worry about it," said Amy. "Everybody! Come down from there, you're going to hurt yourselves. Sorry for the bum's rush, but it's time to go home."

"Come on, Marvy," said Cindy Stokes.

"Amy, listen," said Syl.

"There's no way we're going to leave you alone now," Carla said, and Amy feared this was true. She was frantic now with the need to be alone.

Edna emerged from the dark, brushing leaf debris off her jacket. "What would you like us to do?" she asked Amy.

Amy made sure she could trust her voice, and then opened her mouth to tell them to please leave, when, from far away, she heard a low unmistakable woof, and then another.

"Amy," said Syl, "I messed up. I left the gate open earlier, when I was looking around."

And sure enough he had, wide open, and the fact that Alphonse was still alive was all that kept her from screaming at him. *Get out, you idiot, all of you, get away from me.*

"We'll help you get him," said Chuck.

"No, you won't." Amy took the flashlight from him; she was herself again. "If you want to help," she said, "you'll leave now. I know the neighborhood; I can find him myself. I'll be in touch with you tomorrow."

"I'm sorry," said Syl.

Amy was the one who owed apologies, but they'd need to come later, if at all. "I'll see you all out," she said.

And she did. She stood on her front porch and counted heads as they walked back uphill to their cars, Cindy berating her poor husband ("Well, that was a lot of fun!") and not bothering to lower her voice, and counted the cars as they drove away. When the rear lights from the tenth car disappeared around the corner, she locked up front and back and set out to get Alphonse.

Over their seven years together, he'd escaped twice, both times ending up in the Hallorans' backyard, jumping down into it from a two-foot-high rock wall and then, unable to make the climb out, standing still and barking his head off until somebody let him out. The Hallorans were old and deaf, which was a good thing given the lateness of the hour and the fact that she had to trespass on their property in order to rescue him. There he was in the moonlight, stoically waiting, neither surprised nor especially grateful to see her, but at least he shut up. She grabbed his hindquarters and boosted him up the wall, and together they walked back home. On the way she felt nothing but the chill night air, and she grasped the moment tightly, singing him the basset hound song.

She'd be all right for the night, she thought, as she deadbolted the front door. Tomorrow morning she'd scout out the backyard before letting him out. How she'd actually manage this—literally turning over every leaf on the ground—would just have to wait until then, along with trying to make sense out of the evening. Determined not to think and again court the anxiety that had assaulted her just a half hour ago, she poured herself a deep glass of wine to achieve just this end, knocking it back as she straightened up the living room chairs, and pouring out another. "Go to bed, you boob," she told Alphonse, who kept tripping her up, sniffing out circuitous paths on the ruined carpet. Half the class must have pets at home, and now he browsed methodically through the room, each trail as packed with information as a library shelf. She should have people over more often—more often, anyway, than once every twenty years.

She'd shooed them out in such a hurry that they'd left stuff behind: three copies of the Sniper's manuscript remained on the coffee table. There were no names on any of them, and they were hardly marked up at all. Amy sat down on the couch and gathered them up into a pile to be tossed away, and as she shuffled through them one last time she noticed, in the middle of the pile, a sheet of paper that didn't fit—it was just slightly longer and wider than the other sheets, and whiter, too. She grasped the edge between her nails and pulled it out, that ugly drawing of Edna, naked: the original, in pen and ink, that had been photocopied and inserted into one of the student copies of her story at the end of Fourth Class. Had the Sniper seen her slip it out when Edna wasn't looking, crumple it up, and throw it away? It was the only part of the Sniper's oeuvre that she had left out of tonight's discussion, so of course he'd left it for her, as a kind of reproach.

Quickly she flipped it over, but there was no blinking away the proof that the Sniper had, in fact, been in her house, which of course she knew, that was the whole idea, except that she hadn't really faced it until now, and then, from beneath the cushion on which she sat, came the opening measures of "Memories," from *Cats*, apparently played by a music box on steroids. She lifted the cushion to find a tangerine-colored cell phone which, when she flipped it open, sported a picture of Betty Boop and the dialing number "Pay Phone." At least it wasn't Private Caller. She put it to her ear and listened.

"Who is this?" asked Carla.

Amy stared at the phone in her hand, then held it to her ear again. She heard Carla announce, "They're not saying."

"Carla? What's going on?"

"Amy? Oh my god! It was at Amy's house! Oh, I'm so sorry!"

"What's at my house?"

"My phone!"

Amy hung up and, without allowing a conscious thought, drained her glass. Amy had never done well with sensory overload and did not plan, at this stage of her life, to learn how. The sight of Edna degraded, the echo of that stupid song, Carla's non sequiturs, all instantly evoked competing emotions. Dread, confusion, amusement, fatigue bobbed around her head like circus balloons. *What was at her house?* If I have one more glass of wine, she told herself, I won't give a damn.

The phone went off again, only because she couldn't figure out how to silence it. "We got dropped," said Carla. "Listen, what happened was, I lost my phone and I figured I must have put it in the wrong bag or something, so I was calling to find out who had it, but I never stopped to think it might be you, but since it is, would it be okay if I just swung by to pick it up?" Swung by from La Jolla in the middle of the night? She should be home, or almost home, by now. "I'm not far away, it'll only take a couple of minutes."

"Where are you?"

"Applebees. Harry and Edna and me ended up here, because we were worried about you."

"And people who worry about me go to Applebees?" Amy sat very still and tried to think. "Whose idea was this?" she asked.

"You mean Applebees, or calling you? Well, actually, they were both my idea, and I wasn't really calling you, I was calling the phone." In the background, Harry B. said, *An interesting distinction.*

Maybe, thought Amy, you were doing both. Maybe you knew where the phone was, because you left it here on purpose. This thought was both seductive and sickening, and all at once she wanted more than anything to let Carla in, to see her as she was, not as that annoying-but-lovable cluster of behaviors, but as the mysterious, unknowable creature she must be, because she was not a cartoon, and Amy should have known that. But she mustn't be alone with her.

"I know what you're thinking!" said Carla. "And I'm way ahead of you! We'll come together, in a bunch—right, guys? So you won't be alone. With, you know, anybody. Well, me." She laughed, either appropriately or inappropriately.

"Put Edna on the phone."

For the second time that evening, Edna asked, "What would you like us to do?" What a refreshing question.

"I'd like you to come back, of course."

"We won't even come in!" yelled Carla. "We'll just stand on the stoop!"

Amy assured her that this wasn't necessary. She had just opened a bottle of cabernet, and they were welcome to join her.

"Righto," said Edna. Carla added that this was "incredibly cool."

It was close to midnight by the time they'd settled in before the dying fire, Carla and Edna on the couch, Amy pillowed on the floor, with Alphonse. Harry B., Carla said, had to run to Kinko's, and would be along in a minute. Amy was neither completely sober nor in the bag, and she measured her sips to maintain just this level of Dutch courage: enough to keep the jeebies at bay, not enough to make her reckless. Carla pointed out to Edna the bookshelves Amy had fixed to the wall near the ceiling. "She can't even bear to throw out junky old paperbacks," she told Edna. "Which was my first clue about that book-burning stunt." She was proud to show Edna that she'd been here before, that she was familiar with the place. Her color was high, and she was perspiring, although even with the fire the house was none too warm.

Edna asked Amy how long she'd had Alphonse, and before Amy could answer, Carla said, "Eleven years." Amy and Edna exchanged glances. Amy must have told Carla this at some point, but why would she commit such an inconsequential fact to memory? Then again, she'd done this sort of thing before.

Amy tried to steer the conversation away from herself, her house, her dog, into a rehash of the evening's events and non-events, but Carla would not settle down. Why had Amy moved out to California, and who was her second husband, and what was she working on now?

"Nothing," Amy finally said, in exasperation. "I haven't written anything in years." Carla demanded, on behalf of a heartbroken reading public, to know why. "Because I have nothing to say. When you have nothing to say, you should keep quiet."

"Precisely," said Edna.

"He died, didn't he?" asked Carla. "Your first husband. That must have been so awful. And then . . . you never wrote again."

"Carla, what is wrong with you?"

Carla giggled and lowered her eyes. "Oh, man," she said, and began to fiddle with a loose thread in her red stretch pants, yanking on it until a dime-sized hole blossomed on her thigh. "Do you have any nail polish?" she asked.

The two adult women in the room now regarded Carla closely, neither of them making any attempt to hide her frank inspection. Amy tried to remember everything she knew about Carla—her childhood, her various short-lived careers, her bright, histrionic poetry—and imagine that behind all the drama and jollitude lurked the Sniper's ruthless persona. It made no sense, unless, like Norman Bates, she somehow *became* the Sniper from time to time, and that was just silly—but no sillier than her present, out-of-the-blue behavior, which went far beyond irrepressible and off into the realm of full-blown mania. Amy wished she hadn't thought of Norman Bates, because now she recollected her brief in-person encounter with Mother Massengill, at the beginning of Sixth Class. Amy had spoken to her, she was pretty sure, but had the old battle-axe answered? Still, she'd definitely moved; she wasn't stuffed. On the other hand, Amy had only heard the woman's voice on the phone, or yelling out the window, or from the next room. And what exactly did *that* mean? Amy needed to sober up fast.

"I'm sorry, guys," said Carla, with a deep, catching sigh, like an infant who's cried herself out. *"Vino, por favor."*

If anything, wine might make her more tractable. At Edna's suggestion, Amy brewed a pot of tea for the two of them, and handed over the rest of her bottle to Carla, who proceeded, despite the proffered goblet, to nurse at it for what seemed like a full minute, although the level of the wine didn't go down much. After setting the bottle on the coffee table with exaggerated care, she closed her eyes and leaned back on the couch. "I messed up," she whispered.

Amy held her breath, waiting for the rest of it. "Everyone messes up," she said finally, exchanging a meaningful glance with Edna.

"Not like me," Carla sang, in a child's voice.

"Talk to us, Carla."

"I just wanted . . ." She rubbed her eyes with the heels of her hands, smearing mascara, and yawned mightily. "Easy for you to say," she said.

"What's easy for me to say?"

"*Everybody messes up.* You don't." She opened one eye. "I know all about you," she said. "You're my hero."

Everything knowable about Amy was summed up in three lines in *American Composers and Writers.* Her novels had been out of print for over a decade, and the last time she'd Googled herself she'd found 123 hits, from 113 used booksellers and nine amateur genealogists, plus her blog. "Carla," Amy said. "I've done nothing heroic with my life."

"I know, you don't think it's a big deal that you're a writer, that you got published. But that's just it. That's what's so cool about you. You don't care about any of it."

"I can remember a time," said Edna, "when that description was anything but a compliment. Perhaps you should have some tea."

"You're not needy. You're not the NEEDIEST HUMAN IN THE UNIVERSE." She said this in a voice not her own.

"Carla," said Amy, "what have you done?"

"No clue, Chief." Carla's eyes sprang open and she focused tightly on Amy. "You're my only friend in the whole wide world and you can just almost not quite put up with me, plus I have to pay you. How sad is that." Her gaze slid from Amy's face down to her knees and then slantways all the way down to the floor, like a pinball's lazy glide past the flippers, and then she slumped forward in a heap, a great unstrung puppet. If Amy hadn't grabbed her, she would have ended up on the floor.

Propping Carla up on the couch necessitated embracing and rolling her dead weight backward. Her body was boneless, comically so: it needed to be balanced, delicately, section by section, and the head was particularly intractable, wanting to roll off, now to the left, now the right, as Amy grappled, her own unwieldy body off balance. Carla was as warm as risen dough and smelled of yeast and peppermint and sweat. Amy couldn't remember the last time she had touched another human being so intimately, or for that matter at all. She braced herself for revulsion and was blindsided by tenderness. She could have had a *child*, she could have had just *this,* and there yawned before her instantly, from a dizzying height, the landscape of everything she had rejected in her lifelong flight from pain. How sad was that. Carla's head at last came to rest straight back, facing the ceiling, her eyes rolled up beneath half-closed lids. She was out cold. Her breathing seemed very shallow, though steady. Amy brushed strands of red hair off her forehead. She didn't want to stop touching her. "What on earth," she finally said, "is wrong with her?"

"Grievous bodily harm," said Edna.

Amy sat down next to Carla. "You think she must have been molested, in some way?"

"In some way, surely," said Edna.

Amy nodded, then caught herself, disappointed in Edna for suggesting such a trite explanation, in herself for being so anxious to excuse Carla. "Well," she said, "we're all *molested*, one way or another, and we don't all . . ."

"Georgia home boy," said Edna.

Amy glanced up. Edna had pushed back the sleeve of her Pendleton jacket and was frowning at her watch. Of course—they should check Carla's pulse, and Amy began to fumble with her wrist. "I can't find it," she said. "Actually, I can hardly ever find my own. *You* should probably—"

"GHB," said Edna.

"I beg your pardon?"

"Also known as the 'date rape drug,'" said Edna, still regarding her watch.

"How can we be sure? Why would she take a date rape drug?"

Edna glanced quickly up at Amy, then returned to her watch. "Three minutes even," she said.

Amy gave up. "What are we counting?"

"The time it takes," Edna said, "for you to realize where you are."

"Where am I," asked Amy.

"Alone with me," said Edna.

Carla's unconscious body stretched between Amy and the Sniper like fresh carrion, a barrier easily enough breached, although the Sniper, Amy sensed, was a squeamish predator, disinclined for the moment to lay hands upon it. Amy studied the Sniper's features now in order to save herself—or, more immediately, her clarity of mind. Edna, who had been throughout the evening, throughout the whole nine weeks of their acquaintance, a sturdy, no-nonsense constant in an ever-shifting cast of suspects and therefore never closely regarded, now sprang into marvelous focus. Her old brown eyes, once skeptical and wise, now glinted with malevolence, and of course they always had, but no one had seen, because Edna Wentworth was a construct, a stern old-maid schoolteacher, the most hackneyed of flat characters, and so the most opaque. Now, as opposed to thirty seconds ago, her unadorned, sharp-boned Yankee face was misproportioned somehow, the iron gray brow too low, the jaw too prominent, the teeth just a shade too big and square. She fished in her jacket pocket and came up with a filtered cigarette, the tip of which she held between those ivory yellow teeth as she lit it and puffed. "You don't mind, do you?" she asked. She flicked the dead match into the fire. "Filthy habit," she said, grinning.

"You're not too old after all," Amy tried to say, but her throat seized and she had to clear it more than once. "You're not too old after all," she said, "to run around in the dark with houseplants and masks."

". . . Pushing people off cliffs," finished Edna. "Of course not. I don't do wind sprints, but I stay in shape. For example, I chop my own wood." She deliberately let that image sink in. Really, there was nothing like an axe. "I could take *you*," she said.

Carla's phone went off again, and Edna, not taking her eyes off of Amy, retrieved it from the coffee table, turned it off, and stuffed it back down between the sofa cushions where, obviously, she herself had put it earlier. The echo of *Memories, all alone in the moonlight* hung suspended between them like a gravid cloud.

Amy tried to think. She wasn't afraid, not yet, but she could sense paralysis stealing across her body and her mind, and she fought it hard, calling up the evening she and Max and company had gone to that Lebanese restaurant in Waterville, and upon returning to the parking lot, hilarious with cheap Chianti, had found a scrawny black cat chasing a mouse around and around the left front wheel of the VW, and how she'd picked up the cat and carried it a hundred yards away, leaving it in a vacant lot, and how when she got back to the car the mouse was still there, waiting. They all cracked up laughing while she yelled at the mouse and clapped and stamped her foot so close to it that she almost crushed it, but it was a stone mouse, breathing but dead, and when they drove away it was still waiting, and the cat was halfway back, in no rush. "It is a good day to die," Max's undergraduate had said, infuriating her. She recalled now the name of the restaurant, Saba's Kebabs, and the glisten of recent rain on gravel and tire, the mineral smell in the air, and her own self-consciousness, how foolish and drunk and out of place she had felt, the wrong sensibility, the wrong sex. This memory, which should have been discouraging, instead burnished the present moment into which Amy swooned with alacrity.

Time, while inexorable, was wonderfully divisible, infinitely precious: Edna had not yet struck, Carla still breathed, Alphonse dreamed by the fire, they were all safe for now, and now was all there was. She had imagined she'd known this once—she and Max had made a mantra out of it—but she had been wrong. There really was time for alley cats and stone mice and memories, and there was still time to save the day. There was all the time in the world. Amy grabbed a copy of the Sniper's manuscript—Edna's manuscript—off the coffee table. "Have you got a pen?" she asked Edna.

"What?"

"A pen, a pencil, whatever." Amy held out her hand without looking up. After a while—three Mississippi seconds—a mechanical pencil appeared in it, and she quickly wrote

> Last minute—child, daughter, pulling away, age?—hospice garden—yellow bearded iris—that long sigh—sundial—All the Time in the World

then returned the manuscript to the table and the pencil to Edna, again without bothering to look at her.

Edna snatched up the paper immediately. "You do realize I'm going to burn this," she said, and then apparently read it. "What is it?"

"None of your damn business, Edna." Edna gasped, just as she had on the phone during their last conversation. It was harder to be rude to someone who was right there with you, even someone who probably meant to kill you. "Sorry," Amy said, "but I'm trying to concentrate." She was trying to map out the outlines of a new story in her mind, but she would never have told Edna this even if they were the greatest of friends. If you tell a story, even in outline, you kill it. It was the only magic trick she knew—besides death, in which an irreplaceable scrap of memory and experience vanishes into thin air. There was, Amy thought, nothing twinkly about magic, it was all dark, but you sure had to respect it, and she got another idea, but Edna didn't look in the mood to return her mechanical pencil.

"He's not coming, you know," Edna said.

"Who?"

"Harry," Edna said. "Harry isn't coming."

Amy had forgotten all about Harry B.

"Because," said Edna, "when Carla was in the ladies' room, I encouraged Harry to go on home rather than come here, and he was happy to oblige. When she came back, I told her he was going to Kinko's and—"

Oh, Edna, you hack. Amy snorted. "—and Lady Bastable's alibi fell like a manhandled soufflé, when it was revealed that the angle of the sun at ten forty-five plunged the gazebo into deep shade—"

"You bitch," said Edna.

"Edna, it's just not *interesting*." It felt so good to say this to a student. Amy was amazed at her own calm, which was probably a sign of a looming catatonia, but which nevertheless felt so right. "Obviously you're here without him, so you must have accomplished it somehow. The question is, What do you want?" She almost asked, What is going to happen now, but the wording was wrong—it implied that Edna was in charge of what was going to happen now. No one was in charge of that.

"I want," said Edna, and then waited to find out what she wanted, because she clearly didn't know.

"It's different," Amy guessed, "when you're right here, in the room with us, and not sniping. Frank really *was* an accident, wasn't he? You've never hurt anybody intentionally in full view. You've never stepped up on stage. You poisoned Dot when no one was looking. You—" *You coward*, she almost said, but that would be a mistake. "I'm watching you now. I'm taking you in. I know you, probably as well as anybody ever has."

"Which is not at all," said Edna. "You know nothing about me."

"I've read your story," said Amy, trying to remember its particulars. " 'The Good Woman.' "

"You said it didn't work."

"I said it needed revision. It was about an old woman obsessed by the immoral conduct of her neighbor."

"And from that you surmise what? That I'm an old woman obsessed by the immoral conduct of my neighbor? What a subtle mind you're blessed with."

"That you're observant," said Amy. "That you've always been a watcher, which is a great asset for a writer. That at some point you started keeping score, which is not." She thought she saw Edna flinch. "You're a scorekeeper," she said, and there it was again, a tiny twitch in the corner of the left eye. "It's too bad," Amy said. "You took your eye off the page, where it belonged, and trained it on all those s.o.b.s who didn't *love* what you'd written."

Edna once more reached into her jacket pocket, and this time withdrew a length of dark wood, perhaps ebony, which looked innocuous until she pried it open: a filleting knife, the long slender blade slightly curved back like a scimitar.

So, a knife. Could be worse, thought Amy, and tried to imagine how. But still the fear didn't touch her. It was right there in plain view, like the knife, but it hadn't closed the distance yet.

Edna, who had studied her watch for show, now studied the knife for real. She was alone with it, Amy saw. She was readying herself for it. "I have no set plan," she said, as much to herself as to Amy. "I'm flexible. With luck it will look like *she* did it." She nodded toward Carla. She couldn't use her name, or even look at her directly.

"And you'll be long gone."

"Oh, yes."

"But what about Harry B.? He knows you came here with Carla."

That was a mistake. Edna straightened up and smiled at Amy. "Oh, *now* you're interested in Harry B.," she said.

Amy, a terrible chess player—she could barely visualize a board as it was, let alone as it would be ten moves down the road—tried to imagine Edna's moves. If Carla were to be framed for murder, then Carla was in no physical danger, which left Amy and Alphonse, still carelessly sawing away. Edna was roughly equidistant from both, but it would be easier for her to attack Alphonse first, since Carla wasn't in the way. She would go after him to draw Amy in close. Amy decided to focus on that likelihood. Edna was probably stronger than Amy, but no quicker. Amy, with one eye on Edna, alert for any tensing of muscles that would have to precede a move, began to cast about for possible weapons. Her best shot was the fireplace tools a few feet from Alphonse's twitching, rabbit-chasing feet: there was a poker and shovel and some tongs that she'd never figured out how to use, although the set itself was pretty cheesy, and she got a mental image of the poker flopping over Edna's head like wilted celery.

"This is just totally unnecessary," Amy said.

Edna smiled again. Edna's grins were becoming predictable, as though she were a sneering machine, and if so it seemed she was running on fumes. Perhaps she was just gathering force for the final deed, but Amy suspected not, and that she was seized and bewildered by inertia. "Now you're going to try to reason with me," Edna said.

"No. I'm just pointing out the truth. You've gotten to endgame. You fooled everybody, especially me. You must know that you were brilliant all the way through. You've won. Go home."

"Perhaps I have a fatal disease. Maybe I have six weeks to live and I want to go out with a bang."

"Don't be ridiculous."

"*Why don't they publish me?*" Her voice cracked, her face was drained of color, and for the first time Amy saw that she was unwell, although she very much doubted that Edna had a wasting disease. She had overextended herself tonight: she wasn't cut out for the pirate life. She, who had been effortlessly menacing on the page, had to work too hard to be scary now, and if anything she almost seemed embarrassed. As well she might be. And now she came right out with it, the same dumb question they all asked, like a college junior waving around a notebook crammed with loopy violet paragraphs. "They give two-book contracts to MFA whores with their MFA sentences and their MFA networking and they give me *sorry, thanks, try us again.* I'm better than them. You know it. I've got something to say. I have a mind."

"Yes, but you don't know how to tell a story."

Edna stared at her with loathing.

"You can do scenes, and character, and you write a mean sentence, a better than MFA sentence, and you've got good ideas, but you don't know what a *story* is. 'The Good Woman' started out great and then just ended because it had to. It wasn't a story at all—it was a polemic. If you want to send a message," Amy sneered back, "use Western Union."

"You can't tell that on the basis of a single piece."

"I can tell it on the basis of right now. What's your last line, Edna? Come on. You've got to have a last line."

That did it. Why had Amy pushed her? Edna rose to her feet, not at all arthritically, and began to snake around the table toward Amy, in no hurry but without hesitation, prowling, like that skinny black cat. Amy could stay where she was, a sitting target, or stand up and close the gap that much faster. She stood, pushing the couch back with her calves as she did it, to give herself more room, and marveling at her own ability, still, to view the future in manageable increments. Her sudden movement caused Carla to avalanche onto the floor, where she giggled and crooned softly and began to crawl away. It sounded like she was swimming on the carpet. Amy didn't dare unlock glances with Edna, who seemed not to care about Carla's antics, but at the same time Alphonse, perhaps startled out of sleep by Edna's passing footfalls, scrambled to his feet and shook himself awake. Amy couldn't see him, behind Edna, but she heard the flapping of his great ears and jowls, and then he moseyed over to the window, propped himself up on the ottoman, and peered out into the dark. He hardly ever did this, and Amy wished he hadn't done it now, because Edna studied him, too, as though reconsidering her target.

Amy winged it. "I'll give you a *real* story. I'll show you what a story is." Edna swiveled her gaze like an eagle. "I'll give it to you for free. It's yours."

"I want nothing from you." But she stood still.

"Imagine a young woman. A writer, but she could be a violinist or a sculptor. She could be a legal secretary. What matters is that she marries her best friend, her gay best friend, to keep him out of the draft, and they set up house and live together for sixteen years, married in every way but one. And they love each other. Whatever that means. It can mean whatever you want it to. Your call. And meanwhile other men come and go, many possibilities, she could change her life, she could take chances, but nothing happens, except that he gets sick, and then he's dying. She devotes herself to his comfort, makes lemonade out of lemons. She learns to be hopeless. She's good at this. And just before he dies, her husband sets her up with another man, a man with money, who seems agreeable and wants to marry her. She doesn't care about this man, but her husband, in the time they have left—time that might be spent otherwise, I think you will agree—lays out for her the great advantages presented by this second marriage. The man loves her, the husband claims, and is in a position to support her. Plus they can have sex. "He's got *piles of money*," her husband keeps saying, and "You could do worse." In the very end the husband sends her out of the room for a glass of milk. He dies alone. She doesn't know if he did this on purpose. After the funeral she marries the second man."

"Why?" asked Edna.

"You tell me. It's your story. Does the marriage work out?"

"No," said Edna. She was close enough for Amy to see little beads of sweat standing on her brow.

"One day, when they've settled into a house together—a house very much like the one we're in now—she's rifling through his desk drawer looking for a paper clip, and she finds an envelope on which is written the name of her first husband and the word *settlement*. The envelope is thick. She opens it—and—here you might use Bluebeard, and the stupid expression on the face of that wife as she fumbles with the keys and wonders what that *oddly-shaped one* opens—"

Alphonse woofed under his breath, the way he sometimes did in his sleep. Bad timing. Edna started and took a step forward, the knife gripped in her fist, but she was still listening.

"She opens it, and it's an insurance form, from something called the *Life Escrow Society*. She has no head for legalese and she's about to tuck it away, when she encounters a word. The word is *viatical*. Viatical. It's an important-looking word, a stately homes word. She thinks she knows what the word means. She thinks it's a religious word, a Roman Catholic word, something about communion for the dying, and she wonders how you can have insurance for *that*. But then she figures it out. He had made his *piles of money* buying out the life insurance policies of the doomed. He had bet on her first husband's timely death. She had been living on—" Amy stopped. She had never once told this story to herself. She had thought to lull Edna, like Scheherazade, but instead she herself was turning inward, she had blinked, and in that blink she'd lost so many *manageable increments*, but in even exchange she saw clearly, and what she saw was that the story didn't work, because it wasn't about viatical settlements and being provided for like a faithful old retainer, and it wasn't about the shame of realiz-ing you've shared your bed with a death profiteer, and it wasn't even about a healthy, modestly gifted woman toddling, eyes down, propping herself on walls and chair backs like a shuttered invalid through the only life she would ever have. It was about the glass of milk.

Just like a funhouse pop-up Edna was right there in front of her. She hadn't been listening at all; she'd been concentrating, and now she focused on Amy's throat. Her face was naked, her thoughts legible. She was about to do something deeply contrary to her own nature, requiring obscene intimacy, and she could do it only by imagining the throat as a self-contained thing, unattached to a sentient, complex being. Edna was the one managing time now, preparing to commit a repugnant act in order to emerge whole on the other side, in a better world, where Amy and her story did not exist. Amy could count the fine black whiskers on Edna's upper lip. Edna smelled of tobacco and cloves and rank fear, or maybe that was Amy's own scent, and her breath was hot from a foot away, and then she gripped Amy's shoulder with a steel claw, to hold the throat steady, and this touch, finally, was unbearable to Amy, who knew that if she were to glance down at the hand, it wouldn't be a hand at all. She knew exactly what it was, its flexed furry contours and delicate articulations. To look at it was to fall forever, anything was preferable, even fighting back, and Amy grabbed at the other hand, the one with the knife, which sliced across her palm, and before the pain had a chance to hit, Amy smeared Edna's face with her own blood, coating her chin and cheek, wiping it on her hair, mashing it in, marking her, and then Edna, who should be killing her by now, staggered back wearing a deeply shocked expression and fell flat on the hearth, cracking her head on the bricks on the way down.

"*That* was a creepy story," said Carla. She stood over Edna, swaying in her own breeze, the empty wine bottle in her hand. "Excuse me," she said, then discreetly turned toward the fireplace and threw up. Amy, padding her bleeding palm with a paper napkin, went to help her. "I really liked Edna," Carla said dolefully, "didn't you?" and then, "You better get that." Then Amy heard it, the banging of fists on the door, and there, on her front stoop, were Harry B. and Tiffany and Chuck and a uniformed policeman. "What did I tell you?" Harry berated the cop, "Was I right? What did I tell you?" while Chuck wrapped her hand in a hot washcloth and Tiffany looked after Carla.

Amy sat, her head as light as a weather balloon, taking in the scene from a great remove. There would be time later—time!—to deal with explanations and rituals, not to mention official proceedings, along with shock and the wearing off of same. The room seemed to fill with people. Apparently the class would never end. There was exclaiming and hugging and recapitulation and the comparing of notes; there was a lot of pointing at the prostrate, groaning Edna, and expressions of disgust, and claims of omniscience, and admissions of ignorance and wonder. Dr. Surtees did something to her right hand. Alphonse trotted across her field of view, heading for Edna, intent on licking the blood from her face, and Amy distracted him, waving the soaked napkin like a pennant. He rewarded her with his company, climbing up beside her on the couch, snarfling in the napkin with profound content. This was bliss. "We need to talk, ma'am," said the policeman, bending over her. His voice seemed familiar, though not his face, and Amy peered at the name tag beneath his badge. K-O-W-A-L-C-I-M-I. It couldn't be. "Sergeant Colostomy?"

"It's Colostomy, ma'am," said the sergeant, tipping the brim of an invisible hat.

"Of course it is," said Amy.

For Christmas, Carla had given herself a gigantic replica of one of the Notre Dame gargoyles and parked it outside her front door. It looked like a cross between a vulture and an archangel and was wonderfully hideous. Amy, her arms full of wine bottles and banana-nut bread, rang the bell, twice for good measure, since Mother Massengill was in Palm Desert.

Amy had begged off Christmas Eve with Marvy and Cindy, and also Christmas Day with her choice of Tiffany and her dad, or Pete and his. But Boxing Day with Carla and most of the gang proved sufficiently enticing, because Amy needed a break. She'd been writing every day since Last Class, and she felt confident enough to stop for a bit. In the early stages, she'd approached the previous day's work with dread, remembering how, in the bad old days, lines she'd thought inspired would reveal themselves in morning light as promise-free and just as fascinating as the pontifications of a drunk (which, in a few instances, was exactly what they were). Now they still looked pretty good, or some of them did, and they wouldn't turn feral on her if she took a day off at the Birdhouse.

Carla and Tiffany ushered her in and ensconced her in the comfiest of many comfy chairs while the rest waited on themselves and her. Everybody was there except Marvy, still home with his wife and kids. In the interest of domestic harmony, Amy thought, Marvy was probably going to have to find a hobby he could pursue with his wife.

"Actually," Carla whispered, "Marvy told me Cindy wants him to write a book about it. The whole, you know, thing. He says to tell you he's not going to do it." Good luck, thought Amy, holding out against Cindy.

They all chatted about their families and the gifts they'd given and gotten. They told stories, first about childhood Christmases, and then about everything else—summer camp, college romances, on-the-job hijinks. Harry told splendid yarns about his early days as a public defender, and Ricky was full of tales he hadn't been allowed to run in the paper. It was odd and somehow heartening that the worst writers made the best storytellers.

They pointedly didn't talk about *It*. Nobody mentioned Frank or Dot, or especially Edna. Dr. Surtees glanced at Amy's injured hand and complimented whoever had stitched it up, but immediately changed the topic to *Code Black*, which he had decided to abandon. When Syl and Pete asked why, he said, "Because it sucks." His choice of words was as stunning as the sentiment itself. When Syl asked why he thought it sucked, Dr. Surtees replied, "Because I had a good teacher."

Amy blushed with pleasure. She hated to blush. "Good for you," she said. "Are you going to try again?"

"Absolutely."

Harry B. cleared his throat. "There's something I've been debating about telling you all. I've got courthouse connections, as you know, and Chaz Yanetti's an old friend. Yanetti's representing—"

"Don't!" said Carla. "Do *not* mention her name on this—"

"Yeah, come on," said Syl. "We're having a nice time here."

"Sorry."

After a great yawning silence, during which they all thought of nothing but Edna, Amy said her name. "Edna."

"*Ewww!*"

"Edna Edna Edna."

Chuck began to sing, creating a blues tune around the terrible name.

"Look," said Amy, "you all want to be writers. How are you going to do that if there are words you can't say?" She geared up for her speech about how *unthinkable* was the only truly obscene word in a writer's vocabulary, but then she saw from the looks on their faces, their unwillingness to meet her gaze, that they were batting the word away in order to protect *her*, as though she remained traumatized. How sweet, and how silly. "What," she asked Harry B., "does Chaz Yanetti have to say?"

"Is she pleading insanity?" asked Carla. "Because, forget it, there's no way she should get away with that."

"You think she's sane?" asked Amy.

"I have no idea what she's pleading," said Harry B. "That's lawyer-client business. But I can tell you how she's paying her legal bills."

"Oh, no." Tiffany slowly put down her wineglass and grabbed her head with both hands. "No, no, no."

"Oh, yes," said Harry B.

Everybody else, including Amy, stared at the two in puzzlement. "Oh, no, what?" Chuck finally asked.

"She's selling her stuff," Tiffany whispered. "She's getting published."

The room erupted in outraged shouts and gasps.

"Well, not yet," said Harry B. "But she has got an agent, and a good one."

"*Agent!*"

Amy wasn't outraged. She was trying to figure how she felt. She was pretty sure she wasn't as aggrieved at the rest, whose indignation vaulted to an even higher pitch with the mention of a "bidding war." "Does anybody know," she began, and had to repeat herself three times before she could be heard, "does anybody know if Edna's written any novels?"

"I don't think so," said Chuck after a moment. "I think she would have said. She liked short stories, and that's what she wrote."

Tiffany sneered. "Yes, she was a real *purist*."

"But she must have written a million of them, and now they'll bring them all out in some sort of damn collection, and it'll make the bestseller list, and it'll win the National Book Award—"

"Wrong," said Amy. "The agent and the bidding war are all about notoriety and big bucks. You don't make big bucks with short story collections."

"And your point is what?" asked Tiffany. "She'll still get everything she wanted."

"Maybe, but I'm not so sure. What they'll probably do is force her to turn her stories, or some of them, into a novel. I don't think they could ever get Edna to write a nonfiction tell-all, even to pay her lawyers. It would have to be a novel."

"Well, so what?" asked Carla. "That's worse! She's killed two human beings, and she tried to kill you, and she'll get a big fat novel out of it!"

"And perhaps you're right, and perhaps she'll be pleased with that. But I don't think so." Amy pictured Edna alone in her cell, staring back and forth between book contracts and the precious yellowing pages of "Saving the Whales" and "The Good Woman" and all the rest of her life's work, stories she honestly believed worthy, deserving of publication as written. She'd killed in their defense. Now she'd have to destroy them in order to save them. She'd have to mix and match, and throw away some characters and build up some others out of all proportion, and wrench them into plot positions over which she had no real control. The last thing Edna wanted to write was a big fat novel. At least Amy hoped so.

Pete wasn't mollified. "She'll get over it," he said. "It's just not fair. She's going to be rewarded. She's going to be famous."

"She never wanted to be famous," said Amy. "She wanted to be good."

The silence that followed was, while still gloomy, companionable. "Well," Chuck finally said, "*I'd* rather be famous." Tiffany bonked him in the forehead with a cube of Emmenthaler, which he retrieved from his lap and nibbled on, complaining that she should have thrown a softer cheese, like mozzarella.

"Okay," said Carla, "since we're talking about it, I've got some questions."

"Like what?"

"Well, like the Bundy mask. How did she get it into Tiffany's car? It's been driving me nuts."

"Me, too!" said Tiffany. "There's no way she could have known I'd leave my keys in the trunk."

"Plus she only had fifteen minutes, during break, to get a hold of the mask, which I don't know how she even knew it was there, because mostly I brought show-biz masks, I mean there was Freddy Krueger and all, but nobody really scary, except that one mask, Ted Bundy—"

"Plus," chimed in Pete, "she couldn't have known you were going to bring the masks in the first place."

"What difference does it make?" Amy asked.

"Well, it was impossible, that's what difference it makes," said Pete.

"But it happened, so clearly it *wasn't* impossible."

"But aren't you curious?" Chuck's smile was both mocking and affectionate. "You're always telling us to pay attention to the world and everything in it, and here you are, waving off the how and what and why—"

"I'm not waving off the what and why. I'd never do that. But the how bores me to death."

"—like some snob leaving the help to mop up—"

"Point taken." It was a good thing she didn't have a five-pound wheel of aged Parmesan close at hand. "It's really quite simple, Captain Manley. Our Edna wasn't a micromanager. She wasn't a planner. Our Edna set the wheels in motion and walked away, and if something worked, fine, and if it didn't, there was always tomorrow. Edna knew how to wing it."

"So you're saying she noticed the mask and improvised on the spot? Strolled out to the lot during break just to see what she could do with it?"

"Makes sense to me."

"I suppose you're right. If she hadn't found an open car, or better, Tiffany's keys, she could have just chucked it in the bushes."

Carla sighed. "Amy's always right," she said.

Was she kidding? Carla apparently needed to believe this, which was why they'd never be true friends, which was too bad. *You're my hero.* Amy didn't begrudge her the need, but she didn't understand it, either. Amy had never needed a hero, and even if she were herself deserving of this degree of admiration, she'd be terribly uncomfortable with it. *Idea for a story*: furtive heroics.

"No, she's not," said Chuck. "She's one hundred percent dead flat-out wrong about one thing."

"And what would that be?" asked Amy.

"The sexiest letter of the alphabet. It's Y."

"Why?" asked Carla.

"It's obvious," said Chuck.

"Wait a minute," said Amy. "What did you say?"

"I said Y."

"You've been reading my blog!" Why had this never occurred to her? She'd considered the Sniper—why not the rest of the class?

"Of course we have!"

But it's private, she wanted to say. Which was absurd, as was the fact that she now felt exposed. "We thought you knew," they were saying, as they nominated their favorite entries. It turned out that Carla had found the blog almost immediately upon its inception and had broadcast the address to every writing class she ever took. Community of solipsists, indeed. "Were you all kibbitzers?"

"I was," said Harry B. Now she remembered some suggested legal terms—*privity, bailee.* She'd almost used them both. They were good.

"I suggested three lists," said Syl, "but I guess you didn't like them."

"I liked them fine," Amy lied. "I just ignored them." Syl had to be the one who suggested lame sitcoms, overpriced muscle cars, and funny-looking people.

Amy felt herself blush for the second time in an hour, as she recalled posting her own bad stories and sentences, that *list of lovers.* What had she been thinking? She caught her breath as she remembered the many evenings she'd toyed with posting a list of bad student stuff. It would have been so easy. She'd kept her own private file over the years, and all she'd needed to do was tap a couple of keys, and there it would have been for the world to see, beginning with the very first (and her own sentimental favorite): *He caressed her buttocks in a clockwise motion.* Thank god she hadn't gone through with it. What a betrayal it would have been. I'm not a hero, she thought, but at least I wasn't brought up in a barn.

"So," she said, righting herself, "you were all my kibbitzers?"

Dr. Surtees shook his head, and Ricky and Tiffany looked noncommittal. The others nodded. "But we weren't the only ones," said Carla.

"And which one of you," asked Amy, "was my Number One Fan?"

"That was so rude!" Carla looked genuinely distraught. "I tried to figure out how to delete it, but of course I didn't have your password. That was just mean and rotten."

"Actually," said Chuck, "I thought it was pretty damn funny."

"So did I," said Amy. And so, judging from their expressions, did most of them. Except Pete, whose lowered face was the color of a beefsteak tomato. *Why, Pete, you interesting boy.* "In fact, I tried to figure out how I could include 'the assiest asshat in Assville' in some sort of list, but gave up."

"Is that how you pronounce it?" asked Dr. Surtees. "I thought it had a "sh" in it, like *misshapen.*"

"It couldn't have been any of us," said Carla. "It was some asshat in Peoria."

"Or maybe it *was* one of us," said Ricky, "and you're supposed to guess which one. Make it an exercise in character observation, like 'Guess the Sniper.' "

"That's a tasteless suggestion," said Tiffany.

"What can I say," said Ricky. "I'm a news hack. I'm not a tasteful guy."

Good for you, thought Amy. Tiffany's a nice girl, but you can do better. And kudos to Pete Purvis, her Number One Fan, who didn't exactly hate her but didn't like her either. "I couldn't possibly guess," she said.

For a while they played Ricky's game, theorizing about the asshat poltroon, and when that topic played out, they returned to the one that apparently had not. "Okay," said Carla, "but what about Dot? Where did Edna put the poison, and how did she know who'd drink it, or are you saying that it didn't matter? But it must have mattered, because what if *you'd* drunk it, I know she didn't want to kill *you*, not yet—"

"Yes," said Ricky, "but if she slipped it into Dot's glass—"

Harry B. reminded them that the cops had implied the poison was in one of the *bottles*, and Ricky said they'd been too sloppy with the evidence to know anything for certain, and Dr. Surtees held forth on the probable choice of poison and whether it came in a powder or liquid. Everybody jumped in. They must have been bursting, Amy thought, with all these questions. As the winter sun set, lamps were lit and new bottles uncorked, and Syl Reyes and Pete Purvis raided Carla's kitchen and cooked up an impressive three-course Tex-Mex dinner, and all the while they wrangled and speculated about injustice and fate and the how of things. They offered toasts—to Frank, to Dot, and many times to Amy, who mostly just watched and listened.

People are so interesting, she thought, and *I should really get out more*, and she started to tune them out and turn pleasantly inwards, toward her own life, and the shape of the novel to come. She was interrupted by Chuck with yet another toast. These people needed some coffee. "To Amy's next book," he said.

Which might get finished, and might get published, and might make money, and might be worth reading. But which would surely, in any event, keep her in the world. Amy drank, in private toast to everyone who made this possible. To all of them, to the solipsists, to Max, to Alphonse. To Edna. *Thank you.*